A Principle of Light

A Principle of Light

J. E. Irvin

Çok teşekkür ederim

J. E. Irvin

The New Atlantian Library

THE NEW ATLANTIAN LIBRARY
is an imprint of
ABSOLUTELY AMAZING eBOOKS

Published by Whiz Bang LLC, 926 Truman Avenue, Key West, Florida 33040, USA.

A Principle of Light copyright © 2020 by J.E. Irvin. Electronic compilation/ paperback edition copyright © 2020 by Whiz Bang LLC.

All rights reserved. No part of this book may be reproduced, scanned, or transmitted in any form or by any means, electronic or mechanical, including photocopying, recording, or any information storage and retrieval system, without permission in writing from the publisher. Please do not participate in or encourage piracy of copyrighted materials in violation of the author's rights. Purchase only authorized ebook editions.

This is a work of fiction. Names, characters, places, and incidents either are the product of the author's imagination or are used fictitiously, and any resemblance to actual persons, living or dead, businesses, companies, events, or locales is entirely coincidental or fictional usages. While the author has made every effort to provide accurate information at the time of publication, neither the publisher nor the author assumes any responsibility for errors, or for changes that occur after publication. Further, the publisher does not have any control over and does not assume any responsibility for author or third-party websites or their contents. How the ebook displays on a given reader is beyond the publisher's control.

ISBN 978-1-951150-78-5

For information contact:
Publisher@AbsolutelyAmazingEbooks.com

For the real Nilesen and Jeannie, whose friendship, support and love have made this journey into the light amazing ...

For the Turkish people, whose long history as a crossroads country has given them a rich and unconquerable spirit...
...Sevgiyle

The light we sought is shining still.

Matthew Arnold, *Thyrsis*

... we must live as if we will never die.
Nazik Hikmet, *On Living*

"In the beginning...darkness covered the abyss..."
Genesis 1 - 2,
The New American Bible

A Principle of Light

A Principle of Light

Refraction
1

Diffraction
139

Prisms
195

The Absence of Light
239

The Law of Reflection
297

Işik
345

Refraction

1
... Istanbul, May 2016, 8 a.m....

In a vacuum, light travels 186,282 miles per second.

Nilesen wrapped the gun in a sweater and hid it in the space between the dresser and the wall. The footsteps in the hall receded. She returned to her correspondence. Satisfied with the request for asylum, she addressed it to the British Undersecretary and signed her full name. Nilesen Yilmaz Solaganian. She pushed up from the table with her good hand. Her knees protested, sore after the long walk from the village of Gebze. She glanced down at the trunk, the books within sealed beneath a padlocked clasp. *When I die, who will keep my words?* Now that she had decided to stop writing, the question no longer mattered. Perhaps they were always meant to be lost. Still, it was difficult to let go. Her words were her children, the only ones she would ever bear.

The odor of rotting fruit and mold, reminders of the decay that awaited the discarded and the unwary, drifted in through the open window. A few streets away, tourists shopped or stopped to inquire about the best place to eat in Golden Horn harbor. Few ventured to this block that housed the crush of immigrants seeking what all the self-exiled wanted – a new beginning. Nilesen squinted into the brightness. Odd, how the light bent itself to embrace the trunk, its iron-clad corners rusty yet unbent.

She settled a scarf over her hair, tucking away stray curls. She dropped a handful of coins into a small purse, locked the door, and tiptoed her way down the stairs. Neighbors in this district were suspicious of too-early risers from distant towns who coughed or spat, who prayed too much or not enough. Any action, unnatural, out of the ordinary, could draw the attention of the authorities.

We live in hard times, caught between the darkness and the light. Alain's words, whispered the night they spoke their vows. Only a year ago. Before her incarceration. Before the ambush. She folded away the memory. Today was not a day for such heavy mind travels. As she stepped into the covered entryway, the porter Selim looked up from his newspaper. Worry beads clicked in his hand.

"*Günaydin*, Madam. Did you have a pleasant sleep?"

"*Merhaba*, Selim. Yes, all my demons slept in their own beds last night." Nilesen bit her lip. Why had she answered him with a line from one of her poems? He might recognize it, recognize her. But, no. It was only one line, and many people had bad dreams.

"I see you have another envelope. You must write to many people. May I assist you in mailing it?"

She tightened her grip on the letter. "Thank you, Selim, but this is the last one, and it is something I need to do myself." Again with portentous words. She never would learn to be circumspect. *That is your problem, little hen,* Alain had often chided her. *The truth bubbles from you like water from a spring.* She swallowed the sob lodged in her throat.

The porter lifted his shoulders, dropped them again. "Then, Madam, may you have a successful journey today."

When she crossed in the direction of Istiklal Street, she felt his eyes upon her, bright with attention and worry. If anything happened to her, his reputation would suffer. She had almost reached the intersection when a jandarma stepped out of a doorway, uniform crisp and unwrinkled on his slight frame. As his shadow loomed over her, he put out a hand.

"Nilesen Yilmaz? May I see your papers?"

She glanced over her shoulder. Selim had disappeared into the interior of the building. Several workmen heading her way reversed direction when they spotted the jandarma cap, the ammunition belt, the jop made of malacca wood.

"I am Nilesen Solaganian. I am on my way to the *postane*."

The jandarma leaned so close she could smell his aftershave, a hint of cloves, peppers from his breakfast. The aroma of power, leathery and filled with arrogance. "Ah," he whispered, "so you married the Armenian. And is your husband with you?"

Nilesen shook her head. If she allowed the word to escape, her sorrow, magnified by the lens of death, would fill the city.

"Yes, I forgot. That unfortunate incident at Yenihisar. So sad. But that is yesterday's news." He stretched his lips in a smile that never touched his eyes. "Today, it will be better for you if you just show me your papers. Perhaps you left them in your apartment. Shall we go see?"

The slam of a truck door startled her. A motorbike whizzed by. The street stirred, a pot coming to boil. He took her elbow. "Let us go to your apartment now, Madam Solaganian. To correct any misunderstanding."

In response to his gesture, another policeman emerged from the doorway of the salon across the street. He trailed them as the first man steered her back to her building. Above the rooftops, clouds gathered, blotting out the morning sky, drawing up the light that had illuminated the early hour. Soon it would rain.

Selim had not returned. Inside, the *jandarmalar* herded her toward the stairs. She noted the impatient set of their mouths, the eagerness in their eyes. They already believed in her guilt, certain they would find something in her room that would bring them glory. She began to climb, the second jandarma ahead, the one with the gun and club behind her. Her legs trembled. She tried not to anticipate. So what if they found the trunk. They could not open it without her help, not unless they made a great deal of noise. Which they would not want to do, not here, not now, not with protesters and the media only a short dash away. She would refuse to help them, hold out until pain sucked away even the dignity of denial.

When they reached the third floor, she staggered, as if out of breath. The first man prodded her with his fist.

"Stop stalling. We know you have something to show us."

She drew the key from her pocket, fumbling as she set it in the lock. When she swung the door open, the apartment sighed.

No papers on the floor. No pen and ink beside her chair. No trunk.

2
... Istanbul, May 2016, 9 a.m.

The interrogation room, in the sub-basement of the government complex, contained a table and three stools. An ashtray and a folder, the label printed in heavy, black letters – YILMAZ, N. – rested on the table. She rocked back and forth on the stool where they had placed her, the desire to use the restroom balanced against the need to remain calm. Without the trunk, they had nothing. She fingered the ring Alain had given her on their wedding day, twisting it to catch the fire within. The opal winked just as an older man limped into the room. She recognized his face from the election posters, a smiling portrait of Captain Emre Gazi. But he was no friend.

"Nilesen Yilmaz, where are the books you had delivered from your village?" Gazi pounded his walking stick on the floor, then laid it across the table. Retrieving the folder, he shuffled through the pages. "How old are you now? Thirty-one? Still time to be a wife, a mother. A faithful citizen."

She bit her lips to stop their trembling. She was a wife. Correction: had been. "Why am I here? I have done nothing wrong."

Gazi slapped the file on the table before he opened her purse. When he shook out the contents, the key to the apartment spun across the surface. A handful of *kuruş* tumbled out. Two coins rolled off the edge and bounced on the toe of his polished boot. He lifted the cane and smacked it on the table, scattering the remainder of the money. "Enough. I have no patience to play this game with you."

The missing trunk confused him. Nilesen bowed her head. Whoever robbed the apartment had saved her from a return to prison. But not from brutality. She had drunk from this cup before. She rubbed her crippled hand across her knee. Gazi grabbed the ends of her scarf, pulled until the silk tightened against her neck. She struggled to ease the tension, to gulp air. When he released her, she rocked forward, banging her chest on the edge of the table. *Be silent.* Alain's voice in her ear, the memory of his breath against her skin. *Be brave.*

"Please address me by my married name, Solaganian."

"You think it funny, to trick us with names? I know who you are. A foolish Turkish woman who scribbles verses in the margins of books, who made the mistake of marrying an Armenian subversive. The question, Yilmaz, is this. Do you know who I am?" He rattled the stick against the rungs of her stool. "Do you know what I can do?"

Nilesen held up her damaged hand. "Everyone knows what the *polisi* can do, Captain Gazi, although why the jandarma, the country police, are here in the city is perplexing. Did you have me followed from my village? Because I am not here to cause trouble. I have come to see my doctor."

"Of course, of course. You are nothing more than a simple country girl." Gazi ran his fingers over her file. "A village idiot who writes poetry that inflames the people and criticizes the government."

"I believe you have me confused with another."

"Another what? Agitator? Rebel? Revolutionary?"

"I have done nothing wrong."

"Where is the trunk you had delivered to the pensión?"

"I have no idea what you are talking about."

Gazi prowled the room. His uniformed legs brushed against the back of the stool. He stroked his mustache.

"An interesting hypothesis, innocence." In one sudden movement, he leaned forward, grabbed her hands, and pressed them flat against the tabletop. "What we lack here is proof, and pain is a great lie detector. If you have come to see your doctor, Madam, you will not object to a little experiment."

He nodded at the observation window. The door creaked as the jandarma who had arrested her stepped inside. His belt sagged from the weight of the jop.

"Captain?" The jandarma fingered the weapon.

"Search her."

The jandarma ran his hands over her back, her breasts, her thighs. He pulled the letter from a pocket and slapped it on the table.

"Open it."

The paper rustled as it slipped free of the envelope. "It is a request," the jandarma said, "for an interview with the British ambassador. Something about an academic residency and keeping words?"

"Burn it."

When nothing but ash remained, Gazi nodded again. Nilesen squirmed to pull her hands free, but his grip remained strong. The younger man pulled the jop from his belt, tested it against the palm of one hand, and raised it above his head. Before she could cry out, he swung down, smashing the thumb of her left hand, the damaged one. She screamed and jerked backward against the rigid body of the captain.

"Tell me, Madam Solaganian." He drew out the syllables of her married name, licked at the taste of them in his mouth. "Did you bring anything with you to Istanbul?"

Nilesen stared at the opal gleaming up from her good hand. "I have committed no crime."

"Again," Gazi said. "The other one."

The jandarma hesitated. His shirt darkened with inkblots of sweat as his eyes darted like fireflies from Gazi's face to hers and back again. A tremor rippled down his upraised arm. Staring into the glare of the ceiling lights, Nilesen welcomed the ghost of a poem stirring beneath the fear. The club whooshed down across her writing hand, cracking the surface of the table as it shattered the bones in her fingers. A second blow smashed into her thumb. A starry galaxy of pain pulsed behind her closed eyes. When the captain released her, she slipped off the stool and fell to the floor. He nudged her with the toe of his boot.

"If you are not the poet Nilesen Yilmaz," he said, "you will not mind."

J. E. Irvin

They dropped her at the door of a clinic around the corner from Taksim Square. The street buzzed with vendors setting up kiosks for the next day's book fair and women hurrying past on their way to the markets. Banners announcing the upcoming elections fluttered from hastily erected poles. Along the walkways, protestors marched in small groups, holding signs and chanting *zülüm ölüm*, death to tyranny. A man stepped over her, thinking her drunk or drugged. Two women paused, looked around at the soldiers patrolling the street, and hurried on. A teenager trudged past, his dark head and slight shoulders bent under the burden of a trunk that looked like hers. But, no, this one carried a sign: *Gerçek*. Truth. Rain feathered down in fitful snatches. She licked the blood from her hands.

"I am Yilmaz," she whispered. "I bleed for you."

No one answered.

When the clinic opened, Nilesen crawled inside, panting from the effort not to faint. A nurse helped her up and brought water to soak her hands before propping her in a chair by the door. Beyond the glass, pigeons wove their way among the feet of passersby, pecking for insects and stray bits of grain. A fishmonger strolled by, holding up his fresh catch, bargaining with whoever would return his glance. The sun played a game of darts with the clouds.

It was late afternoon before the doctor set the broken bones. When he lifted her right hand, the fragments of the opal sprayed out across the surface of the examining table, each shard of the fire now scattered, its blaze diminished. She tried to scrape the fragments back together with her forearms until the nurse begged her to stop.

When she shuffled out of the clinic, the groups of protestors had joined together, their voices rising like steam. Night slipped in between the buildings, gathering up the daylight and the last of the sun's stray threads.

"Shall I call a cab for you, Madam?" The nurse was polite but remote. Violence had worn calluses on her concern.

Nilesen shook her head. Pain was all she had left now. How much did Alain feel when the shrapnel tore through his body? Did he think of her as he lay in the road, his blood staining the earth, his martyr's kiss to the land of his ancestors? She ignored her hands, numb from the shots the doctor had injected before he repaired the breaks. She refused to anticipate the evening, when the drugs wore off, and the ache became a throb and then a high-pitched whine as her body tried to separate itself from the damaged limbs.

It took an hour to walk three blocks. She doubted they were following her. Perhaps they hoped she would die and save them the trouble of searching her apartment again. But there was nothing in it, nothing left to find. Slowly, like the taste of last summer's wine, despair settled in her mouth. They had taken the letter, her request to be granted asylum in the UK now ashes in the captain's wastebasket. They had confiscated her purse with the last of her money. Her books were gone, burned in someone's fire or tossed like garbage into a refuse pit on the edge of Istanbul.

At the entrance to the apartment, Selim hopped from his chair. A young man, so much like the porter that he had to be his son, hovered in the shadowy entry.

"I want to die, *abi*," she said. She did not voice the rest of the thought, but it hovered in the air around her. *It hurts too much to live.*

"Oh, my dear madam," Selim caught her as she sagged against the steps. "Be brave."

The echo of Alain's words made her tremble.

"They robbed my apartment, Selim," she said. "They stole my books."

"Perhaps not." He nodded to his son to take her other arm. Together they carried her up the flights of stairs. When they reached the door to the apartment, Selim used his master key to open the lock. "Perhaps they are also on a journey, Nilesen *hanim*, to a place where monsters can no longer find them."

Nilesen staggered into the room. A new stack of writing paper sat on the table, pen and ink beside it. The porter cleared his throat. "The light may be gone, but the night remembers. Fethi, help our lady."

Before she could ask how Selim knew that line, his son had seated her in a chair. When he bent to smooth a blanket over her knees, the gun slipped loose from inside his shirt and landed on her lap. Wincing, she ran her palm across the handle. Fethi snatched it back and shoved it out of sight. "The night remembers, always. Tomorrow, Nilesen *hanim*, I will take you to my cousin's shop in the Cihangir. He runs a café with rooms above for artists. You will be safe there."

She waited until she was alone before she gave in to despair. Every plan had been thwarted. Not even death remained. Laying her head on the table, she allowed the darkness to gather her in.

3

... Istanbul, May 2016, three weeks later ...

When it comes in contact with matter, light bends, decreasing its speed.

I leaned against the open window to trace the sun's path across my skin and squinted at the reflection of the mangled, now-useless luggage tag lying on the sill. Jeanine Maurillac, 90 Seeker's Place, Dayton, OH, USA. The mundane details failed to disclose the resentful spirit behind that name. I swept the tag into the trash and returned to the view of the city. Istanbul, seductive and queenly, spread her wings in the morning sun.

Light streaked across the roof of the neighboring building, dappling the faces of the early risers in gold. Carl had already gone out, his rapid escape one more crack in the façade of our partnership. Why the magazine gave us this fluff piece continued to eat at me. We were no longer a couple, our work relationship tense, yet here I was, researching textiles with him. I resented everything, especially the limited travel allowance that kept me tethered to a crap writer on a crap assignment in the middle of a god-damn uprising. Who cared about the market for Turkish rugs when terrorists were blowing up train stations and nightclubs all over Europe? Despite their startling beauty, my photos of traditional, naturally dyed, and handwoven carpets would win no Pulitzers. And, I had to share a room with him. It was enough to make my stomach ache.

I dropped the sheet wrapped around me, skimmed my naked self with my hands. At least my stomach was still flat. The extra pounds so typical of almost-forty-year-olds had yet to invade my flesh. Bored with so much self-reflection, I slipped into the same clothes I wore yesterday, crammed a stale beignet in my mouth, and gulped down the remnants of last night's coffee. I followed the scuff of Carl's tennis shoes down the dusty stairs to the front door of the building where we had rented the last room available near Taksim Square, two blocks to the west. Despite the early hour, the square already teemed with protesters. The signs they carried, in Turkish and English, attacked the latest wave of immigrant entries into the country. A few denounced one of the candidates.

At the bottom of the stairs, I mumbled a greeting to the porter as I scanned the pedestrian traffic, hoping for a glimpse of Carl and his ever-present iPad. His absence scraped at the anger lodged inside me. Joined by obligation and happenstance, we'd been circling the waters of our dying affair the entire trip, waiting to draw blood. Nevertheless, the contract required me to complete this article, and that's what I intended to do. Take the pictures and get the hell out of Dodge before chaos erupted. Anxiety bubbled inside me. I inhaled the aromas of urban living, gas fumes from the street, cooking oil drifting from open windows, and decided to dial back the attitude. If Carl had gone off by himself, I could concentrate on photographing the city.

"Pardon me, Madam Maurillac. You are seeking Mr. Ruffolo, no?"

Startled out of my tantrum, I acknowledged the porter's greeting. "Yes, Selim. It is Selim, right? Did you see which way he went?"

The porter inclined his head to the left. "Toward the café, I believe, Madam. He said something about a coffee."

"Thank you, Selim. Have a good day."

"You as well, Madam Maurillac. Stay safe."

I adjusted the strap of my camera bag, patted the passport and phone stuffed in the side pocket. I swerved to avoid the women heading toward the hair salon. Aware of a rumbling in the square and another in my stomach, I walked faster, searching for a shock of red hair among the darker ones.

The heart of the arts district beat around me. A violin emitted a siren call from a third-story flat. Bits of conversation wafted above the general clamor, then sank

A Principle of Light

back into the thrum of motorbikes and car engines. Two blocks along, I turned right. The street narrowed, the buildings leaned closer, huddling for support. I stumbled over the uneven cobbles, unable to catch a glimpse of Carl's khaki jacket, the one he bought in Cairo and refused to abandon, even after the elbows wore down and the zipper broke. Where had he gone?

The street wound past a collection of shuttered storefronts before opening onto a small square. Across the intersection of Timsah and Bol Ahenk Sokak, a café sprouted, red-clothed tables and metal chairs empty at this hour. An awning above the door announced **il Phare, Deniz Feneri,** مَنارة**, The Lighthouse**, all four languages printed in green calligraphy against a white background. The hours of operation were listed below. A waiter appeared, apron flashing like a semaphore among the potted geraniums. He used a cloth to brush seeds and petals from the tabletops, then tucked it at his waist. Then he began to sweep the floor. In the window above the café, a woman appeared. She gazed down on the square, drew her headscarf tighter, and retreated. I checked the time and thumbed on the phone, hoping for a message. If Carl had been seeking food, he might have stopped there.

Behind me, a bookseller wheeled a cart through the door of his shop, parking it beneath the display window. Protected by the overhang, the cart bed brimmed with second-hand novels, outdated encyclopedias, and musty textbooks. I set down my bag, took out the camera. and panned the plaza, eager to capture the shadowed nooks and flowered entrances before pedestrians filled the square. Already they were drifting in, mothers leading children, yawning workers, and cigarette-smoking creative types. Click, click, click. I paused to check the images. The sun caught the handle of a passing motorbike, winking as it flashed toward a small volume resting among the items on the cart. The book, a bright ember among the dead coals of the used tomes, sparked in the morning light. Tracing the letters of the title, *IŞIK*, I rescued it from the pile.

"Ah, for a westerner, Madam has curious taste, I see." The proprietor hustled toward me. He wiped the sweat from his lip and cast a nervous glance down the street. Then he plucked the book from my hands. "May I wrap this for you?"

I shook my head. "Thanks, but that's not necessary. That café is open, isn't it?"

A jet passed overhead. Everyone in the square paused to look up. I looked, too, snapping a series of quick shots, most of which I'd probably delete later.

"Best for Madam to take this back to your hotel, no?" he said. He shoved the lens down. "Quieter there, better for concentrating. Safer."

I twisted to see what he was staring at. Across the way, two men wheeled suitcases toward the café. A *polis* approached them, military not municipal by the look of his uniform, the white helmet bearing the words *As Iz*. A polished jop swung loosely from one hand. I turned back to the vendor. "How much for the book?"

"A gift to you, Madam." He pressed it into my hands and, taking me by the elbow, urged me along the sidewalk. "Be safe now. Save your picture-taking for the harbor or the Grand Mosque. Much better scenery."

He stared at the men in the street and scurried back inside. I tucked the book in the camera bag, then focused the lens on the *polis*, who bent his head and gestured toward the taller of the pair. The shorter man took out a cigarette and held it out for a light. I wrapped the strap of the camera around my wrist, slung my camera bag over my shoulder, and angled my way toward the café, pointing and shooting as I strolled. When I reached the first of the tables, the waiter stepped forward to greet me. Behind him, in the dimly lit interior, I glimpsed movement.

"Good morning, Madam. Coffee?" He turned over a cup, scurried away, and returned with a carafe. "You are hungry, no? Perhaps you would like a *simit*? Also, our cook makes the best *menemen* in Istanbul."

I sat so I could keep watch for Carl. The *polis* continued to speak with the men in the square. "I would like some

A Principle of Light

coffee, thank you. And I'll try an order of *menemen*. What is it?"

"Scrambled eggs, madam, with tomatoes and green peppers. You will love it."

"And, " I ran a finger down the menu, "*Sucuk*?"

"A spicy sausage. Very tasty." Touching his fingers to his lips, he slipped away. I removed the bookseller's gift from my bag. Again I ran my fingers over the title, surprised by the impulse to own a book in a language I couldn't read. Poetry? In Turkish? I opened it to the first page. A verse stared up at me, the letters beguiling in their strangeness. I felt at once illiterate and inept, unable to determine the value of the work because I couldn't interpret the words. I placed a finger under the first line and struggled to pronounce each syllable.

The waiter returned with a glass of juice. The square filled with passersby. Down the block, I caught a glimpse of red hair. In the street, the *polis* drew air circles with his cigarette. The travelers moved off, suitcase wheels rumbling as they passed. The man with the red hair drew closer, his bearded scowl familiar, his mouth open and yelling my name. Carl in full howl mode. As he neared the restaurant, he glanced across the square. He jogged around an old man carrying melons and headed for the men with the cases. The *polis* flicked his cigarette into the gutter, stared my way, and sprinted toward the moped parked beside the curb. He mounted, kicked the stand up, and gunned the engine. When he sped past, he cocked a finger at me and pretended to pull a trigger. By this time, Carl had reached the center of the square, so close to the men that he grabbed one of them by the sleeve. The sun rose above the rooftop of the restaurant, winked off a copper weathervane. I shivered at an invisible tug on my vest. The chair tipped, the table, and then the world exploded.

4

... in the heart of the Cihangir, May 2016 ...

1. *The velocity of a projectile depends on the type of cartridge, the effect of gravity, air resistance. A bullet can travel anywhere from 180 to 1500 miles per second.*
2. *Given the vagaries of bomb construction, explosive materials may travel thousands of feet per second.*
3. *Light, bullets, and bombs all travel faster than the speed of sound.*

Nilesen rose from the desk to finger the new passport. Stiff and smelling faintly of glue, the document identified her as an Armenian resident of Paris. Across the room, the porter's son Fethi leaned against the door, hands in pockets, face shadowed by fatigue.

"Thank you, *abi*," she said. "I don't deserve your kindness."

"It is not difficult to be kind to you. Your words give hope to those of us fighting for change."

"Hope, for me, has become a dark tunnel." She tossed the passport on the desk. "I no longer see any light."

"You understand what this means? You are a businesswoman, Nilesen *hanim*." He stepped into the light raying through the curtained window and handed her a brochure. "The conference was held at the Istanbul Hilton."

"They will check the security cameras, you know."

He lifted the sleeve of the niqab she was wearing. "Who can say who breathes beneath the veil?"

She reached out to sweep the dark hair off his forehead. "Why do you risk yourself for me?"

He captured her injured hands and raised them to his lips. "Does the student not follow the teacher? Does the child not honor the mother? Does the lover not shelter the beloved?"

"Careful, little brother. You are beginning to sound like a poet."

"You are not too old for me, Nilesen *hanim*, nor I too young for you. Circumstance ..."

"Do not mistake circumstance for fate, Fethi. I care for you, as a sister cares for a brother. Nothing more. Now, go, please, before you miss your morning class."

They turned at a faint tap on the door. When the footsteps retreated, Fethi carried in the breakfast tray and set it on the desk along with a cell phone. "If you need me."

"*Kendine iyi bak, abi.*"

"And you take care, Nilesen." He stared until she turned away. "Shall I leave this with you?"

When she turned back, the gun from the apartment rested beside the phone. She held up her hands. "It is of no use to me at the moment. Better you keep it, until there is need."

Fethi nodded once, rewrapped the weapon, and let himself out. The door closed with a soft click.

Nilesen fumbled a roll from the tray. She nibbled at the bread as she moved to the window. Her left thumb had almost healed. The table had absorbed most of that blow. But the bones in the right hand were slower to knit. She cradled the bandaged fingers and shrugged. *Tanrinin elinde*. It is in God's hands. She twitched the curtain aside to look down on the square.

Dawn light striped the cobbles, caressed the façade of the shops across the street. The bookseller wheeled his cart in front of the display window. A military policeman putted by on a moped, parked at the intersection, and strolled past the restaurant. Something about the man looked familiar, perhaps the set of his shoulders or the hitch in his gait. A woman with a camera caught Nilesen's attention. She had seen this woman yesterday in the same spot, accompanied by a man. An American, a Brit, or an Australian by clothing and stature,. Careless of her progress, the woman snapped pictures as she walked. She lingered by the bookseller's cart, picked up a book, fanned through the pages. The shopkeeper hurried to take it from her, but the woman snatched it back. Among the morning crowd, two men dragged suitcases over the stones. The wheels on their cases rumbled. The policeman approached, asked for a light. The woman crossed to the restaurant. She paused, looked up, shading her eyes against the flare. Nilesen stepped back from the window, nagged by the image of the *polis*, the men, the suitcases. Circumstance, Fethi had said. She abandoned the roll to stuff the new passport into her bag. She adjusted the niqab and unlocked the door just as the first explosion rocked the building.

5

... Istanbul, in the heart of the Cihangir ...

The air grew still, pulsed, withdrew. The vacuum expanded, fragmenting into shocks. The silent bowl that was the square shattered. Debris pelted my body, the force of the blast pinning me against the ground. Sand and dirt and glass tattooed my skin. A hand dropped from the roof, rings sparkling. Blood sprinkled my forehead like holy water. I clutched the camera tighter. Though I beat at my ear and swallowed hard, I couldn't hear. I worked my jaw around the scream rushing to break free. Blood oozed down my cheek. I opened my left eye. The right one refused to respond to the request. Bits of *menemen* peppered my vest.

"Madam?" Someone buzzed at me down a long tunnel. "Madam? Can you move? We need to go inside."

I gagged on the smell of burning plastic, tasted scorched metal. I twisted toward the woman tugging on my sleeve. She yanked harder before inching back into the interior of the café, shouted three times before I understood her command.

"Hurry." She waved me on. Darkness swathed her small body, black trousers beneath a black blouse, black eyes. The scarf over her nose and mouth slipped free. Beauty and sorrow knit patterns across the planes of her face.

A groan escaped from some deep well inside me. I slithered backward. The camera bag dragged by my elbow.

"Leave it. Hurry." The woman nodded in the direction of the street. "They will be here soon."

Already the bagpipe call of ambulances skirled up the hill. Men shouted. Children cried for their mothers. Above it all, a keening rose as the survivors began to mourn the dead. I wound the strap more tightly around my fist, shoved the book and camera inside the bag, and snapped the fasteners. I refused to leave anything behind. Glass crunched beneath me as I scuttled after the woman through the open door of the café. Beside the register, the waiter who had delivered my breakfast rocked and hummed. When we reached the counter, I pushed to my knees.

"No, Madam. They might see you." The woman shoved me down. She placed her mouth to my ear, spoke in loud bursts, paused until I nodded. "You took photographs of the square, no? Better to leave them behind and save yourself."

Her words made no sense. The camera was my life. The magazine would expect us to complete the assignment. But, no, that was stupid. Carl was dead. I saw him rise, flailing like a marionette in the hands of a mad puppeteer. One minute he was racing toward me, the next he was stardust, a pulverized mass of brains and blood and bone. Horror rose like bile. I shook my head to clear the vision. The swollen eye did not open. I flipped onto my back, balanced the bag on my stomach, and wormed my way down the hall into the kitchen.

"Leave it." My rescuer cautioned me. She pointed at the camera.

"No." I stared. She stared, then shrugged and backed toward a potted fern. I read her lips. *Stupid American.* She shoved the plant aside, revealing a trapdoor. She heaved the door upward and motioned me down.

"Make up your mind." I read her lips, then shook my head. I looked behind me. Dust from the explosion settled in gray furrows over the floor. Stay or run? I had no reason to fear the authorities. Except the *polis* on the motorbike had singled me out, threatened me. Why? My head throbbed in time with my pulse. Out in the square, sirens blared. I tightened my hold on the camera and stumbled down the ladder. My rescuer scrambled after me. Below, a storeroom filled with casks and bags of flour, rice, and beans shared space with a riot of unused and abandoned appliances. The woman pushed me onto a crate, scurried back to close the door, then reached for a rope strung along the base of the trapdoor. A shrill scraping above my head made me jump. The woman patted my shoulder.

A Principle of Light

"The pot hides the opening. The cord pulls it into place." She drew breath, blew it out.

"Why are you helping me?" I leaned forward and threw up. She didn't move away.

"I have no idea," she said.

I wiped my mouth and gagged. Shards of glass rained from my hair, joined the remnants of my breakfast. She offered me a tissue, then touched my shoulder, her breath soft against my cheek. "I am Nilesen Yilmaz."

I stared at her profile in the darkened room. When I understood what she was saying, I nodded. "Jeannie. Maurillac. Photographer."

Nilesen took my hand. A bandage on her thumb scraped against my palm. The bones of her fingers felt as bunched and gnarled as the branches of a fig tree. I pulled away. My rescuer did not.

"I am a poet. Sometimes they make me pay for the privilege. Every obsession has its price."

Her words filtered through my deafness. I shuddered, unable to make sense of them. Pride and pain hissed in her statement, but I sensed no regret. Only resignation.

My eye burned. I winced. Above, the pound of bootheels, a club rattling against the cupboards. Nilesen breathed a warning against my skin. We sat, mute and trembling, as the searchers called to one another.

"*Bul onlari*. I saw the woman outside the café. Bring in the dogs."

The footsteps retreated. Nilesen dragged me to my feet. "Now we must go."

"I can't see very well." An understatement. Even in the light, there would be little clarity.

"You must see enough, Jeannie. They are bringing dogs."

"Who's bringing them?"

"The secret police."

I leaned over, gasped for air. When I could breathe again, I asked, "Where will we go?"

Nilesen motioned me to follow as she felt her way through the dark cellar. When light illuminated a section of the passageway, she pointed toward a gate that opened onto a flight of stairs oozing water and slick with moss. She eased the heavy iron bars open and crept upward. I followed, pausing at each step. My damaged eye wept.

"Where are we going?" I focused on a destination, to keep my mind from rewinding the images in the square.

"I do not know yet, Jeannie Maurillac, but you cannot stay here," Nilesen said. "If they catch you, they will destroy your photographs. And then they will break your bones."

6

... chaos in the Cihangir ...

Distant shouting greeted the women as they exited the cellar. They crossed the alley behind the restaurant and hurried away from the scene of the bombing. Rescue personnel glanced their way, returned to their work. No one approached or stopped them. A cordon of police kept gawkers and distraught family members from flooding into the square. The air trembled with shouts and wails. They traveled two blocks before Nilesen hustled the injured photographer into a doorway. She pulled a scarf from her bag and gestured for Jeannie to bend over.

"Put this on. As soon as possible, we will find you a burqa."

"But, I'm an American."

Nilesen slapped her wrist. "Do not act the fool, Madam. You took photos of a terrorist attack. American, Japanese, or Martian, do you believe they will allow you to leave Turkey with this information?"

"I'm a journalist. They can't detain me."

Nilesen shook a finger at her. "You have much to learn if you want to stay alive."

Jeannie tied the ends of the scarf behind her neck. "I'll just show them my passport. That will keep me safe."

"Good to know." Nilesen settled her bag across her chest. "If they arrest you, you can brandish that as your defense. Now, stay close to me, and, for both our sakes, do not speak."

Nilesen abandoned the safety of the doorway and pushed her way through the crowd. Jeannie hurried after her, stumbled, fell to her knees. The camera bag slipped from her shoulder. One of the clasps snapped open. The contents slipped free and scattered across the sidewalk. The cover on the book tore, splitting the title in two. Nilesen scurried back as passersby flowed around them. She rescued the copy of *Işik* and cradled it to her chest.

"Where did you get this?"

"The man at the bookstore gave it to me," Jeannie said.

"Did he tell you what the book is about?"

"No, but I looked through it. It's just poems."

"Indeed. Just poems."

Jeannie snatched the book, stuffed it in the bag, and refastened the snap. "Do you know the author?"

Nilesen stared at her wounded hands. "Do you?"

Jeannie caught the hesitation before the woman looked up. "You wrote this?"

Nilesen extended an arm to help the photographer stand. "I did. And I am being hunted for it. If you stay with me, you, too, will become their prey."

The photographer glanced around but spotted no police. This woman had saved her. With Carl gone, she had no partner by her side, no colleague to run interference. She also had no desire to return to the site of the bombing. She squeezed the poet's arm and they joined the rush of pedestrians. Guided by the Galata Tower to the northwest, they followed the gulls down the hill toward the harbor. As they walked, Nilesen took out the phone Fethi had forced her to accept. She stabbed a bandaged finger at the numbers until the call rang through. When voice mail kicked in, she left a message for the porter's son.

"Where are we going?" Jeannie scuffed her feet over the uneven pavement and clenched her jaw. Pain dug claws into the skin around her eye.

"Do you have your passport?"

Jeannie patted the side pocket of the camera bag.

"Good. You must leave the country. Today. As soon as we find a taxi, you will take it to the airport."

"What about you?"

Nilesen tapped the new, fake documents in her bag and shrugged. "I have my path to follow. But who knows? Maybe it is our fate to go together."

A Principle of Light

A group of distraught residents spilled out of an apartment building, surrounded the women, impeded their progress. Nilesen ignored the shouted questions. Jeannie covered her injured eye with the scarf. She struggled to erase the sight of Carl's body shredding apart in front of her. Ahead, a trio of soldiers wove through the crowd. One of the men wrangled a large Doberman pincer. Every few steps, they stopped citizens to search their bags and pockets, Nilesen uttered a curse in Turkish.

"Give me your things."

Jeannie rubbed her forehead, then stared at the blood smearing her palm. Nilesen pulled a tissue from her pocket and dabbed at the wound.

"Give me your things now."

The American hesitated only a moment before thrusting the camera bag at her companion. The soldiers drew nearer. Nilesen slipped the bag beneath her shirt. The bulge resembled a pregnant belly.

"Go. Walk ahead of me, so they do not suspect we are together. I will meet you on the corner, there, just past the Sullivant Cahier." She dropped her head and walked on, one more housewife rushing to complete the day's shopping.

Disoriented, in pain, Jeannie tugged the headscarf lower. She passed a dressmaker's shop, the mannequin outside oblivious to her passage. In the doorway of a tobacconist, she lingered to inhale the pungent odor of nicotine that escaped through the opened door. She had almost slipped by the soldiers when the dog turned its head. The handler turned with it, extended his jop, and tapped her arm.

"Madam? Have you come from the accident?" He walked with her a few more steps. "Madam? Let me see your face."

7

... from the Cihangir to the sea ...

I swayed, caught myself on the wall of the nearest building, swallowed back the urge to run. The jop pressed against my ribs. My eye throbbed. Sweat trickled between my breasts. I imagined the soldier could hear my heart thumping, could see the pulse beating in my neck. I tugged the scarf lower, mumbled a reply.

"I ask you again, Madam." He spoke in English, in a tone that chilled. "Did you come from the square? Were you at the scene of the bombing?"

"I'm looking for my cousin. She told me to meet her at the Nusretiye Mosque, but I got lost. All that commotion." I waved in the direction of the square as I eased away from the jop.

"You are injured, Madam."

"I tripped, running from the explosion." I offered a shaky laugh. "Fell and hit my face on the ground."

He raised an eyebrow. The dog circled my legs, sniffing for God only knew what. I avoided eye contact with both of them. The other two soldiers held their weapons casually, the barrels aimed toward the crowd. He prodded my side again, harder. "Let me see your documents, Madam."

I slapped my back pocket, pretending to search for my ID. My passport was in the camera case. I patted the pockets of my vest before I glanced down the block. Nilesen had reached the cross street and waddled forward. She pressed into the milling crowd, wove her way through the tourists who murmured and snapped selfies as they stared toward the square where the explosion took place. I finally located my driver's license.

"Jeannie Maurillac. American. Where is your passport?"

"I left it at the hotel." I almost blurted the name of the pensión where Carl and I were staying, but just as I started, a loud boom drew the attention of the onlookers. A woman yelled a warning. *"Bäm! Burada bäm var."* Others picked up the cry. *Bomba*! Bomb! The street erupted. People ran, heedless of calls to stop. The Doberman barked and lunged at the crowd. The soldiers exchanged looks and shouted more orders. A man barreled toward me, stopped, stumbled against the dog. The handler jerked the leash to prevent an attack and yelled at the *polis* holding my ID. He thrust it at me.

"Wait here, Madam, until we return."

As they moved off, I sprinted across the street, muttering apologies as I collided with harried Turks. I hunched my shoulders, trying to collapse my six-foot frame into a smaller package. I threaded my way down the street, scurrying beneath awnings to hug the buildings. I wandered two blocks farther east until I heard Nilesen call my name. She was standing next to a smart car, waving her arms above her head as the chaos swelled around us.

"*Acele*, Jeannie. Hurry!" Nilesen called.

When I reached the car, I yanked the door open and tumbled in. She scrambled into the passenger side and pounded the seat.

"Go now, Fethi."

The young Turk behind the wheel shifted into drive and inched his way down the hill. In the distance, the waters of the Bosphorus sparkled in the morning sun.

8

... in the heart of the Cihangir, May 2016 ...

As the porter's son inched his way through the narrow streets, Nilesen handed Jeannie the camera case along with a package wrapped in brown paper.

"Put this on before we go to the boat."

The photographer raised her hands. "Wait. Boat? I thought we were going to the airport."

Fethi glanced in the rearview mirror. "You are, Madam," he said. "But not to Atatürk. Too many soldiers. We will go to the Asian side, to Sabiha Gökçen. A water taxi can get you there. Fewer eyes and ears that way."

"Fethi. *Abi*." Nilesen touched his arm. "You cannot come with us."

His lips settled into a firm line beneath the thin nose and dark brows that marked him as a descendant of the Ottoman rulers. His shoulders rose, then relaxed against the seat. He shook his head. "You need my help."

"Your father needs you. Our country does, as well. I will see my friend safely away, and then I will decide what I should do."

"No." The force of his denial rattled both women. "Next time they will not stop with your hands, Nilesen *hanim*. Use the documents I gave you. Go to England. Tell them what is happening here."

Nilesen continued to argue, but he fixed his eyes on the road. Unable to change his mind, she leaned against the headrest and closed her eyes. She remembered another young man with a stubborn set to his denial. Alain, one hand on the wheel, the other clutching hers. *Perhaps we should go to meet your friends,* she told him. *No,* he replied. *This night is for you, for us.* How the shafts of evening shadow striped their clothing! She saw it still, the glint of fire from her ring. The purple of her dress reflected the light as they drove along the tree-lined highway, headed for the villa in Çeşme. Despite the rumblings of dissent, the erosion of civil liberties, she and Alain had embraced the promise of a life together. Then the darkness swallowed them whole. She turned away to wipe the tears, alert to the words unwinding inside her. *You called me from the depth of the dark water, merman warrior, unbound by convention or fear.* His sacrifice fed her work until the fire died, the light faded. All her passion turned to ash and wind. In the back seat, the photographer rocked, lips compressed in pain.

They moved haltingly down the street, stuttering forward, idling for long minutes as the mass of pedestrians flowed around them. Once the crowd separated to allow more military and emergency vehicles to speed toward the bomb site, Fethi scooted forward. Then the throngs closed in and they slowed again. It took more than an hour to reach the docks. Fethi pulled up next to the marina and hopped from the car. When he opened her door, Nilesen waved him off. She hurried to tug Jeannie, now swathed in a burqa, onto the walkway that wound down to the ferry idling below.

"*Sağol*, Fethi. *Sonra görüşürüz.*"

"He's not coming with us?" Unaware of the argument between Nilesen and the porter's son, Jeannie pressed a fold of the burqa to her eye.

"I will see you as far as the airport. Fethi has other responsibilities." Nilesen turned to look out over the water. "Perhaps I should leave with you. But I am undecided. I am a Turk. This is my country. Everything I loved lies in this soil. Is this where I belong?"

"Nilesen." Fethi clenched his fists. "Don't."

She motioned him to silence, then made her way toward a kiosk at the end of the walkway. Jeannie opened her mouth to protest, closed it again. She had no choice. Either she turned herself in to the authorities or she trusted the woman who had saved her life. She gritted her teeth against the pain and wandered toward the gangplank. Across the water, sailboats tacked up and down the strait. Fishermen out since dawn maneuvered their *tekneler* between buoys, the nets

A Principle of Light

that trailed the boats sagging with the morning's catch. Along the dock, housewives and maids inspected the fish as they were unloaded onto the quay. When she shaded her good eye against the glare from the water, she noticed a commotion at the end of the walkway. She hurried back to the kiosk, tugged Nilesen's sleeve. A phalanx of *Ashkeri Inzibat* advanced toward them.

"*Polisi*," Nilesen muttered. She snatched the credit card from the clerk's hand. When he protested, she waved off his protests. "I have changed my mind about the ferry. We need a private water taxi."

The man cursed. Nilesen glared. Finally, he gestured toward a dinghy pulled up on the shore just past the end of the dock. Nilesen adjusted Jeannie's burqa. She steered the photographer around the sales booth and across the grass. An old man wearing a beret and a vest decorated with fishing lures frowned up at them.

"*Selam*, Grandfather." Nilesen inclined her head. "May we employ you for a trip to Sabiha Gökçen?"

The fisherman squinted down the causeway and rocked to his feet. "Trouble compels us to accept the unacceptable, *mi*?"

"Trouble demands that we hurry to escape it. Will you take us?"

He gathered the net he was mending, tossed it into the boat, and extended his hand to Jeannie. "Madam."

"Wait," Jeannie said. "How far is it to Sabiha Gökçen?"

"Istanbul's second airport is on the eastern side of the city, only an hour's journey if we go by water," she said. "From there, you can fly to Paris, and then on to the States."

As soon as the photographer settled in the bow, Nilesen followed her onto the boat. The old man shoved off. He unhooked the rope that anchored the boat to the wooden piling and scrambled over the gunwale. The wind picked up, ruffling the water. The fisherman executed a wide turn. A fishtail of water sprayed toward the shore. Droplets stippled the bench. Several landed on the back of Nilesen's hand, caught the sunlight, winked iridescence. She raised the hand to her lips, tasted the salt spray. A memory jolted free, one she thought long packed away.

They had come to Istanbul with their families to celebrate the engagement and Alain, eager to show her his city, borrowed a sailboat from one of his friends. They set off from the Asian shore, headed out beneath the fierce June sun and the political tremors unsettling the land. She sat beside him, enchanted by the waves and the fishermen casting off all around them. The minarets on the European side reflected the sunlight. Gulls swooped and soared, their raucous, throaty calls reminiscent of oracles croaking out the day's tidings in an ominous tongue. The boat was small, only twelve feet, and easy to maneuver. They had only gone halfway across when the sky turned dark. The advancing storm whipped the water into frothy whitecaps. Alain fought the wind and raced back to the dock before the patter became a deluge. Once more on land, he held out a hand to capture raindrops, dripped them over her lips, then licked each drop away, leaving her aflame.

"Soon, bright one," he whispered against her throat. "Tonight the world will meet you and witness the treasure I have won."

It was there, on the shore, that the messenger found them. The boy wheeled his bike from the path to the shoreline. He handed a letter to Alain, accepted a tip, and retraced his path to the street. They huddled under the eaves of a boathouse until the storm passed on. Soon, the sun peeked out, stayed long enough to steam the path, then retreated behind the clouds, thrusting them into shadow.

"What?" She held his arm as he crumpled the note into a ball.

"A former acquaintance demands to settle an old debt, one he owes me."

His anger faded, his eyes reclaiming the distant light. She mimicked his movements as he secured the mast and settled the floats between the hull and the dock. But when he took her hand, she felt his tremble. "Tell me," she urged. He shook off the question along with the rainwater still hidden in his curls.

"I promise to write it all down, Nilo, for you to read and laugh about when we are no longer young and our children fuss over our old bones."

A pleasant lie that hid a bitter truth. They would not grow old together. No children would care for and love them. Nilesen leaned over the side of the old man's boat. She dipped her hand in the water as she looked back toward the shore.

The soldiers had reached the kiosk. One spotted the boat. He raised his arm and signaled for them to return. The old fisherman ignored the gesture. He adjusted the throttle and headed south toward the Sea of Marmara.

9

... on the Sea of Marmara ...

The day grew warmer. The boat rocked. It slammed down over the whitecaps, sped forward, only to repeat the motion seconds later. Huddled beneath the burqa, I rested my head on my knees. I swallowed hard to keep from throwing up. I shivered, cold then hot, then cold again. The old man spoke to Nilesen in bursts. He glanced my way now and then before scanning the horizon. Nilesen folded her hands in her lap, looked away, looked back. When I caught her eye, she murmured reassurance. The cloth covering my face slipped free. She glanced at me and frowned. I fought the panic inside, wiped the saliva pooling at the corners of my lips. It hurt to breathe.

When I gestured for the camera bag, she only raised one eyebrow before she slid it across the seat. I read the censure in her. *Not a good idea, Amerikali.* I didn't care what she thought. The camera had been my lifeline since college. I couldn't abandon it now. The boat thumped against the waves. I rocked backward, clutching the straps as the bag bumped against my side. Water churned up by our passage moistened the canvas cover. I thought about the data card sealed inside the camera. What exactly had I captured?

Behind us, the European side of Istanbul retreated. Ahead, the Asian shore advanced. We passed a collection of wharves and warehouses before the old man slowed. Nilesen patted my hand. I trailed it in the water, mesmerized by the distortion as light broke the plane. Once, during an experiment on a TV game show, a scientist placed a handful of gel-filled balls into clear water and cautioned viewers to pay close attention. The balls disappeared. A demonstration of a principle of light, the man intoned. Now, running from the unknown, I wanted to be one of those balls. I wanted to bend the pursuit until I, too, vanished from sight.

"I can't breathe." I looked up. Nilesen sat still, her gaze locked straight ahead.

"*Büyük baba*," she said, affection for the stranger evident in her tone. She nodded over his shoulder. "Grandfather. Look there."

"I see them. Get your passports out."

Nilesen pulled hers from a pocket in her bag. I unzipped the side of the camera case, slid mine free, and opened it. "Oh, my God."

The old man swiveled on the seat, his dark eyes intent. "*Sorun nedir?*"

"Jeannie? What is wrong?" Nilesen's concern echoed his.

I held the passport out so they could see the photograph. Nilesen swore softly. "Is Carl the man you were working with?"

"Yes." I leaned over the side of the boat and threw up. When nothing remained but dry heaves, I scooped a handful of water, rinsed my mouth, and sat back down. "He must have grabbed mine by mistake. I never checked."

The patrol boats drew closer. If they stopped us... I couldn't think beyond the moment. Nilesen turned to the old man.

"We are close to Harem Otorgarina?" When he nodded, she gestured toward the land. He hesitated, spat into the water, wiped his mouth on his sleeve. He reversed direction and angled the craft back toward the shore.

"What good will that do?" My stomach cramped, my head throbbed. My eye had swollen to the size of a pomegranate.

"We will do what they least expect. Instead of leaving, we will go deeper into the countryside." She leaned close as if to adjust my headpiece. "Trust me, Jeannie Marillac. I will not let them take you."

The first of the patrol boats had spotted us, yet they made no move toward our position. The fisherman stood, gathered the fishing net, and unfurled it across the water. We trolled our way closer to land. When the net grew heavy, the old man heaved it into the boat, emptied it, and flung it out

A Principle of Light

again. Fish flopped at our feet, gulping air, fanning their gills in a struggle to stay alive. As we approached the dock, more fish tangled themselves in the net and wriggled in panic, desperate to escape. I glanced at my companion, unmoving, unblinking in the noonday sun. I watched the fish, unable to free themselves, unable to return to where they belonged. I unlatched the bag, raised the camera, and snapped the images, one-eyed and off-balance, my unsteady view changing with the direction of the boat and the unforgiving light of mid-day around me.

10

... in Harem Otorgarina ...

Nilesen spotted the ferry first. She tapped the old man's shoulder to direct his attention to the boat approaching off the stern. He dropped the net and settled by the tiller. When the larger craft plowed closer, he swung his craft hard toward land. The ferry tooted a warning as it barreled between the patrol boats and the fishing boat. We drifted closer to shore. The ferry churned on, reversed engines, and bumped gently against the pilings. One of the crew released a gangplank. Passengers scurried off and headed toward Harem Otorgarina, Istanbul's main bus terminal, which sat on a rise above the dock. Behind the station, the Selimiye Barracks loomed.

Alert to the danger coiled and waiting within the military installation, Nilesen fingered the phone Fethi had insisted she carry with her. As the dinghy neared the shore, she called the reservation desk at the station. The phone rang, four, eight, twelve times. Nilesen held the phone so Jeannie could listen in.

"Harem Otorgar. *Efendim*," a harried agent answered. "How can I help you?"

"I need two tickets to Bursa. On the next bus, of course."

"You are calling very late, Madam, to get tickets for today."

"Please, kind sir, my sister and I must go to our mother. She is very ill." Nilesen paused to let the lie settle. "She may be dying."

The ticket agent cleared his throat. "Very well. Perhaps there is space on a bus scheduled to depart at three-thirty this afternoon. Come to the ticket counter before ten minutes pass. That is the best I can do."

Nilesen recommended him to God and hung up. The boat pulled next to the shore several hundred yards north of the main dock.

"Stay in the boat, Madams." The old man grinned to soften the command. While Nilesen looked for patrol boats, he clambered over the gunwale and dropped into the foamy water that

marked the border between the land and the sea. His boots made sucking sounds as he worked his way to shore. While they waited for his return, Nilesen tugged at the burqa."Take this off now. They will be looking for you wearing it." When Jeannie removed the garment, Nilesen checked her injured eye and clucked softly.

"You need a doctor."

Jeannie shrugged. "What I need is to look at my photographs."

Nilesen placed a hand over the camera case. "We will wait until we are safe at Bursa. Can you remove the, I do not know what to call it, the thing that holds the pictures?"

"The memory card?" Jeannie pressed her thumb against her right temple, searching for a pressure point to ease the throbbing. She balanced the camera on her lap, flipped open the panel that hid the ports, and released the data card. "What should I do with this?"

"Can you hide it?"

Jeannie thought for a moment, then checked the pockets of her vest. She pulled out a pack of gum, slipped the card between two sticks of spearmint, and stuffed the package back in her pocket. The bulk of the camera case pressed against her thigh.

"You must leave that behind." Nilesen inclined her head toward the case. "You can put your lenses and wallet in my bag. If anything happens to me, take the bag and run."

Ahead, the crowd from the ferry had dispersed. Only a few stragglers still hiked the red cobbled walkway. Nilesen spotted the fisherman returning along the path that ran next to the shore. Takeout bags dangled from one hand. He set the food down before he approached the boat, then extended

A Principle of Light

his hand to help the women out. After they made their way to land, he opened one of the bags. The aroma of spicy beef and rice drifted out. He removed several cardboard containers and a bottle of water and stuffed them into pouches on his coat before handing the remaining food and water to Jeannie.

"Go now, madams." He cocked his head toward the station. *"Güle, güle."*

"Thank you, Grandfather. You must leave as well. The fish," Nilesen gestured toward the boat, "are waiting."

The old man turned toward the boat. Jeannie struggled up the rise, the rolled burqa clutched in one hand.

"Wait!" he called. "Madam. Your case."

"Throw it in the water," Nilesen said. "Let the fish puzzle over it. *Teşekkür ederim*. Be safe."

"I am honored, Nilesen *hanim*." He touched his forehead. "May you walk in the light."

"You know who I am?"

He reached into a pocket of his jacket and pulled out a copy of *Işik*. "Even an old man can find new words."

Nilesen kissed his cheeks, tasted the tears that coursed down his face. "I will write a poem for you, *baba*."

After he returned to the sea, she gathered her bag and the food sacks and climbed the hill. Jeannie struggled behind her. When they reached the top, the women followed the dirt path until it turned into a sidewalk leading to a wide lane in front of the terminal. A squat, two-story red building stood half-buried among a wall of signs. Beyond the entrance, the building opened onto an immense sweep of numbered stops, buses, and ticketing gates. Vehicles sputtered and roared through the lot. Travelers hustled along the walkways or struggled with suitcases as they sought their departure points.

Jeannie staggered, then righted herself. They passed through the first gate. Posters announcing everything from aftershave to holiday vacations covered the walls. Noise reverberated, announcements of arrivals and departures swallowed up by the voices of a thousand travelers, babbling in a variety of languages. The smell of packed lunches, body odor, and diesel fumes came at them in waves.

Jeannie leaned against a wall to keep from falling. Her head rang with the noise from the lines of people surging toward the doors at the far end of the terminal. "How will we find the right gate?"

"We will ask." Nilesen steered her toward a kiosk in the center. A harried woman shuffled through stacks of paper as the next person in line made his request. When it was her turn, Nilesen accepted a brochure. She tucked it in her bag and steered a path toward the far end of the station. The place swirled with color. Despite the pain, Jeannie itched to document the scene. She lifted the camera and attempted to focus through her good eye.

"No, Maurillac." Nilesen nodded to her left. "Now may not be the best time."

Jeannie followed her gaze. She spied a pair of tourist *polisi* strolling through the crowd. Every few steps they stopped a traveler, examined the person's papers, then moved on.

"There," Nilesen said. "The women's restroom." They detoured around a mother pushing a double stroller. Jeannie bowed her head and plunged ahead as they plowed their way toward the *tuvalet*. They had almost reached the entrance when a hand wrapped around Nilesen's arm. She jerked to a stop.

"Do not run," a man ordered. Nilesen plucked Jeannie's sleeve. The photographer staggered and turned to face a man in a short-sleeved shirt. Despite the heat, he had a jacket draped over his left arm. His eyes flicked over her as he edged closer to Nilesen.

"Gönenç? Is that you?"

Jeannie pushed her way between the man and the poet. He glared at her and tugged Nilesen closer.

"You are mistaken, sir." Nilesen cut her eyes away, blinked twice, and faced him again.

A Principle of Light

"Are you certain?" His insistent shaking of her arm attracted the attention of several women entering and exiting the *tuvalet*. The *polisi* edged closer.

Jeannie shook a finger at the man and again stepped between him and Nilesen. A low growl, something between a warning and a moan, escaped from Jeannie. She poked his chest. Her scarf slipped, revealing the damaged flesh around the eye. When he spotted the injury, the man flinched.

"*Hirsiz*," Jeannie hissed. A crowd formed around the trio. One woman repeated her accusation. The murmur grew. More voices joined in. *Hirsiz. Hirsiz.*

"*Fahişe*," the man said. He released Nilesen and shoved Jeannie. She struck his wrist with the heel of her hand. He cried out and let go of the wallet inside Nilesen's purse.

"So, you are a thief." Nilesen snapped her fingers to attract the attention of the *polisi*. The thief scanned the crowd, pretended to spot a familiar face, and scooted past the circle of women. Shouts and accusations followed him. The policemen noticed the crowd. Jeannie tugged the scarf into place and she and Nilesen pushed through the door of the *tuvalet*. The line of ladies waiting to use the stalls had doubled back upon itself. Wedged into the far end, Nilesen and Jeannie had no choice but to inch slowly forward. In the terminal, the voice of the *hirsiz* rose above the din.

"*Seni bulacağim, Amerikali kadin. Seni bulacağim.*"

One of the *polis* shouted for the man to halt. Whistles and jeers followed. The commotion swelled, burst apart, and settled as the threats receded. Nilesen and Jeannie shared a look. The absurdity of their predicament rolled over them. Jeannie sensed the smile flirting at the corners of her mouth. Terrified by her injury but momentarily relieved at their close escape, she fought the laughter rising inside her. Unable to stop, she held her sides and howled. Nilesen joined her, their howls reverberating in the tiled room. The women around them exchanged glances and leaned away. They clasped hands, savoring the brief moment of reprieve. For now, they were safe.

"What was he shouting?" Jeannie said.

Nilesen picked at her bandaged hand. "What they all say. He promises revenge. After all, we interrupted his thieving."

"I heard him say American." Jeannie's shivers subsided. "I think he plans to find me."

"Do not worry." Nilesen linked arms with the photographer. "I will not let him frighten you."

"Will the police wait for us to come out?" Jeannie hiccupped away the last of the giggles.

"No, I do not think so. They will be too busy chasing the *hirsiz*." Nilesen studied her friend's face. "How did you know what he was?"

"I met one once, on the Metro in Madrid. A pickpocket with seriously beady eyes, wearing a backpack on his chest. He came up behind me, sliced my bag, tried to slip his hand inside. When I warned the others in the car, he followed me to the university. Scariest subway ride of my life." Jeannie picked at a thumbnail. Her eye throbbed. "Where do we go for our tickets?"

Nilesen pulled out the brochure to consult the schedule of departures for Bursa. They shuffled closer to the stalls. "Number thirty-eight. And we better hurry. There is just one small problem."

Jeannie cocked her head, then bent closer to whisper in Nilesen's ear. "How are we going to pay for them?"

"I have an idea."

"So do I." Jeannie slipped a hand beneath the bundled burqa. "Let's use this."

Nilesen stared at the credit card. "Is that what I think it is?"

"Is it a crime to steal from a thief?" Jeannie mimed lifting the card from the *hirsiz*'s pocket and they laughed again. Three more steps and they reached the toilets. Afterward, the lunches the old fisherman had purchased tucked in Nilesen's bag, they made their way toward the ticket kiosk, then followed directions to the waiting area for their bus. Once there, they squatted, backs against the wall, to wolf down the meat-filled pitas, grapes, hummus, and cheese the old man had purchased for them. In the bottom of

A Principle of Light

one bag, Nilesen discovered a bottle of pain reliever. She handed three capsules to Jeannie, who gulped them down. Then Nilesen took two herself.

Jeannie rested her head on her knees. Remorse expanded like an umbrella. If they hadn't fought last night, Carl might have waited for her this morning. But if they had gone out together, she, too, might be nothing but atoms floating in the charged air of the Cihangir.

"Does it hurt very much?" Nilesen peeled back the scarf to examine the wound.

"I think," Jeannie's voice broke, "I've lost the sight in my eye."

"Do not despair, *arkadaşim*. Be strong."

"What does it mean? *Arkadaşim*."

Nilesen hesitated. When she spoke, her words filled the space between them. "Friend, Jeannie."

The photographer stared at her. "Are we? Friends?"

"We have survived a bombing, been chased by polisi, harassed by a thief, and shared a meal. I believe we are. And, I have another friend, in Bursa. She will help you."

Jeannie closed her good eye. "I take pictures for a living, Nilesen. If I can't see, I can't work."

They listened for a time to the rustling of a thousand feet, heard the muttered conversations of a thousand travelers. Finally, Nilesen spoke. "Art, like water, carves its own path through the rock. I am a poet, Jeannie. They broke my hands, yet the words still come. Even when I don't want them. You will find a way."

The terminal buzzed. Buses arrived and departed. Fumes and grit filled the air. They remained still, bound by pain and desperation to the course they had plotted. When the bus to Bursa pulled up half an hour ahead of departure time, they made one more trip to the restroom, then climbed aboard, too weary to notice the dark-eyed man scowling intensely at their backs. The door was closing as he boarded, slid into a seat several rows in front of them, and pretended to fall asleep.

11

... on the road to Bursa ...

I sank into the faux leather seat, too dizzy to ask Nilesen if she preferred to sit by the window. The glass, tinted against the afternoon glare, allowed me to see out. The people along the sidewalk couldn't see in. I settled the camera against my chest, folded my hands, and closed my eyes. Carl's avatar accompanied me, his waving arms and howling mouth fusing with Edvard Munch's screamer as it herded me toward a beady-eyed man with a razor hidden in his coat. Only the jolt as the bus pulled away from the curb rescued me from the horror inside my head. The video of Carl disintegrating was replaced by a series of still shots. The weekend vacation at Niagara Falls when he teased about getting married on the Maid of the Mist. Our abortive trip to Belize to cover lesser-known tourist spots. I wanted to dive. He wanted to party. We came back early when the hurricane blew in. Making love on Sunday afternoons. Breaking up over breakfast at Tim Horton's. Every stupid, funny, senseless conversation ricocheted in my head. I didn't love him yesterday, but I had loved him once. Regret piled up like driftwood, tangled in lost opportunities. Now, there was no more rewind. I fell asleep, a line from "The Raven" floating in my brain. Nevermore. Nevermore.

"Jeannie." Nilesen prodded me gently. "Jeannie. You're moaning. Perhaps you should take more pills."

She held up the bag with the pain reliever inside and offered me the rest of her water. I had finished mine at the station. Now my head pulsed, my mouth was dry, and chills shook my body. I tipped the capsules onto my palm and scooped them into my mouth. I noticed she did the same. When I glanced at her hands, I shuddered at the matrix of scars across the left one, the bandages taped over the right.

"Are you hurting?"

She turned her palms up and shrugged. "Pain, like light, comes and goes. It is what we do with it that matters."

I fought nausea, spoke around the pounding in my head. "Tell me, Nilesen, what do you do with the light?"

She took my hand, held it up against her own. Her small palm nested easily inside my larger one. "I use it to see the truth, *arkadaşim*. Is that not what we all do?"

I thought of my photographs, how I adjusted for the perfect view, how I manipulated the light and the dark to enhance the subject and inform my personal vision. "Not everyone seeks truth. Some of us only search for beauty."

"Are they mutually exclusive?"

When I failed to respond, she started to speak, then held a finger to her lip and lifted her chin toward the front of the bus. Over the top of the headrest in front of me, I spied a man with black button eyes, a shadowed face, and a scowl to match. *Hirsiz*. The thief from the bus station had followed us. I slid lower, drew the scarf over my bandaged eye. Despite our careful planning, we were trapped, defenseless and wounded, on the road to a strange town where I was certain no one would care if we lived or died.

"Nilesen." I shared my suspicions. "What now?"

She liberated her phone from her bag, selected a number, and punched in a message. When she finished, she squeezed my arm.

"Remember what I told you, Jeannie Maurillac." Her words whispered against my neck. "I have friends in Bursa."

I wrapped the camera inside the burqa, the urge to laugh replaced by dread creeping, vine-like, down my back.

12

... on the road to Bursa ...

The afternoon panted on. The sun shifted west, casting long shadows over the olive groves beyond the tinted glass of the bus windows. The thief had not moved from his seat. Nilesen stowed her notebook and pen in her bag, then pressed the back of her hand against Jeannie's forehead. Heat radiated off the photographer's skin. With a scowl, Nilesen thumbed on the phone to check the time. They were still more than two hours from Bursa, long enough for the infection to settle in and spread through the woman's body. Already her rich color had paled, causing the scatter of freckles on her nose and cheeks to stand out sharply. Nilesen burrowed deeper into the seat and studied her companion's bowed head. She should wake her, but perhaps, during sleep, Jeannie's immune responses would rally.

The bus rumbled over the highway, the road winding east, then turning south as it skirted the coast before heading inland. Warehouses and fishing boats gave way to small villages, fields and orchards, the late May plantings already underway. Cars escaping the city streamed past. Semis chugged beside them, then darted forward as the bus motored on. Three rows ahead, the thief draped his jacket over the head rest and scanned the rows behind him. When he stood to use the bathroom in the rear of the bus, Nilesen buried her face against Jeannie's shoulder, peeking out to track the man's progress. Careful not to jar her companion awake, she reached inside the bag the fisherman had given her, his final gift within her grasp.

The thief stalked down the aisle, holding on to seatbacks as he pretended to lose his balance. When he reached their row, he caught her eye and smiled. It was not a friendly grin.

"Payback is coming," he said as he passed.

J. E. Irvin

Nilesen watched until he reached the back of the bus, where he dialed his cell phone and spoke loud enough for her to hear. "They are here." Concern replaced caution,. She took out her phone and typed a message. *Help. We are pursued by thieves.* The *hirsiz* sauntered up the aisle, throwing his weight against her shoulder as he passed. She counted the cars rolling by on the opposite side of the road as she waited for a reply to her text. When it arrived, she pulled the stun gun from the bag and hid it beneath her blouse. The minutes crept by, slower with each turn of the wheels. Shadows from the trees along the road strobed the window. Beside her, Jeannie stirred.

"*Su.*" She struggled to sit up. "I'm so thirsty."

"Here, *arkadaşim.*" Nilesen handed over the last bottle of water. "Listen. The *hirsiz* has called for reinforcements."

"Then it's time to send a picture of our own." Jeannie drank half the bottle and handed it to Nilesen. She braced her legs against the seat, pressed a hand against the window, and forced herself to stand.

"Jeannie." Nilesen hissed a warning.

She patted the poet's shoulder and called out across the rows. "Hey, *hirsiz*, smile."

Startled by the unexpected noise, the other passengers looked up. Those who spoke no English frowned. Those who understood the words glanced her way, then scanned the rows. The thief stared straight ahead. Jeannie repeated the taunt. Her phone jiggled with the motion of the bus, blurring the image. "Hey, *hirsiz*. Now everyone will know who you are."

Protests filled the bus. A man cursed at her. The thief rested a knee on his seat, rose over the headrest, and stared at her. She snapped his picture, once, twice, then sank down. Her left eye teared. She groaned as a wave of nausea hit. "Quick, Nilesen, send the pictures to all my contacts. Someone will know what to do."

Chatter from the travelers increased. The bus slowed, bumped off the roadway, and coasted to a stop. A car pulled in behind it. The bus driver opened the door and called a

A Principle of Light

greeting, then stepped out to speak to two men. One of the them handed over an envelope. The driver slipped it inside his shirt. When he reboarded the bus, he singled out an elderly woman and a teenage boy sitting behind Nilesen and Jeannie. Despite their resistance, he hauled them toward the front of the bus.

"What's going on?" Jeannie clenched her fists.

"Reinforcements. Our *hirsiz* has bribed the driver."

"But the woman and the boy?"

"The next bus will pick them up."

"What about us?"

Nilesen motioned for her to look down. When Jeannie saw the stun gun, she nodded. She searched through the pockets of her vest until she found the key chain with a compass and a whistle. Carl's last gift. *For protection,* he'd insisted, *when I'm not around.* She forced down a sob.

"Perhaps," she said, "this will help."

Nilesen accepted the whistle. They were still a half-hour from Bursa. Two fugitives pitted against a gang of thieves and a complicit bus driver. Terrible odds. Not an auspicious arrangement, a poet might say. Unbidden, Alain's voice reminded her of past challenges, past choices. *Be brave.*

"*Arkadaşim*, that means my friend, right?" Jeannie clutched at the camera hidden in the burqa.

Nilesen nodded. "Remember this, Jeannie. Light conquers darkness."

"*Arkadaşim.*" Despite the problems she had caused, Nilesen had called her friend. Pain lanced through her eye. "But if light conquers darkness, who decides who is the light and who the darkness?"

"That," Nilesen said, "is the job of the universe. Now, rest. Save your strength for the battle to come."

The air conditioning chose that moment to cycle on. A vent beneath the window blew frigid air at their feet. Unfolding the burqa to cover her legs, Jeannie relaxed against the poet's shoulder, too weary to argue, but in her heart, she knew who was *Işik*. Humans may lose sight of the truth, but the camera never lies.

Eyes closed, floating in and out of the shadows thrown by the roadside trees and buildings, she listened to the mumbled threats coming from behind them. The other passengers heard them, too. A chorus of alarm filled the bus, faint at first, then growing louder. Shouts to the driver to pull over. Phone conversations to family and friends. Calls for the thief and his friends to get off the bus. The driver switched on a microphone and pleaded for calm. His excuses were drowned out by the rising panic. Children cried. An elderly man demanded that the police be summoned. That was the last thing Nilesen wanted. When the bus passed a sign announcing Bursa's city limits, she eased into the aisle, then grabbed Jeannie and pushed her forward. As they struggled toward the front, the thief wheeled upright to block their passage. In the aisle behind them, his companions closed in. The bus swayed, throwing them all off balance. Pulling the stun gun from beneath her shirt, Nilesen jammed it into the stomach of the thief and pressed the button. Caught off guard, the man flailed and fell backward. He grabbed for Nilesen, missed, and slid sideways, collapsing onto the floor. She stepped over his twitching body. Jeannie moved closer to the driver. One of the thieves behind grabbed Nilesen's blouse. She turned, thrust the gun at his midsection, and pressed the switch again. Not enough of a charge remained. The gun stuttered and fell silent. Pawing at the sting in his side, the man lunged toward her. She ducked to avoid his fist, shoved hard against Jeannie, and they stumbled down the stairwell beside the driver.

"Let us out."

The driver cursed as he kicked at them. Nilesen staggered, holding onto Jeannie. The doors hissed open and she tumbled through, pulling the photographer with her. They landed hard in the dust. The driver released the brake and pulled away, the wheels of the bus flinging pebbles and dirt over them. Nilesen scrabbled upright. Across the road, a workman repairing a guard rail called out an offer to help. She waved him off. As she and Jeannie stumbled toward a petrol station, they passed a vendor's stand. The aroma of roasting chestnuts drifted toward them. Jeannie's stomach growled. Nilesen raised an eyebrow.

"Bursa is famous for its chestnuts, *arkadaşim*. Would you like to try some?"

Jeannie shook her head. "How can you think about food now?"

"Ah, my American friend, it is your stomach that growls. Besides, when is a better time? We escaped the thieves. We fell out of a bus but broke no bones. Life hands us a moment of respite and we must take it." While Nilesen waited for Jeannie to decide, she peeked at her phone. No message from Fethi. Had he sent someone to rescue them?

Jeannie rummaged in the pocket of her jeans and pulled out three lira. "How many will this buy?"

"Enough." Nilesen removed her scarf, stashed it in her bag, and turned to the vendor. She bargained with him before handing over half their money for two cones of nuts. She gave one to Jeannie and lifted her chin in the direction of the gas station. They ignored the bruises from the fall, limped past the fuel pumps, and hurried into the store. The whoosh of the automatic doors cut off the wail of a police car racing down the highway in the direction of the bus.

13

... in the city of Bursa ...

The ceiling fan mounted above the cash register strained against the heat that greeted us inside the shop. A clerk wearing a ragged t-shirt scurried over to offer assistance as Nilesen half-pushed, half-dragged me deeper into the interior. I hugged my elbows and mumbled a request for *su*. The man set two bottles of water on the counter. Nilesen placed the remaining coins beside them. He rubbed his chin, began to argue, then shrugged and scooped up the money.

"Do you need petrol? An oil change? A car wash? We are a full-service station, Madams."

"We are waiting for a ride," Nilesen said. "My friend is ill. Perhaps contagious."

The clerk raised his hands in a warding gesture and retreated to the farthest edge of the counter. Nilesen ducked to hide a grin before she checked her phone.

"No message?" My legs shook. I needed to lie down, to cover my eyes and forget all that had happened since I left the pensión that morning, but the knowledge that we were pursued by unknown forces kept me upright. I didn't know who scared me more. The secret police, the local jandarmalar, the military soldiers with their dogs, or the thieves who resented our warning potential victims. Despite the throbbing in my head and the images of the explosion scrolling through my memory, I realized two things. One, I was an American woman alone and without documents in a foreign country in the middle of a political crisis. Two, my fate lay in the scarred and battered hands of a revolutionary poet who was considered an enemy of the state. Also, she may have called me a friend, but she wasn't sure she liked me. *Way to go, Maurillac,* Carl would have groused. Poor Carl.

My companion struggled to open the plastic caps on the bottles, then helped me drink. We drifted toward the front of the store. A steady line of cars pulled up, pumped gas, and drove off. A truck driver strolled in for cigarettes. The police car had disappeared, along with the bus. Twenty minutes ticked by. I slumped between a shelf and the wall and drifted in and out of consciousness. When Nilesen poked my shoulder, I jolted up, shouting, "Look out!" The clerk peeked around the register to stare at me.

"Come, Jeannie." Nilesen urged me out the door. "Our ride is here."

Beneath the canopy over the pumps, a van idled. A magnetic sign lettered **Deniz Feneri** had been attached to its side. The driver remained behind the wheel. A woman in a medical coat, stethoscope dangling from one pocket, climbed down from the passenger seat. She propped her sunglasses on top of her head and opened her arms.

"Yilmaz," she said.

"Nepthali." Nilesen stepped into the woman's embrace, their greeting muffled, their reunion cut short by the honking of the van's horn. Nilesen kissed the woman on both cheeks, then gestured me over.

"Caroline, this is Jeannie Maurillac, an American photographer." She lifted the scarf off my face. "She needs your help."

In silent acquiescence, the woman ushered me into the back of the van. She rolled up my sleeve to swab the inside of my elbow, inserted an IV, and attached a drip bag. She pressed me to lie down on a cot anchored to the floor before issuing instructions to the driver. Nilesen settled in the front seat. As the van raced forward, Caroline Nepthali patted my shoulder.

"I am not an ophthalmologist, Ms. Maurillac, but I will do my best."

Nilesen turned to me. "Caroline is too modest. She is the best trauma physician I know."

A Principle of Light

While Doctor Nepthali probed the swollen flesh around my eye, I distracted myself with every question except the one I was desperate to ask. Was I going to lose my sight?

"How do you two know each other?" The doctor touched my cheek. I winced. "Where did you meet?"

"At university." They answered in unison, exchanged glances, laughed.

"I, for one, will never forget that day," Caroline said. "Nilo and I rushing up the stairs of the lecture hall, bumping into each other and falling. The way all the other students turned to watch us tumble down the steps."

"It was a physics class, Jeannie. When we landed at the bottom, the professor proceeded to analyze the event like a collision of particles in a contained space. Soon the entire room was busy constructing a theory and forgot about us. We tiptoed to our seats and have been friends ever since."

"I have always been grateful," Nilesen said, "to Professor Svens for rescuing us so skillfully from eternal embarrassment."

The doctor's hands grew still. "There are glass fragments embedded in the flesh. Perhaps some landed in the eye as well. We must get them out."

"Am I going to lose my sight?" I grabbed her arm, forced her to look at me. "Am I going to die?"

"No, Jeannie, you are not going to die." She shook off my grip and placed a gauze pad over the wound. "Whether there is permanent damage, I cannot say."

She and Nilesen held another wordless conversation. I read the prognosis in the silence that grew until the van screeched to a halt. The driver clambered out and came around to the back. He released the doors, then the lock on the cot, which turned into a gurney. He and the doctor rolled me out and down a ramp.

The van had parked behind a concrete block building painted white. Above the door, the words **Deniz Feneri** reappeared. **Lighthouse**. The same words above the restaurant in the Cihangir. Puzzled by the coincidence and exhausted from the journey, I passed out before we reached the door.

14

... day one in the city of Bursa ...

The light above the transom of the out-patient surgery blinked off. Nilesen stood up as an aide pushed the stretcher bearing Jeannie out into the corridor, down the hall, and into a recovery room. Caroline Nepthali followed. The doctor removed her mask and cap.

"I did what I could, Nilo. Your friend is fortunate no fragments lodged in the eye itself."

"Sağol, Caroline. I am grateful for your efforts." Nilesen waited for the aide to exit before she spoke again. "Do you believe Jeannie will lose her sight?"

The doctor raised her eyebrows, let them fall. "It is difficult to say. Trauma like this can have consequences long after the wound heals."

A bedpan rattled as the aide, returning, set it on a table beside the sedated photographer, bowed to Caroline, and slipped out again. Nilesen gazed after her.

"What about her? And the driver? Will they keep our secret?"

"Adnan, our driver, is one of us, Nilesen. Now, he has gone back to the highway. He can monitor the search from there, warn us if the police or the thieves decide to look this way. Meltem is discreet as well. Her family depends on her earnings."

"We need to leave."

Caroline Nepthali rubbed her temples. "Your friend must rest. The damage was extensive, but she was lucky. Something absorbed most of the blast or she would not even be alive. If there is any hope to retain her sight in that eye, she must remain as quiet and still as possible for the next seventy-two hours."

"Too long. Two days, no longer, that is all we can afford. Then, we must go to Çeşme."

"Why Çeşme?"

"Alain's family owns a villa in the hills. Or they did. We should be safe there for a little while." The poet tugged at her lip. "There is no place else."

Caroline wrapped an arm around Nilesen's shoulders. "Come, *arkadaşim*, while your new friend rests, spend an hour with me remembering old times."

"I miss him, Caroline, more with each passing day."

"Write about your loss, Nilo. Your words have more power than you know."

"I no longer wish to write."

"But, this cannot be. Your pen is your sword. Alain knew that. So did we all."

"Leave it alone, Caro." Despair and resignation echoed in the air. "Nilesen the poet is dead."

Caroline sighed and escorted Nilesen to the outer office. They shared tea and a plate of cheese and olives, spoke of their girlhood, of the long-ago past before the recent past, skirted the wound of Alain's death. When the doctor left to attend to the patients lining up outside the clinic, Nilesen returned to Jeannie's bedside. She opened her notebook, grasped the pen in her ruined fingers. No words came. The compulsion that once ruled her, the urge to place words on the page, to give life to the sorrow within, clawed at her. She touched the lined paper. No new words came, only the embers of an old verse, one to hold up against the darkness growing inside her.

> *Light and matter interact.*
> *The medium bulges, refracts.*
> *Two right angles bend.*
> *One, on the edge of transparency,*
> *changes direction, absorbed*
> *by the dark, unblinking void.*

Although she attempted to erase the lines, her mind refused the effort, traveling backward, revisiting the choices that led her to this place and this moment.

A Principle of Light

~~~
Late Spring, 2010 – Oxford, England

Only two days remained in the academic term. She and Caroline huddled beneath an umbrella, longing for the warmth of their home countries, as they headed toward the library, intent on studying until the last possible moment. Final exams required perseverance and stamina. Neither wished to squander her advantage in the class standings with less than perfect scores. Caroline, already fast-tracked for the pre-med program, planned an internship at her father's medical practice in Cairo. Nilesen had a scholarship to the prestigious Iowa Writers' Workshop in the States. But first they were going to visit the Yilmaz family in Kulu, her mother's hometown south of Ankara. Afterward, they intended to journey to Çeşme, to walk the warm sands and bathe in the sparkling waters of the Aegean.

"Have you ever been to the coast?" Nilesen clutched the book bag beneath her raincoat as she struggled to keep up. Caroline slowed her pace.

"Sorry, I forget that I racewalk everywhere. And, no. Have you?"

"Once, when I was a toddler. But my father sent pictures of the house they have rented. It is so beautiful, Caro, and it will be warm there. Plus, my mother prepares the best baklava."

"That remains to be seen," Caroline shot back. "Perhaps we can have a bake-off. Now, hurry, we have much to do, and I don't want to miss our flight."

The possibility of a competition between the Egyptian and Turkish versions of the beloved pastry added to the anticipation. As the day wound down, they wrote their exams, packed for the trip, and cleaned the apartment. Despite Caroline's fears, they made it to the airport with enough time to eat a quick dinner before boarding. Exhausted by the week's rigors, they slept most of the flight. But when they arrived in Ankara, Nilesen was eager to show her friend around the capital. A phone call home made her change her plans. Her Anne sounded weary, her usual optimistic and cheerful voice hollow and foreboding.

Two hours after their arrival, they set off in a rental car toward Kulu. Nilesen drove, while Caroline discussed their next adventure. Upon arrival, the maid hustled them into the kitchen, where Nilesen's mother greeted them with hugs and dinner. Her father came in late, offered a toast, and entertained Caroline with stories of Nilesen as a child. Something seemed off. Despite their joy in welcoming their daughter home, her parents were strangely subdued.

"Baba, is something wrong?"

Nilesen's father deflected the question. "I am anxious to get on the road." But first, he insisted they return the rental car. She followed him into town, then rode beside him back to their home. He loaded their luggage into the trunk soon after, hustled them into the family sedan, and drove through the night, stopping only for restroom breaks. When they reached the leased villa, Nilesen helped unpack while Caroline swept the house, eager to evict any scorpions hiding in the corners. It was only after the evening meal that the opportunity to question her parents arose. Caroline claimed a headache and withdrew to the bedroom. On the terrace, looking out at the lanterns of the fishing boats bobbing in the night, Nilesen broached the subject again, this time with her mother.

"So, tell me. Something is wrong. What has happened, Anne?"

Her mother moved closer to Baba. She took his hand. "The cancer has come back."

Fear, potent as poison, lanced through Nilesen. Minutes passed, marked by the cry of a gull. Moths fluttered around the candle flame. "But the doctor said..."

"Doctors can be wrong."

"How long?"

Her father raised his head, his warm brown eyes locking with hers before shifting to stare at the stars. "I have the summer, my daughter. It will be enough."

A Principle of Light

Nilesen searched the beloved face, saw the shadow lurking there, the sorrow, the loss, and she knew. The summer would never be enough.

"I will resign my scholarship," she said, "come home, be here for you."

Her father shook his finger. "You will do no such thing. I did not work all my life so you could abandon your goals."

"But, Baba."

"Enough, daughter. And you will write a poem for me, a special verse. Tomorrow or the day after. An ode to honor your father." She heard the smile in his words, the gentle jest as he strolled off, his slippers scuffing over the dirt path. Shaken, Nilesen didn't bring up the prospect of a baklava contest. She didn't write his poem that day or the next. Fate had different plans for her. In the morning, on the way to the roadside market, she met Alain Solaganian.

15

... day two in Bursa ...

I swallowed. My mouth tasted of chemicals and ash. I needed a drink. The IV tube clung, leech-like, to my arm, the liquid drip, drip, dripping down the tube. I touched the bandage over the injured eye, followed the wrapping around my head. The pain morphed from sharp throbbing to a dull, steady ache. I struggled to sit up. Nilesen's mangled hands pushed me back against the pillow. She shook her head, tucked the blankets around my chilled feet, and dragged a chair closer to the bed. Beyond the shuttered window, the hum of traffic reminded me we were still in the busy tourist town of Bursa.

"Tell me a story." I gestured at the bandage. "Keep me from thinking about this."

"You sound like a frog, Jeannie. Here." She held a straw to my lips. I drank from the plastic cup until it was empty.

"Please."

"What would you like to hear? Anecdotes from my childhood? The saga of my university years?"

"Tell me," I said, "about your wedding day."

Nilesen stared at her hands, plucked courage from the air. "Very well. A wedding tale."

I closed my eye. The words flowed over me. How her mother helped her to dress. How she visited the cemetery to pray at her father's grave. How her uncle stood in place of his deceased brother. How the wind carried the scent of pepper blossoms and bees hummed around the apple trees in the courtyard. Each detail evoked beauty and expectation, but I sensed the hesitations, the evasions. A secret lurked beneath the tale. I didn't know what she was holding back, but as she shared her memories one crumb at a time, it was the whole cake that I hungered for.

"Why did you wait so long to marry?" I didn't know why this bothered me, but I needed to understand. About the five years that stretched between her meeting Alain Solaganian and the day they spoke their vows. When I looked up, she was standing by the bed, but her gaze turned inward.

"Alain wished to finish his dissertation, to establish himself at the university."

"And you?" I enclosed her fingers in mine, pressed with care the healing fingers.

"I had an obligation to my art." She tried to pull free. I refused to let go. "Some passions cannot be explained, or mastered."

Although I tried to stay alert, I drifted off, floating in the drugs, awash in the realization that I had my own obsession to answer for. When I woke, the sun was slipping away, pulling the light from the day in one broad sweep of purple and pink.

"When can we leave?" I barked out the words, then choked on my saliva. Nilesen lifted the cup from the bedside table and held it for me. Water dribbled down my chin, but I managed to keep enough down to ease the dryness in my throat.

"Two days, Jeannie. You must lie still for two days if you want to save the eye."

I understood what she said, but I couldn't accept it. The men who followed us wouldn't stop searching. I struggled, and failed, to sit up again. While my fever had gone down, I had no strength.

"You go, then." I grabbed her sleeve. "Take the photo card and go."

"And leave you here?" She snorted. "What kind of woman does that?"

"A smart one." Caroline slipped into the room, folded her arms, and leaned against the wall.

"Two to one. That settles it." I motioned for more water.

Caroline laughed. "The patient, drugged and slightly hallucinatory, has no vote at the moment."

A Principle of Light

While I sipped, they discussed my recovery, argued the merits of our plan, and dissected the options, their voices filled with affection and concern. I imagined the trajectory of their friendship, the strength of their bond. Once, Carl and I had shared such a connection. Now, even that false bird of hope had flown. The cord of loneliness that was my life tightened around me. Down the hall, a telephone rang.

"You must go, Nilesen." The pain medication slurred my words. "They'll be looking for you."

"I am not the one who took the photographs."

I wanted to argue. Caroline shook her head. "Lie still, Jeannie."

"We will go together." Nilesen crossed her arms. "We will take the bus to the coast, to Alain's family villa. In two more days."

"No." I willed the doctor to meet my gaze. "Thirty-six hours total, no more."

"Why did you come to me if you refuse to follow my instructions?"

"Caroline," Nilesen said. "Jeannie is right. Every minute we stay endangers you and your work."

"Fine. Yours is a foolish decision, but I will not hold you here." A shake of the head and Caroline Nepthali turned to go. "If you are determined to leave, I will purchase the tickets. But I cannot buy your sight back."

"A wise wom..." I winced. Pain rippled down my cheek. I struggled for words that wouldn't come. Maybe the bomb had damaged more than my eye. I swallowed hard and spoke again. "A wise woman once told me there is a price to pay for everything. I'm paying mine now."

"Perhaps," the doctor said, "your price is too high."

The moment she moved toward the door, the aide rushed in.

"The police." Melmet hiccuped, caught her breath, and started again. "Adnan called. The police are coming. They are already in the lane."

Without a word, Nilesen grabbed scrubs, a surgical mask, and gloves and slipped them on. The doctor did the same. Then Caroline pulled a sign from beneath the bed and taped it to the wall. She strung caution tape across the door, darted under it, and closed the door behind her. Nilesen unwrapped the bandage around my head to examine the stitching. She took a razor from her pocket, snapped it open. and bent over me.

"Lie very still, Jeannie," she said. "I do not wish to cut you." I felt a tug, then another. Strands of red hair drifted to the floor. I squinted to read the sign above the bed.

Tehlike. Karantina.

"What does that say?"

Nilesen glanced up, returned to her task. She stuffed the shorn locks into a hazardous waste container, rubbed my scalp with foam, and shaved the remaining stubby mess. I couldn't even cry. My price had just gone up.

"Danger." She snapped the razor closed, wiped her hands, and spread lotion over the tender skin. "Quarantine. Do you understand?"

I clutched the sheet as Nilesen rebandaged my entire head. She left openings for my nose and mouth but covered both eyes. Panic swelled. I listened to the rasp of metal chair legs against the tile floor. She touched my shoulder.

"I will not leave you," she said. "*Geçmiş olsun*, Jeannie. May all this soon be in the past. Rest now."

Voices rose outside and drifted toward the room. Footsteps pounded down the hall. Caroline shouted an order to stop. The door handle rattled. Unable to see, gasping to breathe around the strip of cloth that threatened to choke me each time I inhaled, I prepared to rip off the bandages. Maybe I could launch myself through the window. Before I could move, Nilesen shoved something cold and hard against my empty palm. I explored the edges with my thumb. The scalpel felt at home in my hand.

"You are very ill, Madam," she murmured, as though for the benefit of someone listening. "You must lie very still and take calm, deep breaths."

Taking this as my cue, I began to thrash, moaning for help. I pulled the cloth from my mouth, gathered spit, and blew bubbles. Foam gathered on my lips. I had no clue what Caroline had told them, but I was determined to make the disease look good. Someone shoved the door, hard. It swung open and banged against the wall. The caution tape snapped, hissing as it scraped the floor. Boots marched into the room. One giant step. Two. Nilesen rose from the chair.

"*Geri çekil!*" Nilesen warned. "Stay back!" The breeze from her waving arms lifted the bandages. She began to cough, great gut-wrenching hacks. Even I recoiled. The boots retreated. The door slammed closed. The commotion in the hall subsided until only our breathing, ragged, and charged with fear, filled the room.

"Are they gone?" I whispered. Nilesen's shoes shushed across the floor as she moved to the window. The shutters creaked, each slat grumbling as she exposed the room to the light. Returning to my side, she lifted the wrapping off my good eye, wiped my nose and mouth, and sank into the chair. It was only after she nodded that I remembered my hair, stuffed in the hazardous waste bin on its way to the fire, the final remnant of my former life soon to be burned away. I sobbed against the pillow, amazed that tears flowed, even from my damaged eye.

"Be calm, Jeannie. He is gone for now."

Time cantered on. I dozed and woke and struggled with hope. If we stayed here, they would find us. I reached for her. "Tomorrow," I said, but she didn't answer me.

"Alain."

I listened to her whisper. I peeled off the loose gauze around my good eye. Nilesen lay asleep at the foot of the bed, her hands hidden inside the surgical gloves, the razor-sharp scalpel she carried clutched tight against her heart.

16

... night two in Bursa ...

In Nilesen's hand, the cold steel of the blade sharpened the memory. June 6, 2015, on the road to Yenihisar. If she had had the scalpel when they arrested her, she would have slit her wrists and ended it there, on the side of the highway. Now, waiting in the recovery room for Caroline to return, she feigned sleep, while that viper of the past buried its fangs in her memory. What possessed Jeannie to ask about her marriage? On the gurney turned into a bed, the injured photographer drifted in and out of consciousness.

The wedding took place at noon, the ceremony unspooling in fast-forward, the party a crush of color and sound. Her mind scrolled through the day, recording flashes of movement and stillness. Rain at dawn gave way to a wild and brilliant sun that blazed from horizon to horizon until, at dusk, it sank in a rush, leaving them adrift on night's dark waves. She and Alain spent the evening tethered by an invisible thread. As she moved from group to group, greeting family and friends, she felt the tug of their bond, the play of line. Was she the fish or the fisherman? Smoothing the lace of her gown, she smiled and wandered on, catching glimpses of her new husband in urgent conversation with his colleagues from the university or nodding at his father's advice. Once, she saw him alone on the balcony, his face in shadow, his outline backlit by the last touch of dusk. His mother delivered a note and left him there. He read it, crushed the paper in his fist, then tore it into pieces, and flung them into the air. When he caught her staring, he moved through the crowd, into the light and into shadow and back into the light again, until he reached her side.

"What?" she said.

J. E. Irvin

"Only this." He leaned in to kiss her. "Only you, here and now and forever."

The lie tripped so easily from him. It swayed with the music, lulled her into the belief that nothing could separate them. Such a naive little wren she was.

At midnight, they departed from Ankara, heading for a secret rendezvous before traveling south to Antalya. The two nights they spent in Konya reposed, a jewel out of time and space, in the nest of her soul. The following morning they rose early for the trip to the Turkish version of the French Riviera. They swam in the sea, rode a cable car up Mount Tahtali, and explored the ruins of Phaselis. In the old harbor, Alain purchased the earrings she would lose during the ambush. If only they could have stayed in that moment. When the phone call came, bursting the bubble of their isolation, the cell's chime reminded her of a falcon's cry, high, piercing, sharp with warning.

"We must go to Yenihisar," Alain said. Sadness spilled from him like sand from an hourglass. "My friends will meet us outside of town tomorrow. They will be waiting at the temple of Apollo."

"But why, eşim? What has happened, my husband, to make them call for you? And why are they going to Yenihisar?" She struggled to grasp the connection between the friends who had danced and sung at the wedding with the activists driving in haste from Ankara to the coast. True, these were men and women who had collected funds for refugees, agitated against the fundamentalist fervor in the capital, and protested the crackdown on journalists and writers. His friends, warriors, defenders of the truth. And, yes, they questioned every edict coming out of the government. But they were not anarchists, not revolutionaries. Worry tied a knot in her chest.

"I cannot tell you, Nilo, for your safety. It is my job to keep you from harm, little bird. Besides, there's a concert there, in Yenihisar ... the Gypsy Kings."

"A concert." The incongruity was disorienting. "We are interrupting our honeymoon to go to a concert?"

A Principle of Light

"We need to be there by noon tomorrow. Not to worry. We still have today." He distracted her with kisses, moving his hands beneath her clothing until, breathless, she had no interest in what was to come, only in what was now. What a clueless creature she had been, sitting sated and complacent next to her husband, in a car speeding toward a distant town, where their friends waited to provide escort. Her husband's promise of a merry concert caravan concealed a darker purpose, one she chose to ignore.

Alain woke her early, brought coffee and semet. They set out before noon, stopped for a late lunch, winding their way through the hot June day. The sun had drifted lower, streaming banners of delight across the azure sky, when she saw the first of the roadblocks. A truck off to the side of the road pulled out behind them, then turned to cut off any retreat. In the distance, another vehicle, a semitrailer, angled across the highway. Alain leaned across her lap, opened the door, and pushed her out, shouting for her to drop to the ground and roll away. Ahead, a command pierced the air. Gunfire erupted, the slam of bullets striking the pavement, the dirt. She grabbed for him, shaking her head, clawing at the handle, the seat, then falling. She tumbled toward the berm. The soldiers advanced toward the car. Tires squealed. The pavement erupted, a ball of orange fury pulsing in the air. The grind of metal overwhelmed the cries of pain and outrage. The odor of gunpowder and rubber smothered her, and death, a vulture riding the updrafts, circled, waiting for permission to land.

She fought to gain her feet and twisted to look down the road. Alain's body lay sprawled in the dust. The soldiers kicked at the bloody form, then advanced toward her, taunting as they approached. Behind the military convoy, shadows formed, a mirage of camouflaged figures sprinting toward the advancing force. Alain's men. She scrabbled to her feet, ran, dodging the rocks and thyme bushes scattered across the landscape. She made it two hundred yards before they caught her. They placed her in handcuffs and shoved her toward the vehicle that had first blocked the highway.

J. E. Irvin

More gunfire erupted. She slumped to the ground, dug the soles of her sandals into the soil. Her captors refused to be delayed, dragging her to the waiting transport. They tossed her into the back of the truck, clambered aboard, and the truck pulled away, gears grinding, tires crunching, the scene of the ambush abandoned behind them.

The whoosh of wheels over the tarmac provided background noise for the loss building inside her. Alain was dead. Perhaps all his friends had been captured, too. Or killed. Did their bodies lie near his on the bloodied road? Now their famIlies were in danger. Thank Allah that her brother and his wife had relocated to England a year ago, that her sister-in-law's pregnancy was too advanced to permit travel. At least one Yilmaz survived.

She fought the urge to wail, but her grief refused to obey, escaping in sobs that doubled her over, tore at her chest. Two weeks ago she and Alain had wed beneath the apple trees of Kulu. Before they left Antalya, they had packed a trunk with clothing and books and sent it ahead to the family villa in Çeşme. Her engagement gifts were safe in a bank in Izmir, her books boxed and waiting for transport at the postane. The honeymoon, like the temple of Apollo visible as the truck rounded a curve, had fallen into ruin. Only the ambush survived, well-planned and exquisitely cruel. Who had betrayed them?

The drive from Yenihisar to Adalet Bakanlığı took twenty-four hours. Soaked in her urine, desperate for a drink, she refused to feel shame when the soldiers, cursing the smell, hauled her out. She was still in shock when one of her captors brought her fresh clothing, pointed her toward a shower stall, and ordered her to clean up. Then he escorted her to an interrogation room, the next level of hell.

"Nilesen?" Jeannie stirred, groaning as the throbbing around her eye peaked.

"What, *arkadaşim*?"

"I'm cold." The photographer shivered. "I hurt."

The admission cost her. Nilesen noted the clenched fists and the tremble in the photographer's limbs. She slipped an arm beneath Jeannie's shoulders to help her sit up, then shook two tablets onto her outstretched palm.

"Tell me." Jeannie slipped the pills between her teeth and reached for the water.

"What shall I tell you?" Nilesen said. "More pretty stories about weddings?"

"No." Jeannie rotated Nilesen's wrist until their palms met. "Tell me how you broke your hands. How you endure the pain. You're a writer, for God's sake."

"That is not a good story for you to hear now."

Jeannie smoothed her fingers over the poet's scarred thumb. She shook her head, grimaced as the movement jarred her eye. "I may lose my sight, Nilo. I need to know."

"What do you need to know?"

"How you survive. How you go on."

"If I tell you, will you lie back and rest?"

"I promise." Jeannie collapsed against the pillow, its down softness cradling her aching head.

"I will hold you to that." Nilesen smoothed the blanket over Jeannie's legs. "I spent four months in the prison known as Adalet Bakanliği outside Ankara, from June through September. I did not cry. I did not beg. Weakness is what they look for, what they expect. They planned to break me. I thought they failed. I was wrong."

"Why do you say that?"

"To survive, I had to seal myself off from warmth, from emotion, from trusting anyone. Most of all, I banished love from my heart. My husband was dead, and I could not even grieve his passing."

"But now, you care. About me. About our journey."

"I think you misunderstand my motives."

Jeannie frowned, winced, sank deeper into the medication. Nilesen watched her as she slept. But the past, once unlocked, demanded to be acknowledged, and the poet went there, eyes open, heart pounding in the grip of a terror that refused to release her.

The first week they simply asked about the honeymoon. Endless questions in an endless cycle. Where did you stay?

J. E. Irvin

What did you eat? Who did you talk to? After each interrogation, they escorted her back to the cell, handed her a notebook with instructions to write down any details she had forgotten. Each night she copied the initial report word for word, and in the margins, she inked defiance in tiny letters. As she finished each numbered line, she tore the sliver of paper loose and slipped it between the binding of the notebook. When she ran her hand over the edge, the poems made only the slightest of bumps. Each day a new poem, each night, more furtive notes between the covers. After two weeks of insistent questioning, her captors placed a hood over her head and guided her down the hall. Inside the interrogation room, they shackled her wrists to the table, her ankles to the chair. When they removed the hood, she squinted into a light brighter than a star. A voice crackled around her, the identity of the speaker unclear.

"Who are you, Nilesen Yilmaz? Who was your husband?" The question flayed her resolve. A sob escaped. The interrogator laughed. "Where were you going, Yilmaz?"

"My name is Solaganian." The light moved closer, searing her skin. She screamed. "I want to see my lawyer."

"Why have you torn the pages of your notebook, Yilmaz?"

"Perhaps there are mice in the prison. Or bookworms." She blinked to clear the tears. "I demand to see my lawyer."

They released the restraints, tugged the hood back on, and returned her to the cell. Each day a new round of terror. Each night a fresh verse. During the fourth week of questioning, they left her head covered while they beat her. When the lead interrogator entered, jop clacking along the walls as he circled the room, she repeated her request for legal representation. Instead of a reply, the man unshackled her left hand and used the jop to smash her thumb. The bones shattered. Her spirit recoiled, sought refuge in hate. Thirteen weeks passed before they let her meet with a lawyer. Each time she greeted the attorney, she pressed the lines of a poem into his hand. He passed them on to a friend of Alain's, one who had escaped the ambush in Yenihisar.

A Principle of Light

By the time she was released, her words were already on their way into print, the only light to come from that dark mourning.

Outside the door marked quarantine, the *polis* assigned to guard the injured woman shuffled his feet, moved the jop from side to side, then tucked it under his arm as he lit a cigarette. Caroline nodded to him as she came down the hall, pushing a cart with a squeaky wheel. On the bottom shelf, concealed in a box labeled surgical supplies, she had hidden an overnight bag.

"Do not come too close, Officer Kulik." In an effort to hold his breath and avoid contamination, the guard puffed out his cheeks. He backed away at her approach. The doctor ducked under the restored quarantine tape, rolled the cart in behind her, and closed the door.

Nilesen tucked the copy of *Işik* into her bag and rose to greet her friend. Still in the surgical scrubs, she helped the doctor unload the medicines and stashed the travel bag under the sink. Caroline pressed a finger to her lips and gestured for Nilesen to follow. They left the room, forcing another reluctant retreat from the guard. As the two women headed for the office, the *polis* called after them.

"Where are you going, Doctor Nepthali?"

Caroline returned to confront him. She stepped closer. He pressed back against the wall. "I am taking care of business, Kulik. I suggest you do the same. I do not recommend you stay here. You are too close to the patient. What if the air is contaminated? What if you catch her disease?"

The man's eyes grew larger. "What disease are you talking about? What is wrong with her?"

"An affliction no man should ever suffer. If he wants to remain a man, that is." She raised her eyebrows and nodded at his crotch. The *polis* squared his shoulders and shifted his glance to Nilesen. "Do you have it, too, Madam?"

When she met his look with a shrug, he backtracked toward the clinic entrance, slipped out the door, and took up a position under the awning over the walkway.

Caroline locked the door to the clinic and once more led Nilesen down the hall to her office. No bigger than a janitor's closet, the room was lit by a single bulb hanging from a cord in the ceiling. The doctor turned on the light and motioned Nilesen to be silent. Then she ran her hands over the door frame and the narrow shelves, searching for microphones or spy cameras. Satisfied that the policeman had not yet bugged the room, she turned on the radio as an added precaution, leaned across the desk, and reached into the pocket of her doctor's coat. Retrieving an envelope, she handed it to Nilesen.

"Two tickets. To Izmir. First bus in the morning. Adnan will drop you off. There is a bag in the box on the cart. Inside are medicine and bandages. It will look better if you arrive with luggage." She pulled a card from her pocket and tapped it twice before handing it over. "I do not know this Batur Stephanidis, but my colleagues say he is a good man, a fine doctor, and he has helped us in the past. Make sure Jeannie sees him as soon as possible. For the eye. As for the outcome, it is in God's hands."

"You have done all you could, Caroline, and I thank you for that. What is meant to be will be. My friend understands the danger."

The doctor scrubbed at her face. "Are you certain that what she carries is important enough to risk all our lives?"

"Those pictures will open the eyes of the world. Then her sacrifice will be worth something."

"What about you?"

Nilesen reached for her friend. "I made my choice long ago. So did you."

~~~

Cappadoccia, Summer 2011

The earthquake had shifted the town center, cracking the earth and leaving a gap that ran in a jagged line from one end of town to the other. Around the once-bustling square, buildings sagged. Rubble covered the sidewalks. Storefronts lay in ruins. Apartment walls listed, wires and pipes dripped like Spanish moss. Stray dogs nosed at the shattered crockery of a café. Dust puffed beneath the feet of the residents who wandered, shocked and bemused, through the shattered streets. The tires of the truck which carried them bumped over a fresh scatter of sand-colored bricks. An after-shock rumbled. Panicked villagers rushed away from the damaged town center.

Caroline rode in back, clinging to the supplies crowding the open bed. Nilesen sat in front, a map balanced on her knees as she used the GPS on her phone to determine the direction of the relief command post. Their mission to assist Literacy International with voter registration had morphed into a rescue operation. When the Red Crescent and the local government requested additional assistance in the aftermath of the disaster, both women had volunteered.

Ahead, two men, faces covered with bandannas, arms coated with dust, stood in the middle of the broken road. One waved a white flag. The driver slowed. Nilesen stepped down from the truck. She called to them in English, repeated the greeting in halting Arabic. When they did not respond, she spoke a third time in Turkish. The taller of the men removed his mask and rubbed his chin.

"Can we help you?" He stepped to the side to read the logo on the truck. "Are you lost?"

"Perhaps they are sightseers." The other man rolled his eyes."We need medical assistance, not girls on holiday."

Nilesen marched straight toward him. She squared her shoulders and slapped at his chest. "We are not here on vacation, you idiot. That was the first time we met. Or have you forgotten already?"

He rubbed his chest and frowned. "Wait. It cannot be possible. You are that girl from Çeşme?"

"Yes. The world is a small oyster, meh? We have come to help, to do whatever we can, and we need to find the command post. Do you know where it is?"

She smoothed the map and held it out. He grinned as he took it from her and refolded it. "We will show you. Your offer of help is accepted. By the way, in case you forgot, my name is Alain. Solaganian. At your service. Again."

"Who could forget you, Alain Solaganian?" Her gaze lingered, the look passing between them shifting the ground much as the quake had done. Alain gestured toward his friend.

"Do you remember David? He is almost a doctor. And please say you brought supplies."

"We did." Caroline wobbled toward them, two medical supply kits clutched to her side. David rushed to take one of the heavy cases from her before wrapping her in a one-armed hug. "Allah be praised. You are a doctor, too, right? What luck brought you to us?"

David didn't wait for her reply. He shouldered several water bags, hoisted the kit, and jogged in the direction of the mangled streets. The others grabbed what they could carry and followed him toward the triage area.

"Are you also studying medicine?" Alain said. "Or training to be a soldier?"

"Look at me, Solaganian," Nilesen said. "Small hands, small feet. Not much muscle, but big dreams. See that starlight in my eyes? Can you not tell I am a poet?"

~~~

When Nilesen reentered the surgery, the bed was empty. For one second, she believed that Jeannie had run away. Then she spotted the photographer in front of the mirror. Bandages filled the washbowl. Jeannie stared at the reflection of her shaved head and sutured skin. Even in the dim glow of the street light leaking through the blinds, Nilesen recognized the beauty that was only marred but not destroyed. She switched on the overhead light.

"Everyone should look so good with a bald head, arkadaşim."

Jeannie blinked against the brightness. She reached for the scalpel next to the sink. "Perhaps I should finish the job." She made a swift slicing motion under her chin.

"Bah. Then the bastards win."

"Since I have no hair," Jeannie set the scalpel on the edge of the bowl and ran her knuckles over her cheeks. "I need something to mark my transformation. Perhaps a tattoo. A swirl of ink in the shape of a shooting star. And earrings, big, shiny hoops that swing as I walk and draw attention from my face. Not that anyone will see them under the headscarf."

"When we get to Çeşme." Nilesen fingered her empty lobes, the earrings Alain had given her taken from her long before she reached Adalet. "I will take you to the bazaar in the fishing village. I, too, require some jewelry."

Jeannie shuffled back to the bed to pick up the clothes lying there. "Time to move on," she said. She shrugged out of the hospital gown, stepped into a skirt, buttoned her blouse. With a groan, she shrugged into her photographer's vest. The burqa she wore on the bus had been burned, her jeans stuffed into the travel bag. Nilesen collected the dirty linens and tossed them aside as she settled onto the bed to sort through the contents of her bag. The thief's credit card had served its purpose, but they dared not use it again. With a sense of relief, she used the scalpel to slice it into pieces and shoved the remnants into the waste container. Then, with Jeannie beside her, she counted their money. Seventy-two lira between them. Shrugging, she stuffed the coins and bills into a change purse.

"This should be enough to get us to the villa. You must rest now. We need to leave early tomorrow. Adnan wishes to be gone by first light."

"All right." But Jeannie found it difficult to move. She checked the pockets of her vest, tattered from the explosion but still serviceable. The need to know what her photographs revealed burned inside her. She pressed her fingers against the data card she had taken from the gum packet and hidden in a seam of the vest. She teased it free and weighed it in her palm.

Nilesen slid closer. "What are you doing?"

"Maybe," Jeannie flipped the card over, "we should look at the pictures." She dragged out the camera and slipped the card into its slot. She checked the battery power, then initiated a scroll through the photographs. She and Nilesen waited as the activity in the square played out frame by frame by frame, the morning of the bombing captured in a series of clear shots. The early rush of pedestrians on their way to work, the gradual stir as the inhabitants of the quarter swept entryways, watered flowers, soothed babies. The bookshop owner's frowning notice of the *polis* dressed as a jandarma from the country. The arrival of the men dragging suitcases over the cobbled street. Her documentation of the morning life of the Cihangir revealed, scene by scene, each stage in the unfolding horror of the bombing.

"Stop," Nilesen said. "See. There. The jandarma speaks to the men with the suitcases."

"Isn't a jandarma a policeman who works in the countryside?" When Nilesen nodded, Jeannie zoomed in on the picture. "Why isn't he dressed as a *polis* from the city?"

"That is a very interesting question." Nilesen stabbed at the shadowed face of the jandarma. "This man, there is something about him that is familiar, but I do not know why that is. Too bad I cannot see his face more clearly. But you see how he is talking to those men? Standing close to them? It is as if he knows them."

Jeannie jumped to the next frame, to the snapshot of Carl running toward her, panic and something more creasing his face. He looked like a man about to proclaim a revelation. One arm flailed for balance, one stretched forward in an accusatory stab at the men in the middle of the square. But it was the final frame that increased her unease. The jandarma riding past, the glare from the sun hiding his face, his finger like a weapon aimed at her head.

"I didn't realize I took this one."

"You know what this means?" Nilesen placed her hand on the camera. "The bombing in the square. It was not a terrorist attack at all."

17

... day three in Bursa ...

Dawn had barely begun to creep over the city when Caroline came for us. I tugged the hijab tighter around my shaved head, fascinated and repulsed by my naked scalp. Nilesen and I slipped from the back of the clinic into the van and signaled the driver to go. Adnan checked for *polisi*, waved to Caroline, and pulled away. He circled to the front of the clinic. The squeamish guard had fallen asleep, his body slumped against the cinder block wall, the jop tucked under his feet. We coasted down the hill past a cluster of shuttered shops. The sensation of being exposed and vulnerable persisted until we reached the row of three-story apartment buildings that rose, cliff-like, to screen our passage. As soon as the walls closed around us, Adnan gunned the engine and switched on the headlights.

I peeked over the seat, unable to see much through the tinted windshield. The city slumbered in the pre-dawn light. The narrow streets of the shore district pulsed with shadow. Nilesen dozed beside me, but I couldn't stop shaking. Pain, an inconsiderate visitor, commanded my attention at unexpected moments. My worry monitor ratcheted higher with every block we traveled beyond the safety of the clinic. I smoothed the new skirt over my knees. Caroline had insisted we wear plain, nondescript clothing, practical shoes, hijabs in modest colors, and Nilesen agreed. We didn't want to draw attention. But I missed the casual famlliarity of my jeans and tees. Grateful for the comfort the vest provided, I wrapped my arms around my waist and rocked against the drumbeat in my head, the ache in my heart. Alone, intimidated by language and customs I didn't understand, and fighting despair, I became the stranger in the strange land. The realization left me anxious.

The hijab slid free, my bare scalp too slick to provide an anchor for the material. I hurried to tie it back on, pressed hard against the thin line of surgical glue Caroline had applied to keep it in place. The silk rustled like feathers on a duck. I checked and re-checked the travel bag, terrified of losing the tickets that would send us onto the next stage of our journey. We had analyzed the photographs. There was no doubt of the conclusion. I had documented murder. Now, the killers were hunting me.

Adnan stopped the ambulance in front of a house with two overhanging levels. I wondered what would happen if an earthquake struck, toppling the upper floors and sending the inhabitants into a panic. I recalled photographs of temblors in China and South America, images of floors collapsing down and around, burying everyone alive beneath the stucco and wood of the ancient structures. Pictures of Aleppo sprang to mind. Here, in Turkey, what white-helmeted man would come to my rescue? Eager to get moving, I reached for the door handle. Nilesen tugged me back.

"Wait, Jeannie. Look." She lifted her chin. "There."

I stared in the direction of her nod. A dark-colored minicar, unmarked, not obviously police or military, blocked the entrance leading to Bursa Otorgar, the main bus station in the city. A man leaned against the hood, burly arms folded across his chest, the bulge of a firearm visible beneath the drape of his jacket. Adnan motioned to us to get out. Nilesen shook her head.

"No. We must return to the clinic. Now. Quickly."

Our driver grumbled, but he put the van in reverse, glided down the narrow alleyway, and headed back to the **Deniz Feneri**. When we arrived, he clambered out and flung the door open. Nilesen jumped out. I followed, sweating despite the breeze from the sea. My fever had broken, but the weakness in my limbs persisted. The patch over my damaged eye threw me off balance. I misjudged a step, fell to one knee, struggled to stand. Nilesen grasped my elbow and hauled me up. She thanked the driver for his kindness, handed him a wad of lira, and asked him to wait.

After she spied on the *polis* stationed out front, who still dozed against the wall, she herded me back inside. Caroline shuffled from the office, yawning and scrubbing at her eyes. Before she could form a question, we marched her back inside, closed the door, and sagged into chairs.

"The *hirsizlar*." Nilesen paused. "They were waiting for us at the Otorgar."

"*Lanet olsun!*" Caroline said. "Damn it!" She ran her hands through her hair.

"I thought your religion forbade cursing," I said, trying to lessen the tension crowding the room.

She shrugged. "That was a prayer for patience. I thought I had seen the last of you two."

"Cosmic joke," I said. "Call it the boomerang effect."

Caroline choked out a laugh. She steepled her fingers beneath her chin and gazed at us through worried eyes. "Time for plan B. If I succeed in getting you two to safety, all will be forgiven, including my colorful language. Let us hope I am up to the task. Please, wait for me in the surgery."

We tiptoed down the hall to the room we had left only thirty minutes before. I set the bag down, pulled out the camera, and moved to the window. Above the lip of the city, dawn bowed to the day as it lifted strands of golden cloud above the eastern horizon. I stood there, lens cupped in one hand, and watched the rooftops spring like cats from the dark into the light. In the distance, the Sea of Marmara tagged the shore. I cranked the window wide, inhaled the salt-scented air that teased my skin. I aimed the camera at the women of the quarter as they emerged from their houses, heads bowed, shoulders squared, purpose etched in every movement. Caroline returned, explaining in Turkish the details of a new plan as she paced. Nilesen shot me a worried glance. Whatever came next, I wasn't going to like it. With a final admonition to stay hidden, the doctor rolled her shoulders and hurried back to the office. I thought about the thief and his bodyguard watching for us at the Otorgar.

"Are you sure it was them?"

"I am certain, Jeannie. The man by the car was one of the men from the bus."

"How did they find us?"

"Who knows? Every town has rats, those who are poor and desperate enough to share information for a few lira or a bottle of beer. What cannot be changed must be endured."

"But we're stuck here, and time is passing."

"Caroline did the right thing, sending us out early." Nilesen stood on her toes to adjust my scarf. "An hour later and we would have missed seeing him. They would have caught us inside the station. There would have been no way to escape."

"Caroline's a good friend."

"Yes," she said, attending to her hijab. "After today, I will never see her again."

I wanted to reassure her that wasn't true, but the words refused to form. "So, what's our next move?"

The door opened. Gloved and gowned, Caroline Nepthali raised a hypodermic and pointed at me. "You," she said, "are going to a funeral."

"Care to tell me whose?"

"Yours. It is the only way to get you safely out of Bursa."

I backed away, but she continued to approach. Nilesen remained silent. The doctor shoved me into a chair. "Listen to me, Jeannie Maurillac. After I give you the sedative, Nilesen and I will take you into the next room and prepare your body for burial. You must remain calm. We will wrap you in white linens, tie your big toes together, and transport you to a hearse. Your family is waiting for the body in Çeşme. Do you understand? With proper papers, no one will question or stop you."

"How long do I have to play dead?"

"*Arkadaşım.*" Nilesen sat beside me and took my hand. "You must trust us. Caroline knows there is no other way."

I looked at the hypodermic. "What's that do?"

"It will calm you, prevent you from panicking when we close the lid on the coffin."

A Principle of Light

I fought the desire to bolt. With a policeman at the front door and a gang of thieves watching the streets, escape now seemed impossible, but entombing myself in a coffin sounded a whole lot worse. I leaned over the wastebasket and threw up.

"Listen to me, Maurillac. I will place an oxygen tank and a mask beneath the wrappings. If you need it, it will be there."

I wiped my mouth with my wrist, recalling the time Carl and I covered the newest stateside fad on the west coast, funeral celebrations, twenty-first-century style. People throwing death parties, complete with satin-lined coffins, testimonials, and obituaries. The events were supposed to make the participants appreciate their lives more. The resulting photos struck me as weirdly beautiful. Carl, however, thought them macabre. "If you have to fake your death to feel alive, maybe you're already dead," he wrote in the article. That drew a litany of tweets. Now he was truly gone, and the part of me that once loved him wondered what kind of party one had for an atomized body. I glanced from the doctor to Nilesen, noted the worry in their eyes, the grimness shrouding their attempts to reassure me. We were out of options. I rolled up my sleeve and offered a vein.

While they undressed me, I drifted, one of Wordsworth's clouds above the daffodils. At one point, I giggled. Nilesen laid a finger over my lips to silence me. By the time they laid me on the table, I was flying. Each word they spoke floated in a cotton swab of dullness. The cool steel of an oxygen tank rested against my bare skin. I recoiled at its touch. Then I relaxed into the ministrations, soothed and swaddled by the linens they wound around me. I bumped my feet on the edge of the coffin, recalling how unusual this was for Turkey. But then I realized my body did have to travel some distance. Wouldn't do to have it rolling around like a coke bottle in the back of the hearse. Tears leaked down my cheeks, soaked into the linen wrap. I hiccupped twice, and then all the light disappeared.

18

... on the road south ...

The hearse drove away from the clinic at midday, curtains drawn against prying eyes. Dressed in clothes more suitable for accompanying a deceased relative, Nilesen rested her feet atop the suitcase. She clutched her bag to her chest, fought the words that bubbled, spring-like and mineral-rich, from the fountain inside her. No, she commanded as the lines took hold. She had banished her writing, buried it in her sorrow, yet it refused to die. *Above the aerie of dreams, hope circles* ... She checked her watch. The new driver looked over his shoulder. He smiled when she caught his eye.

"How did you manage it, Fethi?"

"My father says a man is not a man until he rescues a woman. I am fulfilling my masculine duty."

"Caroline called you."

He nodded and held up a folder. "She did. The day you arrived. I was already on the road. She handed me all the paperwork."

"Is that all you brought?"

"No, not all." He held up his backpack, tilted it to reveal the contents. The gun peeked from beneath its sweatered wrapping. "Do you want it?"

"Not yet, *abi*. But soon." She locked eyes with him until he returned his gaze to the road. They drove on, ten, twenty, thirty kilometers before she spoke again.

"Are we far enough from the city to wake Jeannie?"

Fethi adjusted his sunglasses against the glare sparking off the car in front of him. "There is another checkpoint ahead. I believe it is the last one along this road. Tell her to be patient a while longer."

When he slowed for traffic, Nilesen rapped on the lid of the coffin. The muffled response from within reassured her that Jeannie still lived. She delivered Fethi's message, then closed her eyes, imagining herself confined in that narrow space, alone in the dark, dependent on strangers for survival. Fifteen minutes later, a soldier rapped his knuckles against the glass.

"Papers." The command mingled with the noise of idling vehicles, irate drivers, and the bullhorn shouts of military personnel. Fethi handed over the documents detailing the contagious nature of the corpse, the need for caution in handling the body, and the necessity of prompt delivery to relatives so the burial could proceed. Nilesen adjusted the mask over her face, hid her hands in her sleeves, and rocked back and forth. When the soldier turned toward her, she began to wail.

Ahead, a semi bearing Bulgarian plates pulled off the road, its driver hauling a load of sheep. The stench from the cargo combined with the fumes of the idling truck caused Nilesen to retch. The soldier stepped back from the car. He raised his hands and gestured them forward as he shouted a warning to the other guards. Then he covered his mouth and nose. A path opened ahead. Fethi eased the hearse past a queue of military trucks. They drove another kilometer, two. The checkpoint receded, shimmering, mirage-like, in the morning heat. They had just cleared the line of sight from the checkpoint when a man leading a donkey wandered onto the road. Fethi swerved into the left lane, wheeled back, then veered to the right. The car bump-bumped over the berm. It plowed across an untended field and breached upward before diving into a ditch.

"*Vay be!*" Fethi slumped forward, caught between the safety belt and the airbag. Propelled across the back seat, Nilesen braced her feet against the side door and reached for something to stop her momentum. In the coffin, Jeannie ricocheted like a pinball.

"Get me out!" The thud of bare feet against the lid of the coffin competed with the tick-tick of a cooling engine. Somewhere beneath the hood, fluids dripped. Nilesen extricated herself from the corner where she was wedged.

A Principle of Light

She struggled to pull a pry bar from the toolbox next to the coffin. Despite the protests from her bandaged hand, she inserted the bar along the top of the pine box and leaned on it. A section splintered and peeled away, throwing her against the opposite door. She clambered back and crawled along the length of the coffin, prying loose more of the wood. Jeannie continued to beat against the lid, her cries for help fewer as light poured into the interior of the box. With one final wrench, Nilesen peeled off the wooden cover. Jeannie launched herself up. Powder coated her face and body, lending her a ghostly glow.

"Clothes." She tore at the linen strips, untied her toes. "Please."

The travel bag had jammed itself between the coffin and the rear of the hearse. Together, Nilesen and Jeannie wrestled it free. Smoke trickled from under the hood. Nilesen used the crowbar to batter the rear doors, then dragged the suitcase out after them. Naked, bleeding where the sides of the box had abraded her skin, Jeannie gulped air.

"Here," Nilesen opened the bag, "clothes." She pulled out jeans, a long-sleeved blouse, the photographer's vest, and a scarf and handed them over. While Jeannie dressed, Nilesen dabbed at a cut on her chin. The creak of a door startled them. They had forgotten Fethi. Backpack slung over one shoulder, he banged his way free just as flames erupted beneath the hearse. Supported by one another, the three limped away from the vehicle. Within minutes, the fire spread through the interior, popping and crackling as it ignited the coffin. They took refuge behind a screen of acacia trees. Jeannie thumbed on the camera and photographed the accident, frame by frame, aware of the irony in documenting her demise, a funeral "party" for the pretend dead.

"I think," she said, "we need another new plan."

Fethi shook his head. "Nilesen *hanim*, you did not tell me the American had such a twisted sense of humor."

Bleating erupted behind the screen of trees. Beyond the burning car, a figure appeared, obscured by the smoke from the fire. They crouched lower, held their breath against the odor of melting rubber. The figure advanced. Had the soldiers found them already?

"Madams? Sir?" A voice penetrated the thick smoke. "Come out, strangers, into the light. Allah has led you to me."

Jeannie strained to identify the man behind the voice. Out of the flames, the traveler from the highway, accompanied by his donkey, trundled toward them.

19

... the path to Eski Deniz ...

In the distance, sirens blared. Although I couldn't see the road, I knew the soldiers were coming. The rumble of heavy vehicles churned up dust that gathered, djinn-like, above the horizon. Fethi grabbed Nilesen and dragged her farther from the wreckage. I stumbled after them. The figure wreathed in smoke approached. With one hand wrapped around the halter of the donkey and the other stretched out in greeting, the man paused, then motioned us to follow him across the field.

"What should we do?" My words popped like fireworks in the acrid air. I thought I had whispered.

"Quiet, Jeannie. You are bellowing like a bull." Nilesen looked in the direction of the road. I raised the camera to snap more photos of the ruined hearse. When I finished, I pulled the scarf across my nose to muffle the smell. The man with the donkey waited.

I scrubbed tears from my good eye. "What are our options?"

Fethi wiped his face. Soot smeared his forehead. "A bad choice is better than no choice." He led the way toward the stranger, who nodded and pushed through a screen of evergreens. Nilesen and I followed, taking care not to get too close to the donkey.

The bushes ceded passage to taller and taller pines. We stumbled past the edge of the forest onto a path, narrow but well-trod, overhung with branches. We stopped to drink at a spring bubbling around a cairn of rocks, then trudged on. No one spoke. The scent of donkey mingled with the odor of fear-tinged sweat made me sneeze. Nilesen walked beside me, one arm around my waist. I tried to shrug her off.

"No, Jeannie, you are still very weak."

Embarrassed by the trembling in my once-sturdy legs, I accepted her support. Fethi walked behind, our traveling bag resting on top of the pack on his back. I listened to the snatches of conversation between our rescuer and Nilesen, but my rudimentary command of Turkish prevented me from grasping much beyond greetings and the simplest of phrases. After a second stop for water, the man handed me a staff he had shaped from a fallen branch. I was grateful for the gift. My bandaged eye threw off my depth perception. Intermittent stabs of pain made me gasp. The camera strap chafed my neck, but I refused to allow anyone else to carry it. I had replaced the card containing the photos of the bombing with one labeled "Turkish vacation." If I survived this journey, I reasoned, I could parlay the travel pics into an article or two, maybe even a full-time job with a bigger salary and better benefits. Besides, the story would make for interesting talks on the lecture circuit. And command impressive fees. If I survived. I stumbled over a rock embedded in the path and narrowly avoided faceplanting in the dirt.

"*Çok uzak değil*," the man said. He waited for me to regain my footing, then went on.

"Not too much farther now," Nilesen translated.

At her words, our rescuer bowed to Nilesen. "When we arrive, I will escort Nilesen *hanim* in first. Do not look so surprised, Madam. Even here, we know of your work."

"How is that possible?" Nilesen narrowed her eyes.

The man placed his palms together and lifted them to the sky. "Did you not write 'even the thickest curtain contains a loose thread'?"

Nilesen nodded. He bowed again and continued down the path. The forest thinned. We clambered up a slope, then headed down the other side. Below lay a fishing village tucked into a narrow harbor. The donkey brayed a greeting.

Overhead, clouds scudded by. Shadows played across the landscape. Near the shore, gulls wheeled and cried out, ever restless for the next meal. When we reached the first of the modest dwellings, the stranger and Nilesen continued on.

Fethi and I squatted under an olive tree. I opened the bag. We shared the bread, olives, and cheese Caroline Nepthali had packed for us. Hidden among the clothes, I discovered a packet of antibiotics and swallowed two capsules.

"What will you do next?" Fethi said.

"Go home." I leaned against the trunk of a *Datça* palm and closed my good eye.

"What will that accomplish?"

"I don't know." The words caught in my throat, as indistinct and uncertain as my decision to leave this country, to escape the memory of Carl and the bombing. What was I doing? What should I do? I had prepared myself for a solitary life, accepted a world without a man to share it, but not this way. Carl might have ceased to be my lover, but he was still and forever my colleague, and, once, my friend. Now I was running from pursuit, separated from every reference point I'd ever known. I mourned the loss of my friend. For years, he had been a constant in my world. Now, he was dead. No center remained, no guidepost. The air rippled around me.

"She needs your support." Fethi offered me the last of the water.

"Thank you." I gulped it down before returning the canteen. "Nilesen? She's the strongest woman I've ever met. And the smartest. And despite her calling me friend, I'm not sure she even likes me."

"Is that so important, that she likes you? Her losses are greater than yours, her journey more demanding. If you cannot be the friend she needs, you should go home."

"She doesn't need me. Even here in the back of nowhere, she is known."

Fethi unbuttoned his shirt and withdrew the package he had carried from the fire. "Does this look to you like the possession of a happy woman?"

I stared at the gun lying within the layers of paper and cloth. "You're telling me that belongs to Nilesen."

"I am. And, she has stopped writing."

"But why would she do that?"

"Do what? Buy a gun? Stop writing. A gun has one purpose, to end a life. When a poet stops writing, she has entered the land of despair. I am telling you, Jeannie Maurillac, our Nilesen needs you, or she will choose a path neither of us wants for her."

He stood to brush leaves from the seat of his pants and slipped back into the trees. I listened to the sound of his passage, horrified by his revelation. After I glanced around, I rewrapped the gun and stashed it deep in the bag. Then, I rested against the palm tree, aware that I had no real plan. I was drifting, unsure of direction, too weary and sad to do more than follow Nilesen's lead. But where was she going and why? For me, returning home had become a metaphor for surrender. Do the job, send the photos, collect my pay, move on to the next assignment, empty and alone. Unmoored by the events in the Cihangir, I had no clear direction.

The sun slipped lower. Below, the man with the donkey escorted Nilesen to the largest building in the center of the village. She hesitated, drew back. They argued until he bowed to her again. When she stepped inside, I rested my head on my knees and took deep breaths. Fethi put a hand on my shoulder.

"Have you made a decision, Madam?"

Overhead, the clouds darkened, clustering together as they blotted out the brightness of the day. I shivered. The decision settled over me like the lid of that pinewood coffin.

"Yes, Fethi." I retied the scarf over my bald head. "I will accompany Nilesen Yilmaz until she tells me to stop."

20

... making plans in Eski Deniz ...

From the hillside perch, Jeannie and Fethi observed the main road leading to and through the village that dozed, waiting for its fishermen to return from the sea. The afternoon drifted to dusk. Hidden from below by the trees, they took turns napping until a boy climbed the path and indicated, with pointed fingers and head bobs, that they should follow him down. With the staff the donkey man had made for her and Fethi's arm, Jeannie made her way down the hill without falling. Once they reached the square of the village, the boy left them as silently as he had arrived. The man who rescued them stepped from behind a row of fishing nets strung up to dry. He extended a hand in welcome and guided them toward the building where he had taken Nilesen.

"Welcome to Eski Deniz. *Benim adim Arif.* My name is Arif. You are safe with me."

"Eski Deniz, that sounds familiar." Jeannie searched through her limited Turkish. "Does it mean Old Harbor?" Although she intended the question for Fethi, again she spoke too loud, her words rising like quail flushed from a field. Embarrassed, she stopped just inside the doorway, waiting for her eye to adjust to the dimness.

"So, you are learning Turkish despite yourself." Nilesen examined the bandage over Jeannie's eye, rested a hand on the photographer's forehead to check for fever, and led them to a bench along the near wall. Fethi remained standing as he surveyed the room. Satisfied that no soldiers or policemen lurked in the shadows, he settled on another of the benches that ringed the tiled foyer. The aroma of cooking oil wafted from the upper floor. In the doorways opening off the central area, girls gathered, their voices bright, their faces eager. Their murmurs whispered through the hall. Arif vanished through one of the doors, returning with a cushioned chair. Positioning it in the middle of the room, he gestured around him.

"This is the Deniz Kiiz Lisesi, a special academy for gifted girls." He indicated the classrooms. "The government was undecided about allowing us to continue instruction in Ankara. To be safe, we have relocated here. What you see and hear within these walls must not be disclosed."

"Are you followers of Gülen?" Nilesen said.

Jeannie recognized the name, Gülen, a controversial cleric living in the United States who was once a friend of Erdoğan. The man had provoked the leader's anger for his views on the future of Turkey and its relationship with Islam.

"No, Nilesen *hanim*," Arif said. "That man is not our patron. We owe allegiance to no political party. In this school, we honor only truth and learning."

Uncertain of the politics at play, Jeannie shifted her attention to the camera. She fiddled with the settings, fighting the urge to document the carved and paneled interior and the girls craning their necks for a glimpse of the strangers. The hush of young voices sifted through the air.

"*Sağol*, Arif *bey*." Nilesen pursed her lips. "We are grateful for your assistance, but we wish to bring no harm to your students. We are simply trying to get to Çeşme."

"Walking, that is a long journey from here, especially for your friend." He raised his brows.

"*Benim adim* Jeannie Maurillac." Jeannie extended her hand.

"You are French?"

"American. Photographer." She held up the camera.

Arif stroked his beard. The students watching from the shadows grew quiet. Even the rustle of clothing had ceased. Fethi approached the headman, fists clenched, body coiled into a protective stance. Arif waved him off.

"Allow me to inquire, Nilesen Yilmaz. What fate brings such a renowned writer to Eski Deniz? Perhaps it is your light I discerned blazing in the fire by the road. Perhaps the gods who once graced this coast have come again to interfere

A Principle of Light

in our insignificant human lives." He chuckled. "Whatever the reason, you are here among us and have nothing to fear. *Kizlar*? Students? Come down."

They clattered down the stairs, sandals slapping against the tiles. The golds and blues of their uniforms flashed as they approached, hands behind their backs, heads bowed in shyness. Only the youngest dared to flash her eyes and flirt with Fethi. "Come, come," Arif said. "This is your opportunity to meet the author of *Işik*."

Nilesen stared at him. "How do you know all this, Arif?"

He reached into his pocket to withdraw a book. "By coincidence, and fate. Thanks to a bookseller in Bursa, I have a copy to add to our library here. I would be honored to have you sign it. Please. Will you sit here?"

The schoolgirls closed in around the chair he had placed in the middle of the room. They jockeyed for a position closer to the visitors, closer to the poet who sat among them. The older girls stepped back, allowing the young ones a better view.

Nilesen looked around, shoulders tense. "Arif *bey*, I will sign, but I do not wish to read."

Fethi moved beside her. "You have a gift to share, Nilesen *hanim*."

She shook her head, looked at Jeannie, the plea obvious in her eyes. *Help*.

"We are all tired," Jeannie said. "Perhaps later?"

The headman shrugged. "Such an opportunity may not come again."

The plea in his voice settled the matter. Nilesen sat, clutched a pen, and inscribed the headmaster's book. Jeannie moved through the crowd to the outside of the circle of students. She checked the battery light on the camera and began to take pictures. No one but Fethi paid her any attention. Seated among the schoolgirls, Nilesen invited them to sit. She traced the title on the front cover, then opened the book and recited the first stanza of *"Güzel kuşlar."*

"Beautiful birds, where do you fly when the air, heavy with words of death, enraptured and jealous, flings poisoned arrows at your swift wings?"

Why did she choose that one to read? When she finished, she noted the tears gleaming on Arif's cheeks. The students and teachers remained silent, entranced by the emotion captured by the poem. A sudden clap of thunder shook the building. Rain pounded the roof. Nilesen ignored the storm. She read three more poems before closing the book to answer questions about her school years and her studies at the great university in England. Although they wanted to know, no one asked, sparing her from talking of her husband or the dark time she spent in prison. Arif clapped to get the students' attention.

"Our guest is tired from her journey to our school," he said. "We will invite her to rest, while you, young scholars, return to your classes.

Nilesen handed the book to one of the girls, then followed Arif as he escorted them to a room at the back of the school. A table had been prepared. Bowls of yogurt and plates of olives, grapes, and cheese sat at each place. A woman carried in a platter of roast chicken. She smiled at Arif and began to serve the meal. The group made small talk, about the storm that continued to drench the village, about the students and their studies, about their accommodations on the upper floors. Only when their hunger had been satisfied and Arif's wife had cleared the dishes did they address the purpose of their journey.

Fethi cleared his throat. "We need transport to Çeşme, Arif *bey*. Is there any way to procure a vehicle?"

Eyes lidded, mouth pursed, Arif toyed with a grape. "The main roads are watched. If I were to go into Banderma to rent a car, people would talk."

"What about a boat?"

"The people of Eski Deniz are compassionate and eager to help, but they must work for a living. No one can spare the time for such a journey."

"We are in your debt, Arif, for bringing us this far." Nilesen toyed with a fig. "You know the roads. What do you suggest?"

Arif rested his arms on the table. "I believe your pursuers believe you will attempt to drive to your destination. The government will not look for you in the past."

Jeannie glanced back and forth between them. "What does that mean?"

Arif called for his wife to bring more water. "We will take my donkeys, ride through the hills to İnegöl. I have a cousin there. He repairs motorcycles. We will borrow several for the ride to Kütahya, where my brother owns a factory. He will take you in his truck to Izmir during one of his deliveries."

"This brother," Fethi said, "what does he make in his factory?"

Arif placed his palms together and brought his fingers to his lips. "The most beautiful clay tiles for the most beautiful villas and resorts along the coast. Turquoise and yellow, each one hand-painted and unique. Highly sought after, which gives him great influence and much freedom to move around as he pleases. Good for all of you, no?"

"Can we trust these people?" Jeannie said. The Turks all stared at her.

"Jeannie, *arkadaşim*, they are family." Nilesen patted the photographer's arm. "There is no more important loyalty than that."

After the meal, Arif's wife escorted Nilesen and Jeannie to a room overlooking the courtyard. The sound of girls singing carried through the open window, the words muted but the melody pure and simple.

Jeannie lay down on one of the mats and glanced at her companion. "Do you know that song?"

Nilesen faced the window. "My mother sang those words to me the day I married Alain. Do not be shy, little bird. No, do not cry, little bird. Soon you will rest in your own little nest."

"That doesn't sound like a wedding tune."

"Oh, but it is. The bride is the little bird about to fly away from her parents' house. The other verses speak of the twigs she will carry, the home she will make, the babies she will raise."

"Did you?"

Nilesen leaned on the sill and hummed along with the girls below. "Did I what?"

"Ever hold your baby?"

"No, *arkadaşim*. And now I never will."

"I'm sorry, Nilesen," Jeannie sat up, "for my words at dinner, for my ineptness. I always seem to say the wrong thing."

"Your heart is good, but your head gets in the way." Nilesen returned to her sleeping mat. "Try to rest now. Our journey will not be easy."

The light leached from the sky. The encroaching gloom wrapped each of them in grief. The veil of dusk masked their tears. As the night coiled around them, Jeannie reached for the lamp. She lit the kerosene and adjusted the flame. Shaking several pills into her palm, she swallowed them without water. Then she stretched out, winding the sheet around her like a cowl. Tomorrow they planned to leave before dawn.

"Tell me something, Jeannie." Nilesen's words were soft, insistent, full of need. "How old are you?"

"Thirty-seven, next month, actually. Why?"

"I will be thirty-one in Aĝustos. Thirty-one. A good age, no? But I have the hands of an old woman and a fossilized heart. My parents are dead, my husband is dead. The poems I wrote now bring me only pain and censure."

"Not from everyone. Remember that fisherman in Istanbul? And Fethi? Think of Arif and the students at this school. You are revered."

"Perhaps." Shrugging off the praise, she rocked back on her heels. "Still, I ask myself, what good is a life of unbearable sorrow? What good are words in the face of evil?"

Jeannie called up the image of Carl running toward her, flailing his arms, already caught in death's mitt, shouting a warning no one heeded. She thought of the photos stacked on the data card, the weight of intention captured in an instant.

"Yet we go forward, don't we?" she whispered. "There's no way to go back."

21

... on the road to Inegöl ...

After a fitful sleep punctuated by nightmares, we left at dawn, climbing the hills, angling our way into the interior of Anatolia. Arif avoided the main roadways. I endured the ride for several hours, as did Nilesen, until the plodding pace of the donkey had rubbed my thighs almost raw. My injured eye throbbed. I couldn't tell if that was a good or a bad sign, but I continued to take the antibiotics. Before she said good-bye, Caroline had insisted I find a doctor friend of hers in Izmir within three days. But twenty-four hours had already passed, and we were no closer to our destination. My time, and the chance to save my eye, was running out.

We stopped for the night at a shepherd's cottage. Arif suggested Nilesen and I sleep inside under the thatched roof, but I preferred to spread my blanket beneath the sky. The route we followed avoided populated areas. The galaxy spilled its milky path above us. In the swirl of clouds and stars, I found a kind of peace.

"Be kind, oh, stars, that light my path, for darkness hovers near. Inside the forge of heaven, the lathe of destiny shapes my fear." As we sat near the fire, Nilesen flung her words into the night, each one a diamond shard that dripped over us. I slipped the cap off the camera lens and captured the moment, uncertain why I did so, obeying a deeply-rooted compulsion to document every step of this strange, ragged flight through the countryside.

It took two days to reach Inegöl. By the time we approached the town, my butt had had enough of the donkey. Arif deposited us in a grove of olive trees while he went to speak with his cousin. Fethi, who had kept mostly silent on the trip, remained with us. He hadn't raised any objection to the headmaster's plan, though I sensed his suspicions in the scowl he directed at our guide. Leaving me with the donkeys, he walked Nilesen out of my hearing. They whispered together, counting the lira they held between them. When they returned to my side, I unlatched the money belt I carried at my waist and held it out.

I shoved the pouch into Fethi's hand. "Use this."

He pushed it back at me. "Not yet, Madam. The time is coming when you will need it, but that time is not now."

I protested. He insisted. Finally, I tucked the belt back under my vest and helped myself to a handful of grapes. Nilesen reminded me to take my medication. I shook the bottle, noting that only a single day's dosage remained. As if on cue, my eye throbbed. I touched the bandage, desperate to know what the wound looked like. When Fethi left to relieve himself, I tugged on Nilesen's sleeve.

"Will you help me with the bandage?" I picked at the gauze wrap. Nilesen stepped closer to pry the ends loose. The heat of the day pulsed around us. The sun evoked a stabbing pain as the flayed skin emerged. I fingered the stitching, pressing gently at the swollen lid. As hard as I tried, I couldn't open it more than a fraction. Light like tarnished silver seeped in, causing the eye to tear up and squeeze shut.

"It is healing." Nilesen's assessment, void of emotion, noncommittal, sent warning tremors through me.

"What aren't you saying?" When she refused to meet my gaze, I held out the camera. "Here. Take a picture."

Fethi came back, looked at my face, and bowed his head. "Jeannie," Nilesen said. "*Arkadaşim*, we can do this later."

I thrust the camera at Fethi. "You, then. I have a right to know."

"Please. Don't do this now." Nilesen put an arm around me.

My words grew fainter. My trembling increased. "I need to know."

Reluctant and frowning, Fethi focused the lens and depressed the shutter. I snatched the camera back, pressed the view button, and stared at my ruined face. Jagged lines of stitching rimmed the eye and curved above the lid, lending a

Frankensteinian flare to the wound. The right side of my face sported green, blue, and yellow hues that deepened to purple and black closer to the eye itself. Even if my sight returned, the woman I once was no longer looked back at me. The fragments of the bomb had cratered the landscape of my face, carving a new surface on which to write my story. I gagged, tried not to scream.

Down the street, Arif struggled toward us, pushing a motorcycle with a sidecar. A man walked behind him, dragging a second cycle, smaller, but with enough room for two riders on the seat. As soon as they reached us, Arif introduced his cousin. Turning away, I rewrapped the bandage around my head. Nilesen moved toward me, but I shooed her away. I couldn't bear the thought of anyone touching the damaged skin.

Fethi held out the money he and Nilesen had counted. Arif's cousin accepted the bills, exchanging them for a grease-stained sack before hurrying away.

"What's his problem?" I mumbled.

"The fewer people who observe us, the better." Arif made the sign to ward off the evil eye and opened the sack. He pulled out containers of rice and fruit and handed them around, then used his knife to slice a loaf of bread. We sat on a low stone wall, absorbed in thought, our conversation stifled by the need to eat and the knowledge that we had no assurance of a future meal. After sharing a jug of water, we stood and approached the motorcycles.

"Do any of you know how to ride these?" Arif asked.

"I thought you did," Fethi said. He eyed the largest cycle with barely-concealed distaste.

"*Olamaz!* Alain and I used to ride these all the time." Nilesen hopped onto the motorcycle and cocked her head at Fethi. "Get in, *abi*."

Eyes downcast, the porter's son clambered into the sidecar. Arif looked at me and nodded. I wrapped the hijab to cover my eye, waited for him to get on, then straddled the bike behind him. "Don't have an accident," I said.

J. E. Irvin

"God willing," he intoned. With a puff of black smoke and a string of staccato pops, the engine sputtered to life, bucked a few times, and headed down the road. Nilesen followed. We passed a sign I couldn't read, roared forward, and arrowed southwest over the mountains toward the river town of Kütahya.

22

... of thieves and refugees ...

The wind screeched in Jeannie's ears, tore at her clothes. Grateful for the protection of Arif's body, she ducked her head against his back to shield her face from further injury. Bugs pinged against her helmet and bounced off her hands, stinging as they struck. It was impossible to speak, impossible to think. The tires chanted road hymns as they crunched over the gravel-strewn pavement. Lulled by the hum of the engine and soothed by the pain meds, she drifted between awareness and sleep. In the stupor induced by the ride and the medications, she allowed herself to stop dwelling on her eye. The drugs eased the physical pain, quieted the emotions rolling within.

By dusk, battered by the ride, tired and eager for a respite from the buffeting, she begged Arif to pull over. He grumbled his displeasure but slowed as they entered a village dominated by a hotel tucked between the postane and a modest mosque. Nilesen pulled up alongside.

"Can we afford to stay here?" She fingered the money belt at her waist. "We have limited funds."

Arif set the kickstand as he waved away her question. "The owner is a friend of my family."

They had barely brushed the road dust from their clothing when the proprietor stepped out of the hotel. He greeted Arif with a hug, hooked his thumbs into his belt, and turned his attention to the group. Arif introduced his fellow travelers. The hotel owner and Fethi shook hands. With a respectful nod to Nilesen and Jeannie and only the briefest of inquiries as to why they had come to his establishment, the man motioned them in. Arif, however, launched into an extended recital of the automobile accident that required the *Americali* to seek medical treatment in Izmir. The man cut his eyes toward Jeannie's bandaged eye and Nilesen's hands as he reached for the room keys.

The night air carried the hint of jasmine. Jeannie wandered past the registration counter, entranced by the inn's interior courtyard. Baskets of lavender hung suspended from the second-floor balcony. Colorful terra cotta pots graced the perimeter. Despite her exhaustion, she headed toward a table near the fountain in the center. A local musician had set up opposite the entrance. He acknowledged their arrival with a nod and returned to playing the oud. A young couple celebrating an engagement strolled through, accompanied by their families and friends. A waiter brought a bottle of wine and a plate of baklava. Arif thanked him before addressing the group.

"This is nice, no? A moment of respite before our journey resumes."

"We are grateful," Nilesen said, "for this kindness."

"Nilesen *hanim*." Fethi turned to her. "I have not seen you writing, but I know you have words to share. Will you read for us, *Lütfe*?"

Nilesen and the porter's son exchanged a glance. "You ask too much of me, *abi*.

Arif raised an eyebrow. "The boy asks only what you are owed. We would be honored to hear your words," he said.

Jeannie nudged Nilesen. "We could all use a little magic. Go ahead."

The music of the oud echoed around them. Nilesen drummed her fingers on the table., then withdrew the notebook from her bag. She shifted to capture the light from the lantern on the table. "Only this night. Then you must not ask me again." She sorted through the pages, selected a poem, and began to recite. Whereas the music had soared, the words whispered, rising over the courtyard, gathering strength. The musician stopped strumming. The wedding party drew closer. Even the owner's children crept in, dropping to their knees and inching near as she read. One boy slipped out of the room. In minutes, he returned, followed by others from the village. Caught by the rhythm of

A Principle of Light

words she didn't understand, Jeannie watched the courtyard fill up.

No one spoke. No one coughed. Mothers held babies on their laps. Lovers held hands. Within the enclosed walls, a fey light grew, shimmering, wavelike, over the assembly. Beyond the circle of listeners, the night listened and held its breath. A breeze stirred the hanging baskets, rustled the trees along the main street. Phantom hair blew across Jeannie's forehead. She reached for the camera. Fethi grabbed her arm.

"Let it go, Madam." He lifted his chin in Nilesen's direction. "This is her moment."

Jeannie shrugged him off, wrapped the strap around her wrist. "I agree, Fethi, and I intend to capture it for her."

Nilesen turned the page and read on. Jeannie adjusted for the fading light and double-checked the battery power. She didn't want to use the flash, to be intrusive, but the compulsion to capture the moment drove her. Careful not to draw attention, she worked her way to the outside of the gathering. From there, she panned the crowd, snapping photos. By the entrance, a teenager lowered a hood over his head, detached himself from the shadows, and slipped out the door.

Jeannie waited for Arif to look up, then motioned him to follow her. She pushed through a knot of listeners and eased through the exit, anxious to catch up with the hooded figure. The corridor, lit by sconces, led to the street where they had parked the motorcycles. When she stepped out, she saw the motorcycle with the sidecar in front of the inn. The smaller ride was missing. Jeannie peered down the lane that ran between the hotel and the mosque and spotted the flash of a tail light off to the left. Camera clutched to her side, she hurried after the retreating bike. The thief glanced over his shoulder. The hood slipped. In the dim light, all Jeannie could see was the profile of a young boy. He turned, spotted Jeannie, and pushed the bike faster. At her back, Arif called out a warning. Soon, Fethi joined the pursuit. The men raced past Jeannie, shouting as they gained on the fleeing figure.

The thief had just reached the edge of the square when Arif grabbed him by the neck. Fethi caught the bike before it fell. The thief kicked and swung his fists, landing several blows before he collapsed into a huddle, arms wrapped around his head, legs drawn to his chest. Arif wiped the blood from one of the blows on the sleeve of his shirt, placed a knee on the young man's back, and slammed him onto his stomach. With a snarl, the thief surged to his knees. His face, scraped and bleeding from a cut on his chin, caught the glow of a streetlamp.

"*Adin ne?*" Arif growled. "*Adin ne?*"

The thief snapped his teeth in an attempt to bite the headmaster. Fethi knelt to hold the boy still. Jeannie set the flash and clicked the shutter as she documented the scene. When she zoomed in for a closeup, she stumbled to a halt.

"Arif," she called. "Fethi. Stop."

"Jeannie." Arif glared at her. "We will handle this."

"No. Please. Let the girl go."

Arif cursed as he released his hold on the thief. Fethi stepped back. Jeannie grabbed the girl and shook her. "Are you Kurdish? Do you speak English?"

The girl closed her eyes. When Jeannie released her, she buried her head in her arms.

"Which is it?" Arif gripped the girl's arm and shook her. "Kurdish? English?"

Baring her teeth, she bobbed her head twice. Arif motioned her to sit.

"Do you promise not to run again?" Jeannie edged closer. The girl trembled as she nodded again. Jeannie pushed the thick fall of black hair off the girl's face. "Why did you steal our bike?"

The girl shivered harder. She looked thirteen or fourteen, not old enough to be traveling on her own. "It's all right, Jeannie said. "They won't hurt you."

She helped the thief up. When she was certain the girl could walk, she escorted her back to the hotel. Arif and Fethi followed, pushing the motorcycle between them. A few villagers stepped out to see what the noise was about.

A Principle of Light

Jeannie ignored their shouted questions. She took the girl to the room she shared with Nilesen, shut the door against the men, and sat her down.

"Do not tell them I am here," the girl said.

"Whose them?"

The girl refused to answer. Jeannie offered a bottle of water, a handful of almonds. The girl accepted both. She gobbled the nuts and held her hand out for more.

While the girl finished the water, Jeannie wondered what it would take to earn the child's trust. Perhaps a promise, one she hoped she could keep. "Are you a refugee? It doesn't matter to me. I won't turn you in."

The girl stared at the wall, the haunted look in her eyes all the answer Jeannie needed. When the door opened, the girl huddled deeper into the shadowed corner. Arif crossed his arms and leaned against the wall. Fethi glared at the thief.

"You are a Kurd." The young Turk jabbed a finger at her. "Do not try to deny it. This village is very far from the border. How did you get here?"

The girl brushed her hands on her trousers and burrowed into the hood. Her tangled hair fell over her face, masking her fear. The door opened again and Nilesen stepped inside. When the girl looked up, she clasped her hands together and issued a string of pleas. Nilesen answered her. The girl reached into a pocket of her jacket and pulled out a newspaper. She spread it on the floor and pointed to a photo. Jeannie crouched lower to see what had agitated the girl. Nilesen pushed past the men, rattled off more questions, then sat back on her heels.

"This is Elani. She is from Diyarbakir, and, yes, that is a long way from here. She was captured by smugglers who intended to sell her to a brothel. She escaped by hiding in the back of a tractor-trailer carrying plumbing supplies but had to jump off before the driver caught her. She has been wandering this area for a week."

"Is that why she tried to steal our motorcycle?" Arms folded, face stern, Fethi shuffled forward. "She enjoys being a thief? Bah, haven't you had enough of thieves, Nilesen *hanim*?"

"Enough, *abi*," Nilesen said. "The girl is terrified, starving, and nearly feral."

"What are we going to do with her?" Jeannie scooted closer to pick up the copy of *Hürriyet*. "Is this what I think it is?"

"Turkey's most widely read newspaper?" Arif said. "It is."

Jeannie scowled at her own likeness. Based on witness accounts from the bombing, the sketch presented a bloated version of Jeanine Maurillac. In the photograph, she still had both of her eyes. And all of her hair. "Great. Now everyone's going to be looking for a red-haired American."

"Except," Nilesen squinted up at her, "you have no hair anymore."

Jeannie touched the scarf that concealed her bald head, and pointed at Elani. "And her?"

"We have no choice. She comes with us to Izmir." Nilesen snatched the paper and continued to read. "The *polisi* are looking for you, *arkadaşim*."

"I'm sorry. I brought this on you." Jeannie turned to Fethi and Arif. "On all of you."

"That does not matter now. We need to move faster." Panic underscored the poet's words.

Jeannie pulled her aside. "What's wrong?"

Nilesen stabbed at a photo beneath the artist's sketch of the photographer. She skimmed her hand down the column and stopped at a name. "I know this man. Emre Gazi. He broke my hands to prove a point. And I cannot be certain, but I believe he was the *polis* in the square."

Chills rippled down Jeannie's spine. "This man, he's chasing us?"

"I believe he is." Nilesen stuffed the paper in her bag and turned away. "We must all go. Now."

"There is no room for anyone else on the bikes." Arif pulled at his beard.

A Principle of Light

"No matter. We will make room." Nilesen knelt to lay a finger on the girl's lips. "She knows who we are. We cannot leave her behind."

23

... arrival in Kütahya ...

A crescent moon slipped lower along the horizon as we made our way to the outskirts of the village. Our host from the inn handed Arif a satchel with food and water, then escorted us through the square.

"You must understand," he said, worry beads clacking. "If even one person makes a call, the soldiers will come."

Arif thanked his friend. Fethi settled behind him on the smaller motorcycle. Nilesen and I squeezed together on the larger one, the Kurdish girl tucked into the sidecar. The rumble of the motorcycles would draw attention, but it no longer mattered. We had lost the safety of anonymity. The newspaper sketch identified me as a person of interest in the Istanbul bombing. That alone decreased our odds of reaching Izmir unnoticed. As we hurtled through the night, I prayed we wouldn't lose our way in the dark.

The landscape enfolded us in ebon arms. We slipped like dreams past the clusters of roadside homes. Sooner than expected, the sun rose behind us, dappling our shoulders, striping the road, climbing like ivy across the undulating fields. We stopped to refuel, to rest our aching muscles, and to eat a hurried lunch. It was nearly sundown again when we reached the outskirts of Kütahya.

Once off the main highway, Arif passed clusters of buildings, searching for the one that belonged to his brother Mehmet. In the early light, I identified kilns perched at the back of each establishment. Each cast off shimmers of heat as the new tiles baked inside. Pallets stacked with glazed wares awaited transport. A convoy of trucks sat idling in front of each factory. Confused by the sprawl of buildings, Arif pulled off the road. He took out his cell, spoke briskly to someone on the other end, then stamped his foot. Although most of what he said escaped me, I recognized a few words, *abi*, *Sağol*, and *Dört*. The number four.

I waited for him to turn toward me. "You're not coming with us?"

He shook his head. I eased off the motorcycle, skipping away from the hot pipes along the side. "How will you return the bikes to your cousin?"

He tapped the phone against his leg. "God will provide."

I wandered away. Thirst plagued me, as it had since the accident. Arif set the kickstand and wiped his forehead with the hem of his shirt. Then he pulled a gun from the waistband of his slacks and waved it in my direction.

"Go stand by the others, Madam."

"What is the matter, Arif?" Nilesen, followed closely by the Kurdish girl, swooped closer, brows raised, hands on hips. "Why do you have a gun?"

Fethi rushed to stand in front of us. Arif shrugged. "Do not be alarmed. It is family business. Please, Madams, stay calm and try not to move."

He raised the gun and fired once into the air. The shot reverberated among the huddle of buildings. Workers rushed from the sheds, cigarettes dangling from their lips, hands coated with clay dust. They shaded their eyes and gestured toward the hill where we stood beside the motorcycles. When they spotted Arif, they ran back inside. At the back of the third building, a door swung open, hinges squealing. A burly man dressed as a Saudi stepped out. He pulled a pistol from beneath his robe and rested the gun over one arm like a cowboy from a very old western movie. Then he aimed it at our group. I ducked and covered my head. A bullet skipped in the dirt next to the motorcycle Arif drove. I covered my mouth to keep from screaming. What craziness had we stumbled into?

Arif shouted, "*Allahu akhbar*." He ran toward the robed stranger. When he reached the man, they embraced each other. Workers peeked from their hiding places behind stacks of tileware, then waved and danced around the

A Principle of Light

brothers, patting backs and laughing. I exchanged a puzzled glance with Nilesen.

"Should we get back on the bikes and ride away?" Exhaustion made my legs shake. My head throbbed with every breath. Elani huddled next to Nilesen, her eyes huge, her body striving to fit itself into a smaller and smaller space. Emerging from the assembly of workers, Arif moved toward the open door, motioning us to follow.

"No, Jeannie. We cannot leave. We are committed to this plan now."

As we approached, I studied the architecture of the surrounding factories. A few of the buildings were modern in design and layout, but most remained as they had been for centuries. The business owned by Arif's brother was Middle Ages old, made of bricks that were most likely produced on the premises. The back door opened onto a narrow, stuccoed hall that branched off into smaller workrooms where the clay was molded, engraved, painted, and set to dry before being fired. The kilns brooded, hive-like, in the yards, hungry for fire and mud to forge into beauty. We shuffled down the narrow corridor into a display room. Arif made brief introductions before ushering us to a tiny office next to an even tinier kitchen. When I looked in, I spotted a dorm-size refrigerator, a basket of fruit, and a water cooler. We crowded into the office. Nilesen and I accepted the offer of the only chairs. Elani perched on my lap.

"So, *erkek kardeşim*," Mehmet clapped Arif on the back, "you are in need of transportation."

Arif swept his hand at us. "Yes, my brother. My friends need to go to Izmir. You have a truck heading there this afternoon, do you not?"

"Perhaps. But your friends have the look of the vagabond about them. Or that of refugees. Why should I do this, risk my fortune for strangers?"

Arif leaned closer to his brother and gestured toward Nilesen and me as he patted his chest. I fiddled with the strap of my camera but decided against taking Mehmet's picture. Something in the look he threw me contained a warning tinged with malice. Plus, he still carried a gun. Arif reached into his pocket, extracted a newspaper, and spread it out on the desk. When he pointed to a sketch on the page, I understood his intention. He tapped the paper and pointed at me.

"Why did you not say we were thumbing our noses at the government?" Mehmet slapped the desk. He set the gun down and looked us over, pausing to examine each face. "Very well. I will transport you to Izmir. However, before you go, you must do something for me."

The room grew quiet. I reached for Nilesen's hand.

"Mehmet." Arif held up a hand in warning. Mehmet shrugged him off.

"Only one small thing." He opened the top drawer of the desk and pulled out an envelope, sealed and ready for mailing. "I need one of you to take this to the postane."

Fethi pushed his way forward. "I will take it."

"No, *abi*." Mehmet pushed him aside. "One of the females must go. They rarely question women."

Nilesen frowned. "One small thing, you say."

Arif's brother nodded. She inclined her head. "I will go."

"What's in the package?" Elani stood up. I moved to stand by Nilesen.

Mehmet shoved the gun into the holster beneath his robe. "Better you do not know."

"And if they stop her?" Nilesen laid a hand on my arm. I didn't back down. "What will happen if the 'rarely' occurs today?"

Mehmet brought his palms together and lifted his eyes to heaven. "The widow Solaganian knows a little something about our jandarmalar. I suggest she avoid meeting them again."

24

... at the *postane* in Kütahya ...

The main post office in Kütahya was located half the city away from Mehmet's tile factory. Despite entreaties from each member of the group, including Elani, Nilesen insisted on going alone. She tucked the package beneath a niqab Arif brought out for her, climbed into the van, and motioned the driver to go. Mehmet had assigned one of the apprentices to escort her, and by the stern look on the young man's face, she knew he took the duty seriously. They drove along the dusty factory lane until it joined the highway leading into the city. The driver crept forward, easing to a stop at every yellow light, inching through the late afternoon traffic. Exasperated by the slow progress, Nilesen slapped his head.

"Ow. Madam, why did you do that?"

"Because, *abi ahmak*, I want to arrive today, not next week. I will drive, if you like. You can direct me."

With a quick gesture against the evil eye, he increased his speed and his appreciation for the woman sitting beside him.

"Are you related to Mehmet *bey*? His sister perhaps? Mr. Mehmet has many siblings, ten in all. His parents are blessed, *Allahu akbhar*."

"Are you a practicing Muslim?" Nilesen was intrigued by his use of Arabic.

"I am a Muslim. My family has worked the tile factories since the late 1500s."

"Did you ever think of starting your own factory?"

When he turned to look at her, the car swerved. Traffic honked and dodged as he veered back into his lane and sighed. "We are master craftsmen, Madam. Would you ask us to give up beauty for business?"

She closed her eyes, struck by the memory of Alain after lovemaking, his arms wrapped tightly around her, echoing these same thoughts.

Never exchange your gift for a less noble one, my love. There is no safety in denial of self.

But if you are in danger, Alain?

I would not have you risk your soul, not even for me.

"Is creating the product more important than selling it?" She fingered the hem of her niqab, the fabric slipping through her fingers.

"Is air more precious than water? Both are necessary for life, but if I had to choose between breath and thirst, I choose that which keeps me most alive."

That which keeps me most alive. Nilesen patted the pocket where she had stashed her notebook and gazed out the window. The arches and towers of Kühtaya rose around them. A chord chimed within her, binding her to all the artists who had created beauty here, then spent their lives sustaining that gift. The van jolted to a stop. A car screeched as it careened around them.

"You can get out now, Madam. We have arrived. I will wait for you there." He pointed around the corner. "Make sure you get a receipt. For Mehmet *bey*."

Nilesen got out of the van, the package clutched tight against her chest. She entered through the double doors of the *postane* and found herself in a room crowded with kiosks and mailing paraphernalia. She rotated the postcards until she found one she liked. Scribbling a message on the back, she pulled out the thick envelope Mehmet had given her and joined the queue that wound around the atrium. Except for an old woman wearing a scarf and a younger one in a fashionable miniskirt, she was the only female. She tucked a stray curl behind her ear and lowered her eyes. At the head of the line, at the spot where customers stepped up to the window, a policeman paced. As the line snailed forward, he tapped random shoulders and requested identification cards. A man carrying a briefcase was escorted to a door next to the post office boxes. When he disappeared inside, the others in

A Principle of Light

the line began to murmur loudly. A middle-aged gentleman with thick eyebrows eyed the female in the short skirt.

"Leave us, woman. You disgrace yourself with this clothing."

A second voice interrupted the first, reciting verses from the Koran. Another man gestured to the girl to cover her head. At first, she ignored them, but as the comments changed from chiding to anger, she shoved at those encroaching on her space. Nilesen stepped forward. "Shame to all of you. Rumi teaches us to listen with ears of tolerance, see through the eyes of compassion, and speak with the language of love."

"Bah! Rumi." The man who initiated the harassment spit on the floor. "What does a dervish know about the Prophet's truth?"

His rebuke increased the outcry. The room boiled with men shaking their fists, pointing fingers, using cigarettes to emphasize talking points. Intimidated by the crowd, the younger woman stepped out of line and hurried from the building. Nilesen rejoined the line and sidled forward. Soon, she and the *yaşli kadin* had moved to the front. Nilesen's grip on the envelope tightened. She glanced up and caught the woman staring at her. One eye slowly winked.

"Foolish men." The old woman waddled closer. "So easily distracted by trivialities, so eager to fight for the wrong cause."

Nilesen eyed the men. "What, then, is the right one?"

The woman placed a hand on the package and winked again. "Truth. It is not what we wear that defines us. It is what we carry in our hearts."

"Perhaps you can help me with my truth, *Büyükanne*. Will you mail this postcard for me?"

The *yaşli kadin* pursed her lips, then held out her hand. Nilesen placed the postcard and the coins in her palm.

"May you stay safe, *Küçük kizkardeş*."

The clerk at the window motioned the line forward. Soon Nilesen would be able to relieve herself of Mehmet's package. The officer by the mystery door examined Nilesen's niqab, sandals, and loose trousers. He tapped his jop against his palm and started toward her. The old woman completed her transaction. When she saw the policeman approach, she cried out and stumbled forward, falling hard against the man's chest. The jandarma caught himself and set the *yaşli kadin* upright.

Nilesen set the parcel and five-lira note on the counter and requested it be mailed today. A clerk emerged through the shuttered door, announced that the *postane* would be closing in ten minutes, and retreated. The patrons in line murmured their disapproval. Nilesen stepped away from the counter and shoved the receipt in her pocket. She eased her way along the wall, avoiding the knots of angry men. She exited the building and started down the sidewalk, anxious to reach the van before the policeman noticed she was gone. Around the corner, the driver sat hunched over the steering wheel, biting his nails. As soon as Nilesen climbed in, he merged into the traffic stream.

"That did not take so long. Any problems, Madam Solaganian?"

"Not today, *abi*."

"You are smiling," he said. "You look very beautiful when you smile."

"A wise man once said that the truth will set you free. Today, I learned a lesson about that kind of truth." She retrieved sunglasses from her bag. The darkened lenses filtered the haze from the afternoon. The cloudless sky blazed, azure and inviting, blissfully unaware of the storm gathering in the wind.

As they approached the industrial park, the tile factories hummed with frantic energy. Workers hustled from workrooms to kilns, anticipating the end of the day's labors. The driver dropped Nilesen at the front of Mehmet Selçuk's warehouse. Fethi rushed to escort her back to Mehmet's office. The brothers were nowhere to be seen.

"We will leave as soon as the truck is loaded," Fethi announced. "Weather reports indicate thunderstorms this evening."

A Principle of Light

The Kurdish girl crouched in the corner, head bowed, arms cradled around her knees. Jeannie greeted Nilesen before plugging the now-recharged battery into the camera. She stowed the charger in the bag that had replaced the abandoned photographer's case.

"How long," she said, "until we reach Izmir?"

Fethi shrugged. "Arif claims it is a drive of five hours or so by car. In a truck heavily loaded with tiles, perhaps the time stretches to six or seven."

"How do you know this man will not simply order the truck to drop us off at the police station?" Elani jumped to her feet, hands fisted on her hips. "How can you trust a man who shoots a gun in the air, then orders us all to march in here?"

Nilesen pulled Elani aside and spoke to her. Gradually the girl unclenched her fists. Nilesen kept the Kurdish refugee close as she spoke to the group. "These are our truths. We cannot reach the coast on our own. Certainly not quickly. Jeannie needs a doctor. Elani needs sanctuary. Fethi needs to return to Istanbul."

The porter's son waved away her words. "I will not abandon you."

Nilesen favored him with a smile and went on. "Arif saved us once. I trust him to do it again."

"Arif maybe." Jeannie touched the bandage on her eye. "Mehmet is another story."

"And what story is that, *Americali*?" The Selçuk brothers banged through the doorway, Mehmet first, Arif following close behind. "You, Madam, are not a very trusting soul. No matter. I do this for my brother, not for you." He took out the pistol and turned it in his hand.

"No more shooting, okay?" Jeannie said.

Mehmet smirked. "We have a running joke, my brother and I, that the gun is mightier than the sword. You know our history, *neh*? How we fought with sabers from horseback to defeat the invaders? If we had had guns, it would not have taken so long to defeat our enemies. So, when we do not see each other for a long time, we greet each other with guns blazing."

Jeannie snorted. "Oh, yeah, that explains everything."

Mehmet tapped the pistol against her forehead. "If I were you, Jeannie Maurillac, I would take care not to insult my host. I am certain the jandarmalar would be most happy to learn of your whereabouts."

He shoved the latest edition of *Hürriyet* at her. She glanced at the first page before handing it to Nilesen, who skimmed through the articles.

"What does it say?" Jeannie asked.

"It says," Nilesen said, "that the authorities have intensified their search for the missing American photographer, Jeannie Maurillac, a suspect in the bombing of the restaurant square in Cihangir."

In the silence that followed, Nilesen folded the paper and stuffed it in her bag. They rechecked their supply of food and water and filed out of the office, working their way through the craft rooms toward the back of the factory. Beyond the giant kiln, a box truck idled, its rear doors open, the incline ramp a claw waiting to gather them in. They thanked the brothers, accepted a small flashlight, and filed into the belly of the truck. When the doors clanged shut, they huddled together next to stacks of tiled beauty, each one encased in a singular and ominous darkness.

No light travels inside a black box.

Diffraction

25

... on the road to the coast ...

*T*he truck rumbles on, pallets creaking and shifting as the road dips toward the sea. Sealed away from the light, the travelers settle into uneasy dreams. Currents of air swirl around them, spinning invisible tendrils of time. Outside, in the luster of stars long dead, the night remembers.

Up from the sea, down from the mountains, the torrent of history strains the seams of Izmir. Settlements rise, flourish, and fall four thousand years before the Christ joins the flood. Alexander the Great conquers here, rules, dies, his tomb drowning beneath the dusty wave of time. The Greeks build agoras above the harbor. The Romans replace them with temples and homes. To the south the great Ephesus sprawls, reigns, abandons the moment to rest, root-draped and silent, in the light that filters through the cracked earth. Luminescence diffracts through the expansive lens of time, illuminating ageless tales. The great ruin dozes under the sun and under the moon, its access to the Aegean silted in by three miles of reclaimed seabed. St. Paul writes letters to the people of Izmir /Smyrna, spreading a monotheistic vision of the Godhead to the descendants of polytheistic tradition. Ancient and prescient, the light bounces off the traveler, who narrows her eyes to peer into history's graveyard. The veneer of modernity sloughs away, the old life unveiling itself, layer upon layer. Light is the baklava of memory, sweet, honeyed, a rich dessert for the hungry pilgrim. Ghosts with hollow, haunted eyes sift among the living, awaiting an invitation to set them free.

~ ~ ~

Thunder shook the truck. Lightning hissed and crackled. Bullets of rain struck the roof of the truck, pinged against the sides. Nilesen jolted awake. No matter how many times she blinked, black night blinded her. A fragment of a Rumi poem unfolded in her mind. *Darkness is your candle.* Alain. Sadness scratched ragged nails on her heart. Once they shared the night, awash in passion, soothed in sleep. A second Rumi line climbed free. *In your light, I learn how to love.* Unable to keep the loss within, she wept.

Beside the poet, Jeannie lay still. The stitches around her eye itched, each thread a tiny worm writhing beneath the skin. She risked opening her good eye, found the darkness so profound that panic tightened her throat. She tried to inhale without gasping, forced her lungs to expand and contract. Listening to the snores and sighs of her companions, she stifled a scream. Entombed in the unlit truck, she could no longer deny the images from the bombing. Like flames in a bonfire, they pranced and flared. Two men with suitcases smoking cigarettes, chatting up a policeman in the middle of the square. The bookseller wheeling the cart back inside his shop. Carl racing up the street, his words chaff floating in a melancholy wind. Fisting one hand over her heart, she released her own tears, a slow drip of water for the dead consumed by fire and hate. Beside her, in the grip of a dream, the Kurdish girl cried out.

"Elani?" Jeannie shook the girl gently, mindful of the dreamer's tendency to lash out.

"What is the matter with her?" Fethi's whisper shuffled across the bare floor between them. He had insisted on lying down near the farthest stack of tiles, his concern for their honor impractical yet touching.

"A bad dream," Nilesen said. Her clothing rustled as she sat up, filling the truck with sighs. She batted at the air, searching for Elani. When she located the girl, she invited Jeannie to move closer. They wrapped their arms around the refugee's trembling body and rocked her between them.

"I wish I could see," Elani said. "I never feared the dark before."

"If you wish for light," Nilesen recited, "be ready to receive light."

"Did you write that?" Jeannie loosened her grip now that the girl was fully awake.

"No, but I studied the man who did. Would you like to hear the rest?" She cleared her throat.

"Please."

Jostled by the sway of the truck, Nilesen spoke into the darkness. "Nourish your ego and be deprived of light. If you wish to find a way out of this prison, do not turn away; bow down in worship and draw near."

"What does that mean?" Elani shifted away from them, drew her knees to her chin. "For me, this is like being in jail, but I refuse to bow down to anyone."

"It feels," Jeannie said, "like I'm stuck in an Edgar Allen Poe tale."

"I remember being so young as you, Elani, so sure of everything. The poem is about love, and the release to be found in acknowledging that love." Nilesen felt along the floor for the bag Arif had given her. She rummaged inside until she located the flashlight. Handing the torch to Fethi, she distributed food and bottles of water.

"Here, I believe we can use some food. Fethi, can you tell us what time it is?"

"Almost ten o'clock," he said. Wedging the flashlight between two pallets, he accepted a sandwich and began to eat. The dim beam illuminated the food pack and the tips of their shoes. Between bites, the porter's son speculated on the time left until their arrival in Izmir. "I calculate one to two hours, no more. Long enough to test our patience and our courage."

The rain segued to a lullaby, pattering in rhythmic drops above them. Nilesen withdrew into the shadows. "When we sit in the dark," she said, "we listen more closely, attend to the smallest of sounds. Do you hear how the storm has gentled? I think Rumi would tell us to cherish this part of the journey. When the light returns, so do our prejudices."

"Maybe," Jeannie said. "But, tell me, what are we going to do when we get there?"

They shared a hushed conversation as they finished the food, discussing and dismissing possible actions once they arrived. They knew of no contacts in the city except for the man the doctor had recommended. Caroline's words echoed in Nilesen's head. *He is not one of us.* But the stranger's was the only name they had, and Jeannie's eye needed attention.

"It is dangerous to wander without a destination in mind." She picked at her thumbnail. "What do you think?"

"I have no way of knowing," Jeannie said. "And I'm too tired to think. Elani?"

The girl raised her head. "I, too, am a stranger here. How would I know?"

Jeannie held her head in her hands. "I trust your judgment, *arkadaşim*. You and Fethi must decide."

They proposed and dismissed several more ideas before Nilesen cut them off. "Enough. Arguing gets us nowhere. Fethi," she said, "no one knows you or Elani, so you will go into the city."

"And do what?"

"Acquire a rental car for the drive to Çeşme. You can pose as students on holiday."

"Wait," Jeannie leaned into the circle of light, her face pale and strained. "If we separate, how will we know they're all right?"

Fethi scratched his head. Finally, smoothing his mustache with his fingers, the young Turk swiped at his phone, typed a message, and set the alarm.

"Once we have the car, I will activate this message." He passed the phone around so they could see the words. **Ready to receive the light**.

"What if there's trouble?" Jeannie handed the phone back to him.

He typed in a second sentence, then recited it. "Find a way out of this prison."

Quiet settled over them, broken only by the sounds of their breathing. Time dripped around them, its steady passage wearing away their confidence. Nilesen fingered the scrap of paper Caroline Nepthali had given her.

"Jeannie and I will find this Doctor, Batur Stephanidis." She expected questions, protests. No one spoke. "I do not believe my friend would send us into danger."

A Principle of Light

Resisting the urge to press the bandage over her eye, Jeannie fiddled instead with the camera strap. "What else is left but trust? I can go alone, Nilesen, if you want. There's no need for both of us to risk being caught."

"No, Jeannie, you will not go alone. Together, we will find this man. Fethi and Elani will bring the car." Nilesen gathered the remnants of their meal, wrapped everything in a cloth, and stuffed it in her bag. "Now, we return to the darkness."

Fethi wrested the flashlight free from its perch and handed it to Nilesen. When the light winked out, he shifted against the pallets, trying to carve a comfortable position out of the unforgiving bed of the truck. The dampness filtering in from outside increased. The women huddled together.

"I will try not to dream again," Elani whispered.

Nilesen hugged the girl to her. "No, Elani. Do not fight sleep. Our dreams, even the scary ones, carry us into the future. Right now, the future is all you have."

~ ~ ~

A breeze slips over the Aegean, caresses the shore, arrows inland. As it passes, it gathers the hum of truck tires, the soughing of trees, the call of predators searching the night. In the rift between what has been and what will be, the air sighs, embracing time. Above, the moon raises a fist of light that shudders across the road. For the travelers, there is only the what-is, that treacherous slipstream of movement spreading across the now.

~ ~ ~

The truck bumped over a rumble strip, downshifted, and screeched to a stop. The bleat of a ship's horn jarred the night, welcoming them to the port of Izmir. Blinded by the dark, shivering and restless, the travelers braced themselves for the next jolt. More time passed. Fearful of drawing attention, they kept still, straining to understand the shouted calls from outside. Something banged the rear of the truck, sending reverberations through the interior. Finally, the driver twisted the locking brace, and the doors swung open.

A spotlight mounted over a loading dock illuminated their release. The driver hissed a warning as they scrambled to their feet. Blinking against the light, they shuffled forward. Fethi sat on the edge of the truck bed and dropped to the ground, then reached up to help the women down. The driver had already turned away, see nothing, say nothing apparent in the set of his shoulders. By the water, a chain banged rhythmically against the quay. Hands entwined, Nilesen, Jeannie, and Elani scampered up an incline leading from the warehouses along the dock until they escaped the glare of the pole light. Fethi followed, the satchel, empty now, banging against his thigh as he ran. He and Elani, then Nilesen and Jeannie, slipped through a gap in the fence, checked for pursuit, and scurried across a road running parallel to the buildings. They stopped to catch their breath, then climbed toward a cluster of bars and marine salvage shops along the access road. At the top of the hill, they paused again, reluctant to separate, eager to be gone. Jeannie glanced at the sky and caught her breath. The night was full of stars.

"Come, Elani." Fethi hesitated before reaching for the girl's hand. "We must hope our Internet search turned up a legitimate business."

"Do you have enough money to pay for the car?" Nilesen said.

The porter's son patted his back pocket. "I plan to use my father's card. He can always claim it was stolen."

"Let me keep your pack for you."

Fethi read Nilesen's silent message. He released the clasp and handed it to Jeannie instead. "Take care of it for me," he told her.

She slung it to her shoulder and groaned. "This thing is heavy. Did you steal some of Mehmet's tiles?"

"Do not pay her any attention, *abi*." Nilesen kissed him on both cheeks. "Take care of Elani. Be safe."

No one spoke again. There was nothing left to say. Nilesen and Jeannie headed one way, Fethi and Elani the

A Principle of Light

other, the faintest of shadows tracing behind them at precisely opposite angles.

26

... night in Izmir ...

*A*nxious to leave the docks behind, Fethi released his hold on the girl and hurried forward. While Elani's sullenness pricked his ego, her beauty unnerved him. Why did she have to have such dark eyes, such full lips? So odd to feel the stirring of desire in the midst of the danger around them. *Be a man*, he admonished himself. He slowed, waited for her to catch up. Even as the girl's manner unsettled him, his worry for his companions kept him glancing over his shoulder. But darkness and the shuttered shops of the harbor had swallowed Nilesen and Jeannie. He thumbed on his cell. The GPS app loaded. He traced the bobbing blue dot into the heart of the harbor district where the auto rental office was located.

"Fethi." Elani caught up. "Someone is following us."

He paused. Behind them, the soft shuffle of footsteps whispered up the hill. He placed his hand in the hollow of her back and hurried her along. "Forgive me, Elani *hanim*," he said, "for being too familiar, but our safety depends on it."

"You sound like my brother, Ali," she said, "always worried about my honor."

"It is my own I also seek to protect. Tell me, where is your brother?"

She gripped his sleeve. The sounds behind them faded, then stopped. "Somewhere on the border. But there is one thing you need to know. I trust you, Fethi, and I am stronger than I look. No one will ever harm me again."

She removed his hand from her waist and pressed it against her chest, revealing the cold metal of the *hançer* hidden there. The outline of the dagger burned his palm. In the dark, closer now than before, the footsteps echoed again. A man called out a greeting. "Weary travelers, do you need a ride? I have a taxi."

Jolted into action, they clasped hands and ran, emerging onto a crowded walkway. The warm night coupled with the wind blowing up from the sea had encouraged the citizens of Izmir to come out for the evening. They slipped into the crowd. Consulting the phone, Fethi led the way toward the car rental agency. The man continued to call out, his voice increasingly drowned out by the chatter around them. Fethi and Elani exchanged a look, acknowledging the unspoken threat. *I know who you are.* Of course, that was impossible. No one knew them. No one could. The son of an Istanbul'lu porter, and a Kurdish kidnap victim from the east were not on anyone's radar. Yet someone was stalking them. Had Arif or Mehmet betrayed them? Making the sign of the evil eye with his thumb and forefinger, Fethi pressed on.

"Perhaps," he murmured, "we are just being paranoid."

Elani squeezed his hand. "Of course. It was only a coincidence."

Unconvinced, they kept up the brisk pace. Ahead, a street vendor held out a paper cone. "Chestnuts from Bursa, honored visitors. Fresh and perfectly roasted."

Fethi waved him off. A woman with a baby strapped to her back offered them *tulipas*.

"The night is beautiful," she called. "The girl is beautiful. Secure your pleasure with a gift of flowers, young sir."

Blushing, he waved the flower-seller away. The farther they walked from the harbor, the more sophisticated and prosperous-looking the people. He tapped the dot on the phone, wondering why they had not yet arrived at their destination. On the map of the city, the shop had not seemed so far away.

"There." Elani pointed toward a sign blinking on and off. *Arabalar.* Fethi shoved the phone in his pocket. They increased their pace, but just as they reached for the door, the sign blinked off. Beyond the glass, a clerk pointed to a placard announcing the hours of operation and shooed them away, mouthing a command to return tomorrow.

"Of all the luck."

A Principle of Light

Elani pulled at her lower lip. "I do not want to stay out here all night. That taxi man may still be following us."

"So then, Kurdish girl, what do you think we should do?" Fethi ran his hands through his hair. The ends stood up like a rooster's tail.

"There is an easy answer to that question, Turkish boy." She rested her hands on her hips and smiled at his unruly appearance. "We must find a place to hide."

"But, of course. Why was I unable to think of that? Now, if only we had enough money to afford two hotel rooms and one car."

"I thought you had your father's credit card."

Fethi turned red. "I do not know how I would explain such a charge."

Elani patted the hidden *hançer*, and winked. Then she grabbed his hand, spread his fingers, and ran them over the hem of her vest, revealing the coins sewn beneath the lining.

"What is this?"

"My dowry," she explained. "The men who took me were too stupid to search properly."

"First a dagger, then money? Are there more secrets you are keeping from me?" Fethi gnawed on a knuckle. "I cannot take your money, Elani."

"Do not be foolish. We can spend one coin tonight. You can pay me back."

Fethi blushed again. "No. That money was intended for you and your new husband. You will see him again, and then you will want to use it for your future home."

"Not going to happen." She gazed at the crowd. "He would never take me back. Besides, I did not want to marry him then, and I do not want to marry him now."

"So, you think you can decide these things because you have escaped from your captors? Because you are free?"

"More things are possible, yes. From this moment on, I am my own person." She stepped away from the *Arabalar*. "Let us try there."

Fethi turned in the direction she pointed. Three shops down, on the opposite side of the street, the neon glow of a

J. E. Irvin

tiny lighthouse flashed on and off above the name of an inn:
IŞIK

27

... night in Izmir ...

Nilesen and Jeannie hiked the darkened lane leading up from the shore. When they topped the ridge, they scurried past the seedy bars and headed toward the restaurants competing for the night's customers. The crowd flowed, tidelike, along the sidewalks. The aroma of fresh fish mingled with that of *lahmacun*, the beef-laced-with-spices street food beloved by Turks. Jeannie's stomach growled.

"You are hungry." Nilesen held up a coin. "Danger be damned. Let us have a treat." She led the way to the vendor's cart, ordered two cabobs, and dropped a coin in the lad's outstretched palm. He handed over the savory meat sticks to Jeannie. Munching as they walked, enveloped in the stream of citizens enjoying the evening air, the women made small talk, about the weather and the food and the need to find a restroom. Neither mentioned the topic foremost in mind, the desire to escape the unknown pursuers. When she finished, Jeannie rubbed her itchy scalp with one of the sticks.

"How are you feeling, *arkadaşim*?" Nilesen said.

"Do you want the truth or some polite response?"

"*Hakikat*, Jeannie. Always speak the truth to me. I prefer not to deal in lies and denial."

"The truth, then. My head throbs with every step. A sadness as heavy as concrete fills my bones, gnaws at my chest. I'm so tired, Nilesen. Even my fingernails ache."

"You need to rest. Come, I see a *dolmuş* waiting." She pointed at a minibus idling on the corner. She checked behind them for pursuit before she signaled the driver. When he drove up, she consulted the directions Caroline had given her and showed the address to the man. "*Karataşa gidiyor musun?*"

The driver nodded as he waved them into the back seat of the *dolmuş*. While Nilesen kept an eye on the street signs,

J. E. Irvin

Jeannie leaned her forehead against the window and gazed at the sea. Lantern lights, swift and bright as fireflies, flitted over the water as the fishing boats made their way to and from the shore. The sea swallowed each dart of brightness, then spit it back onto the restless water. She bobbed, too, her senses dulled by the tug of the stitches and the pain in her heart. Not for Carl but for what Carl represented, her life before she woke up seven days ago to a world shattered by a bomb.

Lulled by the sway of the minibus, she fell into a twilight sleep populated by brilliantly-colored rugs and familiar faces. Her editor shook a finger, urging her to finish the story. Carl exploded into a thousand bubbles of reddish mist. The *polis* on the motorbike pierced her eye with a fingernail ten feet long. When she cried out, Nilesen shook her awake.

The *dolmuş* climbed from the day-bright glow of neon above the bars into the shadow pulse of night. Fever dreams hissed and foamed around her, each filled with regret. She wiped the drool from her chin and stared at the passing homes.

The neighborhood of Karataş slumbered around them, the midnight calm of the residential Jewish Quarter a stark contrast to the bustle of the city and its waterfront noise. When Nilesen reached for her clenched fist, Jeannie surrendered to the poet's gnarled grip. The driver slowed, indicating with his outstretched palm a narrow lane off to the left. They got out and waited until the tail lights dwindled into specks and winked out. Then they made their way down the lane. When they reached the bottom, they approached the door of a one-story dwelling dwarfed by more imposing homes on either side. A six-foot palisade enclosed the side yard. An olive tree branched over the gate. A sign beneath the porch lamp announced **Doktor Batur Stephanidis**, followed by several words and numbers. In the dim light, her good eye stinging from overuse and the other begging to be plucked out, Jeannie failed to make out a single word. It didn't matter. Her Turkish wasn't good enough to understand more than the name and the profession.

"Do you think this man will help me?" She kept her voice low, afraid to alert the neighbors.

"Soon we will know." Nilesen knocked on the door. The seconds stretched out. She and Jeannie huddled closer. A breeze shuffled by, lifting the scarf from Jeannie's forehead, ruffling the hem of Nilesen's niqab. No one came to the door.

"Perhaps Stephanidis isn't home." Jeannie glanced at the stars staring boldly down on them. "Maybe we should go."

Nilesen rapped again, harder. A bush rustled in the yard beyond the fence. A lock clicked and rattled. After a long pause, they heard a second tumbler release. The door sprang open. Backlit by the light inside, a man confronted them, his hands clutching a towel. Taller than Jeannie, his massive shoulders exuded strength and menace. The running clothes he wore revealed corded muscles in his arms and legs, a broad chest, and skin the color of sand at low tide.

"*Ili geceler*, Madams. It is very late to be calling."

Nilesen returned the greeting before handing him a coin. "Doctor Stephanidis. Caroline Nepthali sends her regards. She and David are well, but she urges you to take precautions against the summer flu."

"So," the man flipped the coin and looked past them, surveying the night with owl-like attention, "the season is almost upon us. Are you in need of vaccination?"

Nilesen shoved Jeannie forward. "My companion requires your assistance."

The man rubbed the coin between his thumb and forefinger. When he turned to Jeannie, his profile sharp, she willed herself not to flinch. "Interesting," he said, his deep voice sending shivers down her back, "a person I have never met cashes in a marker, and I am left with hard choices."

"Send us away, then," Nilesen said. "We understand hard choices."

He handed the coin back and motioned them in. After he rebolted the door, he led them to a room to the right of the entry hall.

"It seems the decision has already been made." He narrowed his eyes at Jeannie. "Please, remove the scarf."

Jeannie untied the ends of the scarf and slipped it off. Batur Stephanidis grabbed her chin, turning it gently from side to side, as he examined the cuts and bruising on her face. When he finished, he motioned her to an examination table at the back of the room. Nilesen followed, positioning herself at Jeannie's side as the doctor evaluated the injuries caused by the explosion. He used scissors to cut away the bandage covering the eye. The gauze stuck to the wound. When he finally teased it free, Jeannie flinched. To distract herself, she perused the framed certificates on the wall. Batur Gregor Stephanidis had graduated from Duke University and the Johns Hopkins School of Medicine. He also had certificates from a variety of other renowned teaching hospitals. Impressive. What was he doing in Izmir?

"If you want my help, there must be no secrets. Do you understand?" He directed his gaze at Nilesen, who dipped her chin in agreement. Satisfied, he turned to Jeannie. "Tell me, please. Who are you and why are you here?"

"Her name is Jeannie Maurillac." Nilesen pulled the newspaper from her bag and spread it out on the table. "I am Nilesen Solaganian."

"Did you say Solaganian?"

His voice hitched as he spoke the surname. Did he know who Nilesen was? Did it matter? Before Jeannie could ask, the poet pointed to the article about the bombing in Istanbul.

"This is what we saw. This is why we are here."

Stephanidis grabbed the paper. When he finished reading, he returned it to Nilesen with a frown. "Tell me how you came to Izmir."

In slow and careful English so Jeannie would understand, Nilesen recited the details of their journey from Istanbul. She raised her brows, inviting the photographer to add to or to clarify the account. Jeannie fought the nausea roiling her gut and shook her head. Their story sounded preposterous, a fiction concocted to hide a darker purpose. Stephanidis listened without comment. When Nilesen reached the part about the ride in the back of the truck and the trip to the *postane*, Jeannie dropped her head in her hands, embarrassed and desperate to block out the memories. So far, their luck had held, but they couldn't keep running forever. She dry-heaved. Batur grabbed her shoulders, his touch gentle but his tone fierce.

"Ms. Maurillac?"

Lost in remembering the chaos in the square, Jeannie recoiled. The movement caused her to slip off the table. She tumbled forward. Stephanidis caught her before she hit the floor. He held her until she stopped shaking. When she pushed against him, he set her back on the table.

"You are safe here, both of you." He glanced at Nilesen, turned back to the patient. "I promise. Now, let me have a look at those stitches." He swabbed the skin with antiseptic, picked up the tweezers, and plucked at the catgut. Jeannie studied the lines of his face, intrigued by the dark eyes, the firm jaw, the brooding lips. He might have been a conqueror in another time and place. Her fingers itched to pick up the camera, to sit him in the light and capture the intensity flowing off him.

"Are you Egyptian, like Caroline?" she said, desperate to keep her focus off her ruined eye and the face that no longer resembled her own.

"What a curious question. I do not know this Caroline Nepthali, but perhaps she and I have common roots. My heritage is complicated. My father was from Cairo, yes, but his father was Greek. My mother was Turkish. Stop fidgeting, Ms. Maurillac. You have to sit still, and I apologize, but this will hurt. You should have had these stitches out days ago."

His reproach stung. "We were a bit busy, what with running from thieves and secret police and terrorists."

"So," he lifted one eyebrow, "you are a regular James Bond girl."

She grabbed his wrist and met his stare. "I'm not a joke."

"Forgive me. It was not meant to be funny." Dr. Stephanidis removed her hand. When he leaned in, his breath tickled her skin. "I know who and what you are, Jeannie Maurillac. Another American sent to photograph our complex and struggling country who finds herself caught up in the maelstrom of an imploding democracy."

"How can you judge me?"

"I have met your kind before."

Shamed by his assessment, Jeannie searched for a response. Nothing came to mind. Batur Stephanidis smoothed ointment over the raw skin. "I am right, no? But, tell me, do you know who she is?"

He cocked his head at Nilesen, who had moved to a chair in the corner. Oblivious to their conversation, she sat hunched in thought, her book of poetry resting on her lap.

"I do. That is the poet Nilesen Yilmaz. The people chasing me are after her, too."

"Of course," he murmured. "That explains everything."

Jeannie sat up. "I know there's a reward, but you can't turn her in. I won't let you."

"Steady." He pressed a hand to her shoulder, forced her back against the table. "I have almost finished cleaning it. Then we will check to see if you have lost any of your sight."

She grabbed his wrist again and tugged him closer. "Promise me, Doctor. She has risked her life for mine. You can't turn her in. She's been hurt enough."

Stephanidis met her stare with one more appraising than accusing. "Have no fear, Ms. Maurillac. I will not turn her over to the authorities. That is not who I am."

Tears spilled from her good eye. Jeannie turned away, unsure whether it was anger or relief that moved through her. The doctor confronted her, arms folded across his powerful chest. "The good news, Ms. Maurillac, is your beauty is still intact."

She closed her good eye, retreated into that quiet space where denial warred with reality.

"I hate it when people lie to me."

He placed a palm against her cheek. "Your inner beauty is greater than the scars you bear."

"You Greeks are all alike, *neh*? Fond of bullshit and good conversation." Nilesen shoved the book into her bag and

A Principle of Light

moved to the table. "But perhaps this time you are forgiven. He is not wrong, Jeannie. Look."

Nilesen held up a mirror. Jeannie touched the scar that arced from her temple to her cheek. The lines of stitching rayed above the socket of her eye. She held the mirror steady and tried to open the eyelid, biting her lip with the effort. When a sliver of light pierced her vision, she cried out.

"So." The doctor unfolded his arms and took her hand, his touch warm on her cold fingers. He took the mirror from her, set it down, and taped a clean bandage over the skin where the stitches had been. He drew a small penlight from his pocket and asked her to cover her good eye, then had her follow the light and tell him when and where she saw it. When he finished, he patted her arm, his touch again warm and soothing, as he applied more bandages and tape. "There is a good chance you will regain the sight in that eye. For the time being, we will keep it covered. Come back tomorrow, and I will check it again."

Jeannie looked at Nilesen. "We may not be able to do that."

"You are going to Çeşme tonight?"

"We are," Nilesen said. "We have arranged to meet friends from the city. Perhaps we will have a short rest before we have to run again."

"Please, Nilesen *hanım*, I asked for no lies. The truth is plain." He tidied up the instruments, stowed the bloodied bandages in a hazardous waste receptacle, and washed his hands in the sink. "You are running from the authorities, and you need to know this. The area is no longer secure. There is no safe place to hide along the coast for anyone unfamiliar with the land. Many refugees are hiding there. They break into the villas, steal what they can use or sell. They are not terrible people, but desperation engenders desperate acts. Two women traveling alone increases the danger. And Jeannie's eye needs further attention. Also, I suspect there is more to your story than you have told me."

"We're not alone." Jeannie ignored her friend's frantic, waving plea behind the doctor's back.

Doctor Stephanidis frowned. "How many others?"

The women exchanged a glance. "We have two companions," Nilesen said." A young Istanbul'lu and a Kurdish girl we rescued near Kütahya."

"Where are they now?"

"Renting a car," Jeannie said. "To take us to the coast."

Stephanidis seated himself on a rolling stool and wheeled closer. "If Caroline sent you to me, you are in grave danger. Tell me where you need to go, and I will take you there."

Jeannie felt like a mouse caught in a hawk's talon. She scooted to the end of the table. "We've made other arrangements."

His hand settled around her ankle, cool, firm, strong. "Do you know what will happen if they catch you?"

"They?"

"The secret police. Do you know what happens to someone in their custody?"

Compelled to remain still by the press of his fingers, Jeannie bit her lip. "No," she said.

Nilesen stepped beside them and held out her hands. "I know."

The doctor released Jeannie to examine each curled and cramped finger in Nilesen's hands, swearing softly. When he finished, he cradled the ruined hands in his own.

"The paper says they are looking for you, both of you, because of the bombing." He concentrated on Nilesen. "Why?"

Jeannie hopped down and reached for their bags. Handing one to Nilesen, she tugged her toward the door.

"Let's go, Nilo. Now."

Stephanidis blocked the door, his face radiating concern even as his body broadcast a subtle, definite command. Defy me and face the consequences. She was searching for a way to explain their situation, one he would accept, when Nilesen spoke.

"We know something about the bombing, something they do not want anyone else to know." She grabbed his sleeve. "You have to let us go."

The doctor gripped her by the elbows, lifted her up, and set her down next to Jeannie. "This fire you play with will burn you. Have you read what the government is doing? Have you seen the reports? Jailings. Dismissals. Shutting down newspapers and television studios. Whatever you are running from, it is large and powerful and has tentacles everywhere."

"We have no choice, Batur *bey*."

He ran a hand through his dark hair. Then he pointed at Jeannie. "I may be able to save your eye and your sight, but without further care, you could lose it. Can you return tomorrow?"

Hesitant, she looked at Nilesen for guidance, but the poet wasn't listening. She had withdrawn into herself, head bowed, hands cradled around her phone. "Nilesen? What's wrong?"

She raised the phone so Jeannie could read the screen. "Fethi and Elani." She swallowed hard. "They have been arrested."

28

... midnight in Izmir ...

Fethi guided Elani across the street past the tables of men drinking raki. Smoke from their cigarettes rose with the opinions they cast into the air as they discussed the day's events. Voices barked and cajoled, each man fighting to be heard, to persuade the others of the truth as he saw it. When the young Turk and his Kurdish companion stepped inside the inn, the whoosh of the automatic doors dulled the clamor.

"Must be more bad news from the government," Fethi muttered. They made their way to the front desk. A man in a business suit followed them in, stopping just inside the foyer to place a call on his cell.

The desk was deserted. Fethi drummed his fingers on the counter as he inspected the modest lobby. Three chairs, a table with a beaded lamp, the ubiquitous rack of tourist brochures and, on the far wall, a poster of the president accompanied by the slogan *Milli Irade, Milli Güç*. Elani caught him staring at the face of the Turkish leader. She lifted two fingers to her lips in a disparaging gesture. Fethi swung her around.

"Do not be foolish, Elani." No sooner had he spoken then the clerk strolled out of the back office. At the same time, the man in the suit started toward them. The heels of his shoes clacked against the mosaic tiles. He glared at the clerk, who lowered his gaze and disappeared once more into the back.

"Unless you have your papers," the man said, tapping his thumb against his leg, "you will have to come with me."

Elani stepped in front of Fethi. She raised her fist and began to berate the man in Sorani. Behind her, the porter's son thumbed his cell, swiped to the messages button and hit SEND. The text on its way, he waited until the confirmation icon appeared, then erased the message. The man grabbed him by the elbow and, shoving Elani hard enough to make her stumble, herded them outside and into the back seat of a dark-colored sedan with tinted windows.

As he settled them onto the stained leather, Elani scooted closer to Fethi. "Did you have time?"

He squeezed her hand. Their captor leaned over the seat and raised a gun.

"Be silent." He leveled the weapon at Fethi, then pointed it at Elani. She lifted her chin in defiance, which earned her a rap on the forehead. The barrel of the gun caught the light from the hotel sign. "Do not forget who holds the cards here."

They rode through the streets of Izmir in silence. Elani tapped her foot. Fethi thought about the message bouncing from tower to tower, the text a dagger aimed at the poet's kind heart. *Rumi: Find a way out of this prison.* The hazy view of their surroundings, the unfamiliar city, the unease of the man with the gun ate at his confidence. He shifted his weight, trying to stop the cramping in his legs. The man with the gun ordered him to be still.

"Why have you arrested us? Where are you taking us?" Fethi cleared his throat, conscious of Elani's hand trembling in his. "We have done nothing wrong."

"You bring a Kurdish *Fahişe* to our town to offer to our men. Bah! We should shoot you now and be done with it."

Elani spat at the man. "I am no whore, you Turkish bastard."

Their captor swung the gun. Elani ducked. The man's hand smacked against the window, cracking the glass. He cursed and rested the barrel against Fethi's forehead. The driver grabbed for the weapon, pushed it away.

"Enough! The captain wants them unharmed."

"The captain's a fool. Better to finish them now and hide the bodies."

While the men argued, Fethi squinted through the glass. They had left the harbor area and were heading into a residential sector of fancier homes and less traveled streets. The car slowed. The man with the gun knelt to face them.

A Principle of Light

"Don't be stupid," the driver hissed. "We are to deliver them unharmed." His companion grumbled, but he sat back down. He kept the weapon aimed at them. Fethi swallowed around the tightness in his throat. He risked speaking again.

"At least tell us where we are going."

The gunman rubbed his aching hand and grinned, revealing a mouth full of shiny, artificially-whitened teeth that gleamed in the dashboard light.

"To a place," the man said, "where they have ways of finding out the truth."

Fifteen minutes later the car deposited them at the back entrance of the Izmir Military Hospital.

29

... midnight in Izmir ...

The message faded and winked out. Nilesen tapped the screen until the words reappeared. One fist clenched over her heart, she mouthed each syllable. "Find a way out of this prison." She looked at me. "Fethi and Elani are in trouble."

Doctor Stephanidis reached for the phone and scrolled through the text. The message stared back. "This is from a Rumi poem. What does it mean to you?"

I peered over the doctor's shoulder to read the words. "Find a way out of this prison." Intent on the message, I lost my balance again. When I reached out, I bumped against Stephanidis. The phone went dark. I leaned over and tapped the screen. By the time the screen reloaded, the text had disappeared. I collapsed onto the doctor's stool. "Fethi deleted the message."

"He followed instructions," Nilesen said.

I dropped my head to my knees and practiced deep breathing, trying to clear the fear crackling in my head. "That's not good."

"You are right, *arkadaşim*." Nilesen propped a hand on my shoulder. "They are in danger."

"The companions you spoke of, the ones accompanying you to Çeşme?" Stephanidis interrupted. I looked up, only to be caught in his direct and potent gaze. The falcon had returned.

"Yes." Nilesen and I exchanged glances. I rushed through an explanation of our plan to rent a car. "Now that you know, what will you do?"

"If the government police have them, these friends of yours, they are already gone." The doctor rubbed his chin. "But if the military have snatched them up, they may be at IzMed."

"What is IzMed?" I folded my arms against the lizard chill crawling in my belly.

The doctor headed out the door, speaking over his shoulder as he moved. "There is no time to explain. Wait here."

Stephanidis returned, dressed in medical scrubs, an identification badge clipped to the pocket of his shirt. The uniform added even more authority to his presence while masking the coiled strength. I didn't know how far we could trust him, but one thing seemed certain. In a fight, Batur Stephanidis would be a formidable ally. Or a ruthless opponent.

"Where are you going?"

"To IzMed, Ms. Maurillac. If they are there, I will find them."

"But you don't even know who they are, what they look like."

He folded his arms and shrugged. "So, enlighten me."

"Their names are Fethi and Elani. The young man has helped us since Istanbul. The girl escaped from a slavery ring." Nilesen tugged at my camera strap. "Show him."

Reluctant to reveal too much, I shielded the view screen from Stephanidis as I skipped through the pictures I'd taken along the journey. When I found those of our young companions, I tilted the camera his way. In the first photo, Fethi and Elani stood next to a motorcycle, staring into the distance as they waited to resume the ride. The second revealed them huddled inside the delivery truck, startled from sleep by the snick of the shutter, their eyes blinking, owl-like, into the flash. I had taken the third under the pole light by the docks. Their faith in the promise of the future shone from their tired faces.

Stephanidis studied the photographs, then handed the camera back. Once more he brushed his fingers over the bandage covering my eye. Then he patted Nilesen's shoulder and rattled the keys in his pocket. In the entryway, the doorbell rang.

A Principle of Light

Startled, I staggered up, grabbed my bag, and searched for an exit. Nilesen did the same. Stephanidis hustled us to the rear of the room, clicking off the light switch with his elbow. He clamped his hands over our mouths. His chest pressed against my back, every muscle taut and poised to strike.

Twisting to face him, I hissed through his fingers. "Expecting someone?"

He shook his head and whispered in my ear. "Do not speak. Do not move. Understood?"

Nilesen and I nodded. The bell rang on, as though the petitioner refused to release the button. The doctor released his hold.

"I am going to lock you in. That will be safest. Wait here. Keep the lights off. And do not call out for any reason."

I shivered as the lock clicked into place. Down the hall, the front door scraped open. A voice issued a command.

"Doctor Stephanidis? Come with us, please." Other voices rose and fell before a more chilling question rang out. "Are you alone?"

The doctor's footsteps grew louder as he walked from the entry toward the back of the house. "Of course. Wait here while I get my bag."

"Be quick, Doctor. There is important work to be done tonight."

I reached for Nilesen. We crouched between the medicine closet and a file cabinet, cramped and shivering and afraid to breathe. The camera swung free, grazing the metal cabinet.

"Again, I must ask. Are you alone, Doctor?" The words reverberated down the hall. Boots scraped the floor. The doorknob rattled.

"Sorry. I dropped my keys." The doctor's voice grew nearer, then faded as he headed away from the intruder. "May I take my car? I cannot remain at the hospital. I have office hours here early tomorrow."

"Follow us," the stranger said. "If you do your job quickly, you will be back in your bed, and we will be on our way to Ankara, before morning."

The slamming of the front door sent a shudder through the walls. I counted to one hundred, then clawed my way upright, pulling Nilesen up with me.

"What's going on?" I regretted my weak language skills. Nilesen translated the conversation.

"The doctor is going with them to IzMed." Nilesen groaned. "I need to stretch my legs."

"Me, too." I walked off the cramps in my calves as I listened for the engine growl announcing that the cars had pulled away from the house. "Do you trust this doctor?"

"Do we have a choice?" Nilesen rooted around in her bag. She pulled out two thin metal strips and handed them over.

I juggled the rods in my palm. "What are these?"

"Do not drop them, Jeannie." She tiptoed over to the locked door, then held out her hand. "Now, give them back. I am going to let us out."

"Where did you learn to pick locks?"

"One learns much useful information in prison."

I choked down my next question. Not jail. Prison. How had Nilesen ended up there? Why? How did she get free? That conversation would have to wait for now. I waited while she worked to release the lock. Once the door opened, she fished the flashlight from her bag. She shielded the light with her bag and groped her way along the wall toward the back of the house. I limped after her.

The hall ran straight from the entry to the fenced-in garden beyond the rear entryway. A kitchen opened to the left. On the right, in a windowless den, a television nestled among book-laden shelves that covered the entire rear wall. Nilesen turned on the TV and located the channel carrying NTV, a station known for its emphasis on national and international news. She huddled on the couch, watching films of the protests in Ankara and Istanbul. I paced, chewing my thumbnail. Scenarios of capture and escape ran

A Principle of Light

through my head. My brain, unable to disconnect from the car winding its way toward IzMed, puzzled over the man who had promised to rescue our friends.

"Why did they come for Stephanidis? Are they with the secret police? Is he?" My questions ballooned around the room, bulging with fear.

"I have no idea, *arkadaşim*. We must hope Caroline's contacts know this man better than we do. Besides, we do not know if they were National Intelligence agents."

I resumed biting my nails. The fuzz stubbling my scalp itched. I scratched my head. Nilesen opened her copy of IŞIK. I strained to make out the words she murmured.

The wind shouts a warning,
the crafty sea answers back.
The heart beats on, yearning.
Still, the storm holds its track.
Far along the secret coastline
she finds a hidden harbor
in a cove of his design.
Limned by lightning, she anchors
in the lee of his fading, moaning,
awash in grief and rage 'til morning.

"That's beautiful." I closed my eyes and slumped lower on the couch. "Who's it about?"

"Once, I wrote it for myself. Now, *arkadaşim*," Nilesen said. "I believe it describes you."

30

... after midnight in Izmir ...

Shrouded in dim light, the lowest level of IzMed hunkered down, empty, resting, awaiting release from the tedium of night. In the room where they placed Fethi, the overhead fluorescents hissed, spraying the room with invisible waves. He looked around. Although he was not restrained, his captor had issued stern instructions.

"Remain seated," the guard had said. The unspoken *or else* wafted in the breeze from the ventilator shaft. Fethi sniffed. An antiseptic smell permeated the linen-shrouded tables. They had placed him in a surgical suite. Murmurs, faint and heavy with the thump of interrogation, filtered through the wall of the adjoining room. Elani's voice, alarmed, angry, raged. A male voice responded, demanding and full of menace.

To block out the screams, Fethi covered his ears and looked around. He counted the electrical outlets along the wall, checked the ceiling. When he located the camera mounted in a corner, he knew they were watching him. No one had yet taken his phone, but he hesitated to draw attention to it. He shifted in the chair until he blocked the angle of the spycam. Palming his phone, he dropped his head in his hands and feigned sleep. Grateful that Elani had thought to mute the sound, he swiped to messages. There was only one. **Birds fly free**. When the room plunged into darkness, he shoved the cell back into his pocket and backed the chair against the wall. The door banged open. Several pairs of boots pounded into the room.

"Fethi Keçik." The man who had arrested him flipped the lightswitch. Fethi blinked at the sudden shift from darkness into light. He tried not to flinch when the man slammed a folder on the table. The man grabbed him by the throat and dragged him up. He kicked the chair forward, slammed Fethi back in the chair, and pressed his face against the cold steel tabletop. "What is the son of an Istanbul porter doing with a runaway Kurdish girl in the port of Izmir? Shopping for floor tiles?"

"Where am I?" The mention of tiles increased his unease. Perhaps the soldiers had traced them through the Selçuk brothers.

Releasing Fethi, the interrogator strode to the opposite side of the table and dropped into the second chair. He flicked his fingers at the jandarma by the door, who turned the lock and leaned back, an automatic weapon cradled in his arms.

"You are not under arrest, Keçik, not yet. Tell me. What are you and the girl doing here? If I believe your story, I will let you go."

"We are students on holiday, taking a break from our studies." Fethi noted the tension in the man's shoulders, the tightness around his mouth. This was not a man to suffer lies. But he and Elani had not worked out any story to explain their presence in Izmir. He could only hope that her account would match his, at least in generalities. If this man expected specifics, they were both dead. "Please, sir, where am I?"

The man slapped the table. "Enough with these questions. How does a Turk end up with a Kurdish girl in one of our country's most important ports with no money, no luggage, and no documents?"

"We had those things, sir. They were stolen from us on our way from Kühtaya."

"So, that is what she claims, but I hear a lie. You are a smuggler, *neh*? How much do they pay you to help refugees escape from the fighting across the border?"

"No, sir, I am no criminal. I am a loyal Turk. I would never do such a thing. My father waits for me in Istanbul. My mother expects to hear that I have arrived safely at her cousin's house. Please, allow me to call them."

The man signaled the jandarma to open the door. Both stepped into the corridor. The interrogator returned,

A Principle of Light

wheeling a cart. He lifted the cloth covering to expose two syringes, dental pliers, and a scalpel.

"You asked where we are, so I will tell you. This," the man waved at the air, "is the Izmir Military Hospital, located on the outskirts of this beautiful city. In addition to serving our troops, the hospital welcomes wealthy people from around the world who come here for private medical procedures. In exchange for our protection of these individuals, the hospital permits us to use the underground facilities."

Someone knocked on the door. Fethi's captor tossed the cover over the tray and grinned. "Ah, the doctor. Now we will find out what you know and what you are trying to hide from us."

A powerfully-built man in surgical garb strode in. Fethi couldn't stop the tremble in his hands. He stared at the newcomer. The stranger, face shadowed by a scowl, rubbed his chin, and eyed Fethi.

"The usual, Nalli?" He fingered the instruments on the tray.

"You know what to do." The interrogator folded his arms. "Only tonight, Doctor, my captain requests that I remain in the room."

The doctor stepped away from the instruments. "I am sorry, Nalli, but that is not possible. You know the arrangement. No witnesses, no conflicting reports. I work alone or not at all."

The tug of wills stretched out until Nalli touched the handle of his gun, shook off the doctor's stare, and marched to the door.

"One half-hour, no more. Then I will observe, no matter the arrangement."

When the door closed, Doctor Stephanidis moved toward the captive. He captured Fethi's right arm, tucked it beneath his, and leaned closer. "I am Doctor Stephanidis. Your friends sent me. You must do exactly as I say. Do you understand?"

Fethi met the doctor's predatory stare. He weighed the options and cut his eyes toward the ceiling. His arm already tingled from the lack of circulation. "There is a camera."

"I know." Stephanidis grabbed a syringe. He removed the plastic top with his teeth and spit it onto the floor. While he checked the milligrams on the tube, he eyed the camera in the ceiling, then returned his attention to Fethi. He bent close to Fethi's ear. "I am going to prick the skin, let the liquid run down between us, then place the needle in your arm. A small amount will enter your bloodstream, but it will not be enough to incapacitate you. You must pretend to be sedated. Say no if you understand."

Unable to speak around the dryness in his mouth, Fethi shook his head.

"Good." The doctor glanced once more at the camera and raised his voice. "Since you refuse the easy choice, we shall take the harder path. Let us begin."

A cry erupted from the room next door, followed by scuffling sounds.

"Elani!" Fethi called. The Kurdish girl shouted back. He heard a crash. Something metal skidded across the floor, followed by silence. Stephanidis cocked his head at Fethi's captor, who had stepped back into the room.

"Results, my friend." The man crossed his arms and glared.

The doctor looked at his watch. "You gave me half an hour."

The man called Nalli shook his head. "Time is passing, and my captain sends impatient texts. The best way, my dear young porter's son, to leave here alive is to tell me what I need to know." Nalli picked up the second syringe, removed the cover and squirted a small amount of sodium pentothal into the air. The odor of cat urine drifted across the table. He lurched forward, trapping Fethi's other arm against the top of the table. "The harder way is to shoot you full of this and listen as you spill your guts."

In the hall outside, the squeal of wheels announced the approach of a surgical gurney. There was a knock, followed by the jiggling of the knob. A key scraped the lock and the door burst open. A nurse in blue scrubs and a mask entered, pulling the gurney behind her.

"Forgive me, but we have an emergency and we need this room. Doctor Stephanidis, you must decide. Should I stay or go?" The nurse blocked the sightline of the policeman in the hall and closed the door. On the gurney, a woman lay covered with a sheet. Eyes closed, hair enveloped in a plastic cap, her face lay hidden beneath an oxygen mask. When she opened her eyes, Fethi recognized Elani.

The interrogator dropped the syringe on the tray, wiped his hands on his trousers, and hauled Fethi out of the chair. He shoved the young Turk toward the door. Stephanidis scooped up the dropped syringe and plunged it into Nalli's neck. Elani jumped off the gurney. When Fethi swayed, she wrapped her arms around him to prevent his collapse.

"What are you, Kurdish girl? A superhero?" he whispered. His legs refused to support him.

"Oh, simple Turkish boy, you have much to learn about me." She used her body to brace him against the wall. The nurse who had pushed the stretcher locked eyes with Stephanidis, snatched the sheet that had covered Elani, and tossed it over the interrogator's body. She slipped into the corridor to speak with the jandarma stationed there. A stream of commands followed by a stern order that the man do his duty and find the missing girl sent the guard running. When the hall was clear, she rapped on the door.

Doctor Stephanidis lifted Fethi onto the stretcher. He adjusted the oxygen mask over the boy's face. He also repositioned a cap over Elani's head, helped her put on a nurse's uniform, and eased the door open. He checked for pursuit before pushing the gurney down the hall toward a bank of elevators. The nurse hurried away.

"Who was that?" Fethi struggled to sit up.

"Later. Lie down." The doctor snapped the mask back over Fethi's nose. He squeezed the boy's shoulder. "You have to trust me, *abi*."

As the elevator crawled up to the main floor, Fethi risked another question. "What about Nilesen? Jeannie?"

"Safe," the doctor said. "Be still."

The trio rolled their way past the rooms on the first floor and out the back entrance. When the automatic sensors confirmed that the doors had closed behind them, they breathed easier. The late hour coupled with the privacy of the hospital grounds allowed them to reach the doctor's car without being challenged. As Elani and Fethi climbed in, Stephanidis glanced back.

"*Hoşçakal*, IzMed," he said.

"You are not coming back?" Elani raised an eyebrow.

"I doubt," Batur said, before he pulled into the street, "they will grant me privileges here again."

31

... after midnight in Izmir ...

I covered Nilesen with an afghan and pressed the off button on the remote. The glow illuminating the room died, leaving me in the dark. I felt my way along the wall to the kitchen, peeled back the curtain, and stared into the night. My mind roiled with sorrow and questions. Who was this Batur Stephanidis? When he saw the coin, he admitted us into his home without hesitation, then promised to rescue our friends. He asked for only the most cursory of explanations. Why? Then he responded to the demands of the secret police, or whoever had come to collect him. The man was intense and powerful. He exuded confidence. Everything about him set off alarms. I had encountered men like him on my travels. Strong, fearful of nothing, and ruthless to the bone. They generally fell into one of three categories, military, mercenary, or organized crime. Which was he?

    I shook off the conspiracy theories racing through my mind, opened the refrigerator, and catalogued the contents. Fruit drinks, yogurt, olives, a glass bowl half-filled with a mixture resembling hummus. No milk. No meat. A bottle of white wine. Behind the wine, a bag filled with red liquid. I dragged it out and shook it. The contents thickened, then coated the inside of the bag. A thought skittered, roach-like, pausing to flick its antennae before scurrying into the depths. Was Stephanidis a vampire? The giggle that escaped forced me to acknowledge my exhaustion. Stripped of rational thought by the deep weariness and ever-present sorrow crawling through me, I fought the temptation to curl up in the corner and sob like a child. My stomach growled, reminding me how long it had been since I had eaten. Such a mundane response to the fear building a wall inside my chest. Disoriented, floundering in a current of emotion, I fingered the camera. My undamaged eye stared into the lens of an unpredictable future, while my body demanded food. I cursed that body's need for sustenance, then relented. Perhaps if I ate, the act would settle my nerves and calm the anxiety ratcheting up each time I checked the clock. I replaced the mystery fluid and reached for the olives. Was I snooping? Yes. Did I care? Not sure. If Stephanidis returned to find me rummaging through his cupboards, he would not be pleased. Oh, well.

I snatched a handful of kalamatas, closed the refrigerator door, and slipped into the den. I snatched Nilesen's phone from the table and scurried back to the kitchen to scroll through the text messages before abandoning the effort. Even if Fethi had sent an update on the situation, I couldn't read it. I popped the last of the olives into my mouth. Determined to find out more about the doctor, I shuffled down the hall to his bedroom. If I was going to be a snoop, I might as well do a thorough job.

I flicked on the flashlight app and panned it around the room. The word "spartan" came to mind. A single bed, no headboard, a small dresser, a bedside table. I spied a suitcase tucked in one corner, a sturdy hiking pack in the other. The doctor had tossed his running clothes on the floor, shoved his tennis shoes partway under them. The closet door was ajar, its interior shadowed. I opened the drawer of the bedside table and inspected the items nestled there. A pocket watch. A pair of tiger's eye cufflinks. A broken silver chain. A wooden box with the initials BAS carved in the top. A photograph of a woman in a print dress, a clutch of daisies drooping from one hand. At the woman's side, a boy about five years old balanced on one foot, grinning up at her. Was this Stephanidis and his mother? Who had taken the picture? What had happened to change the joyful boy into the stern-faced man? When I peered closer, I recognized the Galata Bridge rising behind the woman. The picture had been taken in Istanbul. I replaced the items and moved to the closet.

The phone went dark. I switched the light back on as I eased the bifold door open. Three suits, elegant and expensive and smelling faintly of aftershave, hung next to a cluster of surgical scrubs. Shirts and trousers were arranged by color. I ran a hand over the clothing, the material soft to the touch, then dropped to my knees. Several pairs of shoes sat along the back of the closet, toes pointing out. The last, brown leather slip-ons, rested against the butt of a large weapon. I pushed aside the slacks that shielded the gun and lifted out the AR-15. What kind of doctor owned an assault weapon? I set it back against the wall and turned to the dresser. I searched each drawer, lifted up the folded clothing, ran my hand along the sides. Nothing out of the ordinary, except for the Glock nestling under a t-shirt. First an assault rifle, then a handgun. Stephanidis owned some serious firepower. Sweat trickled down my back. I palmed the Glock. The handle rested comfortably in my hand. If the need arose, this was a weapon I could wield.

Headlights raked the window. A car crunched its way down the lane. I shoved the gun in the drawer, shut off the light. and fumbled my way back to the den. When I plopped down on the couch, Nilesen stirred.

"Find anything interesting?"

"What?"

"You have been poking around the doctor's rooms." Nilesen held up two fingers to forestall my denials. "I can tell when you lie, *arkadaşim*. Even in the dark, you look guilty, and your voice betrays you. So, did you discover the doctor's secret life?"

I gnawed on a thumbnail. "He's not just a doctor, is he?"

"No."

I stared at the dark bookshelves, listened to the tick-tick of a clock filling the house with warning. My head said run, but my heart, too tired to beat properly, hammered against my ribs, messaging me to just stay put.

32

... after midnight in Izmir ...

When she slept, Nilesen dreamed of the Solaganian villa, of strange, bloody fingers reaching for Jeannie's eye. Now, awake, she held the photographer's hand as they whispered their concerns. Both went on alert when the front door banged open. The insistent slide of shoes on tile accompanied the doctor as he ushered Fethi and Elani through thr door, checked behind him, then switched off the porch light.

"Stay here. Be quiet." The commands floated toward them. Soon, the shuffling began again. After Stephanidis herded the escapees into the den, he left them to a quiet reunion while he disappeared into his bedroom. Fethi had scarcely begun the tale of their ordeal when the doctor returned, dressed in jeans and a black tee under a leather jacket. The AR-15 lay cradled in his arm. He dragged Jeannie off the couch. In the kitchen, he bared his teeth.

"Did you find what you were looking for?"

"I wasn't ... I didn't." Jeannie shook him off. "I'm sorry. It's just that we don't know anything about you."

"Nor I you. Yet I risk my life for yours. Why do you think that is, Jeannie Maurillac?" He didn't wait for her reply. He wrestled two duffle bags from a closet. When he returned, she caught a glimpse of the Glock holstered next to his ribs.

"Pack this." He tossed a bag at her. "Now that you know where everything is."

Embarrassed by his accusation, she packed the contents of the refrigerator into the bag. Stephanidis issued new instructions. He handed Nilesen his medical kit. "Nilesen *hanim*, empty the cabinet in the surgery. Take all the medications."

"What can I do?" Elani said.

"Wrap that wound. I will stitch it later. For now, scour every surface with these." He tossed a container of antibacterial wipes at Elani.

The Kurdish girl wrapped a towel around the cut on her arm, then hurried to scrub all the surfaces in the kitchen and the den. The doctor returned to his room, emerging minutes later with a second duffle dragging at his heels. The AR-15 was gone. He handed the bag and his backpack to Fethi.

"Take everything to the car, *abi*. Be quick." He tossed the keys to the porter's son.

Lugging the backpack and the heavy duffle, Fethi relieved Nilesen of the kit containing the medications and waddled out the door. Nilesen and Elani followed. Before Jeannie could join them, Stephanidis stopped her. He reached into the bag she carried and lifted out the container of blood. He sliced the bag, flung the contents across the floor, then sidestepped around the scatter pattern. When Jeannie attempted to slip by him, he captured her again.

"What are you planning to do with this?" He lifted the camera from around her neck, thumbed on the power, and flipped the view screen open. When he pressed the video play button, images of Nilesen asleep in the back of the semi scrolled by. Jeannie's voice recorded the date, time, and circumstances.

"I'm documenting our journey." Unnerved by his anger, she stammered out an explanation. "People need to know the truth."

"If the authorities catch you, they will kill you. Unless I do it first."

"Then don't let them catch me, Batur." It wasn't a plea or a request. His grip tightened. She flinched. "Please."

"If you hurt Yilmaz, if you make her suffer," Batur said, "I will make you pay."

"And if I save her?" She refused to blink.

He leaned closer, his breath a flutter against her hair. "Then I will find a way to thank you properly."

Jeannie reclaimed the camera and wriggled free of his grasp. "If I tell her story, no one will dare to harm her."

A Principle of Light

"Then let us pray your arrogant plan succeeds, Ms. Maurillac, for all our sakes." He shoved her ahead of him to the car. He checked the items in the trunk, then glanced at the neighboring houses still slumbering in the night. Lights off, engine at a soft hum, he passed along the narrow lanes, slowing to check for pursuit at every intersection.

"Who was that nurse?" Fethi said. "The one who helped us at the hospital."

Stephanidis spared a glance at the young Turk. "A colleague who shares our politics, and one in need of monetary assistance."

"You paid her?" Elani huffed her disapproval. "One who can be bought by one side can also be bought by the other."

"Perhaps. It does not matter now. Tell me, Fethi, do you see any sign we have been followed?"

Fethi scanned the road behind them. "No, Batur *bey*."

Nilesen, sitting in front with the doctor, strained against the seat belt as she searched for a sign pointing the way to Çeşme. When they arrived at the highway entrance ramp, the doctor came to a stop.

"Which way, Nilesen *hanim*?" He held up his hand to forestall argument. "I know you do not agree with me, but I recommend we bypass Çeşme and head farther south, to the Gulf of Kos."

"No, Batur, that is not the way that calls to me."

"Your path is more dangerous than you realize."

"You must allow me to decide that."

"Very well. There is another choice." The doctor's words were laced with concern and kindness. "We can return to Istanbul. Even that journey is safer."

"No, Batur. We go west." Nilesen pointed to the right. "Toward the last edge of light."

33

... toward the last edge of light ...

Above us, the stars danced along a slipstream of sky. I shivered as I listened to the universe breathe in change, exhale chaos. Elani held my hand, her head resting on Fethi's shoulder while he slept, the stress of his incarceration evident on his face. I stared at the back of Batur's head, then peered out the window, wondering if we evaded one captor only to fall into the hands of another, more dangerous one. The car hurtled on. Nilesen responded to the doctor's quiet questions and murmured directions. Too fogged by lack of sleep and the guilt gnawing a hole in the sugar-plum plan I'd concocted to film the journey and somehow save us all, I failed to grasp most of the conversation. Finally, I heard words I did know. *Ev. Ev onun.* His house. Their discussion had morphed into argument. Heated whispers lobbed across the console between them.

"Make a left here," Nilesen said.

"This is not the best choice, Nilesen *hanim*." Stephanidis switched to English. He must have sensed I was eavesdropping.

"That may be, but it is my choice to make."

He pounded the steering wheel, cursed twice, then swerved off the highway onto a two-lane road. We left the infrequent headlights of fellow travelers and the prospect of comfort stations to wind through the coastal hills. At first, the homes crowded together, a single porch or streetlight marking their existence. The farther we drove along the serpentine lane, the sparser the dwellings became. Soon, stony villas dotted the land like fishing lures. Their solitary lamps bobbed and winked as we drove by, rising skyward to merge with the stars, then dipping to perch, owl-like and predatory, above the restless Aegean. Batur Stephanidis spat out a final question. Nilesen agreed. He coasted to a stop at a scenic overlook along the side of the road.

"Where are we?" I unfolded myself from the cramped back seat. Fethi and Elani slept on.

"Close to our destination." Nilesen whispered, her words an exhalation of sadness and desire. Starlight sketched her in bas-relief. She reminded me of an ancient goddess staring out to sea. Batur Stephanidis rested a booted foot on the low stone wall that kept us from tumbling down the hillside. The AR-15 rested across his knee, its muzzle pointing, arrow-like, to the south. I wrestled my camera from beneath my jacket and centered the two of them in the viewfinder. The night shutter clicked. Batur snapped his head around to glare at me. I couldn't read his eyes, but I felt his wrath as he leaned over to cover the lens with his hand.

"You don't understand." I hissed at him. He growled back.

"What do I not understand? You journalists are all the same."

I removed his hand, my own tingling at the contact. "What does that mean?"

"Reporters are insensitive voyeurs, predators who care not even a little about the lives they invade." He spat at my feet. "You expose people, break them on the wheel of public opinion, and discard them as soon as the next titillating story appears."

"No. Not all of us. But I don't blame you for believing that." I held the camera up. "This, my photographs, it's all about the story, Batur, and the truth only Nilesen and her journey can tell. This is what the world needs to see."

He stepped closer, his body brushing against mine, the contact a talisman of the feral strength lurking in the land around us. I refused to back away, to acknowledge that I recognized the power in him. My body betrayed me, trembling beneath that electric pulse of desire and the ache to be comforted in the only way I knew, the melding of flesh, the losing of self. Here, on this wind-swept hill above the ancient sea, I wanted strong arms to enfold me, soft words to promise that the world would right itself tomorrow. I wanted Batur Stephanidis to forgive me for being true to the only master I'd ever acknowledged, my art.

"Do we have anything to eat?" Elani's plaintive question snapped me back to the moment. Batur shifted his weight and the weapon. His body remained pressed to mine. He moved away then. He scanned our position before drawing out the keys and opening the trunk. Nilesen helped Elani scrounge through the bags, then passed around portions of cheese and bread. I sat on the rock wall and stared into the shadows, unable to dispel the one growing inside me.

Beyond the overlook, the land dropped sharply. Patches of untamed brush competed with terraced swathes of olive trees. An occasional house light sparked on. Farther below, the shush-roar of the sea caressed the beaches that lined the coast, each one shrouded and waiting for the light. A dog barked. Something howled back. I didn't know if coyotes lived in Turkey, or if what I heard was some mythic beast that resided in between the seams of time. By the car, my companions spoke in low murmurs. Fethi climbed out of the back seat to join the pre-dawn picnic. I didn't expect to cry, but tears came anyway, silent trickles of loss and regret. I couldn't see a way back, not to Istanbul or the States, or even to a normal life. All that waited was an unending flight from death. I scrubbed my cheeks with the backs of my hands, squared my shoulders, and delivered my favorite lecture to myself. *Not here, not now. You can fall apart later*. A hand tugged my sleeve.

"Come, Madam," Fethi said, "we are leaving now."

I left my despair on the overlook above Çeşme and followed the porter's son back to the doctor's Saab.

~ ~ ~

Morning broke behind us. When we entered a fishing village along the way to Golden Beach, the doctor insisted that we stop for supplies.

"We cannot hide without food and water. Besides," he rubbed at his chin, then stared at the road ahead, "I want to be certain we have not been followed. Jeannie, come with me. One more American tourist will not raise suspicion."

"No, Batur." Nilesen folded her arms. "I know this village better than either of you. I will go."

"You may be recognized, Nilesen *hanim*. What good will it do if you are lost so close to your goal?"

The argument continued until, exasperated, Batur threw his hands in the air. "Enough."

On the outskirts of the village, a restaurant rested on pilings extending out over the water. Batur pulled in behind the building. He tossed the keys to Fethi, hauled me out of the car, and ordered my companions to stay put. He held my elbow as he dragged me along the waterfront toward the village center. A dog trotted from between two fishing shacks, sniffed at my feet, and lifted his leg. I squealed my disgust. Batur snorted at my reaction and tugged me on.

The main road wound past a block of newly-restored storefronts. Signs in English and Turkish advertised souvenirs. The *postane* shared space with a tobacconist. I identified a three-story structure as the municipal building from the three flags flying atop the roof, one Turkish, one provincial. The third, a weathered squall flag, was used to warn fishermen when a storm was coming. Today it barely reached halfway up the post. An open-air market bustled in front of a more traditional indoor grocery. When we reached the vendor's tables, Batur picked up a basket and handed it over. He placed a finger on my lips.

"Do not speak, Jeannie." His eyes lingered on my mouth. I shivered at his touch, drew a breath, and blew it out around the longing it provoked. He released his grip to stroll ahead, checking the bins, selecting fruits and vegetables and offering them to me. The path between the displays grew crowded. Batur pulled me to his side. We had almost reached the end of the displays when a tray of earrings caught my eye. The hand-made silver hoops gleamed in the early morning sun. I urged him toward the table set up directly in front of the grocery. Before I could decide which pair to buy, movement in the interior caught my attention. I caught the flash of a cell phone. Someone had taken my picture.

"Hey!" I set the earrings down and hurried inside. A short, dark-haired man wearing motorcycle leathers turned and hustled toward the back of the store. The look he threw over his shoulder jogged my memory. The *hirsiz* at the bus station, his shoe-button eyes flat and empty as a shark's gaze. I veered around a display of seascape snow globes to follow him into the back of the shop. The owner blocked my path.

"Employees only, Madam," he said, hands and eyebrows raised in warning. Batur reached my side. He snaked his arm around my waist to hold me back, apologizing in Turkish, I felt certain, for his girlfriend's awkward attempt to greet an old friend.

"Batur." I waited until he paid for our purchases, then grabbed his shirt as we headed back to the car. "That man who took my picture. I recognized him. He's been following me and Nilesen."

"Tell me."

We stopped under the awning of a beauty salon. The women inside glanced up, then returned to their early-morning routines. I rushed to explain our encounter with the thief in the bus station and then on the bus to Bursa, how the man and an accomplice had seemed to find us even there. Batur only interrupted once, to ask what else we had failed to disclose. Chastened, I shook my head.

"There's nothing else. I swear it." I bit my lip. Carl belonged to my past. He had no place in the present, not anymore. Batur pinched my elbow as he race-walked me along the sidewalk. We circled the main block, scuttled down alleys, and strolled past street-sweepers. The smell of the sea accompanied us, along with the cries of gulls. An hour later, we reached the car. Batur stowed the provisions in the trunk, retrieved his binoculars, and scanned the village. When he was satisfied that no one lingered in the shadows or trailed behind us, he started the car. His right hand rested on the holstered Glock. He ignored the questions from Fethi, Elani, and Nilesen as he drove us out of the village.

J. E. Irvin

A mile beyond, the road transitioned from asphalt to dirt. The car bumped over the rutted land. I braced myself against the jolting, but couldn't stop my eye from throbbing. We crawled upward from the wide, white sand beach. The engine labored to climb beside a footpath. Several narrow lanes branched off from the one we followed. We had almost reached the top of the hill when Nilesen pointed out the window and I saw it, the Solaganian villa, the summer house that belonged to her dead husband's family. Three stories of white-washed stucco faded to gray. The front resembled a many-windowed façade softened by the *ardiç* trees that formed a natural windbreak below the parking area. A fig tree loomed in the courtyard, its twisted trunk and wide branches beckoning us closer. The driveway circled the tree, continued on to embrace a fountain, then widened to provide space for three or four cars before disappearing behind the house. I glimpsed an outbuilding to the left of the main structure, perhaps a shed for garden tools or storage. When Batur stopped the car, a rooster crowed. Around us, the new day glowed with purple haze as the sun touched the fields of thyme and oregano scattered over the land. Down the hill, the sea revealed itself in snatches as the sun moved up behind us, white gold and sparkling until it grazed the lumps of volcanic rock brooding in the sandy shore.

We sat silent and observant, waiting for Nilesen to make the first move. She climbed from the passenger seat and looked up at the villa, one hand pressed against her heart, the other waving in denial. I thought she was banishing memories, but perhaps she was calling them to her, beckoning a ghost to her side. Come, shadow, settle here, rub my ankles with your bones and remind me of all I have missed. She took a few steps forward, paused, her face lit by the rosy morning light. I clambered out to stretch, leaned against the trunk, and panned the camera over the view from the hill. Caught in the beauty of the moment, I failed to hear Batur come up behind me. I missed Fethi's curse, too, and Elani's shout of surprise. Batur touched my shoulder. As I turned, Nilesen pushed at the air, desperate to erase the vision ahead of her.

The door of the villa opened. A man stepped out, swung forward on crutches. His right pant leg was pinned up at the knee. His left leg was gone. The cap he wore failed to conceal the scarring that creased his once-handsome face. When he spotted the car, he scowled, caught himself, then stared harder. He turned to glare at Batur. Batur inclined his head. The stranger turned to Fethi, to Elani, to me. He acknowledged us with a nod, then stared at Nilesen.

"No. It cannot be." He started toward us. The crutches shifted. He fell sideways, collapsing in the dust like a damaged marionette. Everyone darted forward. Nilesen reached him first. Kneeling, she lifted his head to her lap and repeated the name she had whispered over and over in her nightmares on our journey from Istanbul. Alain.

Prisms

34

... Monday: Kirmizi (Red)

The sun's light skipped above the villa, searing the tableau into memory. Nilesen, on her knees. Alain, gasping as he struggled to stand. Batur, moving to lift the fallen. Jeannie, Elani, and Fethi, stunned into muteness. Then Batur broke the stillness as he hoisted the legless man and carried him inside. They gathered in the kitchen, a triangularity of solid bodies arranged in groups of two around the farmhouse table. Fethi stood behind Elani, hands in pockets, shoulders slumped beneath the current of emotion roiling the room. Batur leaned against the fireplace, arms crossed, eyes hooded and inscrutable. When Jeannie looked up, she found them narrowed on her. Alain sat with his back to the window that overlooked the hillside. Through the glass, the garden plots of rosemary, thyme, sage, and lavender bowed to the olive tree that spread its gnarled arms over the garden. A path of stones wound through the herbs, transitioning to dirt before it wandered into the cedars and pines that rose like the ribs of a ghost ship above the villa. The dawn glared, red-tinged and screaming, above the hill. Sailor's warning. Passion's flame.

Silent except for the rustle of clothing, the scuff of feet, the travelers sipped from terra cotta mugs the thick, black coffee Batur had prepared. Nilesen held her husband's hand, reluctant to sever the connection, convinced that if she let go, he would drift, a brittle filament of her longing and remorse, only to shatter against the tiles beneath her feet. Jeannie touched her damaged eye. Perhaps today she could remove the bandage for good. Her puckered skin bore no resemblance to Alain's battle scars. If he could greet the days without flinching, she could, too. She ran her thumb over the worn surface of the table and picked at the grained wood until she raised a splinter. Then she fiddled with the power button on the camera. On. Off. On. Off. The itch to document the gathering distracted her. Batur's cough brought her back to the moment.

"Why?" Nilesen bent forward to look him in the eye. Tears fell unheeded to pepper the silk of her blouse. "Why did you not contact me? How could you allow me to believe you were gone?"

Alain brushed his lips across her knuckles. "Forgive me, little bird. I had to believe you were free, alive, untouched by the brutality of this fight. I needed you to go on, to have that better life I had jeopardized for us. Nilesen, *Aşkim*, was it not you who wrote that a cracked vessel no longer holds water?"

"You are no cracked vessel, but one that has been refired in the kiln of life."

He set her hand aside. "The potter forgot to leave me useful parts." He shook his head. "At least you were free."

"I was never free, Alain. I lived no better life." She stared past him, seeing, not the walls of the villa, but the limits of the prison cell. "They took me to Adalet."

The anguish in his cry startled them all. Sunlight poured through the window, gathering them in a fiery embrace.

"I need some air." Jeannie rose, uncomfortable and desperate to avoid the memories Alain's ravaged body stirred. Carl, arms flailing, limbs disintegrating in front of the restaurant. When Batur cocked his head in the direction of the garden, she edged toward the back door. Elani slapped the table and cursed. She rose and scuffed down the hall toward the front of the villa.

"Fethi, come. Help me unload the car," she called over her shoulder. "There is food in the cooler, and I am very hungry."

"You are always hungry." He eased out of the kitchen to follow her. He glanced back, shared a long look with Nilesen, then sighed and walked faster. "I just want to sleep."

"Hurry up, Turkish boy," Elani said when he reached her. "The poet Yilmaz is no longer your concern."

"I admire her, Kurdish girl, that is all. I saved her life."

Elani grabbed his shoulders and propelled him into the morning air. "Time to let her go, *abi*. I understand you have feelings for her, but she is not for you."

"Oh, what do you know? It is I who have protected her, provided for her. Where was her husband all this time? Hiding." He spat into the dirt. "While he stayed safe, she faced down the authorities and published her work."

"You assisted her, yes, as was her due. She is, how do you say this, a splinter in the ass of the ruling party?"

"She is more than a token of resistance. She is a symbol, and one of our country's greatest treasures." He unzipped the duffle bag to stare at the doctor's weapons. "What should I do with these?"

Elani crowded beside him. She picked up a gun, turned it over in her palm, and shrugged. "Nice. If I had one of these when the bastards first took me, I would not be here."

Fethi snatched it back and shoved it in the bag with the rest of the firearms and ammunition. "No. If you had one of these, you might be dead."

"Better dead than a slave."

"Perhaps, for you, that is true. But why do your people always fight?" He lugged the weapons bag to the front door, set it down, and returned for the medical kit, but it was not in the trunk. "Why do you hate us Turks so much?"

Elani rescued his backpack and slipped it on. "What do you have in here, Fethi? Jeannie was right. It is very heavy."

"Put it in the entry and come back for the food."

"I can carry more than one thing at a time." She gathered the bags of food from the market, carried them inside, and returned frowning. "Why do you hate us? We only want what all people want, to be our own masters, to rule ourselves. This president," she made a rude noise, "sends his army to bomb us, shoots at our villages, kills our men. What threat does he see in our autonomy?"

"For a girl, you know a lot about politics. How did you learn so much?"

She lugged the cooler from the car, grunting as she dropped it on the ground.

She turned away to hide the tears, unshed but glistening, and waved at the sea below. "Kurds have no time to be children playing on the beach. You grow up quick, or you die."

35

... Turuncu (Orange) ...

Jeannie ran her hand over the blooms of the lavender plants, the perfume from the flowers rising around her. The air hummed with bees, the fat bumbling bodies already heavy with pollen. As she stepped along the stone walkway, she raised the camera and snapped photos of the garden and the view. When Batur approached, she lowered the lens.

"You know him, don't you? Alain."

Batur glanced at the villa, rubbed his chin, averted his eyes. "Yes. I know Alain Solaganian. I have treated him since he returned."

"I thought you practiced in Izmir."

"Did you?" He scuffed the toe of his boot across the path, almost smiling. "It is unwise to make assumptions based on limited information."

"Why didn't you tell her?

"Because," Batur raised his eyes, "the decision was not mine to make."

She held his gaze for a moment, aware that he wouldn't reveal the whole truth. He captured her hand. "Alain's story is his to tell, Jeannie. We all guard our truths. Even you." She accepted the explanation without comment. Batur was right. Each of them balanced the need to explain against the private nature of their hard choices. She followed him along the stone path to the front of the house only to find herself, mesmerized by the sweep of blue water sparkling below. Sunlight danced across the Aegean, conjuring images of ships plying their way over the sea. Above the waves, in between the frame of sky and water, the ghosts of ancient gods winked in and out of the wind, each jostling for a place in the light-filled sweep of history.

"How do you bear it?" She barely raised her voice, uncertain if she wanted the doctor to hear.

Batur touched her shoulder. "Bear what?"

"This weight of time and space, all that past pressing against the future? Even the air swells with possibility."

"I did not peg you for a philosopher. Americans are rarely so insightful." He turned her to face him, peeled the bandage from her eye, and inspected the scars. "Can you see the light?"

"A little. Colors are coming back, too, rainbows. ROY G BIV."

"Roy G. Biv?" Again that half-smile. She cursed the blush warming her cheeks.

"Something I learned as a child, a way to remember the shades of the rainbow. Red, orange, yellow, green, blue, indigo, violet."

"Clever, that." His thumb stroked the curve of her brow. "Like light through a prism, perhaps, all that whiteness transformed. Like my country, shattered by conflict, shifting to the polar ends."

Riveted by the sorrow in his words, she lowered her gaze. In her rush to escape her own problems, she had forgotten about the people who remained. "Batur, I ..."

He pressed the bandage back in place, his touch light and affirming, and held out a pair of sunglasses. "If you like, you can remove the gauze and tape and wear these. Unless you prefer to remain half blind."

"Do I detect disapproval, Doctor?"

"No, Jeannie, only uncertainty. You Americans see what you want to see. You have a tendency to judge and dismiss, to take and use without investing in the people or the cause."

"Not all of us are insensitive to the world. We just don't have the perspective of your people, the long span of action and events."

"And who do you judge to be my people?"

She paused to check the light. How should she answer him? She raised the camera and focused Batur, seeking a way into his thoughts, his character, willing the lens to reveal the man inside. Her own hypocrisy chided her. Even as she sought to expose him, she hid her own self. She had always found it easier to capture the essence of others, to hide behind the camera than to reveal herself. Now, one-eyed and broken, she could no longer deny that truth. He had asked her a question, waited for the answer. This time she would not shy away.

"Your people? The hurt, the suffering, the innocent, the besieged. I judge those to be yours, which makes you a paradox. Are you a doctor or a killer?"

Batur Stephanidis gazed beyond her, to the hills above, to the sea below. When he stepped past her, she noticed the pack that contained his medical kit riding above the weapon on his hip. The barrel caught the sun, sending orange flashes across the plane of her vision. Her eyes watered.

"Yes." Batur moved on, his long strides taking him beyond her reach. "I am a doctor. I am also a warrior. My people are those who help the helpless. Tell me, Jeannie Maurillac, who do you help, besides yourself?"

She stayed on the path, watching him disappear up the hill toward the scattered villas along the ridge, the censure in his voice scouring away the last of her self-esteem.

In the early afternoon, the travelers gathered again in the kitchen, yawning, stumbling with exhaustion. Nilesen made them lunch, then sent them to the upper rooms, where they slept without dreaming under an orange-tinted, watchful sky and into the starred but moonless night.

36

... Sari (Yellow) ...

*B*irdsong filtered in through the open window. Bread sat cooling atop the oven, its yeasty aroma filling the air. The angry early-morning sun had mellowed to a splash of lemon-colored warmth creeping across the floor. Somewhere beneath the tiles, Nilesen detected the gurgle of a forgotten stream flowing through secret channels of gravel and sand on its way to the azure sea. Alain folded her hand between his, his eyes locked on her face.

"Do you not wish to speak to me?"

Nilesen raised her eyes. "Not yet."

Alain sipped the coffee she placed in front of him. The sun scaled the far wall and crept toward noon. When the silence grew too heavy, he spoke again. "Although I have no right to ask, forgive me, little bird. I beg you."

She dusted the remains of flour from her blouse, uncertain of how to reconcile the pain of the past year with this new discovery. Grieving Alain had scoured her soul. Only bedrock and pain remained.

"Why?" The abyss of a permanent rupture stretched out between them. They balanced on the knife-edge of truth. From the moment Alain opened the door, what seemed inconceivable had come to pass. She had returned to his parents' villa for sanctuary and found him instead. Hiding. Alive.

"Listen to me, *canim*. Hear me." Alain swallowed hard, brushed his free hand over the flap of empty trouser. "After the ambush, my friends arrived. When they pulled me from the wreckage, I was barely breathing, more dead than alive. At first, all I wanted was for you to hold me, to hear your voice, to know that you were safe. I fought the men carrying me, called your name. Then, they laid me in the back of a truck, and I saw the ruin I had become."

"Did you think that would change my heart? Alain." Condemnation rolled like thunder.

"No, *Aşkim*, I knew nothing could change your feelings. But I had led you into this danger. I had squandered our future. I no longer deserved you."

Nilesen moved to the window. She stared at the garden, arms wrapped around her to prevent collapse. "The danger did not go away when you did."

She listened to the scrape of the chair legs as he twisted toward her, the labored breath as he maneuvered the crutches.

"Look at me, Nilo. See me as I am, a crippled man with revenge in his soul. There is only room for hate inside me now. I would not have you share that with me."

She met his gaze, passed, wordless, into communion, searching for the remnants of the husband she had lost and mourned and now grieved again in the flesh.

"What are you doing here?"

He waved a crutch around the room. "Say hello to my war room."

She looked at the maps hanging on the sand-colored walls, the stacks of brochures shoved under the desk. "And where is your army?"

"There is no one that you know left. The new recruits are young, fervent. Their hearts are filled with a zealot's fire."

"How have you managed? To remain hidden, I mean. In Istanbul, there are spies on every corner, conservative fools who think that returning to the old ways will prevent the future from catching us in its talons."

"Such beautiful words for such an ugly truth." He shuffled nearer, ran his hand down the curve of her back to rest at her waist. A yearning long-buried surged through her, coupled with an equally strong desire to run, screaming. How dare he keep himself from her all this time? Did she have enough forgiveness in her to dismiss the past year? Enough courage to welcome him into her body? She had no illusions about allowing him access to her soul. That was sealed from him now.

"You and your friends cannot stay here, Nilesen *canim*. It's too dangerous."

She spread her hands and shrugged. "The world is dangerous. Should I go back to prison to be safe? Or would you return me to the nomadic life I have lived since you died, wandering from place to place, homeless, spreading the gospel of rebellion through my poems? Oh, wait, you are not dead, and I am already in hell."

"Tell me about the prison."

"No." She clenched her jaw around the memory, worried it like a piece of gristle stuck in her teeth, and swallowed hard. "That is a tale I refuse to share."

Thumping his way to the fireplace, Alain dropped heavily onto the bench next to the andirons and scrubbed at his face as though the gesture could wipe away the past. "Who are these people traveling with you?"

Nilesen gnawed the question. How much should she reveal to this evasive, guilt-ridden Alain? Her companions had secrets of their own, and there was Fethi to consider. How best to explain the boy's infatuation with her? Perhaps Elani would help solve that problem.

"What happened to the pepper tree?" She nodded at the unshaded window pane. "I miss the blossoms."

"Last month a storm tore it out by the roots." He traced circles in the wood of the bench. "What did you plan to do, before you found me here? Did you intend to stay in the villa?"

Nilesen thought of the gun Fethi carried for her, of the moment in Istanbul when she traded despair for the pain her writing resurrected. She would keep from him that truth. Death would remain a name on her dance card. Pulling the newspaper from her bag, she pointed to the article on the front. "This is Jeannie Maurillac, and this," she tapped the photograph beneath the sketch, "is the name of the bastard who tried to break me."

Alain stared at the page. A shadow passed across his ravaged face.

"This is what he did to me." She held out her hands.

He gathered them in his and drew them to his lips. When she felt his tears, she slipped free from his grasp. She wrenched the book of poems from her bag and slammed it on the table. "And I did this, mourning you." She ripped out one page, flung it at him. "And this. And this."

The poems fluttered in the breeze from the open door. Alain attempted to rescue them. Unable to reach the ones she'd already torn out, he stretched across the wood and wrested *IŞIK* from her. "If they are mine, if they truly belong to me, you have no right to take them from me."

Nilesen collapsed to the floor, the grief and terror of Adalet escaping in great, heaving sobs. She scrambled to collect the fallen pages. "These words are all I had left of you and your dreams. Now I find even they were lies I told myself."

"No. My beautiful, bright, shining little bird. Your words have flown from town to town, spread hope. Even here in Çeşme they, you, are known and loved." He lowered himself down beside her, cradled her face in his hands. There are no words, *arkaşim,* except the ones you've written. Please. Forgive me."

The sun climbed higher. Shadows crept in to fill the corners. Nilesen rested her head on his chest, listened to the steady beat, felt her answer in each pulse. "What if I cannot?"

"I will wait," he kissed her cheeks, "until you do?"

She raised her hands, allowed him to inspect the damage, wept when he kissed each palm. "Do you believe this man, this Gazi," Alain stuttered over the name, "is still hunting you?"

"Do you doubt me? Because if you do, then truly nothing is left between us."

"The only thing I doubt is myself. Please, my wife, let me hold you."

She struggled to back away, but the comfort of being held, being touched, the desire to be close to him overrode her reluctance. When she settled onto his lap, he kissed her forehead, her cheeks, her neck, her lips. "I could never doubt you," he whispered against her skin, "but this path is perilous."

"We promised to walk it together."

He cupped her face in his hands. "I have no right to ask, but is there still room in your heart for me? I have never, will never, stop loving you. Do you understand?"

She gazed at his ruined face. Her resistance crumbled. Smoothing the dark hair off his temple, she stood and waited until he levered himself up onto the crutches. She matched her steps to his, led him to the bedroom they once shared.

The room echoed with the tick of an unseen clock. As they settled on the bed, shafts of sun trickled through the shutters that graced the window facing west, the light striping their skin in saffron bands.

37

... Tuesday: Yeşil (Green) ...

*F*ethi slammed the hood of the car and dusted his hands on his trousers. He inhaled the fragrance of the roses planted beside the faintly-marked path down the hill to the beach. He had checked the oil and the hoses, just as Batur *bey* had ordered. There was no more he could do at the moment. Elani stood next to the car, arms crossed, legs apart, her gamine features twisted into a mask of defiance. Beneath the bravado, he spied despair.

"Hey," he said, "since we are here, on this beautiful Aegean coast, why not go to the beach?"

"Someone might see us." She cleaned her nails with the *hançer*.

"Bah. No one here knows our names or our faces. Besides, I thought you were a brave Kurdish fighter." Without waiting for her reply, Fethi elbowed past the rosebush and dropped over the crest of the hill. The narrow trail had once been well-tended. Small rocks still lined the path, lodestones for those unfamiliar with the way down, although shoots of thyme and oregano had invaded the scuffed dirt, their green stems eager to reclaim the ground taken from them. When he reached the border of *ardıç* trees, he paused to listen for the scrape of the girl's boots, the rattle of pebbles to indicate she was following.

Elani hung back, pausing when Fethi did, moving forward only when he took a step. The porter's son pressed on. He jogged the final ten minutes to reach the sand. If he had come down in the night, the lumps of volcanic rock might have tripped him up. He shaded his eyes to consider the black sentinels. The forms resembled beached whales, their fins buried in the sand while the eyes looked with longing toward the sea they could no longer reach. Here, in the early dawn, the light sparked off the minerals captive within the stone. The rocks reminded him of sirens signaling to Odysseus, their shadows dark, alien, and seductive. When the light touched their sleeping forms, the truth emerged, solid, unbreakable, shiny in the day's embrace. He checked once more to be certain he was alone, then slipped off his shoes and socks, rolled up his pants and headed toward the water. Waves washed over his toes, an invitation to venture further. Elani slipped up beside him.

"Why do you pursue her?" She kicked at the sea.

"You would not understand." He waded along the shore, dug his toes into the sand, ignored the occasional splash that wet the cuffs of his pants.

"I understand this, Turkish boy. You have romanticized this poet, put her on a pedestal, given her superhuman traits. She is just a woman. An older woman." Elani made a face at him.

"Have you read her work?" He pulled a tattered copy of *Işik* from his pocket. "Before you say another word you might regret, take this."

"What a bossy man you are." She flipped her hair off her shoulder and narrowed her eyes. Fethi scowled.

"Sit on one of these rocks. There. That one has a flat top. Read her book, assuming you can read, then answer your own question."

"She will never love you." Her shout echoed over the water. When he ignored her, she shrugged, settled herself on the rock, and opened the book. Out beyond the foamy stretch of water, the sea rolled from brown to blue to green.

38

... Mavi (Blue) ...

*E*ager to escape the brooding atmosphere in the villa, Jeannie accepted Batur's invitation to climb to the top of the hill. Nilesen and Alain needed more private time and a hike postponed the inevitable decision they all had to make. What next? The path, on a steady, upward slope, led away from the villa. Thankful for the sunglasses he had given her yesterday, she lifted her hand to shade her face and wished she had brought a hat.

When they reached the summit, she counted the five villas strung out like worry beads along the ridge, each a blue-doored guardian poised like a sentinel upon the hill. The past climbed with her. She squinted into the sun-bright horizon. It was easy to imagine Greeks sailing across the water, toiling in the olive groves, torching the orchards when the Turks came back to reclaim their land. The iron of history pressed along her spine, deflating her ego, smoothing the wrinkles of the recent past.

"Once, I thought I could make a difference." Her words skittered in the hot air, pinging against the doctor's shoulders, thick with the sound of regret. Once. Once. "Somehow, I lost my way. When I came to Turkey, the possibility of doing something worthwhile returned. The stuff of vanity, I guess, believing one can make a difference."

The doctor huffed, reminding her of her father preparing to give a lecture or a hug. Sorrow scraped at the scabs of loss. When she looked up, Batur was staring at her, one hand clenched around the strap of his pack, the other rubbing at his chin.

"Did you just growl at me?"

"That," he said, "is part of my bedside manner."

"Good thing I'm not dying," she groused.

"There is always one more chance, if you are strong enough to take it." He folded his arms. "Do you trust me?"

She didn't know what he was offering. Respite? Reconciliation? Resurrection? Whatever bone he planned to throw her way, she found the prospect too tempting to discard.

"Yes," she said. "I do."

"Very well, then. Follow me, Jeannie Maurillac. To make a difference."

He swung off the path, plowed through a thicket of thorn bushes, and plunged ahead until he reached the highest point. Far beyond the villas, she spotted a flash of white.

"I thought we were just going to the top." She used hands to shield her face.

"How about a real hike?" The question stirred inside her, a dare and a promise she welcomed.

"Wait." She squinted at the distant blob of color. "We're going over there?"

"Yes."

She looked back to see how far they had come. "How far is it?"

"Two miles, or four."

"Now you're toying with me." She continued to stare at the flash of white. "Doesn't look that far. Do you know that place?"

Batur gestured toward the villas. "I have visited only Alain this far south of town. The people who live in these homes do not need me. There are others who do. My real work is there. Now, be quiet and try to keep up."

"Charming," she said. When he cocked an eyebrow, she lifted her shoulders. "Your bedside manner could definitely use some work."

Batur shifted the pack on his shoulder and walked away. They hiked higher, following a trail that kept them within sight of the water. The heat intensified. He stopped periodically, waited for her to catch up, then offered sips from his water bottle, a gesture unsettling in its intimacy. In the distance, the sea called, the blue-green water promising comfort and relief. A figure scuffed along the beach, reminding her of Fethi. Down the coast, closer to the village, families strolled across the sand, the women cloaked, the children cavorting like puppies.

"Are you hot?" Lost in the view, she failed to notice Batur until he touched her shoulder. "Here. Use this."

She accepted the cap he offered, adjusting the brim to shade her eyes. She wiped the sunglasses on her blouse and caught her breath again at the sight of the Aegean rolling in from the west. Sunlight swirled over the waves. The shoreline curved in a graceful arc, cupping the water in its embrace. Fishing boats flung their nets out, hauled in the catch, sailed back to land.

"Batur, are we there yet?"

He scowled at her but his shoulders shook. Was he laughing at her? "Patience, Jeannie. You will know when we get there." He set a faster pace. Intimidated by the silence, she stared at his back, noting the ease with which he moved. Batur Stephanidis belonged to this moment. He walked with purpose, every step charged with eagerness and anticipation. She relaxed as the distant white mark grew nearer.

"Are those tents?"

"Yes. When we get there," the doctor stopped abruptly. She plowed right into him, "try not to do anything foolish."

"Love your high opinion of me." She backed away and took out the camera. Her body tingled from the contact with his. "Can I take pictures?"

Batur narrowed his eyes. "Is that not why you are here?"

"Depends on where here is."

He offered another sip of water. When he held the bottle, his fingers grazed her own. A warm flush spread down her arm, across her chest, into her core. She leaned away. He leaned in, tugged on the brim of her cap.

"When we get there, Jeannie, you will see who I am, who they are. What you see, you will not ever forget. Stay close to me." When she looked up, he released his hold on the cap. "Please."

He set off again, leading the way through a grove of fig trees. Although the fruit was just coming into season and the branches should be filled with budding figs, none hung from the lower branches. In the distance, she heard a murmuring, like a wind rushing toward them. Clusters of men, women, and children huddled on the ground beneath the trees. The white object resolved into tents, one, two, ten. Smells assailed her, the wafting of cooking fires, the odor of humans forced to live outdoors. A man with the piercing gaze of a revered elder called out.

"Doctor Stephanidis. *Salaam alaikum.*" The man hobbled over to embrace Batur. He spoke rapidly, punctuating his words with hands clasped in supplication.

Jeannie didn't understand what he said, but she recognized the greeting. Arabic. Batur had brought her to a Syrian refugee camp.

39

... Renk (Indigo) ...

Situated in a chair under the awning that decorated the right half of the villa, Nilesen drew her knees up as she read over the entries in her notebook, the drafts of poems tucked between daily observations and diary entries. A final line, reworked after Alain fell asleep, rested beside a calligraph of his name: *Çiçek'le sapi ayrilmiş birbirinden bir kiliçla adeta. Between the stem and the blossom rides the sword.* Underscoring each word, she double-checked the English translation, then set the notebook aside.

What had they become, she and her damaged bridegroom? Severed from each other, wounded in body and soul, how could they piece themselves back together? She placed her hands over her face, inhaled the earthy odor of their lovemaking still present on her skin. Did hope survive somewhere along the timeline of grief and pain? Above the horizon, the azure sky shaded to indigo. In the distance, clouds curled like question marks, dangling purple strings over the bruised water. Rain was coming.

Down the hill, voice insinuated itself into her reverie. She rose to greet Fethi and Elani, hesitated, then settled down again. Their discussion grew louder, the argument swelling as the young people climbed up from the beach. She didn't hear Jeannie's husky contralto nor Batur's deliberate cadence. Perhaps they had lingered below, pausing to receive the day's final benediction. She opened the bottle of wine, filled three glasses, and set them back on the tray. For this one day, she would forget the troubles pursuing them. Instead, she would invite her companions to share in the traditional Solaganian family ritual. Together they would toast the sunset. Perhaps, having slept away the afternoon, Alain would join them. She cocked her head toward the open window. Inside the house, nothing stirred.

"How can you be so thick?" Fethi said, out of breath and shouting. "It is a poem about death." He batted at the gnats swarming his head as he emerged from the *ardıç* trees, his hair ruffled by the breeze, his face suffused by the passionate defense of his idol. Elani stalked behind him, arms pressed close to her chest. A book peeked from between her small breasts, its cover sparkling with a reflection of the day's last light.

"It is not about death." She lifted the book and shook it at him. "The poems speak about war and loss and the damage men do to women."

"Give me that." Fethi grabbed the book from her. He talked to himself as he shuffled through the pages. When he found the poem he sought, he stamped his foot. "Listen, Kurdish girl, to these lines from *Bahçedeki son erik*. I taste the earth, lick the salt from my wounds. Cast out, I lie, breathless and unbound beneath the heel of history."

Aware for the first time of the prescience in the poem, Nilesen relived the nightmare in Istanbul. Her hands ached. She buried them in the pockets of her slacks and waited for her companions. The debate raged on as they stepped up to the porch. When Fethi paused to catch his breath, Nilesen offered him a glass, held another out to Elani. "What verse has aroused such passion and sowed such discord between you?"

"The orchard poem." Fethi cast a sideways glance at his companion. "Elani thinks it is a feminist rant."

"You twist my words, Fethi." Elani shoved him gently. "Nilesen *hanim* will support my interpretation, I am sure of it."

"Ah, *The Last Plum in the Orchard*. One of my favorites." Nilesen glanced toward the bedroom window. "It is about neither, or all, of those, *öğrenciyimler*."

"Are we your students, Madam Solaganian?" Elani said.

Fethi cut her off. "But, Nilesen *hanim*, you yourself suggested the idea of death to me."

"Did I?"

A Principle of Light

Fethi rolled the stem of the wineglass between his palms. "You did, when we discussed the work in Istanbul."

"We have traveled a long way from the city, have we not, *abi*? Perhaps the poem has also transformed itself along the way."

Swallowing a final word of protest, the porter's son tipped his glass and drank.

"Come, sit. As a student, you must know there are always opposing opinions on a writer's work. Let us discuss this as colleagues. Sorry, there are no plums." Her mouth quivered with laughter as she arranged bread, cheese, and olives on the tray. "But first, tell me, are the doctor and Ms. Maurillac coming back soon?"

Elani shrugged. "We have not seen them since the morning. They did not come with us to the beach."

Unable to shake her disquiet, Nilesen motioned them onto the veranda. "Please, have something to eat. And tell me this. Exactly which of the lines in this verse has caused such disagreement that you are willing to raise your voices to each other?"

Fueled by wine and the heady exhalations of the thyme and oregano plants, the argument regained momentum. The conversation rose in volume as Fethi and Elani considered each verse in the disputed work. Their voices masked the sound of the telephone from inside the villa. Just as Nilesen became aware of it, the ringing stopped. She shrugged away her growing concern and refilled their glasses. The discussion turned to nitpicking over the placement of commas and the use of metaphor. Unable to persuade either one to accept the other's opinion, Nilesen was about to issue an ultimatum when she heard the ragged thump-bump of Alain's crutches. Before she could rise, he passed through the door and swung his way to the table.

"Take your wine and go inside," Alain said. "The jandarmalar are coming."

"What?" Fethi jumped to his feet. "Who is coming?"

In the west, the sun blazed red-orange and fiery. It sparked along the hills before disappearing into the rising wall of an approaching storm. Nilesen splashed wine down her blouse.

Alain shuffled closer. "The neighbors watch the road for me. One of them spotted a military truck entering the village. Nilo, do you remember the *mağara* beneath the stairs?"

"The storage cavern? What about the scorpions?"

One corner of his mouth lifted. "They are more afraid of you, little bird, than you are of them. Take a broom with you, but try not to yell when you kill them. Go. Hurry. Hide."

"You are not coming with us?"

"I have been expecting them for some time." He squinted into the purple haze rolling over the hill. Out on the sea, a curtain of rain raced toward them. "One cannot hide forever."

Fethi and Elani gathered the glasses and hurried inside. Nilesen folded the remaining food into a napkin and tucked it into her pocket. Down the hill, beyond the curve of shoreline, a rumbling rose as the truck geared its way up the hill. Thunder cracked overhead.

"How many?" Nilesen burrowed beneath his arm, steadied the crutch, and embraced his lean body.

"Where there is one, there are more. Too many to fight. You have to hide."

"Do not make me leave you again."

Alain pulled a pistol from his waistband and laid it on the table. Cupping her face, he kissed her eyes, her cheeks, her lips. "Go with your friends, *Aşkim*. Be safe."

Her legs refused to obey. "If only the night were a cloak to cover us in its dark cowl."

"Always the poet, *canim*."

"We have had so little time."

"But." Smiling, he bent to kiss her again. "We have spent it well, *neh*? I carry your scent on my skin, your love in my heart. Forgive me for being less of a poet and more of a man grateful for the gift of your body."

Warmed by his praise, terrified for him, she pulled away. Up the hill, a rustling announced the approach of someone trying to move with stealth. Alain shoved her behind him and raised the gun. They waited as the noises drew closer. Someone sneezed.

"Do not come any closer," Alain called. "I have a weapon, and I know how to use it."

Fugitive raindrops pattered across the awning. A figure stepped from the cover of the *ardıç* trees and moved toward the porch. A second shadow followed.

"Do not shoot, Alain," Batur hissed. "Jeannie and I have returned."

40

... Renk mor (Violet) ...

Long ago, the purplish-blue stone walls of the *mağara* guarded the secrets of traders and thieves. Now, the cave served as refuge for Nilesen and her companions. Huddled and alert, she breathed in the currents whispering in the dark, listening for the furtive rasp of an arachnid advance. Before Batur closed the door to seal them in, he had pronounced the cavern free of insects and mice, but she couldn't shake off her fear. Once he heaved the door closed, the rocks enfolded them in a chilly embrace. The Solaganians had used the *mağara* for storage, then transformed the space into a wine cellar. Now the grotto served as a repository of abandoned furniture, faded linens, and damaged crockery. The hulls of past lives rusted here.

Unwilling to sit on the damp earthen floor, Nilesen squatted. Her knees cracked in protest. Fethi and Batur remained standing, the porter's son hefting a skillet to smash scorpions or pursuers, the doctor with the AR-15 tucked at his side. Elani rocked as she intoned prayers in a hushed voice. Nilesen shuffled closer to Jeannie, steeling herself for what was to come. This was not the first time they had avoided capture by hiding in a lightless, enclosed space. Both were accustomed to tombs. Without warning, the predatory face of Captain Gazi swam into view. She blinked away the image. Blackness surrounded them, the anonymity it offered their only shield against the approaching danger. When the thunderstorm broke, they wouldn't hear it. If Alain called, his words would hiss away in the wind.

Nilesen wished she could pray. The words of the hadiths still resided within her, all the recitations learned at her mother's side, but belief refused to accompany them. Without faith, prayers were nothing more than sighs pressing against the evil around them. She missed Alain. She belonged with him. Above, enveloped by storm, once more alone, her husband faced their enemy. If her heart had any tears left, she would weep for all they had lost and found and lost again.

Beside her, Jeannie flexed one leg, then the other, trying to ease the cramping. She lost her balance, bumped against Batur, and clutched at his calf to keep from falling. When he cradled her head against his thigh, desire stirred anew, older and more primal than the fear of death. His touch, as solid and strong as his convictions, offered comfort. She relaxed against him, seeing again their arrival at the refugee camp, the warmth of his greetings to the people, the easy grace with which he moved from patient to patient. His presence instilled confidence, calmed their fears. She longed to match his courage. When she read the hope in their eyes, she felt ashamed of her own shattered faith. In the dark of the cave, reliving the afternoon's adventure, the chrysalis of the old Jeannie sloughed off and a new Jeannie pushed free.

The sun glared, its caress fierce and unforgiving. Her throat rasped when she tried to speak. Her legs transformed into lead weights dragging her earthward. She sipped water from the bottle Batur pressed into her hand and followed him through the camp. Unnerved by the stares of the refugees, so intense, focused, and fearful, she longed to raise the camera, to hide behind the lens. Batur cautioned her to wait. He tended to patients for an hour before he pointed at the bulge beneath her vest and nodded.

She started with casual shots, always asking for permission, then showing the photos to the subjects. If they objected, she deleted the frame and started over. Caught up in the process, she didn't notice the moment when the people stopped being subjects and became something more than a photo op. Somewhere between their arrival and their departure, her professional distance morphed into empathy. Tears ran unheeded down her cheeks as she accepted the role of witness, through the lens, of their desperation. Each time she paused to recover a sense of self, she found Batur had moved on, always reaching for the

A Principle of Light

next outstretched hand. He belonged here, among these suffering people. His manner never varied, his voice low and reassuring, his hands busy binding, healing. The man was so much more than she expected. When he caught her staring, she turned away before he could read her thoughts.

A scatter of tents, ragged and stained by the elements, circled the crown of the hill. Batur disappeared inside the largest one. When he re-emerged, a young woman followed him, pointing into the distance and wringing her hands. Jeannie searched the compound and spotted the boy at the same time Batur did. Four, maybe five years old, stomach distended from malnutrition, the child lay unmoving in the lap of a woman who was probably his mother. When she spied Batur, she placed the boy on the ground and stumbled forward, falling to her knees at the doctor's feet. Batur crouched to question her, then dumped his pack on the ground and examined the child. He called to Jeannie.

"Spread a cloth on the ground." He nodded at his pack.

The refugees murmured and crowded around them. Jeannie rummaged in the medical kit until she located the sterile sheeting.

"Hurry, Jeannie." His eyes clouded with concern. She unfolded the cloth and slipped it beneath the boy.

"Tell me what you need," she said.

Batur ran his hands over the frail body, assessed the boy's extremities, then palpated his stomach. "Scissors. Bandage. Antiseptic wipes."

Jeannie searched through the kit once more. She located the scissors and handed them over. Batur opened the boy's shirt. A puncture wound, jagged and oozing, marked the midpoint of a massive bruise along the left side of the boy's ribs. Batur dabbed at the wound with a disinfectant while he continued to interrogate the mother. When she refused to answer, he handed the wipe to Jeannie. As she dabbed at the injury, he stood to address the crowd. A man pushed his way to the front and collapsed beside the boy, who moaned and flailed his arms. Jeannie grabbed his thin wrists to keep him still. Batur loosened the pistol in the holster at his waist, motioned the man to put the boy down.

"What's wrong?" Jeannie laid out a suturing kit and more bandages. "What happened to the boy?"

"War," he growled. "Abuse. A father who cares more about fleeing than family. And a possible punctured lung."

"How will you treat that here?"

He met her gaze with a shrug. "With faith."

Inside the tent, a shout rose, followed by wailing. Several of the women stepped away, hesitated, then turned back to the boy. Blinded by tears, Jeannie cursed the wave of human suffering crashing up against the blind eye of the world.

"Jeannie? Focus." Batur sterilized a suturing needle with alcohol and nodded toward the screams. "Can you help out there? If I leave the boy, he will not survive the hour."

She brushed away the flies clustering around the wound. "What's in there?"

"Birth and death. Life's eternal cycle." When he noted her hesitancy, he nudged her with his shoulder. "Go, Jeannie, there is no one else."

She grabbed the last cloth from the kit, searched for sterile gloves, but there weren't any-more.

"Su? Su?" she called as she pressed through the refugees. "Water?" By the time she reached the tent, the screams had become one long note of misery. She lifted the flap and went inside. A girl no older than Elani writhed on the ground, clutching her stomach. Another girl, alike enough to be the first one's twin, mopped the patient's forehead with a damp rag. Bloody mucus stained the dirt beneath the girl's hips. Someone thrust a pot of water into Jeannie's hands, then backed away. On her knees, Jeannie spread the sheet, then eased it under the pregnant woman. In the far corner, an old woman lay gasping for air. The twin shoved at Jeannie, barking orders as she pushed her away.

"Büyükanne. Büyükanne."

A Principle of Light

  Dipping the hem of her shirt into the water, Jeannie crawled over to the grandmother. She scrubbed at the dirt caking the refugee's face until the woman opened her eyes.

  "Easy, now, easy," Jeannie said. "The baby's on its way."

  The büyükanne frowned, then issued instructions through her cracked lips. As the afternoon wore on, the girl's contractions grew stronger and closer together. The baby, when she arrived, echoed her mother's pitiful cries. The sister wrapped the infant in the folds of her robe before placing the child in the grandmother's lap. The air in the tent pulsed. A breeze ruffled the sides. The old woman gripped Jeannie's hand as the mother snatched the baby back. Both girls rocked in sorrow beside the dying woman. When the ragged breathing stopped, the new mother handed the baby to Jeannie, then turned her attention to the dead. Weary, elated, despairing, Jeannie gazed at the tiny face. Birth and death in a single afternoon. Sweat trickled down her face, pooling at the corners of her mouth. She wanted to cry, but no tears came. The baby sucked at the air.

  Batur's touch sent shock waves down her back. He ran a hand over the stubble of hair, picked up the cap that had fallen off, and placed it on her head.

  "Come, Jeannie, it is time to leave."

  "Now?" She held the baby tighter.

  "You did well, Jeannie." His fingers caressed her neck.

  Surprised by her reluctance, she handed the baby back to the grieving mother. What chance did the child have, born in a no man's land of uncertainty and strife? She stumbled from the tent, her back muscles complaining, and followed Batur through the camp. When he reached out, she accepted his hand, grateful for the support. As they neared the outskirts of the camp, she pulled the camera from her blouse to snap one final picture as the parents of the injured boy dug a grave in the dusty soil.

  Jeannie blinked into the darkness and shivered. How long had they been hiding in this damp underground darkness? She allowed Batur to pull her up as they listened for sounds beyond the door. More time passed. They took turns yawning, then huddled closer, trying to conserve body heat. The echo, when it reached them, caught all but Batur unaware.

"No." Nilesen's denial filled the *mağara*, climbed to the ceiling, and slipped into the seams of the rock.

Batur checked his watch. The light from the dial made Jeannie's eye water. Batur cautioned them to silence. They waited another hour, then two. Finally, Batur and Fethi, half-blind now and tense, crept toward the barred door.

"Ready?" Batur's question sliced through the silence.

"Is anyone ever ready for what is to come?" Fethi's answer ended their inertia. The women moved up behind him. The porter's son and the doctor grunted under the weight of the heavy bar. When it slid free, they set it carefully on the floor. Batur listened before he opened the door.

The corridor stood empty. With a curt command to stay together, Batur led the way up the stairs. Jeannie followed, then Nilesen, Elani, and Fethi. They moved with care, anxious to avoid a trip or a fall. Even the slightest scrape would alert any soldiers waiting above. Nothing stirred. The air, thick with the smell of rain, whistled around them. Someone had opened a window.

When they reached the top of the stairs, Batur went into the kitchen. The others remained behind. After he cleared the room, he motioned them out one by one, then moved on down the hall. They stopped frequently to listen for a sneeze, a cough, the scuff of boots over tile. By the time they reached the front of the villa, they breathed in ragged gasps, their nerves on edge. Jeannie's pulse raced, dread riding every footstep. When Batur gave them permission, they crept out into the night. The table where Alain had waited for the *jandarmalar* was empty.

Nilesen darted forward. The book of poems lay abandoned on the table. The pistol Alain had carried was gone. Across the marbled surface, a pool of liquid gathered moonlight as it congealed. Nilesen dipped a finger into the blood and fell to her knees.

Tuesday morphed into Wednesday, the rustle of time a flutter in the wind. A night bird called. Jeannie wandered to the edge of the hill. A sliver of beach lay exposed beneath the crescent moon. Nothing moved below. No boats floated on the water, no lanterns illuminated the night. In the distance, closer than the refugee fires, a skein of lights trailed up the hillside.

"They have killed him." Nilesen's words floated across the courtyard. "They have truly, finally, irrevocably, killed my Alain."

"But, where is he?" Elani knelt beside the poet.

"Maybe," Jeannie whispered, "the wind took him."

Batur gripped her elbow and swung her around to face him. "What foolish thing is this you say?"

"Look." She pointed at the lights bobbing along the path they had walked earlier. "Didn't the boy's mother say her name was Riah?"

On the porch, Nilesen relit the candles. She stared at the open book, recited the lines Alain was reading when the jandarmalar arrived.

"You reside, untouched by time and whole, in the chambered nautilus of my soul." Book clutched to her chest, she sank once more to the floor.

"Nilesen *hanim*." Fethi moved to embrace her. Elani poked him in the ribs.

"Let her be, Fethi." She glanced at Batur and Jeannie and nudged him again.

"Ouch. That hurts." Fethi looked down. Nilesen's pistol, the one he had hand-carried for her all the way from Istanbul, loomed large in the Kurdish girl's grip. Elani held a finger to her lips and pointed toward the driveway.

"She made her choice long ago." She backed him off the porch. "Now be quiet and make yours."

Gaze locked on the gun, Fethi stumbled toward the car.

"No." She gestured in the direction of the path. "That way."

"Are you crazy? Who goes to the beach at night?"

She aimed the gun at the water. "They do."

Out on the sea, a new set of lights swam into view. From the hills around them, a whirlwind of movement as the refugees descended, rushing for the flotilla that would carry them to the shores of Greece.

"This is stupid. Where did you get that gun?"

"Walk. Do not talk." She bit at a fingernail. "I found it in your luggage the day we arrived. I do not know why you had it, but no matter. I told you what would happen if I had a gun."

"It is not mine, and you are ungrateful. Our friends are here. They gave you shelter. Would you repay us with betrayal?"

"I have no choice now, Turkish boy. I needed to pay for my passage. It is a simple exchange. I hand you to the smugglers, they turn a dissident over to the authorities, and everyone else is allowed to leave tonight. A fair trade, all things considered."

"When did you negotiate this trade?"

"When you left me on the beach." Her voice swelled with sorrow.

"I am not going with you." Fethi paused at the hill's edge. Elani lunged toward him. She jabbed the barrel into his back. He dropped down, came up inside her arms, and shoved her back. A shot rang out, echoing over the water. The hillside erupted in shouts as the refugees rushed forward. A handful of rescue boats reversed direction, uncertain of what awaited them on the shore. A searchlight swept the sand. A voice bellowed commands in Turkish and Arabic.

Fethi and Elani tumbled over the rose bush and tangled on the ground. The gun slipped from Elani's fingers and slithered into the bushes. Fethi gathered the girl in his arms and held her until she stopped sobbing.

"I had no choice."

"You have many choices, Elani," he whispered into her hair. "Did you really not understand what you read?"

"Nilesen's hope is not my own."

"It can be. All you have to do is step out of the darkness."

He wrapped his arms around her trembling body and helped her stand. He pressed her deeper into the cover of the trees, trusting the night to keep them safe.

On the porch, Batur drew his weapon. He threw Jeannie to the ground and shielded her body with his own. Struggling under the weight of him, she clawed at the dirt.

"Get off me."

"Not yet." He waited for the echoes to subside. When he was certain the shooting had stopped, he eased off to crouch beside her.

"What just happened?"

He pressed his lips to her ear. "Do. Not. Speak."

He helped her to stand and tugged her toward the cover of the *ardiç* trees. When they reached them, he handed her the AR-15. With a command to stay hidden, he slipped away. Jeannie pressed her back against a tree and looked toward the villa.

On the porch, the candles flickered and danced in the breeze swirling up from the water. Raindrops pinged on the roof, intermittent, lazy, as though the sky couldn't make up its mind what to do. Nilesen, head bare, shoulders hunched, swayed back and forth, a profile of grief as old as the earth itself.

Rifle clutched in her hands, Jeannie wondered where Fethi and Elani had gone. She inhaled the odor of damp dirt and crushed thyme. When no one called to her, she inched forward, alert to movement. She listened hard, but heard nothing above the chaos and confusion rolling up from the beach. Shouts. Screams. The curt orders of police as they rounded up the night's catch. She thought about the baby she had helped deliver. The child had survived, but what good would that do if she and her young mother drowned fighting for a place on a boat? Eyes closed, she saw again the blood and sweat of the delivery. She felt the soft newborn's tiny fingers gripping hers. She envied the exhausted joy in the mother's eyes as she put the baby to her breast. She remembered, too, the grandmother's last breath, the way the light dimmed and sped away as the old woman passed from life to death. She opened her eyes and looked at the bloodstains on her jeans, under her nails, the proof of the afternoon's events tangible. Each moment of the journey and at the camp had marked her, changed her from what she was before the bombing. But who was she now? What had she become? Something Nilesen said in Bursa taunted her.

"We are all becoming, Jeannie. Caterpillar. Chrysallis. Butterfly. We live the stages of our lives over and over until we can no longer go on." Nilesen had teetered on the edge of self-destruction, too. Without Alain, who had been dead, resurrected, now dead again, how would she survive? What stage of becoming would each of the travelers occupy when this interminable night ended?

The stealthy sound of booted feet snapped her out of her musing. She scuttled back and prepared to shoot.

"Jeannie." Batur's call floated on the breeze. "Do not shoot." He moved into her field of vision. She flicked the safety on and stood up. Herding Fethi and Elani ahead of him, the doctor swore softly before helping her up. "This foolish boy has given us a window of opportunity."

"Did you shoot?" Jeannie turned to Fethi.

"No."

"I fired the gun." Elani faced the sea. Rain soaked her hair, drenched her blouse. She shivered. "Look. Some of them are getting away."

Beneath the flashes of lightning, a line of boats crested the horizon, swaying in the swells. Along the shore, those refugees who hadn't found passage huddled within a ring of armed guards. The searchlight continued to strobe the sand in search of stragglers. Farther down the beach, the hills crawled with the unlucky ones, who managed to evade capture only to scuttle back into hiding. Jeannie searched Batur's face. "What opportunity?"

The storm rumbled east. Water dripped from the trees, a chorus of subtle notes in counterpoint to the night insects, who commenced their mating songs. The moon escaped the cloud cover. It sparked in the doctor's eyes before spreading

A Principle of Light

a weak light across the courtyard. Batur ignored her question. He scanned the villa and the people gathered before it.

"Fethi." He shook the boy. "You will take Elani and drive Alain's car to Istanbul. You both will be safe there. You have resources, family to help, places to hide."

"What about Nilesen *hanim* and Madam Maurillac?"

Batur shook him harder. "Do not argue, *abi*. Just do. Jeannie, you will accompany me. No arguments from you, either."

Jeannie met his gaze, accepted the decision, and ran to the porch. She took Nilesen's hands in hers. "Nilo, *arkadaşim*, we have to leave. Now."

"No." Nilesen slipped free. "I cannot leave. Alain will come back. He must come back."

Jeannie stared at the dark liquid on the tiles of the porch. So much blood. She wrapped her arms around her friend, felt her trembling, imagined the strength it took to remain upright in the face of this unfathomable second loss. The others moved in around them.

"Nilesen *hanim*." Batur touched Nilesen's shoulder. "The soldiers will come back. They will come for you next. It is your time to leave."

"No, Batur *bey*, not yet. I have business to attend to. I will not run away again." Behind the villa, dawn climbed the ladder of the sky. Strands of pink and gray and blue and purple laced through the black. The stars yawned and began to fade, pulses of white dispersed by the prism of heaven.

Unaccustomed to being driven, the battered Volkswagen creaked and groaned as Fethi backed it out of the shed that served as a garage. Batur leaned in the window and issued instructions while Jeannie stowed the boy's pack in the trunk. Elani shifted from foot to foot, biting her nails as she hummed indistinct melodies. When the doctor shoved her, gently but firmly, into the passenger seat, she shot him a dirty look.

"Stay on the move." Batur handed over two passports. "These should keep you safe, but they will not stand up to close inspection."

"When did you have time to prepare them?" Jeannie said.

"It is my job to consider all contingencies." He tapped Fethi's shoulder. "Be careful, *abi*. The passports, they are only generic photos. If anyone takes a good look–"

"I understand, Batur *bey*. Nilesen *hanim*?" Fethi glanced toward the porch. The poet sat at the table, the book of poems pressed to her chest, head bent in grief.

Batur patted the younger man's arm. "Your job is to stay safe. Call when you reach Istanbul."

After the car pulled away, Jeannie walked over to survey the beach. In the dim but growing light, the waves curled, inscribing mysterious symbols across the sand. Farther out to sea, a fresh squall advanced, the grey curtain of rain misting the coast and the refugees paddling to the distant land. She watched the slow progress of the car carrying Fethi and Elani, pressed her hands against the hollow fear settling in her stomach.

"Jeannie." Batur touched her shoulder.

"It feels wrong," she laid her hand over his, "leaving her here."

"We are safer when we are not so visible."

"The villa is no longer invisible?"

"No. That is why we are leaving."

"We can't take your car?"

"Is there anything you will not argue, Ms. Maurillac? Of course, we cannot take the car. We are going on foot."

"We can't do that. Nilesen can't hike the hills."

"You said it yourself, Jeannie, and you know the truth of it. I am not leaving." Nilesen gripped the railing as she measured her way toward the front door. Framed by the blue panels, defiant and somehow taller than yesterday, she smiled. "My place is here."

"But the police." Jeannie bit her lip. She couldn't force her friend to accompany them.

A Principle of Light

"Jeannie, *arkadaşim*, I fear them no more than I fear death. Alain is here, in the air, in the walls, in the rooms of this house. I meet his ghost at every turning. Would you ask me to abandon him again?"

"Batur, please. Tell her she can't stay here alone."

The doctor remained silent. Nilesen waved Jeannie over and embraced her. "*Ben yalniz değilim,* Jeannie."

"I don't understand."

"I am not alone. Look." Nilesen pointed toward the ridge.

Jeannie gazed in the direction of the houses upon the hill. A knot of women waited outside the first of the stone villas. Several carried shovels. Others rested baskets on their hips. Heads covered, unmoving, they stared toward the Solaganian villa.

"Did you do what I asked?" Batur urged Jeannie away from the door. She indicated the backpacks lying in the dirt. Batur shouldered one and handed the other to her. He turned to Nilesen, clasped her hands between his, and spoke quietly. Jeannie photographed the women on the hill, then captured the image of Nilesen Yilmaz, unafraid and grieving, the cover of *IŞIK* reflecting the first rays of morning sun.

41

... Wednesday ...

Jeannie trudged behind Batur, dabbing at the sweat trickling between her breasts. The pack grew heavier as she climbed. The sun grew hotter. Removing the scarf from her pocket, she tied it around her forehead, pulling one end down to shade the healing skin, and replaced the ball cap. The image of herself as some bizarre land pirate made her snort. Perhaps a selfie was in order, a record of the trek, one more proof that she hadn't entered a nightmare from which she could not wake.

When they reached the top of the hill, Batur insisted on a water break, then led her south, away from the villas and the refugee camp. Although she discerned no true path through the fig and pepper trees, the doctor never wavered, his steps as sure as those of a mountain goat. She adjusted the brim of the cap, glad once again for its protection. The rain showers she'd spied out at sea had failed to reach the land. The scarf slipped so often, she ended up holding it steady with one hand, which made her progress more halting and uneven. As the morning dragged on, she fell farther and farther behind. Finally, thirsty and sore, she simply stopped walking. Batur was twenty yards ahead before he realized she was no longer behind him. After he retraced his footsteps, he removed the cap, eyed the scarf, and grunted.

"Why did you not tell me?"

She avoided his gaze, choosing to look toward the water instead. "Where are we going?"

Rather than answer, he set down his pack, pulled a gauze pad and tape from his medical kit, and approached her again. She pushed him away.

"I'm fine." She tried to step around him. Batur grabbed her and pulled her close. Gripping the back of her neck, he held her until she stopped resisting. Then he untied the scarf. "Most of the swelling is gone. The wound is healing."

"It doesn't feel like it." She bared her teeth at him. "It itches. And sometimes it burns."

"All part of the process." He forced her to look at him. "There is one thing. You may have lost the peripheral vision in that eye."

She swallowed hard. "Is that all? I thought I wouldn't be able to see."

"Ah, *Jeanniecığim*, no, you are not going to lose your sight, only perhaps a small part of it. Now, will you please allow me to take another look?"

When she relaxed the grip on his shirt, he probed the skin around the wound, his touch sure, tender, soothing. After he cleaned it with antiseptic, she tried opening the eye wider. Light speared her vision, fierce and blinding. She clamped the lid shut, gritted her teeth, and pried it open with her fingers. Batur tipped her head back to add eye drops.

"Wait. Now. Try it now."

More blinking. She tented her face with her hands and stared at the path. White spots resolved into a brown glare, then shadows of grey, before shifting to brown again. "A path?"

He tapped her foot with his boot. "Can you see this?"

But she no longer stared at the ground. "Your eyes," she said. "Are they really that blue?"

"That answers one question." He smoothed ointment over the area, applied a new bandage, and taped it down.. After he repacked his kit, he traced the line of her jaw with his finger. "Pick up the pace, Jeannie. We need to reach the coast by late afternoon."

"Yes, Master," she murmured, not caring if he heard her. Batur shifted the strap of the rifle and moved off. His shoulders rippled. Maybe he was laughing. Maybe he was angry. Whatever he thought, he didn't turn, just walked faster. She forced her legs to keep pace, nursing the sliver of joy swirling in the aftershock of parting from the others. She was Jeannie Maurillac, photographer, and she wasn't blind.

A Principle of Light

The Absence of Light

42

... Wednesday ...

Shards of sunlight danced above the Aegean, racing the clouds. The Volkswagen thumped down the hill, bouncing and groaning over each rut. Fethi gritted his teeth against the constant jarring. Elani wrapped her arms around her knees, jolting from the seat each time they hit a deeper hole. As they bumped from the dirt onto the road and accelerated toward the village, the squall caught them. Fethi glanced toward the sea. The boats tied to the dock strained against the pull of the water. He pitied any fishermen caught in the storm.

Elani remained silent beside him, her small frame burrowed into the worn fabric of Alain's old car. Although the engine ran well, the interior and exterior of the car had not been maintained. Perhaps, Fethi thought, as he dodged the puddles forming in the roadway, Nilesen's husband had kept it that way on purpose. A nondescript vehicle became a useful bit of camouflage for a planned escape or a future attack on the government. Ahead, a few pedestrians scurried from store to store, but the majority of the inhabitants of Denizköy remained indoors. A charter bus idled in front of the tourist center. A line of elderly passengers limped their way into the building, purses, newspapers, and umbrellas held overhead to shield them from the rain. When he slowed to pass the bus, Fethi glimpsed a military transport parked along the side of the road. Elani spotted it, too.

"How long until we are free of this place?" She shifted lower in the seat.

"This car will not go much over eighty kilometers. Istanbul is eight hours away in a fast car on a good travel day. That assumes we do not stop for food or to visit a restroom."

"That is an assumption I refuse to make, Turkish boy. I know you already have to pee." She caught his eye and shot him a shy smile. Her attempt to tease touched him. He grinned back. "Go to sleep, Elani. I will wake you when we reach Ephesus."

"Wait. Ephesus?" When she sat up, she banged her head on the window. "Ow. What route are we taking?"

"The one that offers us the most protection, Batur said."

"Batur insists. Batur commands." She grimaced. "Who is this man? Do you know him? Do you trust him with our lives? I, for one, do not put faith in everything he says."

"Should I trust you? You were willing to deliver me to the police to escape from Turkey, so do not speak to me of faith." The words spun out between them, laden with bitterness. "I should drop you here and let the jandarmalar take you back where you belong."

"No." She gripped his arm with both hands. "Forgive me, Fethi. I am shamed by my actions. But it is not easy to put my fate in the hands of strangers. Doctor Stephanidis may be a good man. Or he may be a devil. But if you trust him, so will I. Please. Do not turn me over to the authorities. You know what will happen."

"Bah, let me go." The windshield wipers squeaked across the window, batting away the rain pounding the glass. "I am better than that, and you know it."

Elani tugged her jacket tighter. She slid her hands up her sleeves, drew into herself. Hunched forward over the steering wheel, neck muscles corded from the strain of peering through the storm, Fethi drove on. The morning gloom grew into midnight darkness. Most of the cars on the road had pulled over, hazard lights flashing, as thunder reverberated above them. Lightning traced jagged paths across the sky. In the absence of light, the twin beams of the headlights emitted photonic bursts. The Volkswagen became a starship hurtling through the galaxy. They had almost reached the turnoff to the ruins when Elani spoke.

"I really am sorry, Fethi." She waited for him to look at her. "Why must we hate each other?"

"Your people," he began, then hesitated. The girl was not her people. She was only a straw caught up in the wind of

A Principle of Light

war, prodded by the past, seduced by old antagonism. So was he. "Tell me about your people. The true story, not the tale created for sound bites and political coin."

"Do you really want to know?"

The question caught him off guard. Did he? What purpose would it serve to hear her explanations? Unbidden, his mind resurrected the image of Nilesen reading to the girls at Deniz Feneri. They had come to listen, to learn, to expand their perceptions. Could he not do the same? That memory triggered others. The students at the university arguing with the professors, their openness to compromise in sharp contrast to the government's intransigence. His father's friends gathered around café tables, smoking and arguing, unwilling to let go of past slights, imagined threats, the loss of identity.

"Did Atatürk not say that the basis of a good country is equal justice for all?" He touched her hand. "I do not want us to be enemies. Tell me about your history."

The storm moved east, but the clouds lingered. Elani spoke with care, her voice rising as passion overcame diplomacy. She related her family history as well as the roots of conflict as she understood them between the factions in the country. Fethi interrupted her only once.

"Why must you seek your own country?"

"Because we are not you. For centuries, my people had their own way of life." She paused, gathered her thoughts. "We were free, until the first World War destroyed that life. The conquerors divided up our lands, took away our independence. My people have been trying to regain our homeland for a very long time."

Fethi banged on the steering wheel. "That is never going to happen, Elani. Atatürk opposed it. So have all the other leaders, all the neighboring countries. Armenia, Syria, Iran, Iraq, they all feel the same."

"You mimic their arguments, but you do not see what they have done. My grandparents died in Saddam's chemical war. My father was crippled by a bomb. I am proud to tell you that I joined the PKK, that I fought beside my brothers and sisters."

Unable to hide his dismay, Fethi slowed the car to stare at her. "But they are terrorists! This fighting is madness. It will destroy us all. Are we not stronger together?"

"If only that were true, togetherness. The possibility sounds so good, of course. But we want to be our own people, in our own land. The 1920 Treaty of Sèvres promised as much."

He shook his head. "And failed to deliver."

"Yes, because no one wants to let us govern ourselves. Why is that, do you suppose?"

Up ahead, a farmer's cart appeared, the driver hunched against the wind and rain, the donkey protesting as it hobbled forward. Fethi wrenched the wheel left, then right, avoiding a collision. As the tires settled once more, he risked a glance at Elani. Fists clenched, face aflame with conviction, she met his stare, her fierce fragility evident. In that moment, he experienced the uncoiling of desire, a need to protect and defend. Disconcerted, he returned his focus to the road.

"Let me tell you this," Elani said. "My ancestors were sheepherders. They traveled the mountains with their flocks, at no man's mercy or permission."

"What about the drugs they ferried?"

"Some did, but not my family. We refused to smuggle that poison."

The rain drummed accompaniment to her denial. Mesmerized by her story and the incessant drone of the storm, Fethi missed the sign announcing the way to Ephesus.

"There!" Interrupting an anecdote about her grandfather's goats, Elani pointed behind them. "Is that where we are going?"

He pulled onto the berm, dragged out the passport Batur had given him, and shook it. A slip of paper tumbled free. "Read that, please."

As Elani spooled off the instructions, Fethi made a u-turn, steering the Volkswagen onto an access road. He passed a turnstile with a broken crossbar and drove behind a row of sheds. Despite the stacks of excavating baskets and specimen trays, he saw no evidence of the scientists assembled to work on the archeological dig. The downpour eased, coughed a few more bursts, and sputtered to a stop. Elani twitched her nose at the smell rising from the steaming earth.

"Are you sure this is safe?"

"Not even the doctor knew that," he said. "We will stop here until he calls."

"What if he fails to call?"

Fethi shrugged. "Then we will go on to Istanbul."

"I thought that was where we were going in the first place."

"There is no need for you to know everything." He smiled to soften the statement.

"Fine, do not tell me." Peering over the dash, she cocked her chin toward the closest shed. "But you might have to tell him."

Ahead, haloed by the emerging sun, a man walked toward the car, one hand fisted on his hip, the other pointing a semi-automatic at the windshield.

43

... Wednesday ...

Gathered beneath the portico of the neighboring house, the women of the Çeşme hills waited for Nilesen to make her way to them. She struggled against the wind gusting up from the beach as she forced her legs to carry her forward. The closer she drew, the clearer the message telegraphed by the slump of their shoulders, the grim stares, the way they linked arms and beckoned her on. These were the neighbors who watched the villa, the women who had accepted her as one of their own when Alain first brought her to the Solaganian villa. When she stepped off the path, they kissed her cheeks, ushered her from one embrace to the next. The last woman, the oldest of the group, whispered in her ear.

"He is here."

Nilesen bowed her head. "Show me, Farraj *hanim*."

Farraj Malamuk hesitated. "Are you certain?"

"Show me."

The women followed Farraj and Nilesen to the orchard behind the house. Surrounded by a low fence, a small plot stood off to the side. Within the enclosed area, a hole had been dug in the sandy soil. Below, encased in white linen, in the hollow carved by their grief, lay the body of Alain Solaganian.

Nilesen fell to her knees and keened. The wind blew away her cries. The others kept vigil as she clambered into the grave to rest a hand on the cloth that covered her husband's face. The rain sputtered back to life, staining the already-saturated earth a darker brown. It pooled around the body, rose over her shoes, then soaked away, searching for the sea. She removed the sheet from his face, traced her husband's features, repeated the vows they had so recently renewed. *Always, ever, faithful unto death.* She bared his shoulders, touched the jagged hole in his chest where the bullet found a home. The women remained above, guarding her sorrow.

The downpour intensified. Farraj Malamuk lowered down a bucket of earth. Then, crouching, she pressed a paper-wrapped packet into the widow's hand. Nilesen mounded the dirt over Alain's chest. She unwrapped the seed and pressed it into the soil. She touched her forehead to his, then kissed him. No warmth remained on his lips, no sign of the spirit that had given him life. She drew the linen over him, then reached up so the women could pull her out. Standing beside them, buoyed by their strength, she listened to their stories. How they witnessed Alain's birth, unexpected and portentous, in the villa he so loved. Followed his passage through the school years, each milestone celebrated with meals and songs. The joining of families to observe Ramadan and Victory Day. Toasting the bride and dancing at his wedding. Each woman's offering wove a chain from birth to death, a necklace of stories to wear through all the lonely years to come. When the final tale had been told, she accepted the finality of his passing, as the women had accepted their own losses. Alain had been the last of the men of the Çeşme hilltop community. Husbands, sons, grandsons, all gone to dust and history. Only the women remained, aging in place as they remembered, mourning losses and defying time, their existence a toll placed daily in the greedy hand of fate.

"Come inside to warm yourself. Stay," Farraj Malamuk urged, "until the torment has passed."

Nilesen waved off the invitation. She headed down the path, welcoming the shock of cold air, the rattle of thunder. Lightning struck close enough to raise the hair on her neck. She did not know how to live with this heaviness weighing down her bones. Beneath the sorrow lay the bedrock of truth. She had lost him twice. The first time broke her will to go on. This second blow promised to destroy her.

Coated in mud, shivering in her rain-soaked clothes, she returned to the villa. She wrenched the door open and fell. She crawled down the hall and staggered into the bedroom.

A Principle of Light

Stripping off the wet clothing, she sprawled naked onto the bed. She pulled her knees to her chest and rocked through the memory of Alain's hands caressing her breasts, Alain inside her, her name on his lips as he came. In the act of lovemaking, she had forgiven him for the deception. Now, he was gone for good and there was only the well of emptiness. The memory of their last time together raised a djinn of loss within this room of shattered hope.

The roof rattled, the windows shook. Tossed by the storm, the furniture on the porch blew over and banged against the house. A shutter tore loose and winged free. It tumbled across the driveway, splintering with a crack against the tree line. Nilesen ignored it all. When she could no longer bear to scream, she pulled the blanket over her head and lost herself to grief.

Be brave, little hen. Alain's admonition whispered at her. She unclenched her limbs and buried her face in the pillow, searching for his scent. If she inhaled deeply enough, could she breathe him back to life? The dark day shifted into a darker night. She remained anchored in the bed, his memory insistent. *Truth bubbles from you like a spring.* Images of her husband, whole and shattered, swirled in her mind. What truth did his shade wish to reveal? Although she did not recall placing it there, the book of poems lay open atop the dresser. She forced herself to rise and plod to the closet. She removed a robe, tied it with a clumsy knot. Gathering her wet clothes, she shuffled into the kitchen, lit a fire, and draped the garments over the backs of chairs. Resolve flared around her, refining her sorrow, burning away all but the need to tell his story.

"I watched from the trees," Farraj had whispered. "He did not kill himself. The soldier forced him to stand, then pulled the trigger. They dumped his body along the lane. We brought him here."

She did not have to ask the soldier's name. She knew it, like she knew the crooked outlines of her hands, the sharp edges of the lies he told. Emre Gazi, who pursued her because once upon a time, in Istanbul, she refused to tell him what he wanted to hear.

The kettle whistled. She poured the water over the apple tea, closing her eyes against another memory, Alain grinning slyly, as he served her tea and teased about the aphrodisiacal qualities of the blend. The taste of apples on his lips when he kissed her. Her world bounded now by one directive, revenge. She found a tin of biscuits and placed them beside the book and her mug. Opening her notebook, she took a sip of tea and set to work. *A Rape At Çeşme.* She recopied the letters in the title, bit her lip until she tasted blood, then smeared it on the page as she wrote.

> *He dwells in darkness, descending*
> *to depths from which no man ascends*
> *while I, laid out like cordwood, mark*
> *the path of his destruction, the stark,*
> *uncharted wasteland, unstarred, moonless,*
> *entombed in ice, a naked, loveless*
> *captive to loss and torment, circling yet*
> *again an endless whirlpool of regret.*

She abandoned the draft to stoke the fire and brushed against a jacket hanging on a hook beside the door. His jacket. Where were the crutches? She raced out the door, searched through the overturned chairs. Nothing. She inspected the lawn, squelched through the mud to the rose bush beside the path. Still nothing. Perhaps the killers threw them in the lane where they tossed his body. That made no sense, but there was no sense in any of this. Back inside, she locked the door, barricaded it with a chair, and returned to the kitchen. She repeated the precautions at the back entrance before she turned on the radio. Static crackled, an affront to her ears. She scanned through the local stations until she found a clearer transmission. A broadcaster interrupted a classical music concert to announce that the United States had ordered the families of embassy personnel in Turkey to return stateside. The government had closed the border to all undocumented foreigners. She thought of Fethi,

A Principle of Light

Elani, Batur, her friend Jeannie, all sealed inside the country, and Alain, already moldering in the Çeşme earth.

44

... Wednesday ...

Fethi kept his eyes on the man advancing toward them, as he grabbed the gun from under the seat. He covered his mouth, feigned a cough, and handed it over to Elani, who had ducked below the dash. "Get out. I will distract him. Stay hidden until it is safe. Then return to the villa."

"You cannot ask this of me, Fethi. I know how to fight, remember?" She released the safety and racked a bullet into the chamber.

He reached toward the glove box, unlatched the passenger door, and nudged her with his elbow. "Go, before he realizes you are here."

Outside, the man shifted the weapon from hand to hand and called out. "Turn off the engine. Keep your hands where I can see them."

"I am staying." She crouched on the floor.

"No. Please. Go, foolish Kurdish girl. Find Batur. He will know what to do."

The windshield wipers scraped away the last of the rain. Fethi drummed his fingers on the steering wheel. Elani chewed her lowered lip. When she made up her mind, he expelled the breath he was holding. "Yes. Go. Now."

"I will bring help," she whispered. "Stay alive." She eased her door open at the same time Fethi pushed on his. While he approached the soldier, she slithered out and huddled beside the car.

"Can I help you, *bey*?" Fethi exaggerated a limp.

"You are injured?" The man raised an eyebrow.

"Just a cramp." Fethi angled to the left, drawing the man's gaze. "Has your truck broken down? I am an excellent mechanic."

Elani inched toward the rear of the vehicle. She low-crawled to the rock wall separating the maintenance sheds from the historical site. When she reached the sheds, she tested each door until she found one unlocked. Once inside, she hid among the shelves of broken pottery and waited for the day to pass.

"Where's the girl?" the man said. Fethi peered at the insignia on his jacket. This was no ordinary soldier.

"The girl? Oh, you mean the hitchhiker? I dropped her off in the village. She said something about relatives in Bursa." Fethi bowed slightly. "Forgive me, Captain. I had no idea you were looking for her."

The man circled Fethi, prodding him with the gun. A younger man in fatigues crawled from the back of the truck. The subordinate lit a cigarette and propped one foot against the tire.

The captain spit into the rain-soaked dirt. "No matter. We will find her. For now, you will come with us. Tomorrow, we will all go back to the villa. I am sure the poet Yilmaz will be happy to see you."

At the mention of Nilesen, Fethi stumbled. The captain jammed the gun into the boy's ribs. "Önder," the captain said, "put him in back, and use the chains. We are returning to Çeşme. Tomorrow we will visit the widow Solaganian."

Önder cut his eyes at Fethi. He crushed the cigarette under his boot and motioned the porter's son to climb up. Inside, he clamped a leg iron around one of Fethi's ankles, tested the chain to be certain it was anchored firmly, and placed the key in his pocket.

"Do not try calling for help," he said. "The captain does not like to be crossed."

"How?" Fethi pitched forward. He grabbed the soldier to keep from falling out the opening.

Önder slammed Fethi onto the bench. "How what?"

"How did you find me?"

"You think we do not know how to track a simple boy like you?" The soldier pulled out an electronic remote. A green button on the case blinked on and off in the dark interior of the truck. A tracking device.

A Principle of Light

Fethi licked the sweat from his lips. "How did you know I would drive that car?"

"You really are a simpleton, no? We bugged every vehicle at the villa, stupid city boy. Now, be quiet. Or yell, if you want to." Önder placed a hand on the pistol. He cocked his head toward the front of the truck. "Personally, I would go out of my way not to anger Captain Gazi."

The engine rumbled to life. Hopping down, the soldier flipped the tarp over the opening and disappeared. As soon as the captain put the truck in gear, Fethi took out the key he had lifted from the soldier and unlocked the shackle around his leg. He replaced it loosely and settled against the seat. "Personally, jandarma," he whispered, "I would advise you not to underestimate this city boy."

The truck rumbled toward the highway. Fethi hefted the key in his palm before he lifted the tarp and tossed it out, watching with satisfaction as it sank into the muddy lane. He removed his cell phone from his shoe. No service. He shoved the phone back in, leaned against the side of the truck, and tried not to worry. At the least, perhaps the captain would not inquire about the reason for his limp.

45

... Wednesday ...

I paused to catch my breath and looked back over the route we had followed. Another storm rolled across the land where the villa stood, yet here, only a few miles farther south, no rain fell. "How is that possible?" I murmured.

Batur halted. "Did you say something?"

Gesturing at the line separating the boil of clouds from our sun-kissed position, I shrugged. "Fethi's driving in that."

"Come on, Jeannie. We can discuss the weather later." He helped himself to water, then handed it over before surveying the terrain ahead. As he moved farther along the ridge, he paused often to check both sides of the hill. "We are too exposed up here. We need to move closer to the shore."

I returned the canteen and rolled my shoulders to ease the burden of the pack. Batur obviously knew where he was going even if I didn't have a clue. Since I had decided to trust him, I had refrained from questioning his decision to remain at the top of the hill. I would have gone down to the water long before now. He must have read my thoughts. He dropped to one knee, took out binoculars, and scanned the horizon.

"The terrain is more rugged below," he said. "Are you sure you can handle it?"

I swatted at the gnats hovering around my eye but said nothing. He cocked his head to study me. "You look tired."

"I'm all right." I pushed past him, slipped on the rocky ground, and skidded to a stop in front of a stand of thorn bushes. I had no reason to be cranky. He had risked a great deal for me. Shame stained my cheeks. I waited for him to start walking, then pushed through the clumps of wild oregano as we made our way down toward the water. The pungent aroma of the crushed plants surrounded me. I suddenly realized how hungry I was, but I didn't dare bring it up. Whatever instinct drove Batur, it was relentless. Finally, the call of nature refused to be ignored. I hissed at him to wait, sprinted into a grove of pepper trees, and relieved myself. When I returned, he was staring at the sea, cell phone cradled in one hand, eyebrows lowered. He looked up. My pulse thrummed beneath the fierceness of his glare.

"What's wrong?"

"Fethi has not called. And he is not answering his phone." He slid the phone back into his pocket. I bit my lip. Panic wouldn't solve anything.

"Maybe he and Elani have gotten far away by now. Or they're simply out of range." The words sounded lame. I reached for his hand, slipped on a rock, and flailed to regain my balance.

"You are tired, Jeannie. We will stop soon. You need to rest, and a patrol boat is due along the coast at," he consulted his watch. "four o'clock."

"We've been walking for nine hours?" The moment I acknowledged the fact, the muscles in my legs quivered. My shoulders ached from the heavy pack.

"We go there." Batur pointed toward a distant rock formation. I squinted into the late-afternoon haze. Relief appeared light-years away. "Not too much farther now. Here, let me help you."

He offered his hand. Hesitant but grateful, I reached out. Together, we crept down the unstable hillside. Half an hour later we encountered the first of the rockfalls, one of which resolved into the ruins of a stone hut. Batur motioned me to silence. He stepped to the doorway, checked inside, then waved an all clear.

"What is this place?" In the dim interior, pebbles spilled from gaps in the walls. A circle of dirt ringed by larger stones occupied the center of the space. A single cot, dusty from disuse, leaned against the back wall. A clay jug squatted next to the door.

"A shepherd's hut. No one uses it any longer. It will serve us for the night."

"We're spending the night?" I ignored the flutter in my belly, the heat flushing through my veins.

"Yes." Batur cut his eyes away. "There is no other shelter nearby."

"You've been here before." I hugged myself against a sudden chill. My companion walked like a man certain of his place in this wild and exotic land. Who was he, I wondered. And what was he to me?

"This is my home, Jeannie. The land has been in my mother's family for centuries."

"This land belongs to you?" I watched him square his shoulders and turn away, ignoring my question. Curiosity piqued, I ignored the caution light blinking in my head. The words tumbled out. "But your name, Stephanidis, it's Greek, isn't it?"

"There is a small spring just over the ridge. I will go for water. Can you fix something to eat?" He dropped his pack, picked up the jug, and hesitated. When he stepped around me, his chest brushed against mine. Our clothes whispered from the contact. When I could no longer detect the shuffle of his boots, I dumped my pack by the fire ring, tested the cot, then lay back, groaning as my body relaxed. I fell asleep to the rustle of wind and the distant heartbeat of the sea, the smell of sweat and dust and Batur Stephanidis shaping my dreams.

When I woke, the light had died. Disoriented, I started up, stumbled over my own feet, and pitched forward. Batur caught me, lowered me back to the cot.

"Go back to sleep, Jeannie." He ran his fingers along my cheek, smoothed his thumb over the healing skin. "You need rest more than food."

Soothed by the breeze swirling through the chinks in the stone, I slipped back into slumber, but not before I noticed him crouched in the doorway, guarding the night.

46

... Thursday ...

*E*lani jerked upright. Awakened by the light seeping under the door of the shed, she checked her pockets, discovering half of an energy bar. The reminder of her journey caused her eyes to fill. She lowered her head to her knees and murmured a prayer for Fethi. Then she ate, brushed her hands over her muddied clothes, and, gun in hand, made her way back to the wall separating the historical site from the workers' area. Once beyond the barrier, she stowed the weapon in her waistband and strolled through the ruins of Ephesus. The past dusted her shoulders, crooned stories in her ear. Her damp clothing made her shiver. The temptation to hide beneath the shadowed walls engulfed her, but she forced herself to walk on. Alert for pursuit, she worked her way toward the main entrance, where she encountered a school group crowded around a tour guide. Teachers prowled the perimeter. She blended in among the students and stayed with the class all the way to a restroom facility.

"What happened to you?" A blue-jeaned girl picked at Elani's blouse, then let it drop with a scowl.

"Fell," Elani said. "Clumsy." She shrugged off further comments about her appearance, rinsed the mud off her clothes, and used paper towels to scrub her face and hands. By the time she finished, the line of texting teens had snaked out the door and curled around the building. A second and then a third group arrived. Unmoved by the history surrounding them, they bustled in, eager to check their makeup and talk about boys. She pushed through the crowd to rejoin the first group. The guide herded them along the designated route. An hour later, certain that no one was paying any attention, she made her way to the public transportation area. When a bus bound for Denizköy pulled up, she boarded quickly, collapsing into a seat close to the rear exit. The local passengers, immune to the wonder of ancient Smyrna, did little more than nod as they passed her spot. Repelled by the odor that rose from her mudstained clothing, no one took the seat beside her. She dozed, slumped against the window, as the bus dieseled its way down the coast. By the time the driver reached the village, Elani, teeth chattering, muscles quivering from dehydration, had decided on her next move.

47

... Thursday ...

The light had fled, rested, returned. Nilesen, scoured by grief, shed the robe and stood naked in Alain's closet. She crushed the shirts and trousers to her face, desperate to recapture him, to rub his essence into every crease and crevice until his scent became her own. The sun had risen far above the horizon before she abandoned the effort and sank to the floor. She could no longer feel her bones beneath the skin.

"You are the shell who held the world," she whispered, "and I the nautilus within your sturdy cage. How can I go on?"

Alain's ghost sent his regrets. No answers remained to be discovered among the cotton threads. The linens had already reshaped themselves, relaxing their grip on his body's contours. Frantic, she clawed at the garments, lost her balance, and tumbled against the wall of the closet. Hangers clanged free around her. The shirts fell, sleeves ballooning as they caught the air. Trousers splayed out, winding their limbless legs around her waist. Something heavy sprang free, speared her foot, and fell away. She kneaded the bruise until the pain subsided, then searched through the jumble of clothing for the cause. Alain's old robe, the one he wore when he prepared his rally speeches, lay beneath his favorite shirt. When she lifted the clothes, she discovered a book, no bigger than a postcard, bound by an elastic band. Heavy, smelling of ink and sandalwood, the journal carried no title. After her hands stopped shaking, she released the band and read the inscription. *Alain Solaganian. For my wife, Nilesen, the light in my darkness.* A long time passed before she found the courage to turn the page.

48

... Thursday ...

The gulls woke me, their calls filling the air as they soared above the hill. Batur no longer stood watch. I stretched, my body protesting as muscles clenched and bones cracked. My stomach growled and my bladder screamed for release. I wandered from the hut, found a bush, and took care of one of the problems. Relieved, I shaded my eyes to search for Batur. I heard him before I saw him, his boots a quiet rasp through the dewy brush. When he saw me, he smiled. Disarmed by the warmth in his eyes, I caught my breath. Before I could smile back, he handed me the water jug.

"Can you light a fire?"

"I was a Girl Scout once," I said, "in my long-ago childhood."

"Good." The smile returned. "I shall be back in half an hour. We will eat then."

"Where are you going?" The thought of being alone rekindled the panic I'd buried. What if he didn't return?

"Fishing." He rubbed his jaw as he assessed my wrinkled state. His eyes lingered on my mouth before sliding away. "You can wash if you like. In the stream just over the hill. Take this. Just in case."

I accepted the Glock. When he drifted out of sight, I followed his directions until I located the stream that flowed from beneath an outcrop of rock. Water pooled in a depression, then meandered down a storm-carved rut on its way to the sea. I peeled the bandage from my wound and shrugged off my blouse. I used the sleeves to scrub at the dust and sweat coating my skin. The cool water eased the cramping in my limbs, removed the stink of yesterday's hike. On the way back to the hut, I gathered sticks. I rummaged through Batur's pack for matches. After I lit a fire, I mixed two packages of dehydrated rice and beans with the water he had brought and set them on stones near the flames. When the food began to steam, I scooped out several handfuls of the mix, relishing the taste. I struggled to stop myself from consuming it all. Batur's reappearance made me jump. He winked and held up a fish.

It didn't take long to gut, clean, and fry the catch. We ate in silence, hemmed in by the walls of the hut and our thoughts. After the meal, Batur went back outside. I wandered after him, the gun he had given me tucked into the waistband of my jeans. He removed his shirt and spread it over the dirt, then removed a small pouch from his pack. His tanned and muscular body gleamed in the sun. He extended his hand for the Glock. I laid it on his palm. Working quietly and efficiently, he broke down the weapon and spread out the parts. I knelt beside him, practicing the words I wanted to say before I spoke.

"Tell me," I said, "about this land, how you came to know it so well."

He looked out over the hillside. "Wild, no, and beautiful? It belonged to my mother's family, and now it belongs to me."

"Is your mother the woman in the photograph?"

Batur slammed the cartridge back into the gun. "You had no right."

"I didn't mean to pry." I ignored his scowl. It was important for me to say this. "We, I, didn't know who you were. Our lives were in your hands, Batur. What if you had planned to betray us?"

"Nevertheless, Jeannie Maurillac, you were wrong."

"Yes," I gnawed my bottom lip, "I was wrong."

He reached for the AR-15 propped against the hut, mouth tight, jaw clenched. "She is dead."

"Your mother?"

"Yes." He paused. I held my breath. "She killed herself, jumping from the Galata the day after my father took that picture."

A Principle of Light

I slumped against the wall, slid down, stared at the toes of my boots.

"Is your curiosity satisfied?" He swiveled to face me. "Do you have enough to fill your American need for drama?"

"No, Batur, that's not, I mean, I didn't." I twisted the ring on my finger, the one my mother handed over the week before the cancer took her. "Please. I want to understand, truly. Why did she do it?"

"Why does anyone commit such an unforgivable act? Even I do not understand it, but I know what she wrote in the letter she left behind. She swore she could no longer live with the prejudice, the dirty looks, the hateful comments of the world."

"Was it that bad?"

Batur stared at me. Shivers raced down my back. This man was fierce, dangerous, in command of my fate. I should stop asking questions, but I couldn't back down. I needed him to see me in a different light. "I'm not merely curious, Batur. I care. About this land, your people. Tell me, please."

"You care." So much bitterness in those two words.

"I have learned to care. Now I want to understand."

The light in his eyes shifted to yearning. "Is it possible to understand? My country is consumed by old hatreds. Turks for Kurds. Turks for Greeks. For Armenians like Alain Solaganian. Istanbul seethes with factions and imagined slights. History spreads a net over us all."

"Who raised you?"

"My older sister. She lives in Athens now." Batur shifted his shoulders, shrugging off the past. "A victim of, what is it you Americans say, reverse discrimination."

"But you became a doctor, a healer." I pointed at the guns, newly-cleaned and ready to bring death. "Why this?"

"My mother named me Batur," he said, "over my father's objections."

"Batur. What does it mean?"

"Warrior." When he stood, his shadow fell over me. The sun flared above his outstretched arms. The sound of engines rattled up from the water. "We need to stay here one more night."

We spent the afternoon in the shade of the hut, moving as the sun moved, its curious light eager to invade our space. We didn't speak, oppressed by all the words that remained unsaid. I scrolled through the pictures on my camera, arranging them on my mind's canvas, startled once again by the truth each one revealed. The power had dwindled, the battery almost out of charge. If I didn't find a way to recharge it soon, I wouldn't be able to document the rest of the journey. That realization chilled me as much as any other. The desire to provide visual proof of all I had witnessed had become an obsession.

A little before dusk, Batur disappeared. When he returned, a rabbit dangled from his belt. I stoked the fire, then watched as he prepared the evening meal. At sunset, he pulled a mat from his pack and spread it in the hut. "I will sleep inside tonight," he said. "You can keep the cot."

But the cot had other ideas. Age and disuse had teamed up to exact revenge for this intrusion. When I lay down, the material sagged, then collapsed, dumping me into a tangle of rotted cloth and broken wood. I yelped as I struggled to right myself, then laughed at my clumsy attempts. I caught Batur trying not to smile and laughed harder. After he pulled me free, he kicked at the remnants of the cot.

"You can have the mat," he said.

"No." I swiped at the tears with the backs of my hands, "you've given up enough for me. We'll share it."

I left the hut to pee, stopping to stare at the horizon, captivated by the sweep of sky and sea visible from the hillside. Once more exhaustion set in, stealing my will to stay awake, but the thought of spending the night next to Batur unsettled me. Perhaps this attraction came from gratitude. No, I refused to lie anymore, even to myself. I was grateful to him for all he had done, but I also felt fascination and admiration and desire. When I stepped back inside the shepherd's hut, he was already asleep. I lay down next to him. He didn't move. I nestled against his back and prayed the nightmares would stay away tonight.

I awoke sobbing. The image of Carl racing toward me drifted away, but the horror it invoked refused to leave. Sadness settled in my chest, carving channels through my resolve. I slipped an arm around Batur. The muscled strength of his body promised protection, his warmth soothed me, despite the growing sense of foreboding. Carl's message had arrived in a bloody spray of lost words.

"Jeannie?" Batur captured my hand, held it to his chest. My breasts pressed against his back. He smelled of sweat and thyme and woodsmoke, so overtly male that my whole body hummed. I lay back. He rolled over and touched my face, traced the tears, then wiped them away. "What is wrong?"

"I don't know." I gulped back a sob. He leaned closer. I told myself to move, to leave the bed, but my self demurred. I waited, aware of the invitation in his eyes. He kissed my forehead, my wounded eye, brushed his lips over mine.

"Do not be afraid," he said. "I promised Nilesen to keep you safe."

"I'm not afraid." I shifted closer, fitting my body against his. He kissed me, this time with an urgency that matched my own. In my mind, a finger wagged, warning of the danger, while the need to be engulfed in his strength urged me on.

"Jeannie, *Aşkim*, are you certain?" He held still, his arousal pressing against me, replacing my sorrow with an ache so fierce and demanding I thought I would faint from longing. "I can leave."

"Yes. No." I drew him closer, cradled his head in my hands. "Stay. For this one night, be with me."

"Jeannie Maurillac, you need to know this." Again he brushed his lips across my cheeks, claimed my mouth, nuzzled my neck. "I am not a one-night man."

"That," I breathed against his skin, "is good to know."

He unbuttoned my blouse, cupped and caressed my breasts. He dipped his head, teasing and stroking my nipples with his tongue. I moaned at the pleasure of his touch and arched against him. Desire blasted away all my reservations. How could I have ignored the attraction, the need coursing through me? Inside the stone ring, an ember cracked, scattering sparks, illuminating his body poised above me. I shrugged out of my blouse, skimmed off my jeans. Batur rested on one elbow, watching me disrobe, his gaze reflecting the fire inside me. When I reached for him, he pushed me down, fit his body between my legs. He drew a nipple into his mouth and sucked until I arched against him once more. Despite my pleading, he refused to rush, blessing me with his hands and his mouth until I sobbed for release. When he entered me, the anguish in my heart morphed into a fierce and terrible joy.

49

... Thursday ...

Dressing as quickly as her fingers permitted, Nilesen tucked the diary inside her blouse, then checked that the doors were locked, the windows closed. Despite the heat building up as the day marched on, she refused to open herself to the outside world. She would read Alain's words in solitude, sucking whatever life they still contained through the pads of her fingers. In the bedroom, she put the kettle on the hot plate on the corner table, lifted down the tin of tea from the shelf above, and opened the lid. She inhaled the aroma, rubbed her thumb across the spoon Alain had used to prepare the drink in between their lovemaking. Eyes closed, she replayed his comic lecture on the aphrodisiac qualities of Turkish apple tea. When the water boiled, she steeped a cup, blew on the liquid to cool it, and settled among the pillows. Her body ached with the memory of what had been and would never be again. More time passed before she opened the diary.

The second page had been removed, leaving only a ragged edge and the first letter of each line. She fingered the raw wound before inspecting the next complete entry, dated a month before their wedding. A section of that one was also missing. She traced the words that remained.

... called. Again. Demanded to know about the movement, threatened ... wants to expose the group, pressured me to reveal the names of my compatriots, offered insinuations, hinted at favors to be gained or lost. The others laugh at his threats, but vipers are cunning, patient. This snake harbors a secret, one he longs to share with me ... but there is no bond between us, no true connection, no intimacy. Nilesen, if ever you read these words, know this. Once I made a boyhood promise to this man, but that debt is canceled. I said no. When he spoke

your name, to frighten me ... almost I came close to betraying us all. Almost I sacrificed truth for love. Was I wrong, Aşkim?

The tea had cooled. She traced the rim of the lacquered cup, remembering when she gave the set to Alain, always remembering. She puzzled over the description of Alain's tormentor. The ink had smeared down the edge of the page, disappeared into a black blot. To whom did Alain refer? Could she determine a name? She held it up to the light, desperate to unmask a clue to the face of an associate or a colleague, someone to blame. Nothing appeared. Perhaps this caller was an old friend, one she had not met. Or one of the myriad Solaganian cousins. She returned to the diary. According to the date at the top of the next page, a week passed before he wrote again. Lists filled the space, names of friends to invite to the wedding, arrangements to be made for the honeymoon, the minutiae of planning for their new life together. A ghost of a smile creased her lips. Then the lists stopped.

Aşkim seni seviyorum. I want to be with you under the night stars and the morning moon ... when I look at you I see time stretch out before us, a river of days ... I long to paint your skin with my fingertips, to learn your body, to hold you close ... You cannot know my eagerness to lie with you, to have you touch me ....

She gathered the words like shells and layered them onto her soul's beach. The tea grew cold. Shadows crept in like a stray cat. The pages rustled with her weeping. She pushed on. *Damn. My tormentor refuses to stay gone. Today at the market, he shadowed me like a falcon. Forced me to hide in the scarf seller's stall ... how you would have laughed, Nilo, to see me mumble an excuse to the vendor, to wrap the scarves around my head ... he waited for me to emerge, followed me into an alley ... I lashed out, held him by the throat ... he mouthed excuses but his eyes blazed with fury ... something sly lies coiled within him, something secretive ... I warned him again ... ordered him away. I tried to hide the truth ... that the movement has grown beyond us, but jealousy and hate rule him ... someday you may need to know what he said. These are the words he threw at me. "You are mistaken, Solaganian. Armenians like you, Kurds, Greeks, Jews, all will be whispers in the wind when the jandarmalar come to call" ... can he be right? ... some schoolboys wandered down the alley. I let him go, but I fear for my companions, for you. Once this fiend walked with us. Now he stalks us. We are the herd. He has become the predator.*

She needed a name. Fractured memories of Alain's work with the anti-government movement came back to her, fragments of conversation overheard, references to times and places unknown to her. Was this the man who betrayed her husband's first mission, the abortive raid on the arms depot in Ankara? How did he learn of their plan to disrupt the elections, the scheme to challenge the government at Yenihisar? The answer hid among her grief, but who cared now for all these political machinations. She flipped back through the journal, searching for the words about her, hungry for more proof of his love. She skipped over the mundane, promising to return and savor each dinner description, the accounts of his daily activities. She stumbled across a line from one of her early poems, composed the summer they first met. She had not realized Alain kept her early drafts, yet here they were, folded and clipped to the page above a line printed in caps and underscored in black marker: <u>HE KNOWS</u> ...

The room grew dark. She shifted to catch the final rays of light from the window. *Last night he called from the Denizkoy ... Anne fetched me to the phone ... I left you sitting on the porch, your face lit by the Aegean sunset... you, Aşkim, so luminous, anticipating our wedding and our life to come.* Pain lanced through her, the scene crystallizing in her mind. Wine glasses spread across the table, the blaze of dying sun across the horizon. Her mother was scheduled to arrive the next day, her cousins the day after. The ladies of the hillside, Farraj Malamuk and the others, had offered rooms to accommodate the extra guests. Her future shimmered in the evening air, beckoning. And then it fell apart.

Anne passed the phone to me ... the viper spoke in unctuous tones, his words dripping with venom ... he knows that you are all that matters to me. He does not know you write poems for the movement, but he suspects ... promises no more warnings ... I believe him ... there will be no more stalling, no negotiating ... I am out of time ... save your family, he tells me. Save hers ... he insists on meeting in the village ... I am to bring the information he seeks or he will come for you ... so I excuse myself, avoid your questions, hike down the path to stand by the water weighing the choices before me ... my dilemma ... save the movement or save you, my life ... fight ... flee ... do you remember Atatürk's warning? "... the struggle for existence is inevitable" ... words meant for the battle for our nation, but at their most basic they speak to our struggle, yours and mine, to survive against the forces determined to divide us .... if I betray the cause, he will hold all the power ... if you ever read this, you will know I made my decision ... with the sea washing over my feet, your laughter flowing down the hillside ... losing no matter which way I turn. Damn Emre.

The air hummed with loss. Nilesen hugged the journal to her as she burrowed beneath the covers, swept back to the interrogation room, to the sound of the jop whistling as it descended, and the triumph in her torturer's final words. *If you are not the poet Nilesen Yilmaz, you will not mind.* That voice, full of malice. Alain's nemesis and killer. Captain Emre Gazi.

50

... Thursday ...

The storm scoured the grit from the air, laid the dust to rest, polished the shoreline to a glossy sheen. Light tripped off the dock and scampered along the roadway, causing pedestrians to stumble as they blinked into the dazzle. Elani followed the travelers off the bus and into the rest stop. Several twenty-somethings, Brits by their accents, cut their eyes at her, shrugged, and fingered the trinkets in a kiosk inside the door. She skipped the line for the women's *tuvalet* to wander among the souvenirs until she was out of sight of the driver's watchful eye. Drawing her hijab around her face, she left the shop, strolled toward the harbor, then cut across the road. When she reached the lane that led to the Solaganian villa, a golf cart careened down the path. It jolted and jumped over the ruts. The old woman driving slowed, bowed to Elani, then passed on. Malamuk, the matriarch from the neighboring villa, the leader of the women who had gathered on the hill. Elani feared the message in the woman's slumped shoulders. It must be true. The soldiers who had killed Alain were the ones who had taken Fethi.

The hill grew steeper. Elani pressed on. She kept to the shadows, checking over her shoulder each time she paused to catch her breath. When the labored approach of a military truck sounded behind her, she moved into the cluster of *ardıç* trees. How had they caught up so fast? As the vehicle rumbled by, she spotted Fethi peeking out from beneath the tarp covering. The sight doubled her over. Not dead, then, but captive. She stepped out of the trees to signal him. Before she could raise a hand, he flipped the tarp covering higher, scooted to the edge of the truck bed, and jumped.

The truck rumbled on. Elani cupped her hands to her mouth and called his name. Startled, Fethi hunched his shoulders, anticipating a blow. She called again. This time he spotted her. With a furtive glance at the disappearing truck, he scurried to her side. She hugged him, then pushed away.

"What did they do to you?"

"That," he flinched as she ran her fingers over his bruised face and swollen nose, "is a tale for another time."

"How did you get free?"

"Do not be so demanding. I have some skills, Turkish girl." When she continued to ask questions, he relented. "I stole a key, unlocked the irons. Then I just pretended to be shackled. They left me in the truck all night. Under guard, or I would have escaped sooner."

She urged him into the cover of the trees. "We must warn Nilesen *hanim*."

"We will try. Are you all right?" When she nodded, he set off through the brush. Climbing up the hillside, they shadowed the vehicle, pausing each time the truck slowed to navigate the rutted lane. When it made the turn to the villa, Fethi shielded her behind him.

"Can you see anyone?" Elani crouched in the bushes, dried mud flaking from her jeans.

He signaled her to be quiet. From their vantage point, they could see the truck parked beside the villa. Önder had resumed his position at the back of the vehicle, smoking again. He had not checked on the prisoner chained in the back of the truck. Fethi returned to Elani.

"Stay here. Please, Elani."

"What are you going to do?"

"They have Nilesen." The words hung between them. "What shall I do?"

"Take this." Elani pulled her *hençer* from its sling and held it out. "If they cannot drive the truck, they cannot take her away."

Above their heads, a dove cooed. Fethi closed his fingers around the hilt of the dagger. He dropped to the ground and crawled toward the truck. Once underneath the vehicle, he inspected the undercarriage. When he located the brake line, he got to work.

A Principle of Light

"Private." Captain Gazi called from the doorway. Önder stamped out the cigarette, picked up his rifle. and joined Gazi at the door of the villa. Fethi scooted clear of the truck. He checked on the soldier and began his retreat toward Elani's hiding place. At his approach, the dove in the tree fluttered up. Alerted by the noise, Önder whirled. Fethi raised his hands.

"Don't shoot, *abi*."

Önder glanced over his shoulder. Gazi nodded. The soldier fired. Fethi tightened his grip on the dagger and staggered to his feet. He stared at the blood running down his arm. A second burst struck him just below the waist. A third pierced his chest.

"No!" Elani exploded from the brush. She scrambled forward until she reached Fethi's side. "Animals!"

Captain Gazi lifted a hand to knock at the door. "Bring the girl, private. We shall see what she knows."

Önder lowered the weapon and sprinted toward Elani. He grabbed her hair and jerked her to her feet. When he pulled her against him, she raised the dagger and slashed it across his neck.

51

... Thursday ...

Swept deeper into memory, Nilesen listened to the murmur of lost voices. She wandered through the labyrinth of time, embraced the pain coiled in the corner, preparing to strike. *See me. Taste, touch, merge with me.* She saw the sunlight dancing on the water, felt the music dancing over her skin. Alain, whole, unburdened by regret, reached for her, each touch of hand or thigh a promise of delight to come. Nights of starred pleasure, followed by the trip to Yenihisar. Confusion, panic, the choking dust from the explosion. Alain, bloodied, unaware, and she, clawing her way toward the wreckage, retreating when she spotted the attackers, dodging the bullets, rolling out of range and scuttling out of their sight, searching for a cave in the hills.

Gunfire rattled the windows. Another round, and a third, followed by a knock at the door. The pounding, deliberate, measured, demanding, echoed like the crack of the jop all those weeks ago. Each blow dragged her back from the past, the repetitive, rhythmic sounds like the tick of a metronome. Gone, gone, gone, they insisted. Dead, dead, dead. Shoeless, she hustled to the kitchen. She hid one of the kitchen knives in the pocket of her robe before she answered the door. *Be brave,* Alain's ghost whispered. She set the chair aside, released the lock, then stared, with undisguised hatred, at the smirking visage of Captain Emre Gazi. Elani, hands bound, knelt at his feet.

"Murderer. Assassin." Nilesen spat the words as she helped Elani up. Blood smeared the girl's hands and chest.

Gazi shoved both women inside and slammed the door. "Ah, but you knew I would come."

"What do you want?" Nilesen backed toward the kitchen, half-carrying Elani. The hidden knife scraped at her thigh. The girl shook with sobs. Gazi kept his weapon trained on them as he inspected the room. He grabbed the Kurdish girl and shoved her onto a chair.

"Tie her up. Tight, so she cannot escape again." He stroked the barrel of the gun down Elani's cheek. "She has a taste for death, this one. We will see how she feels after a day of thirst and inducements."

Nilesen stepped between them. "She has nothing to do with this, Gazi. What is between us is not her concern."

"Do it now, Yilmaz." He watched her fumble with the plastic ties, then did the same to her. Satisfied that the women could not escape, Gazi explored the house. They heard him clomping from room to room, the sound of drawers opening, furniture overturned. When he returned, scowling, Nilesen laughed.

"You did not find what you were looking for, did you?"

Gazi set the weapon aside and struck a match to the kindling in the fireplace. As the flames spiraled upward, he leaned against the wall and grinned. "We will see how brave you are, Yilmaz, when hunger bites, and your mouth is dry, and your skin burns from the touch of hot iron."

He slept for two hours. Then he began the torture.

52

... Friday ...

The last of the embers flickered, throwing low shadows against the walls. I lay in Batur's arms, dozing, then coming awake to the brush of his hand along my hip, the quiet insistence of his erection against me. Rising to my knees, I straddled him, guided him inside, exulting in the way he filled me so that the fear and terror of the past weeks floated beyond my grasp.

I fell into dreams again, waking to sunlight pouring through the chinks in the wall, striping the dead fire and my naked body in gold. Batur was gone. Stretching, I touched the small bruises that marked our last frantic coupling and smiled.

"Do you have regrets?" He stepped into the hut, buttoned his shirt, ran a hand through his hair.

I suppressed the urge to cover myself. It wasn't like he didn't know my body. I waited for him to move closer, open his arms, hold me in those large, capable hands. I waited for him to kiss me. When he didn't, I reached for my clothes. Did I regret last night? Sobs built up within me, I used my blouse like a shield. Batur grabbed it away and pulled me against him.

"Jeannie?"

I pushed at his chest. "How can you ask me that?"

He pinned my arms against him and waited. I relaxed in his embrace, realized his body was ready again. "If you only needed me for the night, I understand. But it was not that for me."

A line from one of Nilesen's poems came to mind, one she had shared during our stay at the clinic in Bursa.

"Desire, like light," I said, "illuminates the darkness and you, laser-bright, are my light."

He ran a hand over the fuzz on my head and closed his eyes.

"What are you doing?"

"Pretending," he rested his forehead on mine, "that I am lifting your beautiful hair and wrapping it around my fingers."

"No, Batur. I don't regret it." I trembled.

"You are a flame, Jeannie Maurillac, and I the moth seeking your light." The kiss, when it ended, floated like a sigh under my skin.

Outside, above the trees, the thwap-thwap of helicopters reverberated in the morning air.

Voices, distant but drawing nearer, called back and forth, some curious, others demanding. Batur released me and strode to the door. He glanced out, unbuckled his sidearm, and set it at my feet.

"Hide the camera," he said, "and this."

He handed me the rifle. I rested it beside the camera before shoving my discarded clothing into my backpack. The shouting drew nearer. I shimmied into my jeans and blouse and the photographer's vest. Then, on my knees, I clawed at the rockfall until I had a depression carved in the soil near the back of the hut.

"Put on your scarf and sunglasses, Jeannie. Hurry." Batur rummaged in his backpack while I worked at the hiding place. He pulled out two armbands. "*Vous parlez français, oui?*"

Distracted by his question, I forgot to remove the photo card from its slot. Uncovering the half-buried camera, I slipped the card free, inserted an empty one, then shoved the full card into the secret seam in the hem of my vest. Now I carried hundreds of photographs, evidence of the people behind the bombing and a visual testimony to the plight of the refugees. I had compiled a startling documentary of the journey from Istanbul. In color and in black and white, each frame in the dark recesses of the thin microchips offered proof of what I had witnessed. Each picture revealed enough truth to endanger my friends, more than enough to get me

A Principle of Light

killed. My hands shook. I didn't have to take the chance. I could bury the cards, hide the evidence. I stared at the dirt under my nails and counted to ten. Then, I shoved dirt in the hole, piled rocks over the cache, and dusted my hands on my jeans.

"*Oui,*" I said, "*je parle français.*" The slap-slap of the helicopter blades grew louder as it hovered above the hut. I scuffed at the dirt, grooming it to look like the rest of the hut, recently disturbed by occupants but otherwise of no consequence. I shook out Batur's sleeping mat, rolled it up, and stuffed it in next to my underwear. The memory of last night's encounter washed over me.

"Here." Batur tugged an armband up my arm. *Médicins sans frontières* stared up at me in French and English. **Doctors Without Borders** "You are my nurse. I will do the talking. Follow my lead."

"Batur." I pressed a kiss into the palm cupping my cheek before pointing at his pack. "The sidearm."

"You did not bury it." He paused. I picked it up.

"I did not."

"If they find it on you." He spoke so low I barely registered his words. "They will kill you. Better to leave it behind."

"They won't find it. And we might need it." I tucked the weapon into the back of my jeans and pulled my vest down to cover the bulge. I could no longer allow Batur to take all the risks. The old me would have argued against taking the gun altogether. But that woman no longer existed. If the need arose, I knew what to do.

More shouting from the hillside. Dust stirred as the copter set down. Pebbles rattled against the side of the hut. Batur raised his hands and stepped into the sunlight. The soldiers aimed their weapons at his head.

"*Ateş etmeyin. Bizde hiçbir silah yok.* Do not shoot. We have no weapons."

I shrugged on the pack and followed him, head bowed, knees shaking, praying that my college minor in French would be enough to convince them of our claims.

A soldier approached. He greeted Batur, spoke quietly for a few minutes, then turned to me. I greeted him in halting Turkish, then switched to French.

"*Médicins sans frontiers*," Batur repeated, patting his breast pocket where paper crinkled. When the soldier nodded, he drew out his credentials. He pointed to himself, then to me. "*Docteur. Infirmière.*"

"*Doktor.*" A man dressed in civilian clothes motioned us forward. "I am interpreter. Madam. Please, you come with us."

The soldier jabbed Batur with his gun to emphasize the request. More soldiers moved forward. One grabbed Batur's backpack. They didn't take mine. Batur used his body to shield me from the men herding us down the incline toward the beach. We straggled behind the interpreter, scrabbling across the rocky land, our boots slipping on the loose scree. My eyesight had improved, but the unfamiliar ground, the anxiety pumping through my system, and the lack of breakfast made me stumble. Batur held my hand as he guided me down, but he didn't speak until we reached the bottom.

"Steady now, Ms. Maurillac," he said, his touch firm on my back. "Almost there."

I swallowed the urge to curse our captors and concentrated on navigating the unsteady ground. When the soldiers halted, Batur and I stopped, too. I raised my head and scanned the beach.

Along the shore, boats bobbed in the surf. The wood and metal crafts were outnumbered by clutches of inflatable rafts that drifted against each other with every swell. Soldiers lined the shore, weapons pointed at the men driving the rescue boats. Farther down the coast, more soldiers drove stragglers along the beach.

"I didn't realize the refugees had traveled so far down the coastline," I murmured.

Batur slipped an arm around my waist. "The gods of war drive them, Jeannie. No place is untouched in these strange times."

A Principle of Light

Anxious to outrun the soldiers, the dispossessed men and women drew closer. I wished I had brought the buried camera. Then I remembered my cell phone. I faked a leg cramp, hopped around, and bent over. I took out the cell and propped it against my thigh, snapping pictures as the families rushed, slid, and rolled down the hills, landing at the feet of an army determined to send them back where they came from. When the interpreter looked my way, I shoved the phone back in my pocket.

The soldier who ordered us to the beach moved off to speak to his superior. Separated from me by the crush of refugees, Batur nodded toward his backpack lying discarded on the sand. I snatched the pack containing the medical kit and held it close as I fought my way through the line. When I caught up to Batur, he frowned.

"What?" I said. "Aren't they letting the people board the boats?"

He gave me a curt nod, but his eyes continued to scan the assembly.

"I don't understand. Why are they lining everyone up?"

"There is more going on here than chasing fugitive Syrians." He moved me away from the crowd of refugees. "They are searching for someone."

I noted again the armed men stationed between the boats and the refugees. As each adult approached the shore, a soldier asked for documents. If the person had none, the soldier asked more questions. Men were required to remove their shirts. Women had to uncover their heads. Bags and belongings were searched. Often, a refugee would be ordered to go to a tent set up farther down the beach. Only when the soldiers were satisfied did they allow anyone to wade out to the boats idling in the water.

"Who?" I dug my boots in the sand. "Who are they looking for?"

"The soldiers," he steered me toward a tent flying red crescent and red cross flags, "are looking for you."

53

*T*he medical tent steamed in the noonday heat. Batur and I bypassed the refugees waiting to be examined. A soldier stationed at the entrance rose from a camp chair. He stopped us with his jop. "Who are you and what do you want?"

"I am a doctor." Batur pointed to his armband. "This is my nurse."

"You must be here for the commander." He lifted the flap and ushered us in. Three tables stretched across the interior, flanked by portable units of supplies. On one of the tables, an officer sprawled. He groaned as he sat up, looked at our armbands, and waved off the younger man. "Go. Now. Keep everyone out. Do not disturb us until I call for you."

The dismissed soldier saluted before he hurried from the tent.

"*Vous, Doctor? Infirmière?*" The injured man gestured us forward. He pressed a blood-soaked cloth against his left arm. When his fractured French got no response, he switched to Turkish. "*Bununla ilgilen.* Take care of this."

"Officer." Batur removed the cloth to examine the wound. "That must be very painful. Nurse Maurillac, please clean this man's wound."

I opened his pack, retrieved the kit, and laid out the instruments he would need to stitch the wound. Head down, hands sweaty inside a pair of plastic gloves, I swabbed away the blood on the man's skin. Something very sharp had sliced through muscle and nicked the bone. While I worked, Batur prepared an injection to numb the area around the torn flesh.

"You know what you are doing, right?" The officer barked in Turkish. He stared at me. "*C'est bon doctor, oui?*"

Careful to keep my face averted, I murmured a reply. "*Doctor Stephanidis c'est notre meilleur chirurgien.*"

Our finest surgeon? Batur mouthed the words at me. When he raised his eyebrows, I bit my lip to keep from smiling. The officer swore, then switched languages again, his English considerably more polished than his French.

"A Greek. Figures."

"My mother," Batur said, "was a Turk."

"She was a traitor if she married a Greek."

Exchanging a look with Batur, I scraped away the last of the dirt and clotted blood.

"Nurse, please hold the officer's arm." Batur washed his hands and inserted the first stitch. "How did you receive this injury?"

The officer tried to pull away. I wedged his arm more firmly between my elbow and ribs. He glowered at me.

"These damn refugees. One of the miserable scum had a knife, but no documents. I grabbed her as she tried to escape. Pah."

"Careful, sir," I said, "you don't want to cause more damage to the muscles."

Instead of sitting still, the man grabbed my chin with his good hand, forcing me to look at him. "You remind me of an American film star, the one who starred in that war movie about Bin Laden and that raid on his compound. Let me see your head, and I will tell you her name."

Startled, I relaxed my hold. Blood bubbled up from the wound.

"Captain," Batur said. Ignoring the warning, the captain snatched the scarf from my head.

"What happened to your hair?"

"I prefer it this way when I'm on assignment." I retied the scarf. "What were you saying about a film star?"

"You look like her, that actress, Jessica Chastain. I know American movies." Batur pressed the man to the table, stretched the injured arm, and continued stitching the wound. The officer turned to me. "But no, that is not quite right. I have seen you somewhere else."

"Nurse," Batur motioned me to his side. "Fetch my bag."

A Principle of Light

I grabbed the backpack and moved out of sight of the patient. The air grew thick with heat. Dust kicked up by vehicles passing down the beach filtered into the tent. I coughed. The man twisted to stare at me but turned back when Batur yanked his arm. I eased the gun from my waistband and slammed it against the back of the man's head. When he jerked upward, I hit him again. Batur caught him. He lowered him to the table and administered a sedative while I repacked the kit. We listened for voices before slipping out the back of the tent. Once more on the run, we headed south across the empty stretch of sand.

"Where?" The word escaped in a single burst. How quickly I had learned to speak in shorthand.

"There is a boat. Farther down the coast. You have to leave Turkey. Now."

"We have to leave."

Batur refused to meet my gaze. He kept us moving, tense and focused, as though he expected pursuit. One of the soldiers headed in our direction. Batur waved him off, shouting that he would return with more supplies. The soldier fingered his weapon. Batur increased our pace. I risked a glance backward. The line of refugees had crowded closer to the medical tent. Afraid to incur the commander's wrath, confused by the doctor and nurse rushing away from the camp, the soldier took two more steps toward us, shrugged, and resumed his post before the entrance to the tent. Batur and I resumed our trek through the sand. Ten minutes passed before we slipped beyond a tumble of rocks and out of the soldier's sight.

"Faster, Jeannie. Before they realize we are not coming back."

"Did I kill him?"

He tugged me close and kissed my forehead. "It does not matter. He would have exposed you."

I rested against his chest, then slipped my hand in his. We walked on while the day wilted around us. The clamor of the refugees dwindled, and the soldiers, exhausted and hungry, forgot to be vigilant.

54

Thirst consumed me. The muscles in my legs quivered with fatigue. Glancing back, I watched the shoreline curve. Soon, the soldiers and the refugees disappeared. The land settled into an uneasy calm, broken only by the susurrations of the sea, the shuffle-crunch of my boots over the sand. Above, the gulls cried out their solitude. Batur and I scurried from one volcanic rock to another as we made our way down the coast. The hours passed in quiet contemplation. Finally, only the light spraying skyward from the distant campfires remained, blurred by the fine sea spray and the hillside rising to our left. Too exhausted to ask questions, I obeyed every command Batur gave, stopping when he signaled a halt, slogging forward when he waved me on. When a cluster of cabana-like structures in the distance resolved into a compound, I rubbed my eyes and whispered a thank you to the gods.

Weathered but sturdy, the village shimmered in the light of the dying day. I saw no sign of tourists, no neon come-ons or waterfront restaurants, only a string of fishing boats drawn up on the sand, nets draped over the bows. My throat ached. The adrenaline spurring our flight had long since evaporated. Remembering the look of recognition on the wounded officer's face, I shuddered and fought the dread creeping over me. The need to escape, to elude my pursuers and the catastrophe bearing down on me warred with concern for the fate of those left behind. I stared at Batur, saw the tension in his shoulders, the resolve that drove his decisions. He didn't run away from suffering. He embraced it. Subdued it. Made it his own. I pondered the duality of the man. Healer. Soldier. Which one was the essential Batur? I didn't know how to reconcile the contrasts in his nature, the gentleness with which he cared for patients against the wild, insistent demands of his lovemaking, the cold calculation of the warrior. An ache spread up my thighs, pooling in my center. I wanted him as I had never wanted Carl or any man, with a need so compelling it left me breathless. When he suddenly stopped walking, I plowed into him, stepped back, then reached out to draw him to me.

"What?" He tightened his embrace.

Unable to articulate the hunger inside, I sought solace in the melding of our bodies, the joining of our lips.

"Jeannie." He breathed my name, kissed me fiercely, and let me go. "Only a little farther now."

The sand dragged at my boots. Stars rose like fireflies, filling the canopy above us with ice-cold desire. The chant of the sea, as old as the earth itself, mocked my fear. I resisted an urge to tear off my clothes and dive in, to swim beyond the reach of land and invite the silk caress of the water into my lungs. The spirits of all who had passed through this land pressed at me. My past, atrophying within this present reality, sloughed off around a new consciousness. I touched the scar around my bruised eye, traced the puckers of flesh, the jagged truth of a Jeannie Maurillac reborn.

"There." Batur took my hand and rubbed his thumb across my knuckles before pointing ahead. Thirty yards offshore, a sleek cigar boat rocked in the evening swell. Beyond, the sunset glowed like a blast furnace.

"My boat," Batur said, his voice low and filled with pride.

"We're leaving now?" The sooner I stepped off the land, the easier I would breathe.

"Not quite yet." He guided me toward the first of the fishing sheds. "Soon. I need to get something first."

"You're leaving me?" Panic tripped up my spine.

He grabbed my clenched fist, opened it, and placed a knife on my palm. "You will be fine, Jeannie. You are stronger than you know."

"And what if you don't?"

"Don't what?"

"Return."

"Then you must go on without me. If I am not back in three hours, swim to the boat. You know how to operate one?"

"Maybe." I slipped the knife free of its sheath to finger the blade, wondering if I dared to plunge it into a real person.

"Do not tease me. You are better than that."

"Why do you have to go?"

He stared up the darkened hillside. "I need the rifle, and you need your camera."

The tension between us expanded, punctuated by insect calls and the rush and clutter of the waves.

"Jeannie?"

"Yes." I answered every unspoken question embodied in my name.

"Thank you," he said. He touched my cheek and headed toward the hillside. I watched until even his shadow faded into the night.

The bond between us stretched, then drifted free. Huddled next to the shed, I clutched his memory closer. My damaged eye barely opened. The good one blinked at the stars, dead or dying, their reflections only now arriving. Each twinkling wave sent a message from the universe in a language only the gods could read. I searched for a comfortable spot on the uneven ground, lay back, and admired the constellations until sleep snatched me away.

The scrape of men's voices woke me. I didn't know how long Batur had been gone. I had forgotten to ask for his watch. As the voices drew nearer, I debated whether to remain where I was or make a break for the boat. The smell of tobacco perfumed the night air.

"*Neredeler? Onlari gördün mü?*" The speaker spoke in smooth and measured tones

"*Ben imseyi görmedim.*" A deeper, more abrasive voice responded.

"*Doktor. Amerikali kadin.*"

"*Ben imseyi görmedim,*" the man insisted. The cigarette smell drifted away, along with the voices. When I peeked around the corner of the shed, I caught the glint of an ammunition belt, the outline of a jop above a shoulder. I gripped the knife so tight the sheath bit into my palm. The soldiers were looking for us. If Batur didn't return soon, I would enter the water and take my chances in the sea. I counted to one hundred and stood up, prepared to dash for the beach. An arm snaked around my waist. A hand clamped over my mouth, cutting off the scream working its way out.

"Quiet," Batur hissed. "It is only me."

When my heart fluttered back into my chest, I nodded. Batur removed his hand, but he didn't relax his hold.

"How many?" I managed to squeak out.

"Three. A soldier and a fisherman together, another soldier trailing behind. Do not worry. The villagers will say nothing."

"Wait." I faced him. "The people of the village, they know we are here?"

"This is my land, Jeannie, my real home. Of course, they are aware of us. And they will keep the jandarmalar occupied while we go to the boat."

"How do we get there?"

Batur pursed his lips to hide a grin. "How do you think?" He guided me past the boats. We skirted the sheds lining the road, slipped down the sandy embankment, and stopped at the edge of the water. Removing his clothes, he tied them into a bundle and stepped into the water. I followed his lead, glad for the darkness that hid my naked body. My underwear remained stuffed in the backpack. The memory of his hands on my skin ignited a deeper heat. I glanced at Batur, his sleek and powerful body limned by the stars. Danger and desire warred inside me. I wrapped my clothes in a ball and handed them over.

I waded past him, the warm sea a caress on my tired muscles. Clothing balanced above his head, Batur strode in behind me and floated away, swift and graceful as an otter. A strong swimmer, he soon left me behind. I crawled along, searching for courage. *Don't think about the sea creatures scouting below*, I told myself. *Or the man waiting on board.*

When I reached the boat, he hauled me up, started the engine, and moved away from shore. I crossed my arms against the shivering as we cruised parallel to the land. When Batur judged us far enough out to be safe, he cut the engine. He moved up behind me, massaged my puckered hands before enveloping me in his arms.

"No regrets?" he said.

"Only one." I turned to kiss the corners of his mouth, trailed my fingers down his chest. "That we do not have more time."

"Then we will make do with the time we have." He lifted me, molding my hips to his hardness. "*Aşkim.*"

He planted kisses down the soft curve of my neck, tongued my nipples. When he eased my legs apart and lifted me up, his thrust was fierce and eager. I urged him deeper, opening my eyes to watch as he came. When he cried out, I welcomed my own climax, the echo of our joining rising to the stars.

The Law of Reflection

55

The moon reflected along the crest of each wave. The sea sparkled like a black diamond. No sound carried across the water. Only the sky marked the moment when we fell away from each other. I pressed my nose to my lover's skin, savoring the smell of salt and sweat and passion, aware of each second pulling us apart.

Batur raised the anchor and we dressed slowly. I ran a hand over his shoulder and down his chest. He cradled my breasts in his hands before buttoning my blouse. Desire rushed through me again. I rested against his chest, then straightened and moved to the helm. While he started the engine, I familiarized myself with the controls. We followed the coastline north, running without lights, relying on his knowledge and the underwater sonar to keep us away from the rocks. When my stomach growled, Batur offered a handful of figs, which I ate in greedy gulps. I drank from the last of the bottled water, then passed it to him. Our fingers wove together, mine tingling with remembered pleasure. I pressed my lips to his neck, tasted his skin. He pulled me close and kissed me deeply. I felt shy and brazen and cherished and unafraid.

"Batur." I pointed at the guns bundled in the waterproof bag. "Why do you need those?"

He brushed a hand over my chia-pet hair. "It takes more than desire to survive in this land."

"But you care so deeply for your patients. You know what damage guns can do."

"I know you care for me, *Aşkim*. But do you see me, really see me?"

"I want to. Help me." I traced the calluses on his hand, followed the heart line on his palm.

"Each of us," he said, "has a warrior and a healer inside. I choose to honor both my natures."

"And a killer? Is there one of those lurking beneath our skin?" I turned away, ashamed of asking the question, for even as I said it, the truth revealed itself to me. Batur saw it, too.

"You know the answer to that question."

I balanced on the knife-edge of decision. To acknowledge his dark side was to validate my own, accept what I would do, had perhaps done, when I raised the gun against the officer in the medical tent. Back in Istanbul, when Carl raced toward me, I froze. Now, I would not hesitate to defend myself and the ones I cared about. Moving into Batur's arms, I embraced him and all our contradictions. As we stood together, riding in and out of the moonlight, I allowed the last of the barriers between us to fall.

"Does it matter if I am?" he asked at last.

"No," I whispered, because it no longer did. "Tell me the plan."

"Take the helm," he said. When I did, he stepped aside. "You know how to navigate?"

"My father and I sailed every summer on Lake Michigan." I swallowed around the memory and checked the compass. "I have decided something. I have to go back for Nilesen. You know that, don't you?"

"What if she refuses to come? What will you do then?"

I bit my lip and considered the possibilities, wondering if I had the right to force my friend to leave her home. But she had saved me more than once. Now it fell to me to save her. "Batur. Please. Her words deserve to be heard beyond these borders. Her voice must not be allowed to die."

"You have the poems. Why do you need her?"

A gust of wind raised goosebumps on my arms. Batur's eyes pinned me. The question demanded an answer.

"I don't need her, but the world does. She, not the poems, is the light. With time, she will realize that truth." In the stillness shrouding us, I heard my heart beating, felt the weight of the journey settle more comfortably on my shoulders. There, afloat on the Aegean, I finally understood

A Principle of Light

the message of this journey. Nilesen was the light, and I was the lighthouse keeper. It fell to me to keep it lit.

"Very well," Batur said. "After we get her, if she agrees to leave, we will try our luck on Chios. I have a contact there who helps refugees reach Greece. How much money do you have?"

"I don't know. Only a few *kuruş*, I think, in my pack. Maybe Nilesen has funds hidden in the villa. But if we make it to Athens, I can contact the U. S. embassy there, request their protection."

"It's a good plan," Batur said. I wanted to ask if he was coming with us, but the words refused to come. Instead, I counted the stars as the boat sliced a path through the aging night.

For two hours we hugged the coastline, taking turns steering as we skirted refugee boats and the searchlights strobing the water. Using night-vision binoculars, Batur scanned the shore, seeking familiar landmarks. When he finally located the villa tucked high up on the hillside, he slowed the engine and dropped anchor. The boat drifted just off the beach below Alain's family home. I stared up at the light burning in the front bedroom of the Solaganian villa and pondered how best to persuade Nilesen to leave the past behind.

Batur handed me a small, water-tight sack. The healer retreated, replaced by the soldier. Purpose radiated off him like a fever.

"Gun?"

I fished it out of our bundled clothing. When he shoved it in the sack, it thudded against another object.

"I don't want you to go alone." I placed a palm on his chest, felt the beat of his heart, strong and steady and unbroken. My own flipped erratically. For a moment, fear threatened to choke me.

"Same plan as before, when I left you in the village. You remember? Stay here. This time wait only one hour. If I do not return with Nilesen, use the charts and head for Skiros."

"Before you said Chios."

"Without me," he cupped my chin in his hands, "you must go elsewhere. Skiros is better for a woman alone."

"Without you." The statement dropped like a stone between us. "You might not come back?"

Batur glanced up, seeking guidance, but the stars kept their counsel. "You will be safe on the boat, Jeannie. Please, *Aşkim*."

The sea paused mid-swell, anticipating my reply. I was tempted. Batur didn't expect me to accompany him. I could wait for his return, hidden, protected, allow the others to face the danger. I watched him strip and prepare to risk himself again. He had interrupted his life to help us. What kind of person would I be if I hung back now?

"No. I'm going with you."

"*Aşkim*." He leaned his forehead against mine and sighed. "No."

"Yes. Where you go, I go."

He shook his head. "Stubborn *Amerikali*. Stay close, then. Stay hidden."

Off came the wrinkled vest and blouse. I shoved them into the pack along with the med kit. Then I slipped off my jeans and joined him at the rail. "I think, from now on, underwear will always be completely optional."

The corners of his mouth twitched. He pulled me close and whispered, "If only we had time."

I climbed over the gunwale, pinched my nose, and jumped, swallowing a shriek at the moment of impact. Batur climbed down the rope ladder, carrying our clothes in one waterproof bag, the gun in the other. He swam away, stretching the distance between us until only his wake was visible. I stroked faster this time, squelching the voice that ticked off a list of creatures waiting to drag me under. Octopus. Squid. Eel. Shark. Despair. Naked and lightless, I became a pale streak of phosphorescence spearing toward the land.

Once on shore, Batur hurried to the rocks that marked the path to the villa. When I reached the sand, I struggled to pull the jeans on over my wet thighs while he scouted the

A Principle of Light

empty beach. For the moment, no refugees had wandered down from the hills, and no soldiers waited to capture them. Satisfied we were unobserved, he started up the hill. We ascended in stages, pushing forward, then stopping to scout the horizon, to listen for sounds of human traffic. Below, the put-put of a motorcycle, the muffled voices of scavengers, or lovers, intruded. Unbidden, the face of the *hirsiz* popped into memory, black button eyes boring into me. "I promise I will find you, American devil," he had shouted in the bus station. But soon he and the other monsters would be left behind, his threat only a bad chapter on this torturous journey.

Distracted by my thoughts, I missed my footing and fell. I scrabbled at the rocks in an attempt to stop the slide when my hand settled on something that was not a rock. My boots dug in. I pulled the smooth metal object toward me and recognized Nilesen's gun, lost during the fight between Fethi and Elani. I shoved it into the waistband of my jeans and called to Batur. He helped me up. Assured that I was not hurt, he climbed on. The weight of the gun distracted me. I cocked my head toward the sounds from the beach. The whispers morphed into laughter. Lovers, then. I envied them the time and space to be carefree and untroubled, just as I had envied Nilesen and Alain the strength of their connection. I gazed at Batur, wondering if our bond was strong enough to last.

When we reached the top, Batur moved ahead to crouch in the brush. When I caught up, he grabbed my hand, traced letters on my palm. *Stay.* I shook my head. He signed it again and continued up the trail. I crept up behind him. The villa came into view. He circled the rosebush, crept into the courtyard, and halted.

"Jeannie. Stop." Pain layered the request. Dismay. He moved to shield my view of the house. "You have to go back. Now."

I pushed him away and stepped around his outstretched arm. When I saw the body sprawled next to a military truck, my stomach heaved. I stumbled over to the dead soldier. Blood had formed a pool beneath the man's head, a darker stain among the shadowed blackness of the courtyard. Two yards away, outlined by the spill of light from the bedroom window, I spotted a second body. Fethi.

56

Nilesen hobbled down the corridor. Pain from the burns on her hands gnawed at her. Elani struggled beside her, whispering threats as Gazi herded them toward the bedroom. The long hours of daylight had fled along with their screams. Now, certain of success, he saw no reason to keep them in bondage.

"Turn on the light," he ordered Elani. She slipped to the floor, crawled to a corner, and buried her head. Nilesen switched on the overhead bulb, throwing all of them into high relief. She cocked her head, listening for the echo of Alain's ritual words. *Be brave, little bird.* Then she joined Elani.

Crossing to the table, Captain Emre Gazi opened the container of apple tea. He sprinkled the crystals across the bed, where they glittered like stardust against the dark blue of the comforter. When the last of the leaves fell, he swiped a finger over the rim, licked off the residue, and tossed the tin at the women crouched in the corner. Nilesen batted it away, her eyes full of disgust. Elani retreated deeper into herself,. Careful not to touch the burns on her arms, she drew her knees to her chest. A keening rose from her. Nilesen reached out to comfort the girl. but one look at Gazi changed her mind. Rage bubbled anew. So few options. Such grave danger. Gazi smirked.

"Such a terrible sound, the song of loss. Tell me, Nilesen Solaganian, how does it feel the second time around?"

"Go to hell, Gazi. They are waiting to welcome you there."

"Now, now. Such ugly words from one famous for writing beautiful ones." He stroked his mustache. "But enough of this small talk. Where is the other one?"

"You know there is no one else here, only me and my assistant."

Gazi ran his eyes over the Kurdish girl and dismissed her. "The red-haired photographer from the square. Maurillac. You were together. Where has she gone?"

"The American woman? She flew back to the states when we reached Izmir."

"More untruths." Gazi wiped his mouth with the back of his hand. "Such a crafty liar you have become. Despite the losses. Despite the torture. What is to be done with you, Yilmaz?"

"My name is Solaganian. Leave us be." She tightened her grip on the knife hidden in the pocket of her robe. "You have already taken your revenge."

"Ah, but there you are wrong. Your husband's campaign against the government earned him a traitor's death. Your crime, however, is more cunning. Secret messages. Consorting with terrorists. Anti-government propaganda hidden in your clever little rhymes. The list is long and damning."

"Do not think to convince me of your innocence, Captain." She spat the title at him. "I know the truth about the bombing."

Gazi shuffled closer, his back to the door, the gun he carried pointed at her chest. "Be quiet, woman. You have no proof of those accusations. And we have more important items to discuss. Tell me, Nilesen *hanim*, did you ever consider how your husband might have saved you? All he had to do to protect himself, to protect you, was to share with me the plans for the demonstrations, the disruptions. I simply pass the information to my superiors, and everyone wins. I earn a promotion. Your Alain survives the scorn of his compatriots, and you go on living the happy marriage fantasy. No need for cryptic messages in poems and requests for asylum in the mail. Alain gives me one small piece of information, and everybody lives."

Nilesen spat on his boot. "These are the real lies, every word. Once, you promised to join us, to work against the very men you now support. You are the true traitor to our country. You offer allegiance to no one but yourself. You will

A Principle of Light

never be a hero, Gazi. You are a small man with a small mind."

He lifted the gun to strike her. She drew the knife and he backed away. "So, the poet holds a weapon sharper than words. Pah. Empty threats, little bird. I hold the power here. I write the rules and set them in motion."

The use of Alain's pet name for her landed a blow his hand never could. Tears ran down her cheeks. When she pushed herself upright, her hand shook with the effort to hold the knife steady. The blade caught the light, the flare arcing toward Gazi. He raised a hand against the brightness. "You follow no rules." Nilesen took a step forward. "If you did, you would have taken Alain, me, the girl to the authorities. But, no, you are here instead, playing the bully. Tell me, Captain, where are your government soldiers? Your *polisi*, your loyal jandarmalar?"

"You do know I can kill you." He fingered the trigger. "Faster than you can strike."

"You could, but you will not. A bullet robs you of the pleasure you take in torture." Nilesen shifted the blade from one hand to the other, drying the sweat from her blistered palm on her pants. "But you are right about one thing. I no longer have a heart, and I am stronger than you, more resolved. Your need to hurt others is the only creed you live by. But know this. You have no rights here in my home. This girl and I have done you no harm. You have no reason to detain us."

"But you are all alone, with no witnesses to aid your cause. There is a soldier in your courtyard whose death demands reparation. Whose version of the night do you think will carry more weight?"

Nilesen glanced at Elani. The girl stared back, blinked twice, and returned to her mourning.

"He tried to force himself on her." Nilesen lashed out with the knife. The captain dodged to the left and rushed forward. He slammed the butt of the gun down on her arm. She screamed but kept her grip on the blade. He grabbed her wrist and squeezed until the bones ground together. The knife slipped from her fingers, bounced across the floor, and skidded under the bed. Gazi shoved her. When she fell, he laughed.

"When they find you," she gasped at the pain clawing at her arm, "Alain's comrades, they will kill you. Slowly and with much joy."

The captain stroked his mustache again. "The resistance is over. With Solaganian gone, the others will scatter like cockroaches caught in the light. But not to worry. We will find them and make them disappear for good, taking their dissension with them."

"No." Nilesen reached inside her blouse and pulled out the copy of *Işik*. "These words expose you and all who try to extinguish the truth."

"You stupid revolutionary, your words mean nothing. The time has come to join your husband in the darkness. But first, I want to hear you beg." The captain swung the gun at her head. She ducked, arms raised to ward off the blow. Elani leaped up and lunged forward. Wrapping her arms around his legs, she sank her teeth into his calf. Gazi pivoted to beat at her. Dizzy from the blow, Nilesen crawled toward the bed. She lifted the hot plate and swung it at their tormentor. The blow glanced off his shoulder. Enraged by the attack, he shook free of Elani. Blood from the bite on his leg soaked through his trousers. He stepped back, raised his weapon, and aimed at Elani's head.

"Why?" Nilesen collapsed on the bed, her fingers kneading the tea into the cover, blotting out the bright shimmer of the grains against the cloth.

"You took him from me." Gazi's roar shook the room. "Alain was mine, my friend, my companion, my ticket to greatness. Together, we planned a rise to power. We were comrades in arms. Until you seduced him away."

"You were students at the same university, fool. Nothing more than that."

"I knew what you were the first time I read one of your poems."

"What is he saying, Nilesen *hanim*?" Elani said, spitting out a mouthful of cloth fibers. She clutched her head where the blow from the weapon had stripped away a patch of hair and skin.

"Nonsense, *benim küçük arkadaşim*, nothing but nonsense." Nilesen stretched a hand toward the girl. "While my husband and his friends took action, this one daydreamed and plotted, fawned and lied his way toward power. It was nothing but a coward's fantasy."

"Liar. Whore." Gazi wiped spittle from the corners of his mouth. "Alain admired my tenacity. He praised my ideas. I worked with him and his companions all that summer, among the people, cataloging grievances, soliciting signatures. We were prepared to take our concerns to the president."

"Yet here you are, nothing but a tool of the secret police, mouthing lies about protecting the country. There is nothing but hate in your heart. Listen now to the real truth. Alain never loved you, not even a little bit. Tell me, Emre, did you beg for his affection, or did you just threaten to expose him if he didn't give you what you wanted?"

The captain tossed the rifle aside. He grabbed Nilesen by the hair and lifted her off the bed. Then he forced her to her knees. When he pulled the jop from his belt, Nilesen struck at his wounded leg. He relaxed his grip and she fell against Elani. Together, they tumbled over the floor, scrambling to evade the blows.

"I never threaten, Yilmaz. I do." He lifted his arm and stopped mid-threat. He grabbed for the arm hooked around his neck. Batur increased the pressure until the jop clattered to the floor.

"Batur." Jeannie laid a hand on Batur's shoulder. "It's the man from the square, the one I saw talking to the suicide bombers."

"Then he deserves to die." Batur tightened his grip. Gazi clawed harder, eyes bulging as he struggled to free himself.

"Let him breathe, *sevgili*. He will pay for his crimes."

"Jeannie is right, Batur *bey*. Let him reap what he has sown." Nilesen stalked toward the captain. "Enough, Gazi. No more pursuit. No more threats. This ends here."

Elani crawled under the bed. She rose to her knees, knife in hand, and launched herself at the captain. Gazi twisted to the side, but Batur's hold did not ease. Elani screamed as she rushed forward. She raised the blade and buried it in Gazi's chest. Batur did not release him until the man stopped struggling, until, lifeless, Captain Emre Gazi slumped to the floor.

Elani stood over the body and shouted. She stooped to wipe her bloody hands across his uniform. Then she spit in his face.

57

The moon had gone into hiding. An owl hooted twice before retreating among the midnight ghosts. Batur and I strapped the bodies of the captain and the soldier inside the military truck. I gagged but managed not to throw up. He leaned in to steer the truck toward the lane while I pushed from the passenger's side. When the vehicle picked up speed, I slammed the door and waited for him to join me. The whine of the engine pierced the night as the truck charged downhill. A thin cloud scraped across the moon as, hand in hand, Batur and I made our way back to the villa. One more task awaited, the saddest of them all.

I knelt beside Fethi's body. Batur stood guard as the truck careened down the lane. It sliced through the brush and crashed into one of the rocks guarding the shore. The impact sent tremors over the landscape, followed by the whoosh of an explosion.

Batur touched my shoulder. "It is ended."

I returned my attention to the porter's son. Easing him onto his back, I crossed his arms over his chest and smoothed the hair off his forehead. Dear Fethi, loyal, devoted, one more sacrifice to the gods of discord.

"I'm so sorry, *abi*." I ignored the blood on his face as I straightened the collar of his shirt.

"Come, Jeannie." Batur laid a hand on my back. "Let me take care of him, and then it will be time to go."

"Not you, Batur. You have done enough." Nilesen moved out of the shadows. Elani shuffled beside her, the pain of Fethi's loss hovering over them like fog. "They will take him."

When I looked up, the women of the hillside, led by the widow Malamuk, stepped out of the woods. Only their moon-bright faces were visible above the dark garments they wore. Farraj embraced Nilesen, then gathered the Kurdish girl into her arms. Silent and sorrowful, the women placed a linen sheet next to Fethi's body. Together, they lifted him onto the cloth, wrapped him with care, and carried him away.

"Another fearless warrior returning to the dirt," Nilesen said. We watched until the procession faded into the cover of night.

"You must go. Now." Batur swept his gaze over us. "All of you."

"This time, Batur *bey*, I believe you are right." Nilesen glanced back at the villa. "Although I do not wish to leave, it is no longer safe to stay."

"*Arkadaşim*," I wiped the tears from my face. "You saved me. Let me return the gift. Your life is too precious to waste."

Elani stood, hands fisted at her sides, and shook her head. "I cannot leave him here alone."

"I agree it is important to honor Fethi. He fought very hard for you, which is why you must remain free." Nilesen grabbed the girl and turned her to face uphill. "Be at peace. My friends will take care of him. He will not be alone."

I touched the gun at my back, then waited as Batur returned to the villa. Soon, the house stood dark, silent and shuttered. Batur handed the key and a small, paper-wrapped package to Nilesen. "One day, Nilesen *hanim*, you will return."

"Perhaps. But pain lives on this hillside. Death stalks me here. I can feel it sharpening its claws. The next time I return will be the last." Nilesen tucked the key and the package inside her blouse. Without a backward glance, she and Elani headed to the beach. I followed more slowly, torn between the loyalty I had to my friend and the man who held my heart. Halfway down the path, Batur took my hand. I moved into his arms and rested there, my mind stumbling over arguments and entreaties. He traced my spine, caressed my neck, stroked the bristling new growth of hair. I leaned into his touch, unable to free the dagger of loss buried in my heart. When I looked up, he stepped back.

"What you need is in here, Jeannie." He thrust the small sack in my hands. "Make it count."

A Principle of Light

I ran my fingers over the contents, detected the camera inside. Batur had rescued it from the shepherd's hut and carried it from the boat. For me. I started to thank him, but he was gone. Not even a whisper remained to mark his leaving. Another loss, greater than all the ones that had come before, shadowed by his final words. *Make it count.* I could go after him. I should go after him. I hesitated. *Make it count.* I squared my shoulders and headed to join my friends.

Without a light to guide them, Nilesen and Elani stumbled down the path, tripping over roots and small stones that littered the trail. It took them a long time to reach the sand. I was about to follow them onto the beach when I spotted two motorcycles parked ten feet from the path. A man leaned against one of the bikes, arms crossed, helmeted head folded on his chest. He watched as Nilesen and Elani moved clear of the trees. Then he removed the helmet. A second figure popped up from behind. He swept a light over the women and shouted. He flashed the light on and off and on, then doused the beam. Nilesen and Elani threw up their arms to shield themselves from the light. I froze.

"Nilesen," I called from my hiding place. The thieves from the bus station had found us. "*Hirsiz.*"

"Run, Jeannie."

The thief from Istanbul tossed his helmet onto the sand. His laughter echoed over the water. "Ah, now the evening begins."

"Run," Elani yelled.

His companion pulled a knife, flipped it open to test the blade against his thumb, and jabbed it in the air. Elani exchanged a glance with Nilesen.

"Another blade," she said.

"You did not think I would forget about you and the American, Madam?" The thief circled their position, slipping in and out of the shadows cast by the rocks and the looming trees. "No. I am certain you remember my promise to her. And I am willing to bet the secret police will pay good money for both of you. Tell me, how long can she hide, the other bitch, the tall one?"

"Bah." Nilesen kicked sand at his feet. "Go find another woman to frighten, *hirsiz*. I've been threatened by the best."

He staggered forward, the sand dragging at his boots, and placed the blade against the burns on Nilesen's cheek. One of the blisters popped under the pressure. Blood trickled down her neck. He shoved her aside. When he grabbed for Elani, she kicked his shins. The first thief came up behind, grabbed her by the hair, and dragged her across the sand.

"And who is this, then? Another runaway. No, wait, something more than that. Ho, three for the price of one. I expect the red-haired witch thinks she has escaped again, but we will find her. In the woods, in the water, no matter. She will bleed just like you. In the meantime, if you do not care to beg for your own life, perhaps you will consider saving this one. Sami."

The thief called Sami directed the flashlight at the Kurdish girl. The larger *hirsiz* released her hair to wrap a hand around her arm.

"So, tell me who you are, girl. A Syrian? A Kurd? Perhaps you are a PKK infiltrator. A spy sent to gather information on the military forces along the coast. This night grows ever more interesting." He barked a command at his accomplice. Sami tucked the flashlight under his arm. He held a rope. "Bind them tightly. We will load them onto our boat."

From my hiding place, I located Batur's craft rocking up and down on the midnight sea. Closer to shore, I recognized the silhouette of an inflatable raft skimming over the water. I shuffled farther away from the open sand, calculated the distance to the next grove of *ardıç* trees, and weighed my chances of reaching their protection before the thieves could catch me. My legs felt like jello. My body ached with sorrow. If I ran, they would capture me before I could help my friends. Unwrapping the bundle Batur had handed me, I took out the camera, tightened the strap around my wrist, and removed the gun from the sack. I released the clip, checked it. Elani had fired two bullets. I reloaded the

A Principle of Light

weapon, tucked it under my arm, and thumbed on the camera. I set the shutter speed for night lighting and prepared to raise the lens. Around me, I sensed a tsunami of movement. The hillside trembled. Perhaps the gods had sent an earthquake to swallow us all. Or maybe the land had chosen this night to cough up its ghosts beneath the starred and watchful sky.

The man called Sami wrapped an arm around Nilesen. The other *hirsiz* sheathed the knife and drew a gun. He placed the barrel against Elani's forehead. I peered through the lens, waiting for the shutter to adjust. If only the man wouldn't pull the trigger. When the readout shifted to ready, I pressed the button. The flash strobed. I snapped another picture. And another. The *hirsiz* tossed Elani aside. He aimed into the darkness. I let the camera dangle, steadied the gun, and squeezed the trigger. The thief rocked back. His left arm dropped to his side. He stared at the blood trickling down his arm. Startled by the light and the gunshot, Sami relaxed his hold on Nilesen. She wriggled free and collapsed to the sand. The beach rumbled to life. Refugees scrambled down the hillside, spilling from the trees. Clumps of desperate people shouted as they ran toward the boats approaching from the west. The crowd slammed into the thieves. The crush of bodies overturned the motorcycles. People fell on top of each other, cried out for help, scrambled to regain their footing. They rushed past, a clutch of human turtles obeying the instinct to reach the sea.

Elani kicked her captor in the shins, lowered her head, and rammed into his midsection. Jostled free by the attack, his gun arced upward, bounced off a rock, and wedged itself in the sand. Nilesen sprang toward the Kurdish girl. I shoved my way through the crowd. Suddenly, Batur was beside me.

"Run. Now." He snatched the gun from my hand as he tugged me toward the water. "Go to the boats."

"But you." The mass of bodies propelled us forward. He freed the watertight bag from my waistband, tucked the camera inside, and hung the strap around my neck. Cupping my face in his hands, he teased a lock of hair between his thumb and forefinger. When I nodded, he used his knife to sever a tiny curl.

"Go, my flame. Tell the world what is happening here. Make a difference." He raised my mouth to his and kissed me deeply before steering me once again toward the water.

"Your boat, Batur." Water splashed my face. My vision blurred. Refugees battled their way forward. I gripped his sleeves. "We can take your boat."

"No, *sevgili*." I remembered the word from our lovemaking. Dear. Beloved. He pushed me away. I lunged toward him. He shoved me harder, backed away into the crowd. "There is no way to reach it now. *Polisi* will be waiting for me on board. You are safer without me. Go."

The beach boiled with refugees who clawed and shoved and clamored for help. I fought against them, but they swept me along as they ran. Unable to retreat, I checked the strap around my neck and looked for Nilesen and Elani. When I saw them on the shore, I bulled through the crowd until I reached them. We locked elbows, supporting each other as we moved into deeper water. The rescue boats glided closer. I splashed through the waist-deep swells, dragging them with me. The first of the rafts bumped against me. More boats drifted in behind, thudding against the people trying to climb aboard. A boy slipped beneath the waves, came up sputtering as he clung to the forearm of a man already in the raft. Chest-deep in the sea, I picked Elani up and tossed her onto the closest raft. I grabbed Nilesen by the waist and boosted her onto the boat.

The raft, overloaded and rocking in the heavy swell, began to pull away. I clung to the rope along the side while the sea swirled around me. I took a breath, went under, came up to take another. Wave after wave crashed over my head. A hand closed over mine. I choked and sputtered, kicked hard, and heaved myself upward. I banged against someone's knee, splitting my lip. The camera dragged at my neck. Drenched and shivering, I huddled among the unwashed bodies.

A Principle of Light

"Nilesen? Elani?" The feathery sound of my voice failed to override the laboring of the boat as the captain revved the engine and drifted across the sea on a course toward Greece.

"We are here, *arkadaşim*, we are here." Nilesen's assurance sifted between the shouts and curses. I gazed toward the shore, anxious for a glimpse of Batur. From the direction of the fishing village we had left hours ago, a military convoy bore down on the civilians still clustered on the beach. I shared the panic of the ones who had failed to reach the boats. My heart pumped erratically in my chest. I clenched my fists against the sensation of falling, Alice-like, into the unknown. No way out, my rational mind chanted.

At the bottom of the road leading down from the villa, a fire blazed, filling the air with the odor of burning rubber. The truck carrying the bodies of Önder and Captain Gazi blazed on.

"Good riddance," I whispered. Above the roil of sea and shore, barely visible on the hillside, the Solaganian house sat alone, its shuttered windows a blind oracle whose time had come and gone. A flare shot up, showering the manic scene with sparks and there, among the refugees, I found him, Batur Stephanidis, my love, one hand lifted in farewell, staring out at the inconstant sea.

58

Light poked through the eastern blanket of clouds as the raft crested over the increasingly restive sea. Shivering in their wet clothes, Jeannie, Nilesen, and Elani wrapped their arms around each other to stay warm. The families on the boat huddled together. When a baby fussed, the mother gave it her breast. Children whimpered. The men stared at the wake, contemplating the swells of loss. As the sky lightened, Jeannie unsealed the camera to record a final view of the Çeşme coast.

The raft struggled to maintain speed. It began to take on water before they reached Chios. Reluctant to proceed, the pilot detoured to a cove a half-mile from the main harbor on the island's leeward side and ordered them all off the boat. Before the last of the group reached the shore, he and the ailing craft had disappeared. Once on shore, the refugees scattered. Nilesen waited until the crowd dispersed before she took out the pouch plastered to her skin beneath her blouse. Too tired to do more than raise an eyebrow, Jeannie watched her friend count the damp bills. Elani snatched the money and counted it again.

"You did not tell us you were rich." The girl pretended to pout, then grinned as she danced in the sand.

"Hush, *arkadaşim*. This will do little more than keep the wolves away."

Dawn opened rosy eyes. Mist swirled at the water's edge. The air carried the scent of salt and fish and sorrow. An eagle startled from the cliff above their heads and angled out to sea. Nilesen urged them to hurry as she hiked up to the road and set out for the buildings clustered around the main dock on the island. When she reached the first of the fishing sheds, she ordered Jeannie and Elani to shelter under an awning sporting a weathered image of the sea god Poseidon. Exhausted, cold, and hungry, the photographer and the Kurdish girl huddled beneath the canted overhang. Jeannie rested her head against the weathered boards. Elani scooted close to touch the skin around the photographer's eye.

"Does it still hurt?"

"Only when you push on it." Jeannie captured the girl's probing fingers and examined them. "Do you need more ointment for your burns?"

"No." Elani continued to stare at her. "What can you see? No, do not tell me. You probably do not wish to discuss this."

"It's all right, Elani. I ask myself that same question hundreds of times a day." She closed her good eye and concentrated. "What can I see? Colors. Shapes, the outlines of large objects. Your bright eyes."

The girl tried to apologize again. Jeannie cut her off. "No need to excuse your curiosity, Elani. We are more than friends. You see, I have some depth perception."

"Your face reminds me of an ancient statue," the girl said, "weathered by time and the elements, but still beautiful."

Jeannie blinked, bruised by the memory of Batur kissing the scars. *You are my Amazon warrior, brave, bold, fearless.* She had tucked his praise into her heart, savoring the words of comfort and caring until there were no words, only his body fitting into hers, two abandoned puzzle pieces finding their connection. His loss carved a new channel in the valley of her heart. She didn't know how to bear it, didn't know how Nilesen and Elani endured such anguish.

Out of words, they drifted into sleep. Nilesen kicked their feet to wake them. "Come. We have a boat."

"Where are we going?" Elani stumbled up.

Nilesen exchanged a glance with Jeannie. "To Athens. I have the passports he gave me."

"Batur." His name spilled out like a sob.

"I cannot go with you. I have no passport." Elani hugged herself. "They will send me back."

"No, they won't." Jeannie shook her gently. "You will request political asylum, and I will persuade them of the need to protect you. To protect all of us."

A Principle of Light

Elani shrugged her off. "I have nothing to prove any of it. Only my word."

"You're right, Elani. You don't have proof, but I do." Jeannie patted the photo cards zipped into the seam of her vest, then inspected the camera for water damage and checked the battery level. Eighty percent. Batur must have charged it while they were on the boat. She framed Nilesen and Elani in the viewer, zoomed to the background sign, and took their picture. Later, if the photographs ever went public, critics could argue the symbolism of the sea god and the trident, but Jeannie thought she would always title this picture "Rescue By the Sea."

The boat captain reminded Jeannie of the old fisherman who transported them from Beyoğlu to Harem, slow to speak, cautious, kind. He asked few questions. Dr. Stephanidis, he said, had treated his wife, his daughters. They were friends. The mention of Batur reopened the wound of their parting, but Jeannie shoved down the stab of self-pity. Elani lost Fethi. Nilesen lost Alain twice. She had no right to claim a deeper grief than theirs.

The trip from Chios to Athens lasted ten hours. Usually the crossing took less time, the captain said, but he wished to avoid any confrontation with other vessels. When another boat appeared in the distance, he changed course. The women spent the time sleeping or washing their clothes. They refused to speak of the past. Once, when the captain anchored for an hour to keep from being swept up in a coast guard raid, Jeannie dove off the boat to bathe in the sea. Floating, eyes closed, she abandoned herself to the sun and the waves. The dust of the journey rinsed clean, but the wounds in her heart still bled. She could not scrub away the sight of Carl disintegrating, of Fethi unmoving in the Çeşme dust, of Captain Emre Gazi splayed out on the villa's bedroom floor. Nor could she stop remembering the taste of Batur Stephanidis, the salt and sweat and tears, and his body invading hers with such tenderness and strength. When the grieving waned, she climbed from the water to stretch out on the deck. Nilesen tapped her foot.

"Would you like to hear my new poem?"

"I thought," Jeannie sat up, "you gave that up?"

"I did, and now I start again." Nilesen fiddled with the collar of her blouse. "Yes or no."

When Jeannie nodded, Nilesen took a breath and recited the draft.

> *The hearth no longer binds me.*
> *The sea churns at my feet, blindsided,*
> *by a random current that sucks me under.*
> *Silent scatter of blood in the water.*
> *Memory surfaces in the water.*
> *And light bounces, quiet thunder,*
> *while I, finless albedo, surrender, wide-eyed.*
> *to the depths, where Death dances with Lethe.*

"Oh, Nilo." Jeannie closed her eyes against the pain. "What poem is that?"

"I call it In the Bathyal Zone," Nilesen said.

"What is that?" Elani asked.

"The shallowest region of the ocean," Nilesen explained, "where no light reaches."

Jeannie leaned into her friend's sorrow. Elani shifted in her chair. They joined hands, towed under by the tide of remembering. Hollowed by their ordeal, they listened to the boat churn west toward Greece, uncertain of the trials still to come.

As the captain glided into Athens harbor, a coastal patrol intercepted their boat. They rehearsed their stories one more time. When the armed militia boarded the craft, it didn't take long for the captain to establish his innocence.

"I am only the poor owner of a chartered craft with a large family to support and many bills to pay. I know nothing about my passengers. They pay their money and I carry them into port. Here, search my boat. I have nothing to hide." He wrung his hands and prayed.

During the interrogation, a soldier checked Nilesen and Jeannie's passports. Then he turned to Elani, his voice rising with each question. When he attempted to separate the women from the Kurdish girl, they tucked her between them and refused to let go. Nilesen argued in Turkish. Jeannie yelled in French. Unable to break the guard's resolve, she switched to English.

"Asylum," Jeannie said. "We are seeking asylum. Please contact the American Embassy."

"*Iltica*," Nilesen echoed. "We are in danger."

The interrogator threw his hands in the air, muttered a command in Greek, and motioned them onto the patrol boat. They sat together, arms locked, feigning confidence. As soon as they docked, the harbor patrol escorted them to a two-story building with a tourist information booth and a spacious indoor waiting area. He spoke to a superior, who gave them the once-over, rubbed his chin, and swore loudly before he disappeared into his cubicle. Through the frosted glass panel separating the office from the anteroom, Jeannie watched the man initiate the requisite calls to his superiors. His voice carried, but she only caught snatches in English. When the call ended, the man returned, beckoned her to follow him, and led her into his office.

"Madam, I need to hear from you again, just the facts, please. Who are you?" He tapped her passport on the desk.

"I am Jeanine Maurillac, an American journalist. I have been on assignment in Turkey. I have information about a bombing in Istanbul. My friends," she gestured toward Nilesen and Elani, "are in danger from the same people who have been chasing me."

The Greek raised his eyebrows. "Chasing you? Is this another American conspiracy theory? Or are you perhaps filming an action movie?"

"Please, *Kirie*. Please, sir." She schooled her voice not to shake. "Just let me talk to the Embassy."

"What happened to you?" He stared at the scars around her eye.

She touched the skin, reading the ridges of tissue, the puckers of flesh, remembering Carl and Fethi and Batur. She must finish the journey for them. She swallowed the urge to cry, turned instead to stare at the Greek flag hanging behind him. "I witnessed a bombing. What I saw cannot be unseen."

Half-rising from his chair, he fingered a strand of her shorn hair and frowned. His attention shifted to the telephone. When he caught her staring, he squared his shoulders. "Return to your seat, Madam. I will call you when I need you."

Back on the bench, Jeannie shared the information she had gleaned and tried not to fidget. The passport Batur had prepared would not stand up to more intense scrutiny. If the Embassy refused to admit them, the Greeks would send them back to Turkey. They needed a backup plan. She glanced around. The waiting area, nearly empty when they arrived, had filled with tourists. She made eye contact with a middle-aged blonde wearing flowered shorts and a neon pink blouse. The woman's companion was decked out in a Hawaiian-print shirt and khakis. The couple cast worried glances around the room.

"I have an idea." She squeezed Nilesen's shoulder and patted Elani's cheek. "Wait for me here."

Jeannie pretended to look out the windows. She stopped to talk with a group of teenagers on a school trip. Then she made her way toward the American tourists.

"Hey, hi. Where y'all from?" She cursed the southern that slipped out when she was stressed. "Isn't this just the worst thing? My friends and I only arrived from Chios this morning and they won't let us in without giving us the third degree."

The man tugged on the woman's sleeve. "Don't talk to anyone, Nancy."

"Listen, Nancy." Jeannie leaned closer. "If you let me use your phone, I can get us all out of here in a New York minute. I'll call my editor and ..."

"You're a reporter?" The woman caught her breath, stared at Jeannie's damaged eye, and looked away. Uncertainty replaced suspicion. "Jim, she's a reporter. Maybe she can help us. We don't speak Greek. Can you just tell them we didn't know we couldn't take this home?"

The woman pointed at the bag wedged between her sandals. A stone carving bearing the likeness of an ancient

A Principle of Light

deity peeked out from between the handles. Authentic or fake, Jeannie couldn't tell, but the couple looked scared.

"I'm sure it's just a misunderstanding." She held out her hand. "I'm Jeanine Maurillac, from Ohio. Do you have a phone I could use? I lost mine."

Despite her husband's objections, the woman handed over her phone. Jeannie checked the time before she placed the first call. The automated receptionist at the magazine shunted her to the internal directory. She punched in Boyd Fenton's extension. When the editor growled his name, she took a deep breath. Don't give him space to object, she reminded herself.

"Mr. Fenton? Please, don't hang up. It's Jeannie Maurillac." She waited through his exclamations of relief, consternation, and annoyance, cutting him off when he started in on disappointment. "I've got a real story here, sir, and it's much better than carpets. This is one you're going to want to run, and soon. But first, you have to get me out of Greece."

"Greece? What are you doing in Greece? Every police agency in the country's been crawling all over us since you disappeared." Fenton popped his gum. "Where the hell have you been?"

"I know, sir. I'm sorry," she said, even though she wasn't. She'd been too focused on survival to think about how her disappearance had affected her colleagues and friends. Glad, for the first time, that her father had passed and her mother was drifting farther from reality, she interrupted his next question. "And, no, I did not have anything to do with the bombing in Istanbul. But I did witness it. I have pictures. Lots of pictures." More shouting, this time of a celebratory nature, followed by a machine-gun Q and A and a long pause.

"Maurillac." Fenton resumed cracking his gum. "I'm glad you're safe, and I'm sorry about Carl."

Jeannie cleared her throat, dropping her request in the space between heartbeats. "There's one more thing, Mr. Fenton. I'm not alone. The women who helped me escape, they're with me. You have to help them, sir. If they're sent back to Turkey, they'll die."

The editor stopped her. "I've alerted our legal team as we speak," he said, "and I sent a heads-up to our sister paper. How many women are we talking about?"

"Two."

"Two, you say? Turkish?"

"One. The other's a Kurdish girl. Seriously, Mr. Fenton, their lives depend on it. You have to help."

"I'll contact the State Department as soon as we hang up. You need to call the Embassy from your end." He rattled off a number. She searched her pockets for something to write with. Then she spotted a container of pens next to a display of travel brochures. She cut through the crowd, grabbed a postcard hawking Acropolis tours, and scribbled the number in the margin. Fenton kept talking.

"You'll be safe there until we can get you out. Oh, and call the AP correspondent in Athens, Tony Welsh. Here's his number. Tell him what you can. He can help get the word out. Publicity is your friend now."

The tourist couple trailed behind her, sending dirty looks as the call dragged on. Mr. Shorty-Pants mumbled about the cost. His wife worried about germs. "Maybe she's got some disease, Larry. Her eye's almost touching the screen."

With a promise to call as soon as he had news, Fenton hung up before Jeannie could tell him that wouldn't work. Mouthing thank you to the couple, she moved farther away to place the second call. She introduced herself to the receptionist at the American Embassy and hurried into an account of her journey. When she stopped to catch her breath, the receptionist asked her name. His pleasant but bored tone changed to a charged rush.

"You are Jeanine Maurillac?" he said. "The reporter implicated in the Istanbul bombing?"

"I am Maurillac." She pressed her fingers against the photo cards hidden in the lining of her vest. "But I didn't bomb anyone. The poet Nilesen Yilmaz is with me. We are in danger." She decided not to mention Elani. Once the embassy staff came for her, she would insist they take the girl, too.

"Do not, under any circumstances, leave the waiting area," the voice on the phone intoned. "Your escort will arrive within the hour."

Assured that help was on the way, Jeannie considered advocating for the couple who allowed her to borrow their phone. She scanned the now-bustling waiting room. When she located the tourists, they were engaged in a discussion with a customs official. As Shorty-Pants slipped bills into the official's hand, she decided they were doing fine on their own. She squeezed her way through the crowd, slapped the phone into the woman's purse, and hurried back to the bench. She settled in between a dozing Nilesen and a scowling Elani and slumped against the wall. The camera thumped against her chest, reminding her of Coleridge's albatross. She felt again for the photo cards. Their presence demanded a commitment. The images of the people she had come to know and care about weighed on her, their stories more important than her own. But it wasn't the faces of the bombers or the girls at the school in Deniz Feneri or the women on the hill above the villa who haunted her most. Instead, she saw Carl running to warn her, Alain sitting at the table on the porch, Fethi teasing Elani, and Batur, gazing at her with a desire that matched her own. The demands of the moment, of the place and the circumstances where they found themselves, required she sacrifice that desire. So much light and goodness found and lost, fading now unless she brought it back.

"Ms. Maurillac?" A marine in full gear carrying a semiautomatic rifle shook her shoulder, stepped back, called her name again. Jeannie set her pack on her shoulder and answered him. Nilesen and Elani had moved from the bench and now stood by the entrance. She took a step toward them. "You need to come with us, Ma'am."

"I'm ready." She reached to pull her hair back, touched the fuzzy new growth, and sighed. "I just need to get my friends."

While she slept, the waiting area had cleared of travelers. Only a handful of tourists remained near the information desk. They cast wary glances at the armed American soldiers and the young diplomat with the stern expression. He stepped to her side, obstructing her view of the door, and took her elbow.

"You need to come with us now, Ms. Maurillac, if you wish our assistance."

"Of course." She tried to peek around him. "My friends …"

The man pressed her forward. "We need to leave now, ma'am."

She wrenched free, stepped away from the guard, and stared at the entrance. Nilesen and Elani were gone.

59

After a two-hour interrogation, a shower, and a meal I could barely eat, I spent the night at the United States Embassy compound in Athens. Everyone was kind, understanding, efficiently suspicious. I should have felt safe and protected. Instead, I stewed over my statements, anxious about Nilesen and Elani. Where were they? I still had my phone, but no cord to charge it. I hesitated to reveal its existence, afraid one of the guards might confiscate it and the pictures it contained. Escorted to a room with a cot and a private bath, I tried to sleep, but the itch of guilt kept me scratching at my decisions. If I hadn't left my friends ... except I didn't leave them. While I, exhausted, nodded off, they left me.

Early the next morning, a sweet-faced young man from Georgia, drove me to the airport. He refused to leave my side until I boarded a military transport that flew me to Ramstein Air Base in Germany. During the flight, I felt weightless and detached. The chatter of airmen, the hum of engines, disturbed the onslaught of memories. As the plane touched down, I lost the last of the light that had sustained me for the past month.

Another pleasant airman escorted me to the hospital, where I was assigned a room and subjected to a barrage of physical and mental exams. They confiscated my belongings and my phone. The doctors were competent, the nurses bustling and cheerfully noncommittal. No one answered my questions. How long would I be here? When could I go home? The black hole around me grew darker. After reviewing the diagnosis, dehydration and mild malnutrition, a medic explained my treatment options, scribbled orders on a clipboard, and left me alone. I spent the next twenty-four hours hooked up to an IV and begging for a phone. Finally, a nurse took pity on me and handed me her cell. As soon as she left, I called Boyd Fenton.

"Mr. Fenton." I paused to order my questions. "New number. What's going on? Where are my friends?"

"Look, Maurillac," he growled through the connection, "I'm doing everything I can to get you home."

I tried again. "Nilesen Yilmaz and the Kurdish girl, Elani. They are in serious jeopardy."

"The Greek government," he intoned, "denies any knowledge of their whereabouts. Your friends, Nilesen and Elaine, is it? They have disappeared. Even my best sources don't know where they are."

We argued for a few more minutes until I lost the connection. Maybe a different form of communication would work better. I punched in a message to Nilo.

Not my phone Where are u?

I pressed SEND and waited. Five minutes, ten. No response.

The nurse bustled into the room, my backpack and camera in her arms. She stowed the pack in the closet, placed the camera on the bedside tray, and held out her hand.

"I need it back, Miss Maurillac." She glanced over her shoulder. "I've already broken one rule."

"Please, I just need a few more minutes."

She wiggled her fingers. I hesitated. Down the hall, a call bell chimed. "I'll be right back," she said.

I slipped the phone beneath my gown and prayed that my caregiver would develop temporary amnesia. I needed to make more calls, but my head ached and the loss pressing down on my chest threatened to crush me. Still cold, I burrowed beneath the nest of blankets, considered requesting more. No matter how many they brought, I couldn't get warm enough. I tucked the phone under the pillow and dozed off. The ping of an incoming text woke me.

Safe arkadaşim oxford poets society

Dopey from sleep, I struggled to make the connection between Nilo's safety and the reference to a group she was no longer part of. But the mention of poets gave me an idea. If the government refused to help, and the media struck out, maybe the creative world would rally to her cause. I clicked on the web to search for arts organizations. When I found a listing for European poets, I used the back of the morning menu to scribble down the information. By the time I finished, my head throbbed and my mouth felt like a desert. I checked the time. In the hall, med carts rumbled, followed by murmured instructions and shuffling feet. That nurse would return soon. *Hurry*, Nilesen's quiet voice urged. "Hurry," I whispered above the drip-drip of the IV.

I turned my back to the door and hammered out several emails. What else? I looked up addresses for Ohio's congressmen and senators. If I didn't have to give the phone back, I could send those out later. Finally, I located an online contact form for the Oxford Poets Society. On the long, dark ride in the tile truck, Nilesen had shared a little of her undergraduate days, how she had joined the group as an undergrad and how, later, as a graduate student, she had given a reading. I had planned to make a list of writing magazines and literary journals, but the battery was running low and again I didn't have a charger. I folded the menu and tucked it and the phone under my hospital gown right before the door banged open. Four men, two in suits, the others in camouflage gear, filed into the room.

"Ms. Maurillac?" The man in charge straightened his tie and gave me an appraising stare. Then he held out his hand. "CIA, ma'am. Agent Frank DiVicenzo. This is my colleague Steven Handy. Bill Freyer and Marcus Thwait are with Homeland Security."

The men took turns shaking hands as they arranged themselves around the bed. Now I understood why I had no roommate.

DiVicenzo moved closer. "We need to talk."

"No, we don't." I pulled the blankets up to my chin. "I want a lawyer."

"A lawyer? You're a United States citizen, Ms. Maurillac, and you witnessed a terrorist attack. Why would you need a lawyer?"

Snatching the camera off the table, I cradled it against my body. "I need to protect my intellectual property. And my friends."

"Any photographs you took are part of an ongoing investigation, Ms. Maurillac. Your country needs your help."

I released the photo card from the slot before holding it up. "I agree that the pictures I took in Istanbul may be valuable. However, the others are of no interest to anyone but my employer." I snatched the card back from his outstretched hand and slipped it into the camera. "I want to speak to a lawyer first, to see what my rights are before I release them to you."

"We can take them by force if we have to." He folded his arms, his posture aggressive. The others shuffled closer.

"Respectfully, Mr. DiVicenzo, the press is already hounding me. I've had a million requests for interviews. They'll be on me like flies on roadkill the minute I leave the base."

Although no one had contacted me yet, a bit of bluffing was in order. The lie was worth the breathing room it bought me while I figured out what to do. I looked out the window. In the distance, a van cruised, its broadcasting antenna aimed at the hospital. So far, Ramstein had refused admittance to the media, but I knew they were out there, salivating for the story only I could tell.

"Don't pull a Snowden or a Winner, Maurillac," DiVicenzo said.

"I'm no traitor." I drew the blanket up to my chin. "Just an artist trying to survive in a dangerous world."

He stared at me. I stared back. The heart monitor continued its steady beep-beep. Oxygen hissed through the tube in the wall. Finally, he shrugged and ordered his companions from the room. After they left, he leaned over the bed.

"Be careful, Ms. Maurillac," he said. "You're playing with the big boys now."

I didn't bother to reply. I'd been playing with the big boys for two months, and I was still alive. Damaged, heartbroken, remade in more ways than I could tally, but alive. The nurse bustled in. She shooed DiVicenzo from the room, pushed a cart closer to the bed, and grinned.

"Nothing I like more than bossing men around. Here. Take these."

I swallowed the pills and asked for a razor. When she raised her eyebrows, I laughed.

"Don't worry," I said. "I'm not suicidal. I just want to shave my legs." I stuck my hairy shins out from under the sheet and wiggled them.

"I'll see what I can do." She checked my pulse and oxygen levels, wrapped the blood pressure monitor around my arm, and pursed her lips.

"Your hair's growing back," she said. "It's a beautiful color. Reminds me of a campfire, all those reds and golds shining in the light."

I rubbed at the bristly curls. Batur had called me his flame. But when the fire goes out, only ash remains. The nurse wheeled the cart away. She had forgotten to ask for the phone. When she returned with a disposable razor and a can of shaving cream, I didn't remind her.

"It's not very sharp." She ran a thumb across the blades. "But it should work for your legs."

As soon as she left, I locked myself in the bathroom. I spent some time staring at the new Jeannie Maurillac, cheekbones prominent beneath the scar tissue, new worry lines etched across my brow, I remembered Batur cradling my shorn head as he moved inside me. His flame, he called me, a spark to ignite his passion. What might have sounded clichéd had become precious, words of love to balance against the hate surrounding us. When the grief passed, I got to work. It took a while to reshave my head with the dull razor. After I swept the cuttings into the waste container, I studied the face again, trying to rekindle that fire amid the pale skin and amber eyes of loss.

60

The lawyer showed up after lunch, ID badge pinned to her waist, lipstick a splash of red against the Army green of her uniform.

"Captain Rao," she said. We shook hands. "I understand you requested legal representation."

"I did." I waited for her to settle in before I spoke. "I'm a photographer, Captain. I have a great many pictures from my journey across Turkey. These pictures represent my life and the lives of my companions. They constitute an intimate portrait of all the people I met along the way. I want to know how I can keep them out of the hands of the government and the press. Can you help me safeguard my work?" I choked out the last word. The record of our odyssey was more than work. The photographs comprised a love letter to the courage and humanity of my saviors. I refused to let that become fodder for supermarket tabloids and TV talk shows.

"I'll have to do some research before I can answer that, Ms. Maurillac." Rao made notes on a yellow tablet she pulled from her briefcase. "Is there anything else?"

"Please. Call me Jeannie." I sipped water from a plastic cup, aware of how I must look to her. A woman with no hair and a scarred face, sadness flaking off me like rust. I stared at my hands, pondering how best to address the matter of Nilesen and Elani. Finally, I cleared my throat and plunged ahead. "I have friends, two women, who need political asylum. How can I help them?"

"Go on," Rao said. I described the situation as clinically as I could, but I couldn't stop the tears. The captain wrote for several more minutes before looking up.

"I can explain how a request for asylum works, Jeannie, if you're certain that's what you want to do, but I can't promise you'll be successful. It would be better to focus on your own issues."

"Nilesen and Elani are my most important issue."

Captain Rao waited for me to look up. "Give me their information, Jeannie. After you tell me your story, I'll begin the inquiry process."

I spent the next hour reviewing the information I had already supplied in several interviews. Rao asked questions, clarified details, insisted on specific times and places. I revealed what I could, but I kept Fethi and Alain out of the narrative. Their stories belonged to Nilesen, to Elani. Batur belonged to me. If by chance or luck he had survived, if he wasn't a prisoner, I would do what I could to keep him safe. And if he had died on that beach in Çeşme, then I would grieve in private. I would not share him with the world just yet. Maybe never. The captain kept the questions impersonal until the very end of the interview.

"Be assured that what you have told me is privileged information, Jeannie. I just have one question." Rao tapped her pen on the notepad. "Have you told me who you're mourning?"

My hand fluttered to my head, dropped back to my lap. "What do you mean?"

"You have shaved your head, and I know you are not Hindu. I recognize the symbolism of your action. It has long been a custom among the people of India to do so," she paused, "when one has lost a loved one. My grandmother followed this custom when my grandfather died. You will speak to the press, the journalists will notice, and some will ask questions. There may even be a few who understand the significance, who will wonder, as I do, what this beautiful woman is hiding. All will speculate, and what they suggest you may not like. Unless you tell them the truth. Will you?"

"When I'm ready, Captain." I sat up straighter. The cell phone tumbled from beneath the blankets and clattered to the floor.

"Shaveen, please." She picked up the phone, swiped the screen, and studied the calls. Before I could reclaim it, she slipped the cell into her pocket. "I'm guessing this doesn't belong to you. It's best if I return it."

A Principle of Light

I started shaking. The tremors grew stronger. I feared losing the best, maybe the only, link to my friends. The last time I felt this alone was the day the bomb exploded.

"I promise," Captain Rao stood by the bed until I stopped shaking, "to do all I can to save your friends. And I'll erase your searches."

The following day, DiVicenzo returned, alone. We played cat and mouse with the facts. I offered what I could. He asked questions I refused to answer. It was a most unpleasant conversation. After he left, dissatisfied and scowling, the hospital discharged me. Shaveen escorted me to a small apartment on base. She also brought me my cell phone. I spent hours sending emails under her watchful care before the agent showed up again. This time he brought his partner. That's when the debriefings began in earnest. DiVicenzo and Steven Handy trooped in, placed a recording device on the table, and rolled up their shirt sleeves. Shaveen sat by my side, taking notes and whispering instructions. I had never felt more vulnerable.

The official interrogation, two hours in the morning and two in the afternoon, took a week. Pressed to explain why my "journey" lasted more than a month, I recounted the route Nilesen and I had taken from Istanbul to Çeşme, but, claiming a lack of language skills, I denied any knowledge of the identity of those who helped us flee. I also concealed the existence of the second photo card. Shaveen supported my effort to deny them permanent custody of the original set of photos, although she did allow the agents to view and make copies of the images of the square, the jandarma, the men with the suitcases, and Carl rushing to warn us all.

Each evening, I sent texts and emails. I scoured the Internet for any scrap of information that might tell me where Nilesen and Elani had gone, whether Batur was dead or alive. At the end of the week, the order arrived to release me, along with instructions regarding my return and a warning to keep our discussions private. I boarded an Air Force transport and flew home. By that time, the state department had persuaded the administration to treat me as a hero, not a traitor. Turkey wanted me back for questioning, but the country was scrambling in the wake of a coup attempt. The Kurds were demanding access to Elani, accusing the Greeks of illegally detaining their citizen in an undisclosed location. No mention was made of the missing poet, Nilesen Yilmaz.

    I stared out the window as the plane touched down at Wright Patterson Air Base. My eyes were swollen from crying and my stomach ached. Sorrow was a leaden band tightened around my heart. Off to the west, the land shimmered in the haze of a July afternoon. Along the horizon, the sky had purpled. Wall clouds rumbled as they raced east. I had borrowed a charger from one of the flight crew and slept while the cell battery returned to full power. Now, the weather app on my phone flashed. Meteorologists were predicting severe thunderstorms over a third of the area. Escorted to a waiting limousine, courtesy of Boyd Fenton and the newspaper/magazine conglomerate I worked for, I reached my condo before the storm hit. The sky lit up with lightning strikes while I paced, anxious and frightened for my friends. Despite the intense search for Nilesen and Elani, I still had no idea where they had gone.

61

The view from the window looked out over Dinokratous and Evzonon Streets. Leaning on the sill, Elani stared at the traffic below. Ignoring the girl's brooding, Nilesen opened the notebook and wrote *Aşk ve kayip*. Love and loss. She was writing again, not a poem but an essay. Her grief, she decided, demanded a wider lens. The thought reminded her of Jeannie, another loss to grieve.

"There." Elani pointed toward a sign just visible through the trees. "I see a Metro stop. We could escape that way."

Nilesen abandoned her work to embrace the girl. "And where exactly would we go, Kurdish girl?"

"Somewhere." Elani rested her head on the poet's shoulder. "Away from here."

"We know no one in Athens. We have no contacts and no money."

Elani fingered the coins sewn in her blouse. "We have my dowry."

"No, that money is your future. I think, for now, we must trust our British friends."

"Westerners, bah." The girl stomped on the floor. "We have been imprisoned here for twenty-one days. If they were going to help us, they would have done so by now. Anyway, Nilesen *hanim*, they might help you. But not me. You are educated. Your poems are famous now. I am an anonymous girl from a war zone in a country crawling with displaced people."

Before Nilesen could respond, a trio of embassy staffers filed into the room. One of them carried a stack of notebooks. Another wheeled two small suitcases behind her.

"Ms. Solaganian? Ms. Goran? I apologize for the delay." The woman who spoke wore a navy polka-dot blouse and a tailored skirt. Efficiency ruled her every move. She gestured to the table that dominated the room. The staffers placed the materials there and left. She stepped closer to shake

Nilesen's hand. "I am Sara Andreas, and I have come to expedite your request for asylum. Now, Ms. Goran, kindly go to the room next door. My associate, Miss Patton, will speak with you while Madam Solaganian and I talk here."

Nilesen touched her temple, a reminder to Elani to stick with the story they had rehearsed. When the adjoining door clicked shut, she folded her hands in her lap and waited for the Andreas woman to begin the interrogation.

"Can you tell me, Ms. Solaganian, about your journey?"

"We have already given this information. Many times."

Sara Andreas folded her hands on the table. "I understand your frustration, Madam Solaganian. Please. Tell me again."

Beginning with the bombing, Nilesen recounted how she rescued Jeannie, how the soldiers searched for them. She told of their journey down the coast as they fled from their pursuers. She did not mention Caroline Nepthali or the Arif brothers or Batur Stephanidis. She did not include the women of the villas or the *hirsizler* on the beach. Nor did she reveal what had happened to Fethi or the truth about Alain's death. Some details were best left hidden for now.

"Do you have reason to believe that Captain Gazi is still alive?" Ms. Andreas leaned in, her English tinged with the rhythms of her native Greek.

Nilesen closed her eyes. "I saw the truck burning," she said. "He could not have escaped."

"Why is that, Mrs. Solaganian? Surely he and his driver would have realized what was happening and made every effort to exit the vehicle."

Nilesen met the skepticism in the woman's eyes with a smile. "I suppose that may be true, but I never saw anyone run from the truck."

"Why did he not take you with him? After all, you say he was chasing you across the country. Once he caught you, why did he let you go?"

"Because I gave him what he was after." Nilesen smoothed her broken hands over her thighs. "He wanted my husband's diary."

"Why?"

"Alain's journal contained evidence that implicated Gazi in the recent coup attempt, as well as in the bombing in Cihangir."

"And you believe that diary burned with him?"

"I am certain of it." Nilesen gazed at the wall above the woman's head. "Emre Gazi was a cruel man, Ms. Andreas. He intended for me to suffer all my life, to live knowing he was the one who killed my husband and stole back his secrets."

"Secrets." Andreas flexed her ankles, causing her jeweled sandals to wink and sparkle. "So you admit your husband and this Gazi had more than one thing to hide."

"My husband has been dead for more than a year. Whatever secrets he kept died with him. I only know about Gazi."

"Why is that, Ms. Solaganian?"

"Because he told me himself when he came to the villa to retrieve the diary. He expected to return to Ankara, to blame Alain's followers for the explosion, and to continue with his plotting. How better to stir up more trouble than by bombing his own people and blaming the dissenting element?"

Andreas fingered the recorder on the table. "It makes no sense," she said.

Nilesen reached over and took the woman's hand. "That I understand. Because you are not an evil person. Trust me when I say this. Captain Gazi was a tortured, ugly soul. He deserved to die. Allah saw to it that he did."

An unexpected rap on the door interrupted the interview. Nilesen turned to the new arrival. "Wesley?"

She hurried to embrace the tall man striding into the room. He returned the hug before nodding at Sara Andreas.

"Mr. Boatwright." The Andreas woman rose to her feet. "There was no need for you to come, sir."

"Nilesen *hanim* and I are old friends, Sara. I have spoken with her before. You and your associates may break for lunch now. I'll handle the rest of the interview."

Bowing to her superior, the woman hurried away.

"What are you doing here?" Nilesen said.

Wesley Boatwright sat down beside her. "Oxford Poets' Society. Our code survives the years. Apparently, your photographer friend activated the network with her emails. I'm sorry that I couldn't come sooner. And I am so very sorry about Alain."

"He was alive, Wes, at the villa." Nilesen bowed her head. "All this time I did not know. Changed, in body and in spirit, but alive. But before we could leave, Gazi found us."

Wesley grasped her clenched hands. "Is it certain that he is truly gone?"

"He is gone. All that promise destroyed by Gazi's ambition, his twisted love." Nilesen drew back, disentangling from his grip. "I have buried him twice now, once in my mind and then on the hillside."

"You and Alain have served us well, my dear friend. I'm deeply sorry for your loss."

"I am done with this, Wesley. No more. When you sent your messenger to Adalet, I had no choices left to me. That is why I agreed to spy for you. It is a decision I regret deeply."

"Not spy, Nilesen. You observed and recorded and sent information, but we never expected you to ..."

"No more deception." Nilesen shook her finger. "The time for lying has passed. I did what you asked and more. But I am finished with that part of my life. I have lost everything but my art. Now that is the only master I will serve until I die."

The head of the MIA Middle East Division exhaled loudly. "I agree. You have done enough. Who would have thought, all those years ago when we met at university, that we would be here, in a room in Athens, trading secrets?"

"There has been no trading, only taking." She held up her hands. "They crippled my left hand in the prison, I suspect on Gazi's orders. When I finally reached Istanbul, I tried to seek your help, before the bombing. Did you receive any of the notes I sent?"

Opening his case, Wesley Boatwright extracted an oversize envelope and emptied the contents onto the table.

A Principle of Light

"Here are your letters, and every postcard from every small town. But you never mentioned the pursuit. Had I known Gazi was chasing you, I might have intervened."

"How would you do that, Wes? The man was deeply embedded in the military. In the city, before I could contact you, he caught me again, and then he watched while his jandarma broke my other hand. I lost Alain to a roadside attack and found him again hiding in the villa, plotting, a dark shadow of the bright light he once was." She held her stomach, the nausea building. "Do you know what he lost? His legs, his faith in the goodness of others, his conviction that I would love him despite the damage. So much loss. Both of us caught up in other people's plots. You asked too much."

Boatwright bowed his head. "We did."

"So." She patted her knees, stood, and walked to the window. "You owe me."

"More than I can repay." He gathered up the communications and stuffed them back in his case. "You and the girl, Elani, will you come to England?"

The day had passed into dusk. On the street, horns honked, cars screeched, vendors called out to pedestrians. The odor of cooking oil insinuated itself from the hall. Nilesen flicked a dead fly from the sill.

"Oh, to be in England," she said. She turned from the view and threw up all over Wes's shoes. He caught her as she fainted. When she recovered consciousness, she was lying on a sofa. A nurse sat nearby, a blood pressure cuff dangling from her hand. Elani paced the room.

"What happened?" Nilesen struggled to sit up. Elani pushed her down.

"Lie still, Nilo. You passed out. Do you not remember? But that man, Mr. Boatwright, he says we can leave this place. We can go to England. Tomorrow. We can be free there."

Nilesen pulled herself up. When the nausea returned, she lay down again.

"Nilesen *hanim*, please, say we will leave this place."

"Very well, my little thorn, we will go. If you promise not to frown anymore." Her cell phone pinged. She stared at the words on the screen. Another message from Jeannie. *Arkadaşim*. It was way past time to let her friend know they were safe. Propping herself with a pillow, she sent a text that her friend would understand. *Ready to receive the light.*

Early the next morning, a limousine whisked her and Elani to the airport. In the car, Nilesen suffered a second fainting spell. Unsettled by the vertigo, she refused to eat. Elani coaxed her to drink some lemon soda as they waited for their flight to board. The anti-immigration climate sweeping the United States was also roling England, but with Wesley Boatwright and his caseful of diplomatic passports, no one questioned their departure. In England, the British government settled them into a tiny flat near the railway station in Oxford.

Elani studied hard, passed her exams, and was admitted to a prestigious prep school for girls interested in mathematics. Nilesen established a pattern of reading and writing, of quick trips to the market and nights full of frightening dreams. In between the dizzy spells, she worked on her essays about freedom, intolerance, greed, and loss. She dedicated the collection to Alain. The nausea intensified, but after three months, the episodes grew less severe. She waited for a doctor to confirm the diagnosis before she called Jeannie.

Işık Light

62

... May 2018 ...

"Light is both a particle and an electromagnetic wave capable of transferring energy from one point to another."

-Elani Goran's introduction to
her senior physics project,
Oxford Preparatory
School, October 2016.

"Light, like love, reaches us long after the star
that generates it has ceased to exist."
-Nilesen Yilmaz, "*Aşk ve kayip*:
On Love and Loss," **Essays from
the Edge of the Galaxy**,
HarperCollins, 2018.

"Twinkle, twinkle, little star, how I wonder what
you are."
-Elma Solaganian singing to
her mother. April 2018.

The string of white lights lining the façade of The Gallery at Fifth and Washington blinked like fireflies in the late spring evening. The show wasn't scheduled to open to the public until seven, but patrons already lined the sidewalk, buzzing over the promised appearance of the photographer and her famous subject. Although the owner had requested access for the artists through the back of the shop, the crush of traffic prevented the limo from entering the alley. Protected from the crowd by the tinted windows and the bodyguard riding shotgun, Jeannie tightened her grip on her friend's cold hands. Nilesen squeezed back, as if to reassure them both that they could do this. Jeannie tossed her hair over her shoulder. It had grown in a darker red-gold, thicker, and more luxurious, solid shiny proof that not everything had been lost. She glanced at Nilesen. Most of the poet's pregnancy weight was gone, although her breasts were fuller, her face plumper. They both looked healthy, the scars they carried hidden, Jeannie's beneath the tattoo around her eye, Nilesen's under the gloves she wore.

"Maybe no one will recognize me," Nilesen said as they climbed out of the car.

"No such luck, *arkadaşim*. You're even more beautiful than ever." Jeannie refused to acknowledge the shadow of grief in her friend's eyes. Even Elma's birth could not dispel the sorrow, and the fact that the child resembled Alain so strongly reinforced that loss every day. "How is our little Apple doing?"

Nilesen smiled as they pushed through the queue and headed for the rear door of the gallery. "Elma is growing well, despite her premature arrival."

Mitzy Goldman swung the door open. "Thank goodness," the gallery owner said, "you made it just in time." The woman ushered them past the caterer and into the front room. When Jeannie spotted the photos, she caught her breath and swore.

"*Kaşar*. I didn't realize how big they would be."

One wall had been dedicated to the story of the poet, Nilesen Yilmaz. The pictures documented the journey from Istanbul to the coast. Below each photograph, a line from one of her poems anchored the visual narrative. Nilesen waved her hands in the air. "No, no. This is too much. I feel naked. How can I stay here? How can I watch these people inspect my life?"

Mitzy escorted her to a low table set up on a dais. Jeannie followed. The woman waved at the photographs. "This is a tribute to your art, Mrs. Solaganian."

"Nilesen, *arkadaşim*," Jeannie said, "Alain would be so proud. This is your story, and Elma's legacy."

A Principle of Light

Under the glare of the track lights, Nilesen turned to the opposite wall. She gripped Jeannie by the chin. "You think so? Look there. Observe your wall. Then tell me about a legacy."

"Oh, my God." Jeannie covered her eyes, then peeked at her half of the gallery. The walls were covered, floor to ceiling, in the photographs that had won her the Pulitzer. Those on the left detailed the story of the Syrian refugees. A center section was dedicated to the early stages of the journey from Istanbul – the old fisherman who took them to Harem, Carolyn at the clinic, Arif and his donkey. A poem from *Işik* accompanied each image. To the right hung the portraits of Fethi, the porter's son who became a hero, and Elani, the Kurdish girl who escaped sexual slavery to study international relations in the States. The photos captured every mood, serious, frightened, resourceful, alarmed. One portrait, taken as dawn lit up the sky, captured their joy as they smiled at each other.

"I did not realize you took so many pictures of them, Jeannie. Does Elani know?"

Jeannie moved toward the artwork. She trailed a hand along the wall, reliving the journey. "She helped me decide which ones to include."

~ ~ ~

The third-floor walkup off Delancy Street overlooked the harbor. Elani rocked baby Elma against her shoulder and stared at the lights along the marina, content to be alone with the baby.

"Such a good girl, Elma," she crooned in Arabic, repeating the praise in Turkish and English. "You'll be trilingual by the time you are two, little Apple."

After the child fell asleep, Elani took out a sheet of the fine linen stationery Jeannie had gifted her.

"*Dear Fethi. Dear benim Türk oğlan.*" She listened a moment. Elma did not stir.

"*I am well. The baby is well. Nilesen and Jeannie are at the gallery, showing the world the story of our journey. You look very handsome in the photos. We also look very scared in some of them, but now the world will know what we accomplished, how we worked together to survive. They will know that our differences matter less than our humanity. Ah, I hear you say, big words for such a little Kurdish girl. But I am now grown enough to admit I miss you. My studies are going well. Imagine. They permitted me to enter the political science program at Columbia without graduating from high school here in America. Never did I believe such a thing was possible, but it is true. Experience counts for something then. How are you, Turkish boy, in your hideout by the sea? Has Alain bey's tree grown taller than yours? Are the hills covered in purple blooms? Does the aroma of thyme drift in the breeze? I wonder if your father has visited yet? Jeannie tells me he has permission to go to England. If they do not grant him a visa to travel to New York, we will go and meet him there. I miss our discussions, Fethi. Do not forget me. I will never forget you. Kisses on both cheeks from your Kurdish girl."*

She sealed the envelope, took a stamp from the desk, and addressed it in care of Farraj Malamuk. Then she set the letter on the table beside the door. Tomorrow, when she took Elma for a ride in the stroller, she would mail it. Mrs. Malamuk would carry it to the graveyard and bury it by the roots of the apple tree growing above Fethi's grave.

~ ~ ~

Threads of conversation wove around the room, snaring Jeannie's attention, then unraveling as she shifted from group to group. Unexpectedly, she found herself alone in a pocket of silence, staring at the image of Batur tending to the injured child in the refugee camp. The ache that had been forming in her chest all evening doubled in size. Why had she agreed to leave him? Her heart remained in the Çeşme hills, beating in concert with the man who saved their lives, the one who stayed behind.

"Ms. Maurillac?" Mitzy Goldman tapped her shoulder. When she turned, Mitzy handed her a glass of wine. "What a night! Successful and lucrative."

"For you or for our charity?"

"Both, my dear. Donors are eager to support the causes you champion in these photos." The woman gestured at the wall before looking at the photographer. "Are you all right?"

"I'm fine. I just need a little air."

"Don't stay away too long, dear." Mitzy gulped the remainder of her wine and set the glass on the tray of a passing waiter. "Your adoring public is eager to speak with you."

Jeannie fanned the collar of her dress over her heated cheeks as she elbowed her way through the crowd. At the front of the gallery, she nodded to the clerk at the register and slipped outside. A few more patrons waited in line to enter and view the displays. An elderly couple strolled past, holding hands and murmuring to each other. The streetlight cast their shadows over her, obscuring the profile of a man leaning against the pole, arms folded, head bent in thought. She followed after them, hands fisted against the pain in her heart. Under the streetlight, the man looked up.

"Jeannie. Jeannie Maurillac."

Her name whispered in the air between them. She bit her lip. How did this stranger know her? A hustler, then, come to ask for an autograph, or a paparazzi, or a con man. Maybe a stalker. As each possibility occurred, the man called her name again, stepping toward her. She backed away, twisting her ankle. When he reached out to steady her, she clutched his arm. Not possible, she thought, not here.

"*Aşkim.*" Beloved. Batur.

She closed her eyes, regained her footing, voiced the first thing that came to mind. "Why do I always lose my balance around you?"

Batur gathered her in his arms. He traced the tattoo that disguised the scars around her eye.

"I should have known you would choose a firebird."

"Batur." His name escaped, a sob and a prayer. "How?"

"Like a moth to your flame, *Aşkim*. How could I stay away?"

J. E. Irvin

She raised a hand to trace the strong jaw, the sensual lips, the fierce hawk features that sent her blood racing. "I thought you were gone forever. How is it you are here?"

"That is a tale for tomorrow." Shadows flickered in his eyes. "All that matters is now."

"All that matters is now," she echoed, moving back into his arms to meet his kiss under the streetlight with the evening crowds breaking around them, the pulse of the city like the murmur of the sea along that ancient Aegean coastline.

~ ~ ~

The patrons drifted away, abandoning wine glasses and napkins, dropping cards in the fishbowl on the counter. The copies of **On Love and Loss** had dwindled. Only a handful remained, the light from within raying out like flashes of starlight. Nilesen stood in front of the photograph Jeannie had taken the day they all sat in the kitchen staring at Alain, risen from the dead only to return there less than forty-eight hours later. She placed her hands over her stomach, marveling at the miracle those hours had given her. Reaching into her pocket, she withdrew the latest note from Farraj Malamuk, recounting the daily activities of the women of the Çeşme hills. She held up the picture of the seedling apple trees, one for Alain and a second for Fethi, pushing through the orchard soil from the graves below, stretching, like Elma, like all of them, toward the light.

Acknowledgements

My deep and sincere thanks to all who helped in the shaping of this book:

To the fabulous Nilesen Gökay, the inspiration for the fictional Nilesen, and my dearest friend for over thirty years ... Rest In Peace, arkadaşim. Now you share your light with the stars. (Please read the invitation following the acknowledgments regarding raising funds for ALS.)

To Nilesen's husband, Cem Gökay, and Cem's sister, Demet Gökay, who advised me, corrected me, and made sure my language and cultural references were accurate. Any errors are mine alone.

To the most amazing, talented poet Myrna Stone, who not only read the novel multiple times but who also encouraged me to allow the fictional Nilesen to share her poems with the world.

To my early readers, Jeannie Smith and Joanne Huist Smith (not related!). You gave me courage to keep writing until the tale was complete.

To the amazing Donna Laugle, whose editorial skills and advice helped me make this novel a reality.

To my family and friends, who never admitted to growing tired of my Turkish story.

Bibliography

There are many fine books I consulted in researching this story. Here is a partial list of those I found most helpful.

Mustafa Kemal Atatürk **The Speech** Metro 1995

Pamuk, Orhan Istanbul **Memories and the City** Alfred E, Knopf 2004

Reminiscences of Atatürk Trans. By Önder Renkliyildirim

Istanbul Eyewitness Travel Guides DK 2004

AN INVITATION: TEAM NILO or TEAM JEANNIE?

My friend Nilesen Gokay suffered from ALS. During the last difficult years of her life, she provided consistent support and belief in this novel. To honor her, I pledge to donate 10% of the proceeds from this book to the **ALS Association,** "an American nonprofit organization that raises money for research and patient services, promotes awareness about and advocates in state and federal government on issues related to amyotrophic lateral sclerosis (**ALS**), also known as Lou Gehrig's disease."

Your purchase will help us work toward a cure for this debilitating and deadly disease. I invite you to visit my web site – janetirvin.com—where you can sign up for TEAM NILO or TEAM JEANNIE, compete for prizes and exclusive previews of upcoming books, and meet other authors whose writing will inspire and entertain you.

Join me at janetirvin.com ... put your name on the emailing list, select your team – NILO or JEANNIE – and make a difference!

THANK YOU!

P.S. If you would, please leave a review of *A Principle of Light* on Amazon or Goodreads ...

... and help me grow the contributions to ALS

BOOK CLUB QUESTIONS

1. Given the situation in which the women find themselves, do they make a wise decision to run away?

2. As they travel down the coast, Nilesen and Jeannie begin a tentative friendship. What do you think is the most important element of that friendship?

3. During their travels, others join the women. What does each newcomer contribute to the journey?

4. Conflict is an essential ingredient in all the relationships in the book? Discuss the types of conflict and how each is resolved.

5. Initially, Nilesen questions whether she wants to go on living? What incidents or events change her mind?

6. Each woman begins the novel with a goal. How do their goals change as the story progresses?

7. Confronted with the truth about her husband's death, Nilesen must decide whether or not to forgive the deceit. Does she do the right thing?

8. Which of Jeannie's experiences serves as the greatest catalyst for change in her perception of herself and her goals?

9. In the end, *A Principle of Light* is a story about the strength and courage of men and women in the face of adversity. Discuss how each of the characters meets that test and deals with it.

10. In using the metaphor of light, the author contrasts the dark deeds of the mysterious pursuers with the actions of Nilesen and Jeannie. How does this metaphor inform the reader about the world we live in?

About the Author

J.E. Irvin is a career educator and the award-winning author of three mystery novels: *The Dark End of the Rainbow*, *The Rules of the Game*, and *The Strange Disappearance of Rose Stone*. Her shorter works have appeared in a variety of print and online publications, including Alfred Hitchcock Mystery Magazine, Sherlock Holmes Mystery Magazine, FLIGHTS, and SPARK. An avid canoeist and hiker, Irvin and her husband reside in Springfield, Ohio, on the edge of a nature park.

The New
Atlantian Library

NewAtlantianLibrary.com
or AbsolutelyAmazingEbooks.com
or AA-eBooks.com